WITCH
WAYWARD
WARRIOR

WITCH WAYWARD WARRIOR

THE SILVER CURSE BOOK THREE

ANNA ORR

Podium

WITCH
WAYWARD
WARRIOR

Prologue

Behind him, the ominous snap of brittle twigs trampled underfoot grew louder. The beast's gait had picked up, transitioning from a slow lumber to a trot. The low-lying brush rustled as whatever was following him plunged brazenly through the undergrowth in pursuit. With his heart drumming against his ribcage like a frantic bat fluttering from its cave, Faris quickened his pace.

Tried to, anyway. His efforts resulted in him missing his next step and tumbling head over heels over a fallen log and down the subsequent hillside just behind. Faris's battered body rolled to a stop among a bed of ferns at the base of the lush knoll. He tried to stand and screamed instead as pain rocketed up his ankle. "Muck!"

A gruff growl sounded above him.

No, no, no! A paralyzing chill blossomed within his chest, threatening to cut off his airway. With ice coursing through his veins, Faris forced his aching body back onto his feet. Not like this. He got to die in a fabulous house surrounded by money! Not by a bear. Gods, he hated bears. Why was it always bears?

Figures. Here he was on the hunt for his idiot witch best friend, whom he desperately needed in order to save his family and his village, and a damn bear had to go and muck it all up! It was hard enough with half the United Territories falling into open rebellion and his own ugly mug plastered on every wanted poster from Adderwood to Castle Bay, but noooooo. This misadventure couldn't possibly have been complete without something trying to eat him!

Croak! A raven descended from the upper boughs of a paper birch and flapped its dark wings at him, uttering unintelligible noises.

"For the last time, I don't know what you're saying," Faris hissed under his breath. He really should have learned how to distinguish the ravens from one another, because he honestly had no idea which member of Rasp's family he was currently yelling at.

Croak.

"Yes, a bear. I'm aware, thank you."

The crunch of approaching footsteps reminded Faris that he was supposed to be running for his life. Gritting his teeth, he limped along, certain he could hear the huffing breath of the beast grow louder as it slowly closed the gap between them.

CHAPTER ONE

That's Cannibalism

Look, I like charred snake as much as the next person. Nothing hits the spot better when you're stumbling home after a night at the tavern." Rasp tore another chunk of piping hot meat from the skewer with his front teeth, feeling the warm juices dribble down his chin. He wiped the grease from his scratchy beard with the back of his sleeve as he wandered between the busy vendor stalls, sweeping his cane across the cobblestone street ahead of him.

A flood of blurry citizens flowed around him as if he were a turtle among a stampede of rabbits. As most passersby avoided acknowledging him, Rasp felt inclined to return the favor. He carried on, still chewing, "All I'm saying is that the local kebab business could do with some variety. Remember that muskrat we had a couple months back? Practically orgasmic."

Croak.

"What do you mean you preferred the chicken?" He lifted the half-eaten skewer higher, allowing the raven perched on his shoulder to tear a morsel free with a violent shake of its head. "You're a bird. Isn't that, like, I don't know, cannibalism or something?"

Unable to speak clearly around the beak full of meat he was scarfing down, Father gargled his reply instead.

"I know you're not a chicken! It's just weird, is all."

Croak!

"For the last time, I did not eat that man's foot. I bit down a little too hard and a piece got in my mouth. I panicked and swallowed. Me accidentally ingesting the tip of someone's pinky toe is not the same as you going out of your way to eat another bird because you enjoy the flavor."

Although the mass of festivalgoers shuffling around him constituted little more than hazy shadows, Rasp was certain he saw a number of heads turn in his direction. In all fairness, the blind vagrant sharing a skewer of crackled pork belly with the raven perched on his shoulder was probably reason enough to stare. Even without proper eyesight, he knew he looked a mess. His silver hair had grown out and now hung around his ears in a dirty, tangled mess. He had several months' worth of a patchy beard on his chin and the layer of filth was probably the only thing keeping his traveling clothes from falling apart at the seams.

Around them, the late-evening air was crisp and laden with the fragrance of bloomed chili spices, roasted meats, and enough cut onions to make his eyes weep. The dark sky was held at bay by countless twinkling yellow lanterns strung between the food stalls that lined either side of the bustling street. The Hanover city market was alive with activity as vendors cried out their wares to the passing patrons. The swaths of festivalgoers swarmed around Rasp, going out of their way not to touch him. As much as he would like to pretend this was out of conscientiousness for his cane, he suspected the odor from his unwashed skin was probably equally responsible for their wide berth.

Under Father's semi-helpful direction, Rasp was able to navigate the throng of blurry shapes until the street widened into a piazza of some sort. A structure rose up out of the cobblestones at the center of the city square. Rasp struck out toward it, certain he now knew what this curious landmark was. As he drew nearer, the soothing trickle of babbling water reached his ears, confirming that this was another one of the realm's curious creations known as a fountain.

The more of the realm Rasp explored, the less of it he understood. Fountains, for example, had no function other than something to be enjoyed. Apparently, you weren't supposed to drink or bathe in them—a fact Rasp had learned the hard way. Lucky for him, Whisper had managed to talk the local authorities into releasing him with a warning after explaining that Rasp had been kicked in the head by several horses as a child.

He rested his cane against the lip of the fountain and sat on the damp stone. Mist from the water feature pitter-pattered against his shoulders each time the evening breeze changed direction. Ignoring the chill, Rasp tugged a steaming chunk of pork from the skewer and tossed it into the air above him. Father leapt from his shoulder in a flurry of dark feathers and claws to retrieve it.

With his traveling companion temporarily distracted, Rasp scarfed down the rest of the food as quickly as he could. The last charred morsel was being shoved into the side of his cheek when Father landed on the stone lip beside him with an undignified screech.

"Wha'?" Rasp managed around the mouthful. "I'm bigger than you. I get more."

He regretted his gluttony almost immediately. The coarse salt crust was so thick it made his tongue burn. Attempting to chew the pork into a more manageable size, Rasp instinctively reached for the waterskin hanging from his hip when he remembered he wasn't wearing it. The waterskin was back with the rest of his meager belongings, stashed under a bush—coincidentally, the same place he was supposed to be.

Waiting for the other members of his party to return from their errands was boring, though. And with the enticing sounds and smells of the Hanover Harvest Festival calling to him from within the city walls, Rasp had no choice but to abandon his post and wander aimlessly inside. For strictly educational purposes, of course. After all, how could he expect to learn to blend in as an ordinary citizen of the realm if he spent all his time hiding in the bushes? That sounded more akin to a pervert and he didn't wish to be mistaken for one of those. Again.

A blurry passerby drew closer. Rasp felt his heart rate spike, fearing they were going to strike up a conversation. His fear was for naught, he realized when something struck the cobblestone between his feet with a metallic *clink*.

Rasp squinted at the mysterious shadow as they shuffled back into the indiscernible tide of moving bodies. Forcing down the rest of his food with a difficult swallow, he asked, "Did they just throw something at me?"

And Whisper said he could never pass for an ordinary citizen, ha! These people weren't so different from him after all. They, too, threw random objects at strangers. The thrower could stand to work on their aim though. It hadn't even gotten close to hitting him. Every experienced antagonist knew you aimed for either the head or the nuts. Those were the fundamentals of being an asshole.

Croak.

"He threw money at us?" Rasp tilted his head to the side curiously. He saw Father's blurry shape start to move for the prize and leapt into action, shooing the raven back as he scrambled to be the first to claim it. "Get your dirty talons out of here! You don't even use money."

Croak! Croak! Croak!

"I don't care how shiny it is. He threw it at me, therefore it's mine!" His grease-covered fingers were just grasping the coin when Father's body struck him in the back of the head. With an awkward squawk, Rasp toppled over onto the cobbled stone. He twisted and turned, flailing his arms and legs in order to keep the persistent raven at bay.

Father's talons skittered against the cobbled road as he hopped just outside of Rasp's range, croaking up a storm.

"Of course I'm acting like a child! I *am* a child. Your child, specifically! What's that say about your stellar parenting, huh?"

They continued in this manner for several moments more before Father gave up. It was a good thing too, because Rasp was now completely winded and in severe need of something to drink. With a groan, he rested his head against the rough stone and stared up at the lantern-obstructed sky as he considered all of the poor decisions that had led him to this new personal low.

Traveling the land with his mentor, Whisper, wasn't all bad. In fact, it came with some very unique upsides. In addition to learning how to actually use his powers, Rasp was also getting to see life outside of the Iron Ridge. Well, not actually *seeing* it. *Experiencing* it was probably a more accurate description. But he got to taste it, and smell it, hear all of its terrible sounds. And sometimes, amid the ever-present chaos of running from one territory to the next, scouring the realm for some ancient artifact he didn't care about, he got to kick a few asses too.

It almost made it all worthwhile—was what he told himself every morning as he dragged his protesting carcass out of whatever hidey-hole they'd bunkered down in for the night. Some days, the lies were all that kept him going. Tall tales such as: one day this will all be over; your enemies can't possibly come after you for the rest of your life; maybe you'll get to see Faris again.

"Is there a problem here?" The blurry outline of a person loomed over the top of him where he still stared pointlessly upward.

Rasp couldn't make out anything distinct about their features, but from the authoritative tone, he assumed they were wearing a uniform—the kind that usually came equipped with a little shiny badge pinned to their breast pocket, a baton hanging from their hip, and a false sense of superiority. Best to play it safe then. "A horrid creature attacked me," Rasp said. "I barely escaped with my life!"

There was a notable pause as the looming shape appeared to twist his head this way and that, searching the surrounding area for the creature in question. "All I see is a bird."

"Ah, well therein lies the problem, good sir. For I cannot see anything. I had no way of knowing whether the foul beast was a bird or a small, feathery dragon."

The officer's voice changed from mildly concerned to *it's time to move along, sir.* "We received several noise complaints—"

"Yes, it seems it was a very noisy bird," Rasp agreed.

"You were referring to it as 'Father'?"

Croak!

"Hey, you stay out of this! No one asked you," Rasp snapped before realizing this probably wasn't making his case. "I call anyone who attacks me Father. Ingrained childhood trauma and whatnot. It's a bit of a reflex."

Rasp pushed himself into a sitting position and scanned the area around him in the event things took a turn for the chaotic. He could barely make out his cane resting against the brim of the stone fountain several paces away. If he moved quickly enough, he could probably grab it before the officer grabbed him. Whether or not he'd be able to get any farther was a question he wasn't sure he wanted the answer to.

"I see. Do you have somewhere to stay tonight, sir?" The officer probably already had a convenient place in mind. The kind of room that came devoid of all furniture with white, padded walls and a padlocked door.

"I do. In fact, it's probably time I get headed in that direction now." Rasp rolled swiftly to his feet and was moving back toward the fountain when the officer's hand clamped firmly over his shoulder, yanking him to an abrupt halt.

"I don't want to make any assumptions about your circumstances, but if you would allow me to help, I think I might be able to find you someplace with a nice bed, maybe a hot meal, a bath . . ."

Some fashionable wrist bracelets, a nice shiny chain or two, Rasp's brain kindly filled in the blanks. Ducking low, he slipped the man's grip and whipped around, moving steadily backward until his calves struck the fountain. "Oh no, no, no. That won't be necessary."

Croak.

"More than one?" Rasp's eyes darted back and forth across the muddled city square, realizing he could make out the faint outlines of three other officers closing in around him. "Fuck! Why didn't you say something before?"

Father's reply was idiotic as expected.

"Because I wouldn't give you the damn money, really? Fine, take it! I'm not going to need it wherever I'm going, am I?" Rasp hurled the offending coin in the direction of the officer, whose shadowy figure was edging noticeably closer.

His attacker dodged, narrowly avoiding a collision with the squawking ball of feathers and fury that chased recklessly after the coin. "Easy, old man."

"Old man?" Rasp felt the drum of his heartbeat quicken as heat flushed across his face.

"Let's not make a scene here. Come quietly and we can get all of this sorted out for you."

Rasp was still caught up on the "old man" part. He'd thought it had been bad when everyone used to call him "boy" all the time, but this was so, so much worse. Just because his hair was silver didn't make him old. It was times like this, Rasp found, that the best way to prove he wasn't some old geezer was to act as immaturely as possible. Granted, the argument could be made that this was his solution for everything, but there wasn't any sense in fixing what had been broken for too long already.

"Good sir," Rasp said as the familiar warmth of magic lit a fire within his weary bones, "I'll have you know I refuse to do anything quietly!"

CHAPTER TWO

Father-Son Bonding

Alright, easy does it. Time to exercise some of that control Whisper is always hammering into your thick head.

Magic flooded down Rasp's forearms and pooled in his hands until each greasy fingertip thrummed with energy. He held it, allowing its intensity to build until his core was near bursting. With an idle flick of his fingers, a rush of water spilled over the side of the fountain behind him in a single, rolling wave.

The cries around him were more surprised than terrified, which meant his strategy was working. The water wasn't meant as a means of destruction. It was simply the first step in a brilliant plan of escape that would, ideally, harm as few people as possible, including himself.

Rasp leapt backward onto the fountain, ensuring his feet were not touching the tide that rolled soundlessly across the open city square. Already, he could see several of the advancing figures had overcome their shock and had remembered they were supposed to be catching him. According to Father, there were four pursuers in total. Rasp could hear their footsteps splashing through ankle-deep water toward him.

Father landed on his shoulder in a dark flutter of wings, voicing his concerns regarding the validity of Rasp's plan.

"I know they're getting closer. Stop rushing me."

Blocking out the raven's unhelpful response, Rasp drew inward. He pictured the energy burning within him and redirected it into his hands. Channeling his concentration, he tempered the raging fire, transforming it from hot to cold. He waited, allowing the magic to complete the change before casting it downward with a wave of his hand. Below him, the cobblestone crackled and popped as a layer of frost spread across the surface of the water, rendering it to ice.

So far so good. Twice now he'd managed to tap into his powers without awakening the beast within. This was good. This was working.

"What in the name of chaos?" the closest officer cried.

When Rasp opened his eyes again, he saw the man's blurry form lurch to a halt, unable to move forward with his boots stuck within a sheet of ice. A quick visual sweep of the surrounding area confirmed that the shadowy outlines of his cronies appeared to be having similar difficulties.

It was a shame Whisper wasn't here to see his accomplishment. His mentor might have actually been proud of him for a change. Of course, in order to brag about it later, Rasp first had to ensure he actually got away.

Ignoring the impulse to jump from the fountain and attempt a swift escape, Rasp eased his way onto the ice, checking to be sure he had his footing before skidding out across the slippery square. He was making slow but steady progress when he heard the ice shatter behind him. A glance over his shoulder confirmed that the lead officer had broken a foot free and was working on the other. Rasp attempted to pick up his speed but succeeded only in losing his balance and falling over.

Father took to the air above his head. *Croak!*

"My stick?" Crap. In a valiant effort to control his inner rage, Rasp had gotten so caught up in the getaway, he'd mistakenly left his cane behind. "That would have been helpful to know back at the fountain!"

Father's explanation was as petty as could be expected.

"Because you didn't get your coin, really?" So much for his valiant effort. Rasp could feel his temper beginning to stir along with his rising panic. "I will make it up to you, I swear. Now help me figure a way out of this!"

A second shattering of ice warned that his pursuer now had both feet free. Amid a slew of cursing, the officer's hazy shape started to move, shuffling rather comically in his direction. Rasp pulled to his knees and scrambled away on all fours, wincing as his bare skin tried to fuse with the passing ice. He continued despite the pain, focused on making sense of whatever nonsense Father was croaking up a storm about.

"Just like ice-skating?" he repeated. It was official. The damn bird was out of his pea-sized mind. "I never learned how to ice-skate. You said it was for pansies!"

Father continued to shout unhelpful advice at him from above.

Despite his best efforts, he wasn't getting anywhere very quickly on all fours. Additionally, two more pursuers had broken free from the ice and were now in slow pursuit. Whispering a silent prayer to whatever deity might be listening, Rasp rose shakily onto his feet, keeping his hands out in front of him in case he toppled over again. "Alright! We'll do it your way. Tell me what to do."

The large raven landed on the ice several paces ahead of him, squawking instructions as he hopped and skipped along the path he wished for Rasp to take.

"I don't have time to put my socks over my shoes. Jump to the next step!"

Rasp listened to Father's instructions, feeling the icy grip of panic spread throughout his body. No time to think, just do. Filling his lungs with what was sure to be his last breath, Rasp bent forward and repositioned his center of gravity until it was over his feet. With one boot firmly planted, he pushed off with the other. To his absolute shock, he slid smoothly across the ice without falling. Excitement bubbled in his chest as he repeated Father's instructions a second time, both amazed and utterly delighted to find the results were the same as the first.

"Dad, look, look! I'm doing it!"

Rasp heard the ice crunch behind him as one of his pissed-off pursuers started to gain on him.

Croak!

"Don't think, just do" rang through his head once more. Per Father's instructions, Rasp pushed off once more, this time pivoting with his stationary foot in order to change direction. The motion threw his body spinning sideways, barely escaping the dark shape that leapt at him from behind. Rasp bent his knees to regain his balance until he slid to a successful stop. This time, when a second hazy form staggered closer, he was ready.

Rasp pivoted out of their grasp with relative ease. Emboldened by his newfound skill, he pressed forward, alternating feet as he built speed. Looking over his shoulder, he saw that the blurry shadows of his pursuers were so far in the distance they were now indistinguishable from the background. Rasp kept moving, certain at any moment, he would reach the edge of the ice floe and fall flat on his face, but the end never came. The ice stretched on even after he reached the towering buildings and slid into an adjoining side street.

The fleeing, alas, was made more difficult by the sheer volume of people who refused to get out of his way. It was only after his third collision that Rasp realized it was not intentional. From the frantic shouts and crunching of ice, a fair amount of the festivalgoers were trapped in place. Under Father's watchful direction, Rasp dodged and weaved his way through the confused crowd.

He was making decent progress when an uncomfortable warmth seeped from the soles of his shoes upward. Glancing down, he saw a faint pulsing glow illuminating the ice beneath his feet. The unfamiliar magic shot upward, shattering the surface layer with a resounding *crack!* A swirling mass of broken ice and stone lifted him in the air and whipped him sideways. Rasp slammed into a nearby vendor cart, snapping the stand from its wooden wheels along with what he imagined were several, if not all, of his ribs in the process.

Rasp lifted his head with a groan and tried to make sense of the twinkling specks of light dancing along the edge of his muddled vision. Through the shifting gloom, he saw the newest player advance toward him.

"By the order of the Division of Divination, I hereby order you to surrender!"

One of these idiots, great. As if fleeing from a squad of city police hadn't been bad enough, apparently Rasp's antics had drawn the attention of something far worse.

"Put your hands where—" The rest of the division member's words were cut off by a violent gust of wind that sent her careening back down the icy cobbled street like a dried leaf caught in a tornado.

"Fucking witches," Rasp cursed, attempting to roll to his feet but succeeding in landing face-first against the slick stone pavers. "I hate witches!"

"You are a witch," an unfamiliar voice said.

"Don't remind me," Rasp muttered. "Figures you were watching along the sidelines this whole time, being unhelpful as usual. Were you planning to step in at all or just watch me crash and burn?"

"I did step in."

"A little on the late side, don't you think?"

"I would not have had to step in had you stayed with the bags as instructed." A hand reached down and grasped his wrist. From the lack of concern in the stranger's voice, Rasp knew this wasn't a stranger at all, but one of his mentor's many disguises. Traveling in their true form, after all, would have simply caused more problems—primarily the kind involving pitchfork-wielding mobs.

"Now, if you're done making a spectacle of yourself, I suggest we make a quick exit. Where there is one member of the division, there are many." Whisper did not pull Rasp to his feet. Their hand on his wrist was simply to remind him that if he didn't make the effort himself, the fae would overcompensate with magic.

"You should be thankful it was as little of a spectacle as it was." Rasp stood and hooked his arm through Whisper's, starting off at an awkward limp as he attempted to match their stride. "Believe me, I could have made that way more spectacular."

Whisper pulled Rasp behind a random building and out the other end into a narrow alleyway. Dark and stinking of garbage, the street was thankfully free of ice, making passage much faster. "They'll have eyes on the main gate by now. We'll have to find another way through."

Rasp found himself wondering if this other way through would involve obliterating a portion of the city wall. Not that he was opposed to it, of course, but such methods did seem to be in direct conflict with their agreed-upon *try to be subtle, dammit* way of doing things.

"We are not blowing a hole in anything." Whisper increased their pace from a fast shuffle to a clumsy run.

"Stop reading my thoughts!"

"Stop thinking stupid thoughts and I won't have to read them to tell you they're stupid."

"You know, I'm starting to think most mentors don't spend half their time calling their apprentices stupid." Rasp tightened his grip on Whisper's arm as he struggled to keep pace. With the absence of the lanterns, he was unable to make out anything more than vague passing shadows.

"Correct. What does that say about you, little bird?"

"Stop turning this around on me! Did you see what I did at the fountain? Problem-solving without overreacting. I dipped into my magic without stirring the darkness. You're welcome."

"Yes, yes." Whisper veered to the side, tugging Rasp around a corner he hadn't seen coming. "The performance was exemplary. Your reluctance to set anything on fire was particularly commendable. Well done."

Rasp was continually impressed by his mentor's ability to turn even the most benign of compliments into an insult. He opened his mouth, prepared to volley a barrage of venom-laced insults, when a sudden hiss from Whisper cut him short.

Rasp fell silent not so much out of a willingness to obey, but because he was already short of breath and shouting while running was only exacerbating the fire burning within his lungs. Over the rasping pant of his own breath, he heard the echo of fast footsteps close in behind them.

CHAPTER THREE

A Heartfelt Reunion

Get your hands off me!" Daana's voice reverberated against the vaulted ceiling with such magnitude, the entire palace was probably aware of the disturbance taking place in the grand entryway.

Startled by her volume, the guard slightly lessened his crushing grip on Daana's elbow. She ripped her arm free and staggered several steps backward. The worn tread of her boots slid on the slick gold and white marble tile as she put space between her and the palace guard, ensuring she had adequate room to dodge in the event he tried to grab her a second time. She supposed she could kick him between the legs as she had done to the guard who intercepted her on the steps, but that would only add to her growing troubles.

The palace guard overcame his momentary shock and, with a firmly set jaw, moved toward her again. His right hand shot out to grab her, but Daana sidestepped him. "I already told you," he snarled. "No one enters the palace without an appointment. Either you leave now, willingly, or you shall do so under arrest."

"For the last damn time, I don't need an appointment because I live here! I am Daana Lazuli."

"That joke gets less funny every time you tell it."

She caught a glimpse of her grimy reflection in one of the gold-plated mirrors mounted along the wall. At the very least, the guard's reaction was understandable. Daana looked more like a street urchin than she did the proud member of a noble house. She wasn't even going to address the fact that if it weren't for the dress, it would have been next to impossible to tell she was a lady.

"Alright, I admit this looks bad." Daana steadily backed away, keeping a watchful eye on the second palace guard, who was slinking up along the hallway from behind. The grand entryway staircase was only ten yards to her left. With a little skill and a heap of luck, there was a chance she could reach it before either of them nabbed her. "I only jumped the fence because the sentries at the gate wouldn't let me in. And yes, I might have kicked the guard that intercepted me on the steps . . . several times, but he was being unnecessarily rough. If you would just fetch my uncle, Geralt Lazuli, Speaker of the People, he could clear up this little misunderstanding right away."

The rear guard rushed forward without warning, the heels of their boots clacking thunderously against the tile. Daana dodged the approaching guard but flubbed the footing. While her coordination was subpar, her timing was not. She threw her momentum into a roll and sprang into a low crouch, saving her face from a most unpleasant encounter with the floor.

With a horrendous squeak, she slid across the freshly waxed marble until she came to a stop several feet from the bottom of the staircase. The fact that she was facing the wrong way did little to dampen her astonishment. *Damn,* she thought, whipping around in order to face the oncoming enemy. *Why couldn't I have done that when one of the others was watching?*

Not the guards, obviously. The pair had witnessed her unexpected feat of agility and were steadily advancing with more caution than before. They even had shortswords drawn. She didn't know whether to feel flattered or insulted by that.

"What is the meaning of this?" a harsh voice rang out from above.

Even after months away, Daana still flinched at the familiar tone. The guards halted in their tracks, allowing Daana a brief second to glance over her shoulder. An elf with light brown skin and tightly braided hair stood at the top step. The hem of his long, black robes pooled at his feet. His eyes were ice gray, like frost-coated silver.

The elf's gaze settled on Daana and his lower lip fell open with a slight tremble. "Daana?"

She'd thought she was prepared for this moment, but dread fluttered like an injured butterfly in the pit of her stomach regardless. On cue, a tight smile pulled mechanically across her lips. Daana threw out her hands to welcome him, nearly choking on the word as it squeaked free from her dry throat. "Uncle!"

An amalgamation of various emotions flickered across his sharp features, none of which Daana could identify with any certainty. Her unannounced arrival must have come as a surprise even to him because, for the first time in her life, Uncle appeared to be at a loss for words.

"How?" he managed, finally.

She swallowed hard, fighting the instinct to open her mouth and let it all come pouring out in a desperate bid to win his approval.

"I will explain everything, I assure you." Daana tilted her head at the sword-wielding guards. Thankfully Uncle's presence appeared to be keeping the pair at bay for the moment. "Do you think you could do something about my present situation first? This is, after all, a heartfelt reunion and not an interrogation. I'll pretend not to be offended that your muscle didn't recognize me."

"I will take it from here, thank you." Geralt dismissed the palace guards with a wave of his hand as he skittered down the stairs, his dark robe billowing majestically in his wake. Somehow Uncle managed to make even a rushed descent look regal. He reached the bottom of the staircase and pulled Daana into his arms.

Her heartbeat doubled as she stood frozen, unsure of whether to pull away or give in. Uncle had never been the affectionate type. In fact, she couldn't remember the last time he'd hugged her. Was this proof that she'd misjudged the situation? That maybe things between them weren't as horrible as she'd been led to believe?

The embrace was as awkward as it was short-lived. Geralt pulled swiftly away, the edges of his sharp nostrils wrinkling in disgust. "Why do you smell like a dung heap? Dear girl, in all of this time away, tell me you haven't forgotten how to bathe."

Ah, there it was. Cruel reality right on schedule.

"This may come as a surprise, but there weren't many opportunities to freshen up while trekking through lawless territory on my own, Uncle," Daana replied in an overly chipper tone. The filth was an added layer of protection as well. Overeager soldiers and suspicious townsfolk would have noticed the highborn elf passing through, but no one batted an eye at another bedraggled traveler. With war waging across the territories, displaced refugees had been turning up in the capital in record numbers. No one had noticed the stowaway that slipped through the gates among them.

"Yes, of course." Unless he was weaponizing the impact of uninterrupted eye contact to make a point, Uncle Geralt's gaze never lingered in the same place for long. His stare lifted from Daana as he spoke, sweeping the area around them. "I want to hear all about it. But perhaps somewhere private. Come."

He led her into the stateroom, pausing at the doorway to speak with a passing servant. Daana drifted into the room ahead of him. The blue-and-gold stateroom stretched around her in a glimmering display of bloated opulence. Three of the four pastel-blue walls sported spiraling columns of gold and ivory. The spaces between the columns were lined with tufted chairs and lounges, above which hung giant, tastefully boring paintings all depicting variations of the same floral garden. The fourth wall proudly displayed a gilded hearth nearly the size of a small storehouse, fashioned to look like the mouth of a snarling dragon. The polished marble flooring was obscured from sight by the plush blue rug that sank nearly half an inch under her weight. Overhead, three crystal chandeliers showered the stateroom in pale, flickering light.

Among the lavish furnishings, the only detail out of place, regretfully, appeared to be her.

Daana shifted nervously, clasping her hands in front of her in order to avoid adjusting her poorly fitted dress for the umpteenth time. The garment had been nabbed from an unattended clothesline several towns over. Despite her best efforts to adjust the fit to conform to her body, the waist still cut uncomfortably deep into her stomach. No matter how she tried, her gaze kept wandering back to the pedestals that lined either side of the hearth with various shiny treasures.

The doors closed behind her softly, disrupting Daana's internal debate over which valuable would fetch the best price on the street.

"I have food on its way." Geralt imparted one of his tight-lipped smiles. The kind that never seemed to reach his eyes. "In the meantime, I want to know everything. Starting with how it is you got here?"

"Walked mostly."

"Yes, but how? Your last known whereabouts were in Adderwood, held hostage by the enemy. I have the ransom notes to prove it. How did you manage to escape and make your way all the way here without anyone knowing?"

While Uncle had used the word "anyone," he actually meant "me." All her life, he had insisted that information was the greatest power and wielded it with far more accuracy than any weapon. The fact that Daana had managed to break out on her own without his notice was probably eating away at him from the inside. "Oh, so you *did* receive the ransom notes." Daana couldn't deny the sting of disappointment that pulled tight at her throat. It was one thing to be ignorant of your niece being held captive. But to know and purposely do nothing? Rat bastard. "Didn't ever get around to paying them, I guess. You did read the part where my captors threatened to cut off my fingers, right?"

Uncle's mouth parted, horrified. Daana laughed it off with a playful shove. He stumbled several steps backward before regaining his composure.

A pity. Perhaps she'd give it another try near the top of the stairs.

"I'm kidding, Uncle! Although I suppose it's good I took care of things when I got the chance." Daana lifted her hands, wiggling her fingers at him. "Else I might be short a few of these."

"Daana . . ." His frosted gray eyes were focused on her arm and not her words. Uncle Geralt reached out and grasped her wrist, gently pushing back her sleeve to get a better view of the black, branching veins that snaked up the inside of her forearm. "What happened?"

Oh yeah. *That.*

Daana had run this same conversation through her head so many times, she was certain she'd covered all her bases. And yet, somehow the explanation for the dark magic writhing beneath her skin had slipped her mind completely. If she was being honest with herself, it was because it scared her to think about.

Honesty, however, was the last thing on her mind and Daana offered Uncle Geralt a nervous smile instead. "Did you say there was food coming? Because I don't know about you, but I could really go for a strong cup of tea about now."

And a few shots of gin for added measure. Or a bottle. Maybe a case.

CHAPTER FOUR

Threatening Silence

Uncle Geralt traced the outline of the dark veins on Daana's wrist with his index finger. He stopped when he reached the edge of her tattered sleeve, tapping his fingertip against the underside of her arm as his eyes narrowed in concentrated thought. She searched his expression for clues, but found none. The skin on Daana's face was unbearably hot. Sweat dripped down her forehead as her heartbeat intermixed with the sound of her own racing thoughts.

How was she supposed to explain the markings on her arm? *Oh, you know how it is with evil, dark entities, Uncle. One moment you're trapping it within a powerstone and, in the next, you're accidentally absorbing some of its power. Also, I may have infected two other people while doing so. Whoopsie!*

"Daana?"

Uncle's voice snapped her from her inward spiral. Daana's teeth sank into her bottom lip as she stared back at him, refusing to say any more.

"Daana?" he repeated.

Hold the silence, Daana. You can do it.

"Child, you haven't blinked in ages."

Hold it. Hold it. Hold it!

Uncle Geralt's gaze lifted from her arm to her face, bearing down on her with the full weight of his attention. Something about his expression changed. Daana didn't know how exactly, only that it was suddenly taking every ounce of her nerve not to squirm out from under his scrutinizing stare.

Finally, having reached some unspoken conclusion, he imparted his thoughts with slow, methodical care. "This is not like any sort of affliction I have ever seen before. By its appearance, I would hazard that it was not exacted on you by a mortal either."

Daana's brow furrowed. Of course the first thing out of his mouth was about the damn magic! Not "Daana, my dear, I was so worried. I missed you terribly. Your absence made me realize all the ways in which I mistreated you, and I would like the chance to do better."

With her stream of consciousness running rampant through her thoughts, Uncle Geralt's next question caught her by surprise. "Is it causing you harm?"

For the briefest of moments, something flickered in her chest. Was it possible? Did he actually care? She had spent the past few months so utterly furious at him that she hadn't considered the possibility that Uncle might have actually been worried. "I don't know." Her voice was small. "I was hoping to find that out myself."

"I've heard mixed reports detailing the battle on Mount Hook. Without any eyewitnesses on our end, it has been difficult separating fact from fiction." This time, when his somber gaze lifted, it remained fixed on her, watching her reaction for tells. "Was this the ghost's doing?"

And just like that, the flicker of hope snuffed out. Daana jerked her arm free of his grasp, working her loose sleeve back over the markings. "The ghost, really? That's what you think to ask me? Not, *Daana, how are you? Are you alright? Can I get anything for you?* For fuck's sake, next you'll be asking me if I captured the damn thing."

His dark eyebrows rose as if to say *did you?*

"It still counts if you say it with your face!"

Uncle Geralt picked his words carefully. "I am getting the sense that you are upset with me. If it is about the ransom, please know that I have been attempting to negotiate your release for months now. Regretfully, communications from your captors have been unreliable at best."

Daana found herself unable to form a reply that didn't rely exclusively on the use of profane language. "Mhm."

Geralt's gaze swept to the nearest lounge. He frowned, as if debating whether he wanted to put a towel down first. "Let us sit and discuss this civilly. As you can imagine, I have so many questions."

"Yeah, I don't think so. You don't get answers. Not before I get some first." She folded her arms over her chest and broadened her defiant stance. "I learned some very interesting rumors during my time away. You're not getting another word out of me about the Palace Ghost, or Oralia, or the rebellion, until you give me the truth."

"Oralia?" Uncle Geralt looked as though he had bitten into an exceptionally sour lemon. "Oralia Dawnsight? Traitor to the realm, responsible for sparking widespread civil disobedience and turning at least two out of the outer territories into active rebellion against the current governing body— that Oralia? For the gods' sakes, child, she held you prisoner against your will! You, above all else, should know better than to believe a single word out of that traitor's mouth."

"Actually, it was Ellisar that told me." Daana tapped her foot, watching his reaction as carefully as he watched hers. "I wonder if she's returned to calling herself Captain Pride by now. That's a name you should recognize, isn't it, dear Uncle? She's not a chatty one, but she had an awful lot to say about you."

He stared at her like a predator determining whether to meet the opposition's challenge or turn tail and run.

"No? Well, what about Larkspur Denari? Is there anything you'd like to tell me about her?"

Uncle Geralt's unnerving stare continued to try to pin her to the carpet.

"Uncle, Uncle, Uncle." Daana tsked at his efforts. She stepped closer, pushing her face nearer to his, hoping to crack his fixed expression. His nostrils twitched at the smell, but to his credit, his resolve remained otherwise undeterred. "The threatening silence, really? You know Oralia practically invented that, right? Frankly, she's a lot better at it, too. Let's leave the hostility to the experts, shall we?"

Uncle's voice was low, spoken through clenched teeth. "What do you want from me?"

"The truth."

"The truth? The truth is Larkspur Denari was a magical extremist. She didn't care about freeing her fellow witches any more than she cared about you, Daana."

"So it's true then? She was my mother?" She didn't wait for his answer. Fighting the sudden onslaught of angry tears, Daana threw her arms out from her sides. "Don't you think that's something you should have told me? I deserved to know!"

"It did not matter."

"Of course it mattered!"

Uncle Geralt's downturned mouth doubled its efforts. "She didn't want you, Daana. What good would it have done to grow up knowing that? Forgive me for trying to spare you this pain. I thought it was better to keep you in the dark than to know your mother abandoned you."

"Putting me on a boat does not count as abandoning me," Daana replied stiffly. She met his frown with a raise of her eyebrow. "Yes, that's right. I know about that part, too. And how you paid off the goblin that found me so you could claim me as your own."

"What was I supposed to do? You arrived at the palace doorstep as an orphan. No charity would have taken you in, not with your familial history. I forged the papers and your background, yes. But what of it? Did I not give you everything your actual mother couldn't? A roof over your head, the finest schooling, and the greatest asset of all, a purpose. And now, after everything I have done for you, you're willing to throw it all away on the word of a deranged criminal claiming to be some long-dead revolutionist?"

Daana's scowl must have been one for the record books because it caused Uncle to falter. Finally, after an uncomfortable silence settled between them, he drew himself to his full height and allowed the weight of his words to settle. "What is your end goal here, Daana? Was it enough to hear me admit my deceptions out loud? I would like to think our relationship can recover from this, but that would require compromise on both our ends."

"I already told you what I want! Stop trying to rearrange me on your stupid chessboard and tell me about Larkspur Denari."

"The answers you seek will not fulfill you."

Daana gritted her teeth together. "Tell me about my mother."

"As you wish." He stepped around her, hailing someone lingering on the other side of the ajar door. "Guards, secure her."

On his command, a trio of hired muscle stormed into the stateroom. They were dressed in plainclothes without an emblem or insignia to identify their employer. Meaning, of course, that they worked for her uncle exclusively. The only similarity shared between the three goons stalking swiftly toward her was the abundance of weaponry hanging from their belts. Each one openly carried a shortsword and a dagger.

As her own knife had been stripped by the palace guard who intercepted her on the front steps, Daana had no realistic means of defense. She may have learned how to throw a decent right hook and kick below the belt during her time away, but she was still no match for three professionals. Two of the unmarked guardsmen took up positions on either side of her as the third secured her hands behind her back with a set of heavy iron manacles.

Daana winced as the metal snapped over her wrists with a heavy *clink!* "You're putting me under arrest? Really?"

"I'm afraid my hand has been forced."

"Is that just how lowly you think of me, Uncle? In case you've forgotten, I grew up in this palace. I watched you play this game with the common folk." Daana did her best to look unbothered by the fact that the manacles were entirely too tight. "You place me in chains, have your guards haul me out the door. Just as I'm being dragged away, I have a sudden change of heart and agree to tell you everything I know in exchange for my freedom. Am I remembering that correctly?"

"You are," Uncle Geralt said. "Unfortunately, such information will only serve to make this next step awkward between us."

Daana gazed around the room, avoiding direct eye contact lest he see the fear hidden behind her mask of indifference. Amid the various replies rampaging behind her eyes, she chose the one that would be sure to antagonize him the most. "To be honest, I'm not convinced you even have a dungeon at this point."

"Several, actually." He started toward the double doors, with his hands clasped behind his back as his long robe swayed behind him. "Escort her to the carriage, gentlemen."

Daana dug her heels into the plush carpet as the guards shepherded her toward the double doorway. Uncle Geralt awaited them in the hallway, watching with an expression of callous indifference. No, it was worse than that. The fucker looked bored! Ugh, Daana couldn't wait to wipe that stupid look from his face the moment she got her hands free.

She had to settle for glaring daggers at him instead. "This isn't funny! Tell your men to unhand me this instant!"

Geralt strode casually alongside as the guards whisked her out of the stateroom and down a separate hallway. The corridor was dark and narrow, leading to the servants' entrance. "You asked to learn about your mother, Daana. I am merely sending you to the one person who knew her well. You should be thanking me, honestly."

CHAPTER FIVE

The Full Dungeon Experience

It was times like this that Daana regretted swearing off magic for good. Yes, there had been legitimate reasons for doing so: her diminishing sense of control; the unintended, often disastrous consequences that immediately followed; and, most importantly, that the use of magic seemed to directly correlate with the spreading darkness within her veins. But so what? If anything, her present situation called for drastic measures. Unfortunately, without her armlets and with no immediate way to awaken the magic buried inside her, Daana was forced to rely on more practical means to escape.

Dragging her feet into the carpet proved both ineffective and impractical. No matter how she struggled, Daana was unable to slow their swift progress. The third henchman reached the end of the hallway and held the door for them. A stark channel of sunlight poured in from outside, temporarily obstructing her vision. The same could not be said for her escorts, who carried on without missing a beat.

Uncle Geralt stopped at the doorway and waved the procession down a series of worn stone steps. There was an unmarked carriage awaiting them in the empty courtyard below, its door already swung open in preparation for a swift departure. "Oh, and do be sure to remember the blindfold," Uncle called after them. "It would be a shame to rob my dear niece of the full dungeon experience."

Well, shit. He wasn't playing around anymore, was he? Daana had meant to push him over the edge, of course. She simply hadn't expected it to be this easy. Uncle Geralt had always been a fickle fiddle to play. After so many years of being on top of his game, had he finally lost his touch? A troubling thought settled over Daana's thoughts. What if he hadn't? What if he'd somehow anticipated her move and was now stringing her along as a means to fuck with her in return?

Don't let him get into your head!

Right. Stick to the plan. Daana willed her limbs to go limp, causing the guards to nearly drop her, as she revisited her mental checklist. Break into the capital, check. Confront Uncle and piss him off, check and check. Make it look convincing. Ah, yes, that's where she was. By all accounts, she was nailing it so far. It probably helped that the fear she was supposed to be feigning was one hundred percent authentic. All that was missing now was a desperate escape attempt to really drive the performance home.

Springing back to her feet, Daana kicked the guard to her left in the back of the knee. He crumpled to the ground with a surprised yelp. Wrenching free of the other, Daana spun around to find the third henchman hurtling toward her. She dodged him, inadvertently tripping over the fallen body of the first, and struck the cobblestones, unable to use her hands to cushion her fall.

"Ugh," she groaned, rolling stiffly onto her side. While she had known the escape would fail, she hadn't meant for it to fail so spectacularly. Or quickly, for that matter. For the gods' sakes, she'd managed to roll *closer* to the damn carriage!

A slow clap emitted from the top of the steps. "Well done, Daana," Geralt congratulated. "You always were full of surprises. Now be a dear and move this along quickly. I have a nation to run."

The obligatory "fuck you" died on Daana's tongue as a dark hood was pulled over her head. She continued to fight every step of the way until one very exasperated henchman abandoned all sense of propriety and swung her over his shoulder. Muttering under his breath, he clambered into the back of the awaiting carriage with Daana kicking for all she was worth. He set her onto the wooden bench with an ungentle slam, knocking the remaining air from her lungs.

The carriage frame rocked as the second guard climbed inside and took a seat across from them. The third jumped in next but was prevented from sitting alongside the second.

"On the other side of the prisoner," Guard Number Two ordered.

"There's barely any room!" number three protested.

"She's already given half the palace force the slip. We're not taking any chances. One on either side of her."

". . . But the smell."

"Oh please," Daana muttered. "I can still smell the whore on your breath with this bag over my head."

"You, shut up. And you, *sit*."

With a reluctant groan, guard number three made room by shoving Daana farther down the wooden bench seat until she was pressed firmly against the body of the first.

Uncle's voice rang out, fainter than before thanks to the stupid hood. He must have abandoned his post at the top of the stairs to see her off. How generous of him. It was a shame she couldn't reward his kindness with a nice headbutt to the nose. "This pains me as much as it does you, Daana," Uncle Geralt said. "I do hope that you come around on your own. Until that time, enjoy your stay. I assure you, you will be in the very best of hands."

Without further ado, the door slammed shut and the carriage lurched forward, picking up speed as it barreled down the uneven cobblestone road. Daana ground her back molars as her backside slammed against the un-cushioned bench seat as the driver seemingly went out of his way to drive over every bump and pothole in the city.

Daana squirmed in her seat, attempting to work her wrists free of the heavy iron manacles keeping her hands fastened behind her back. She suc-ceeded only in rubbing the skin on her wrists raw against the unyielding metal—that and earning a firm elbow to the ribs from the guard on her left.

"Sit still," he grunted.

There was a time in her life that such rough-handed treatment would have frightened her into an obedient stupor, but that was Old Daana. And Old Daana would not even recognize the version of her that now sat shackled on the bench, headed for a dungeon, running poorly thought-out revenge plots through her head. Using the toe of her boot, Daana searched the floor for Guard Number One's foot until she found it. She lifted her boot and brought her heel down upon it with as much force as she could muster.

Daana was rewarded with a cry of pain, immediately followed by a sec-ond elbow to the ribs. This one was noticeably harder than the last.

She doubled over, barely able to breathe as hot tears sprang from her eyes and trickled down her face. An unnerving laugh filled the cramped carriage. What was even more unnerving was the fact that it was coming from her. Oh dear. After months of being stretched thin, her mind had finally snapped.

"What the fuck is wrong with you?" Guard Number Three struck her across the back of the head. "Sit still and shut up!"

With each gasping laugh, the coarse fabric of the hood pressed farther into her mouth, threatening to cut off her dwindling air. Daana closed her eyes and focused on slowing the rampant drum of her heartbeat as a maniacal smile pulled across her mouth. "What was that? A love tap?"

"Muzzle it, or I'll give you another one."

As her ability to defend herself had steadily improved over the course of the past four months, so too had her aptitude for shit talk. Unfortunately, the latter was not always to her benefit. "How about you unchain me and I show you what a real hit feels like?"

Oh gods. Had she really fallen so far? Considering she was sitting shackled in an unmarked carriage destined for a secret dungeon, the answer was equally as uncomfortable. Pushing the thought from her mind, Daana put on her best smile in spite of the hood and said, "We could take turns if you really want."

She felt the guard's body shift as he twisted his torso around, winding up for what would surely be a painful swing. The officer across from them was quick to put a stop to it. "Back off, man. She's not worth it."

The rest of the ride was carried out in silence. Eventually, the terrain beneath the clackity wooden wheels shifted from stone to dirt. Daana assumed this meant they were on the outskirts of the capital, perhaps beyond the city wall itself. The cart took an unexpected turn and Daana squeezed farther against the shoulder of the guard on her left until the whole thing rolled to a gentle stop. A poorly oiled door creaked open seconds before she was half pulled, half pushed from the bench and onto the awaiting ground below.

She twisted her head to either side, her eyes straining against the dark cloth to make out any sort of detail as to her surroundings. It was a futile effort. What she could tell was that the air was fresher here. The deafening hustle and bustle associated with city living was absent as well. Definitely outside of the capital, she concluded.

"Walk." The guard on her left yanked her forward. The crunch of loose dirt underfoot soon changed to stone. From the sudden chill and decrease in light, Daana suspected she'd been herded into an airy building. If Uncle's chilling words were to be believed, it was a dungeon. Probably just one of the many dungeons that those in power claimed didn't exist.

One quick, whispered conversation later, and Daana found herself being delivered into a different set of hands. These ones came attached to a much larger body. One that smelled like cheap cigars and unwashed armpits. She felt a warm, sweaty hand wrap over her shackled wrists as the other pressed flat against her shoulder. Pressure from the palm on her shoulder told her that it was time to move again.

The warden, jailer, guard—whomever this person was—walked her several paces and then took a sharp turn. The stairs came next. The stone steps were small and poorly spaced, spiraling upward in such an endless manner, Daana feared the guard was taking her all the way to the top just to prove a point. The putrid stench of overflowed chamber pots and mildew permeated her burning lungs as they climbed steadily higher.

She heard a muffled scream in the distance. Or at least she thought she did—still kind of hard to know for sure with the damn hood muffling everything going on around her. Perhaps it'd just been the wind. Or a mouse, or a creaky door, or the tortured soul of one of the many ghosts that undoubtedly haunted the dark corridors in the dead of night.

On second thought, this was a terrible plan. Why in the name of chaos did she agree to this?

To the relief of her aching feet, they eventually reached the desired floor and the guard herded her down a poorly lit passageway. The hand wrapped over her wrists yanked her to a halt. Daana heard the jangle of iron keys on a keyring next and then nearly jumped out of her skin when the guard raised his voice. "Stand at attention, back wall!"

Daana had a sickly feeling that he wasn't addressing her.

The door swung open with a shrill creak moments before Daana felt her shackles unlock and the hood was yanked from her head. An ungentle shove sent her careening into the open doorway. Catching her balance, Daana spun around in time to see the barred door slam behind her. The guard tested the integrity of the lock and then left, his heavy footsteps growing softer as he disappeared down the unlit corridor.

Flexing the life back into her numb fingers, Daana turned and took in her gloomy surroundings. Her vision adjusted rather quickly, which she normally would've been grateful for, except that in this case the shadow that loomed over her turned out not to be a trick of the low light at all, but a person.

A low voice rumbled over the top of her head. "I hate it when they make me slaughter my own dinner."

CHAPTER SIX

No More Lone Martyr Shit

The steady *drip-drip-drip* of water leaking from somewhere within the dilapidated walls faded into the background as Oralia crept along the deserted passageway. She'd hear the occasional scuttle of feet, followed by a scuffle, sometimes a scream, and then nothing. The ominous silence would eventually give way to the steady drip of water once more. There weren't many stragglers left. From the sounds of it, her team was making short work of the few soldiers foolish enough to have stayed behind.

The old military settlement she was currently picking her way through had clearly seen better days. Nearly all of the mounted lanterns were missing, adding a layer of darkness to an already unpleasant experience. It was times like this that made her grateful she was no longer the Protector of the Realm. Had Oralia visited this particular settlement during her service, she would have ripped the command a new one for allowing their regiments to live in such squalor.

That was all in the past, however. And instead of inspecting the grounds, Oralia now found herself in the unique position of actively hunting its former occupants. She and her small force had split at the last four-way intersection, intent on flushing any stragglers toward the exit and into the awaiting arms of the recovery team—any that survived, that is. Certain members of her crew were more eager than others and did not quite grasp the concept of capturing their quarry *alive*.

For the first time in what felt like ages, Oralia found herself alone. The silence itself was a small blessing. Well, would have been, were it not for the nagging whisper that infiltrated her thoughts. **You can feel it, can't you? The hunger that flows through your veins? That's the call of magic. And we're getting closer to the source. To the left, now!**

Doing her best not to roll her eyes, Oralia ducked right instead.

Daft, orc. You're going the wrong way!

This portion of the building looked to be the officers' barracks. She crept down the gloomy passage with its bowed, planked walls and sagging ceiling. Around her, the musty air reeked of water damage and wood rot. Oralia checked several open doors as she passed, all of which were in various stages of abandonment. These chambers were bigger than the ones she'd seen on the way in. Each room was outfitted with a wooden desk and a single bunk—the sign of rank when it came to military strongholds.

In the distance, faint footsteps grew louder. Whatever officers were still trapped in the barracks were being driven her way. And, judging by the speed of the oncoming footsteps, had abandoned all sense of stealth in favor of a desperate run.

The powerstone hanging around her neck thrummed against her skin. **Turn back around! It's getting farther a—**

Oralia shut herself off from the voice that rippled across her mind. Now was not the time to get distracted. With her broadsword gripped in her dominant hand, she retreated into the protection of an open doorway and waited for the approaching footsteps to draw within striking range. The reason for the runner's speed was soon apparent. Oralia's heightened hearing picked up two additional sets of footsteps. There were voices as well. Male, human voices with which Oralia was regretfully all too familiar.

"Will you shove off?" Lingon snapped. "This one's mine! I had to tear down an entire barricade just to flush 'im out! You can't jump in mid-chase."

"What? And let another elf outfox you? We've got a namesake to uphold, Dingle. I'm not gonna let you tarnish it 'cause you're too proud to ask for help."

Oralia glanced around the edge of the door. The runner was nearly to her, crossing the intersection where the current hallway crossed the next with the next, when a dark shape took the soldier out at the knees. Oralia leapt from the protection of the doorway and started toward the scene to help. There was no need, however. The struggling soldier was subdued with neat, practiced precision.

Mul and Lingon's slogging steps reached the intersection only seconds ahead of Oralia. "Dammit, Rali," Lingon whined. "That one was mine!"

"Don't use that tone when speaking to my future wife," Mul said.

"What's that, Mulberry? You want to join the prisoner on the floor?" The threat in Rali's tone bordered on lethal. "Keep it up then. There's plenty of room down here, bucko!"

A shit-eating grin stretched across Mul's heavily bearded face. "Pickle, we agreed we wouldn't fight in front of company. You can wrestle me all you like in the privacy of our bedroom."

With a look of absolute disgust, Rali stood and dusted her hands together. "This here's number three for me. Remind me what score you two are at again? Still in the negative?"

Lingon crossed his arms over his chest, muttering, "It ain't fair that it counts against me each time I accidentally kill one. I can't help that their necks are so fragile!"

"To the losers goes the grunt work." Rali stepped over the bound soldier with a familiar swagger in her step. "Which one of you dingleberries is going to deliver him for processing?"

The cool, smooth exterior of the pendant grew inexplicably warm against Oralia's skin. It hung heavy and pulled at her, like an anchor. **To the left, orc. To the left! The source of power is near. It's hiding, but I can find it for you.**

It was then that Oralia noticed Rali gazing up at her, her nose wrinkled in scrutiny. "You alright there, boss?"

"Fine," Oralia lied.

"That thing's talking to you again, isn't it?"

There was no sense in denying what Rali obviously already knew. "It senses a witch nearby."

While trapping a dark, magical entity in a powerstone had prevented it from wreaking havoc on the mortal world, the aftermath was not without complications. What to do with the stone afterward, for example, was still being debated. Despite Ellisar's insistence that they drop the gem into the deepest trench at the bottom of the ocean and hope for the best, others felt it was only a temporary solution. A magic this strong attracted attention and eventually someone, somehow, would find it.

There was also the issue of the dark lines burrowed beneath Oralia's skin, tagging along like a cursed parasite. Back on the mountain, unbeknownst to them, the entity had splintered during the final spell. And while the powerstone housed the majority of it, she and Daana each carried a piece. Rasp may as well, but considering the last time she'd set eyes on him he was being carried off in the clutches of a dragon, Oralia had no objective way of knowing for certain.

Thus, she elected to keep the powerstone close until its fate could be decided. Without magic of her own, it was incapable of corrupting her. This, regretfully, did not prevent the damn thing from constantly whispering in her ear.

"Fucking witches." Lingon shuddered. "Tell you what, you all deal with the magic nonsense. I'll go deliver the prisoner and those of us still with heads can go raid the cantina for a drink afterward."

"Nice try, bucko. This is an all-hands situation." Rali reached out and grabbed him by the collar before he could slink away. She turned and employed a tone of voice that gently reminded Oralia what she was supposed to be doing. "Shall I signal for the rest of the team then?"

"Yes, of course. Thank you." Oralia's days of carrying out a mission single-handedly were over. Rali referred to the new policy as *no more lone martyr shit*. Between her and Sascha, it was a miracle Oralia was permitted to go anywhere without someone holding her hand. She knew it was out of concern, and tried to view it from their perspective, but it felt like overkill nonetheless.

Rali's infamous bird screech rang out, echoing along the empty corridors like a lost banshee in a labyrinth. Lingon waited until it was safe to uncover his ears again before voicing his complaints. "If you've got backup coming, then you definitely don't need me. You always complain that I just get in the way."

"I, for one, support our fearless leader's tactical decision," Mul congratulated with a hearty pat to Rali's shoulder. "Well done, Quartzey. I do hope our children take after their mother."

Quartz Ralizak was, by nature, not the type to let a fickle thing like virtue get between her and her revenge. Anyone who earned her wrath generally had the shattered kneecaps to prove it. The fact that the dwarf was actively restraining herself from seizing Mul by the wrist and flipping him head over heels onto the floor should have been commendable. Unfortunately, Oralia knew it was her presence and not personal growth that was keeping the bothersome man alive and well.

Rali clenched her jaw as her normally pale skin took on a hue similar to that of a ripe tomato. She locked eyes with Oralia, communicating her displeasure through the placement of a well-furrowed brow. Over the years together, they'd honed their ability to hold a silent conversation, or—in this case and, regretfully, almost all cases—argument. Oralia imagined Rali's protest went something like: *One more word, that's it, and this human's already short lifespan is going to get significantly shorter!*

In turn, Oralia's unamused expression replied, *You cannot kill him.*

Can and will, boss. Watch me. Look, I'll even do it with the bucko's own knife. Ha! Killed by his own weapon, wouldn't that be a scream?

No. Oralia was forced to rely on several hand signals to properly convey her line of reasoning. *We are guests in this territory. We must maintain a united front. Turn on each other now, and those in power will cast us out.*

Rali rolled her eyes as if to say, *What's the point of being an outlaw if I can't murder as I see fit?*

Outlaws do not murder their teammates.

Fine. I'll settle for a light stabbing. Deal?

No stabbing!

From the corner of her vision, Oralia saw Mul lean closer to Lingon. "Why's it look like they're fucking each other with their eyes?"

"It's a form of non-verbal communication," Lingon replied matter-of-factly. "So they can converse without us hearing all the juicy details, I'd wager." While Mul was loud, abrasive, and bullheaded, Lingon was also these things, but craftier. The younger Stoneclaw was always watching, always learning, always finding new and inventive ways to make Oralia pull her hair out. There was an undeniable spark of intelligence disguised beneath his slimy, rough-and-tumble exterior—which was saying a lot for a man who currently had a blasted finger shoved up his nose.

Mul was simpler. There was often only one of three things on his mind and, judging from his eager eyebrows, Oralia could already guess which of the three was currently rattling around his large head. He gave Lingon a playful nudge. "Juicy, huh? Are they fighting over who gets to have their way with me first?"

"Yeah, something like that." Lingon flipped his long hair over his shoulder in order to peer at Rali without it obstructing his vision. "Since bossy britches here ain't letting you have your fun, can I earn extra points by hitting Mul for you?"

"No!" Rali looked as though she was fighting the sudden urge to stomp her foot. "Nobody does my hitting for me. The only person who does Rali's hitting is Rali!"

The brothers exchanged glances before Lingon's mouth pulled into a wolfish smile. "Is Rali swooning so hard she talks in the third person now?"

"Mul thinks there's nothing wrong with talking in the third person," Mul said. "Also, Mul is an excellent swooner. Thank you for the compliment, Lingon. You are re-invited to the wedding."

Rali balled her hands into fists, but said nothing. Even in the low light, it was not difficult to see the shade of tomato on her face had turned deep crimson. Oralia considered coming to the dwarf's aid, but doubted Rali would appreciate it. In the end, it would only encourage the Stoneclaw brothers to double down on their efforts to . . . woo her? Torture her? Push her into a frenzied killing spree? Oralia still wasn't one hundred percent sure what their objective was.

"I can't believe I'm saying this," Rali groaned as she turned back to Oralia. "But can we get back to finding the witch already? The sooner we're out of here, the sooner I can go start digging some unmarked graves."

"We are awaiting the rest of the team," Oralia reminded her. She could hear at least two of them in the distance, steadily drawing closer as they navigated the labyrinth of dark passageways.

"They'll catch up easy enough," the dwarf said, eyeing the brothers with a rather unnerving twinkle in her eye. "Should be pretty straightforward given the blood trail we'll be leaving behind."

"I said no stabbing."

"Exactly. You mentioned nothing about bludgeoning."

CHAPTER SEVEN

Magic Smells of Lies and Deception

Movement from farther down the corridor spared Oralia from having to listen to her team's ceaseless griping. She recognized the first of the approaching forms from his quiet confidence. The dwarf captain, Almas Bernstein, walked with his head high and shoulders squared. His second officer trailed in his wake, gripping her ax with less confidence as she gazed up and down the dark passageway. The third arrival was more difficult to spot. They slunk along the curve of the dilapidated walls, utilizing every shadow to disguise their swift progress.

"Captain Bernstein," Oralia greeted the lead dwarf. She addressed his lieutenant next in a similar fashion. It was the third arrival's name, however, that took effort to say. Not through any fault of their own, of course. "Snag."

The goblin that stepped from the shadows was most certainly not Snaglebrag. The simple truth was Dewpetal looked nothing like Snag. She wasn't even the same species of goblin, for crying out loud. As Dewpetal was the only stand-in they could muster on such short notice, Oralia was making it work the best she could. Not that the discrepancies in appearance seemed to matter. A goblin was a goblin, as far as the realm was concerned. If her intelligence was to be believed, Geralt Lazuli was still unaware that the real Snag and Ellisar had already slipped past his defenses.

Rali's spirits perked at the rest of the team's arrival. "Alright, spill it. How many did you guys get?"

"I don't find it necessary to make everything a competition." Captain Bernstein spoke for him and his lieutenant, unconsciously fiddling with the ends of his beard as he often did in Rali's presence.

"None again, huh, Almas? That's alright, at least you're not in the negative. What about you?" Rali turned to the goblin and displayed three fingers.

Dewpetal held aloft seven clawed fingertips with a triumphant smile.

There was a collective groan from the others. One of the Stoneclaw brothers hissed under his breath, "She cheats worse than the real Snag!"

"We cleared the north and west corridors," Captain Bernstein said to Oralia. "Is there something we may assist you with, Madam Pro—"

"Oralia."

"Madam Oralia."

"Just Oralia." As she did not intend to stick around long enough to earn a title, Oralia insisted upon being referred to strictly by her name. Old habits were hard to break and her former rank had a habit of slipping out of people's mouths. "We have a witch on our hands. I believe they are holed up in one of these rooms, employing some sort of anti-detection spell."

Locating the witch would not be difficult thanks to the powerstone that hung from the chain around her neck. The entity trapped within the gem fed exclusively on magic to survive. Its constant thirst for power made it quite useful when tracking down witches. Captain Bernstein didn't know of the stone's existence, of course, and Oralia intended to keep it that way.

Captain Bernstein saw the terror that flashed across his lieutenant's tawny face and took pity on her. He gestured to the bound elf sprawled across the ground with his iron-tipped boot. "First, we will need to do something with our friend here. Lieutenant, will you see that they are safely escorted from the danger?"

"Yes, sir." His lieutenant heaved the prisoner into an upright position and marched them toward the entrance.

Lingon watched her go, pouting. "Not fair! I called dibs."

Captain Bernstein's concerned gaze returned to Oralia. "My encounters with people of the magical variety have been few and far between. I'm afraid I don't know the first thing about witch tracking."

"Oh, don't worry about that, Cappy," Rali assured him with a playful elbow to the breastplate. "Oralia's got a nose for magic. Just hang back with the rest of us; she'll lead us right to the scoundrel."

The captain's copper-colored eyebrows furrowed in confusion. "Miss Ralizak, if that was meant to be informative, it has only left me with more questions. Most notably, how?"

A glare from Oralia served to only encourage Rali's boundless imagination. "Well, it's a bit of a newfound ability, you see. Something she picked up on the mountain after the whole—" Rali waggled her fingers over her head, simulating an explosion, which, alas, included sound effects. "Being that close to potent magic can have unintended effects on the body, you know. It sort of imprinted into her internal synapses and made her extra sensitive to spellwork. Effectively, the boss can now smell magic."

His eyes grew wide in awe. "Unbelievable."

"Truly," Oralia agreed, taking the lead.

Captain Bernstein formed rank beside her and lowered his deep voice to a whisper. "What does magic smell like?"

Like lies and deception!

This was why she insisted on being excluded from Rali's games. Oralia had never been good at fabricating untruths, at least not without hours of extensive rehearsal beforehand. Her ability to ad lib on a moment's notice was not an ability at all, but an invariable weakness. ". . . Celery."

She heard several stifled snickers behind her.

Oralia navigated the dim corridor with the voice of the entity rippling across her thoughts. **Closer, closer, stop!**

She signaled for the others to halt. Alone, Oralia ventured forward and examined the entrance to the room that lay before her. The paint-chipped door was sealed shut with no light coming from underneath. Ignoring the tarnished handle, Oralia placed her hand against the wood instead. Tiny, magical vibrations shot up her arm and slammed into her chest, nearly knocking the breath from her lungs.

Shit.

She pulled away, wringing the sting from her fingers. Incapable of escaping its gemstone prison, the dark entity had a way of attracting outside magic toward it, utilizing Oralia as a conductor between it and its intended food source.

Signaling for Mul to keep watch, Oralia retreated several yards back down the corridor, where their hushed conversation would be less likely to be overheard. "I cannot tell how powerful our quarry is," she whispered. "We will have to proceed with absolute caution. Ralizak, do you have any more powder charges?"

"Two, I think."

Lingon wrapped his arms over his scrawny chest in a self-embrace, grumbling, "Would have been more if you'd let me carry 'em."

The charges had been a parting gift from Snaglebrag. His recovery after the mountain had been spent experimenting with his mysterious black powder. The charges were not only effective, but downright terrifying. Fearful the

Stoneclaw brothers would use them on each other, Oralia had appointed Rali as the designated carrier. The occasional distant *boom* in the night oftentimes made her wonder if that decision had been shortsighted.

"We will use the charge to take out the door." Oralia reached into the pouch on her hip and withdrew a folded slip of parchment and a chalk stick. After witnessing the symbol's power on the mountain, she had been sure to copy a number of runes from Daana's green spellbook. "Lingon, etch a seer's trap onto either side of the corridor, several yards from the doorway. There is a chance whoever is inside will flee once the door comes down. I would rather catch them through smarts than brute force."

Lingon's gaze dropped to the items deposited into his hands. "Why's it I always get tasked with the hedonistic symbolatry?"

Rali's response was sufficient in sending him on his way. "Because any time I try to use you as the bait, you run away."

"I do not mean to call your strategy into question," Captain Bernstein whispered. "But all of this sounds incredibly dangerous, possibly lethal. As the Adderwood representative on this mission, I do feel it would be proper to offer the individual inside the opportunity to surrender first."

"And give away our element of surprise?" Rali hissed. "Are you out of mind, bucko? There's no etiquette rulebook at play here. This is war!"

"More of a revolution, actually. One in which you and your commanding officer—"

"Friend," Oralia corrected.

"—have been brought on as temporary consultants."

Rali took a daring step forward, locking eyes with the slightly taller dwarf. "The whole point of hiring a consultant is to listen to them, yeah? Well listen here, bucko. Your plan is stupid and shortsighted. Not only are you taking away our main advantage, but you're going to give our enemy the opportunity to throw the first punch."

Captain Bernstein was not accustomed to being talked down to by someone he considered a subordinate. Most officers in his position would have been infuriated by the blatant disrespect. He merely gazed back at Rali, twisting his beard in what might have been amusement. "Technically speaking, you're not hired consultants, as the New Adderwood Republic does not possess the funds to pay you."

"Kinda feels like you're focusing on the wrong details here, Cappy."

"Your warning was heard loud and clear, Miss Ralizak. I appreciate your expertise. We will be doing it by the rulebook, regardless."

As much as she agreed with Rali, Captain Bernstein was their designated military escort and, therefore, in charge. The last thing Oralia needed was to have active warrants for her arrest in more than one nation at a time. Besides, it wasn't her war. So what if they did poorly? Her role was simply to act as a distraction, focusing Geralt's attention away from the capital, until which time Ashwyn could be found and freed.

Oralia stepped between the dwarfs, preventing Rali from ripping the captain's beard from his face. "If you feel it necessary, Captain. We will follow your lead."

When the others were in position, Captain Bernstein pressed himself flat against the mold-speckled wall beside the door. He slammed the butt of his ax against the ground with such force, a portion of the roof sprinkled down over the top of his helm like rotten, crumbly rain. "This is Captain Almas Bernstein of the New Adderwood Republic. We have you surrounded. All who surrender will be unharm—"

Oralia felt the wave of magic before it struck. She managed to yell for the others to take cover a split second before the oak door ripped from its hinges in a shower of white sparks. A cloud of smoke rolled through the musty corridor, choking the air. As the buzzing in her ears lowered to a tolerable hum, Oralia uncovered her head, suddenly aware that there was an additional body pressed against her.

"Ralizak?"

"I told that fucker this would happen!" Rali had her limbs spread wide, as if to shield as much of Oralia as her squat frame could allow. The dwarf tilted her head upward, squinting through the haze at Oralia. "You alright, boss? Still got your head? All ten fingers and toes?"

"Please stop doing that. The armor I am wearing is perfectly adequate. You checked it yourself only this morning." Through the smoke, Oralia saw a shadow dart from the smoldering room. "On the move! Southwest corridor."

There was a cacophony of sound as several bodies leapt from the protection of the wall and gave chase at once. A channel of pale green light flared farther down the passage, highlighting the chalk circle etched over the floor. Lingon reached the seer's trap steps ahead of the others. His nasal voice rang out with indignation. "Mul?"

The larger brother stood stock-still, with his arms held midair, eyes wide and petrified. "Lingon, what the fuck did you do to the symbol? It's supposed to catch witches, not me!"

"Where'd the witch go?"

"The little fucker sidled past!"

"Sucks for you then." Lingon pressed his shoulders to the wall and awkwardly shuffled around the seer's trap, mindful not to step inside.

"Oh, come on!" Mul bellowed as Rali and Captain Bernstein's respective shapes bounded across the symbol, unaffected by the anti-magic spell. "Don't leave me here, you bastards."

Oralia stopped and smudged the chalk symbol with the toe of her boot. The eerie glow of the magic faded, rendering the corridor dark once more. "Mul, this is the second time you have been caught by a seer's trap. You do realize this means—"

"Yeah, yeah, I've got ground to cover. I know!" He took off at a headlong sprint.

With a shake of her head, Oralia caught up to him as he rounded the corner. The chase was over as quickly as it had begun. The others stood in various states of frustration only a short ways away. Oralia slowed her step as the reason for the sudden stop became apparent. A human was strewn across the ground with their hands bound, groaning. Focused on the captured witch, Oralia nearly missed the goblin lingering in the shadows beside the body, proudly holding eight fingers aloft.

CHAPTER EIGHT

Level the Playing Field

Rasp's feet pounded against the cobblestone, sending jolts of pain coursing up his leaden legs. He ran, unable to focus on anything more than setting one stubborn foot in front of the other, as Whisper guided them deeper into the mazework of back alley streets and unlit ginnels. Rasp didn't know where they were going and had a sneaking suspicion that Whisper didn't either. He continued to slam his aching heels against the buckled street regardless.

The sounds of their pursuers grew fainter in the distance. He and Whisper were gaining the lead. Which was a good sign, because Rasp wasn't sure how much longer he could carry on. Already, his lungs felt as if they were folding in on themselves. Everything hurt—his knees, his bones, the steadily growing throb that tightened on the inside of his skull, threatening to send his brain matter shooting through his eye sockets.

"So dramatic," Whisper muttered.

He may have been short of breath, but that didn't keep him from complaining when the opportunity presented itself. "You know, when you first kidnapped me—"

"I did not kidnap you. I relocated you. By surprise." Whisper added, "Very suddenly."

"Yeah? Well, you failed to mention there would be this much running!"

Prior to his surprise relocation, Rasp hadn't had much experience with cities. Zero experience, to be exact. Lonebrook had been the largest populated settlement he'd ever visited and he'd found that overwhelming at times. The idea was somewhat laughable now. Rasp's newfound career as a fugitive witch acquainted him with cities of all shapes and sizes. As much as running down narrow alleyways to evade the law could acquaint one, that is.

There was one thing that stuck out to him. Be it a wealthy cityscape straddling coastline, or a landlocked sprawl surrounded by expansive farmland, there was a common denominator that united all of the cities of the realm: the seedy underbelly. It didn't matter if the city had iron gates and the finest towering stone walls to keep the rabble out. You could bet your last coin that beyond the cobbled pavers and lantern-lit streetways, there existed a district the rest of society turned a blind eye to. It was in these such places, Rasp discovered, that he usually found himself neck deep in trouble.

Tonight was no exception.

"Curse this abysmal city!" Whisper's fingers dug into Rasp's forearm and pulled him to a stumbling halt.

"What?" Rasp whipped his head from side to side, resisting the urge to keel over from exhaustion. The sparse moonlight filtering down through the dense cloud bank stopped at the terraced roofline, rendering the surrounding alleyway impossibly dark. A light wind whipped through the stone alleyway, carrying bits of garbage and the stench of spoiled food and manure.

Rasp's dry words came out between desperate gulps for air. "What is it?"

"A dead end."

"So? We just up-and-over it." It wasn't like this was the first time such a thing had happened. Being a blasted witch had to have some advantages, after all.

"Normally I would agree, but one of our pursuers presents a problem with that plan." Before Rasp could ask how, Whisper turned him to face the mouth of the alleyway. "Do as we have practiced. Reach out with your magic and listen to what it is telling you."

Old Rasp would have protested the idea, insisting their remaining time was better spent finding an alternate escape route. Current Rasp felt similarly. The only difference being that he now possessed the wisdom not to mock Whisper's suggestion out loud. Stifling a sigh, Rasp sucked in a lungful of dingy alley air and focused on his heartbeat, allowing its rampant drum to drown out his other senses.

His magic intermingled with the breeze and allowed the current to pull it farther down the dark alleyway. A series of faint energy pulses glowed within his mind, growing stronger as their sources neared. "I sense three witches," he said.

"Good. Dig deeper. Tell me what type."

Rasp tried to focus on the energies but the effort succeeded only in making his head swim. "Red, green, and blue?"

"Are we in primary school, little bird? Those are colors, not magical classifications."

"I don't know, alright?!"

"An earth elemental, an energy caster, and an alchemist." Whisper kindly provided the answer. "The reason we cannot up-and-over it, as you put it, is because the energy caster would strike us down the moment we tried."

In other words, they were trapped and the only way out would be to go through the enemy. Lovely. Rasp tilted his head, listening as three sets of footsteps flooded into the narrow alley. Try as he might, there was simply not enough light to distinguish the new arrivals from the rest of his environment.

"You are surrounded!" a voice bellowed across from them, reverberating off the surrounding stone buildings. "Surrender now and—"

Rasp didn't bother to listen to the rest of the witch's instructions. Having heard one overconfident call for surrender, you'd heard them all. They ended basically the same anyway: give us what we want or we hurt you. Rasp leaned closer to Whisper and said, "What's the plan?"

"I don't know. What is *your* plan?"

"My plan?" he sputtered. "You're the mentor! You're supposed to tell me the plan and I half-ass my way through it."

"I would not be a good mentor if I spent your entire training handing you the answers, little bird. I have full confidence that you can devise a competent strategy all on your own."

A crackling ball of green energy zipped between them and erupted against the wall at their backs. Shattered bits of brick and stone ricocheted across the alleyway amid the downpour of green sparks.

"Hey! We weren't ready!" Rasp's temper flared as he drew inward, hastily searching for the nearest element. The breeze responded, whispering into his ear as it tousled his hair. Rasp reached out with his magic, harnessing the power of the wind, and channeled it into a single force. He could feel the warm heat of the energy caster's power building into another attack across from him. With seconds to spare, Rasp unleashed the torrent of air into the narrow alleyway. Over the howling wind raging in his ears, he was rewarded with the panicked screams of his attackers as they were buffeted backward.

It wasn't a lasting measure by any means, but it did provide him with the opportunity to round on Whisper. "That was too close, even for you. You depleted your magic with that little spell back in the square, didn't you?"

"Regrettably, yes. But I still maintain that it's important for you to learn to rely on yourself." Whisper sounded remarkably unconcerned for someone whose current power was but a shadow of what it had once been. The latent effects of iron poisoning, unfortunately. "Now, stop thinking about me and focus on the fight at hand. You are outnumbered and your opponents currently have you on the defensive when you should be on the offensive. What is your first prerogative?"

Level the playing field. If Rasp couldn't rely on vision to aid him, then neither should his opponents. He reached into his pocket and withdrew a single matchstick.

"Oh dear gods," Whisper groaned.

"You told me to do this my way. This is how I'm doing it." Before Whisper could knock any sense into him, Rasp struck the match against his belt and a flicker of flame ignited the gloom. Fire was one of the easier elements to manipulate. Control, no. Manipulate, yes. Burn the town down in the process? Sometimes. All that mattered now was that he and Whisper got away.

Rasp pictured a blazing ball of flame and willed it into existence. In a single pulse, a beacon of light flared across the alleyway, chasing the darkness away and blinding his pursuers with the sudden transition from dark to light. It remained solid for several seconds before the magic broke loose, shooting tiny fireballs in every direction.

"Crap!" Rasp realized several of the burning balls of fire were hurtling in *his* direction.

A shimmering blaze of blue light leapt up around him, shielding both him and Whisper from the fiery onslaught. Rasp uncovered his face and then checked his hands, realizing the magic was not his own. With a heavy sigh, he turned once more to his mentor. "What happened to your magic being depleted?"

"I thought perhaps a sense of false urgency would cause you to make better decisions. Obviously I was wrong."

Whisper's protection spell dimmed, allowing Rasp to get an idea of what sort of damage he'd inflicted to the alleyway. The scattered flames spread by his fireball provided enough contrast for him to pick out the outlines of his attackers from their muddled surroundings. One looked to be down for the count and possibly on fire. The other two, unfortunately, were no worse for the wear and had regrouped a sensible distance away from the worst of the flames.

Before Rasp could ask which of the three he'd managed to take out, the buckled cobblestone heaved beneath his feet, sending him flat on his ass. A hazy swirl of red magic lifted slabs of broken street into the air across from him. Shouting a spell at the top of her lungs, the earth elemental hurled her arsenal in their direction.

Rasp threw his palms out in front of him and the debris jerked to a stop midair. Gritting his teeth, he staggered to his feet as raw magic poured from his hands, forcing the shrapnel in the opposite direction. Yellow sparked against red as his magic combatted the other. He was gaining the upper hand, having forced her into retreat, when a stray flash of green struck the building above him, sending a cascade of broken clay tiles onto his head.

Rasp rushed forward, dodging shattered roof tiles as he went. Blood trickled from a fresh split in his forehead. The pain faded as fresh rage pumped through his veins, fueling his magic. The earth elemental was weakening. Rasp could feel her concentration slipping. He swore he could see her magical signature pulsing against the dark of the alleyway. He followed it, like a beacon, barely conscious of the strange sensation stirring to life within his chest.

Power, cold like ice, snaked and slithered beneath his skin. The sensation started at the base of his neck and spread downward, wrapping his body in its icy tendrils. Amid the chaos, a startling realization occurred to him. He was suddenly very, very hungry.

CHAPTER NINE

The Darkness

The earth elemental's spell was fading. Her crimson aura, once mouth-wateringly bright, was dimming, growing smaller as her energy drained from her body. Rasp held back her arsenal of broken cobblestone with ease. He paused, allowing the power in his hands to build for the final push, when he noticed two additional magical signatures pulsing out of the corner of his murky vision. His breath caught in his throat as he realized he wasn't seeing flashes of magic, but the witches themselves. Their tantalizing energies glowed against the dark, one blue and the other green, darting about as they tried to obliterate another.

Whisper's aura was a weak flicker compared to their opponent. Rasp's poor, weary mentor was barely a mouthful at this point.

Mouthful? Raps didn't have time to question why he was suddenly describing Whisper as if they were roasted meat on a stick. Still keeping the stones airborne with one hand, he reached out with the other and harnessed the breeze. He willed it stronger, and then did something he had never thought to try before. He combined two separate magical sources into one.

His warning rang out a split second before he unleashed all of the chaos onto the alleyway. "Whisper, run!"

Broken cobblestone and earth whipped around him in a deadly whirlwind, picking up speed as it grew in size. Rasp stood at its center, protected from the desperate flashes of green and red as his victims did everything in their power to combat the inevitable. He couldn't find Whisper's signature anymore, but it didn't matter. His mentor was smart enough to stay the fuck out of his way.

Magic coursed through Rasp's veins, buzzing in the air around him in a deadly yellow glow as the wind whipped faster, faster, faster. And then, unable to hold it a second longer, Rasp released. Wind surged from his hands, blasting the surrounding walls with rock-laden debris. The buildings rattled and shook as shrapnel struck around him on all sides. As the noises around him stilled to a deathly quiet, Rasp at last opened his eyes. The surrounding fires had gone out, leaving the alleyway impossibly dark once more. The air was thick with smoke and dust. He waved a hand in front of his face, attempting to keep it from invading his mouth and nostrils.

A blast of green energy flared in his direction. Without thinking, Rasp lifted his hand and a wall of stone rose before him. The energy blast struck the other side in a blaze of green sparks, unable to penetrate the makeshift barrier. Another flick of Rasp's fingers sent the wall hurtling in the energy caster's direction. The stones found their mark, burying the witch beneath a pile of loose rubble.

To his annoyance, their intoxicating aura still pulsed ever so faintly. Still alive, Rasp realized. But not for long. He could see to that himself.

The blood in his veins had turned to ice. Rasp felt his breath turn colder with each exhale as the magic writhing beneath his skin wormed deeper. He didn't even have to think about his next move. It was coming to him all so clearly now, as if the instinct had been buried within him all along. A single flick of his wrist, that's all it would take, and he could cave the buildings in over the top of his foes.

Little bird, no. This is not the way.

Seriously? Whisper was stopping him now? After he was finally showing a knack for this? "The Division of Divination is your sworn enemy," Rasp reminded them. "They've been hounding us for months. You never hesitated to thin out their ranks before."

This is not about them. This is about you. A faint blue aura appeared beside him. **You are not the one in control. Drop your magic, now.**

There was urgency in Whisper's words. The magic pulled against Rasp's flesh, urging him to continue, to ignore Whisper's warning and release his wrath on those that wished to harm him.

Raspberry Stoneclaw!

The full name treatment wasn't necessary. Rasp already realized what was wrong. The magic writhing beneath his skin was not his own, not entirely anyway. Like a parasite, the darkness had latched its hooks into him and used him for its own devices. Fuck that. It was bad enough the darkness had hitched a ride inside of him like a bloodsucking leech; that didn't mean he had to feed it.

Rasp snapped his eyes shut, searching for something to latch onto and pull him from the darkness's grip. He listened for his heartbeat, but the dark magic fought back, wrapping tighter around him. His left hand spasmed, fingers curling with a will of their own as his arm lifted in the air independent of his control. *Oh fuck! No, no, no, no!*

Rasp grabbed his disobedient hand and bit down. Pain flooded his senses, drawing tears to his eyes, as his magical connection dissipated. The sudden drop in power caused him to stumble backward. He cursed softly under his breath as his senses returned to him. Rasp rubbed the life back into his numb arms. Cold. He was so fucking cold. It felt like all of the blood had been drained from his body and replaced with glacier water.

When will you fucking learn? That was stupid of you! Stupid, stupid, stupid . . .

Rasp nearly jumped out of his skin when he felt a hand touch his own. "That was close, little bird," Whisper said, their voice notably soft. "Do not be angry at yourself. You stopped the darkness before it seized control. That is a feat not many could accomplish on their own."

Rasp stomped his feet, attempting to rid them of the awful pins and needles sensation coursing through both legs. "Don't do that."

Whisper removed their hand, confused. "Do what?"

"Don't act like you're proud of me. You've done nothing but belittle me all night and now, suddenly, you want to treat me like I matter? Fuck off with that."

"Had you stayed outside of the city, as instructed, none of this would have happened."

"Should have thought of that before you kidnapped me."

"How many times must we rehash this same argument? You are here because we made a deal."

"You know what wasn't a part of that deal? Being cursed with dark magic! How the fuck am I supposed to learn to use my power if every time I do, that thing wakes up inside of me, huh? You're asking me to do the impossible here!"

"Did I curse you with dark magic?" Whisper, sensibly, didn't wait for an answer as they already knew Rasp had no intention of giving one. "I am here attempting to find you a cure, am I not? Which, by the way, would be far more successful if you stopped trying to pick a fight with every living creature that crosses your path, including me."

Why not? It sounded like a great idea. A brilliant idea. Possibly the best idea he'd had all day. "Finding a cure? Is that what you call this? Pointlessly running from one city to the next, getting hounded everywhere we go?"

"As much as I would love to have this conversation with you, now is not the time."

Working the last tremble from his arms, Rasp glanced around him, realizing he could sense a growing magical signature from where the energy caster had fallen. "How the fuck is he still alive? Do yourself a favor," he shouted to the stubborn energy caster, "and quit while you're still breathing. I am seriously not in the mood!"

His opponent's response came in the form of a channel of crackling light. Rasp threw himself to the side. The energy blast narrowly missed, singeing some of the hair from Rasp's arm as it erupted against the wall behind him.

Whisper sounded notably farther away than they'd been before. "His energy is dwindling, but without your magic, we may have to find a creative way to get around him."

"I know just the thing." The realization that he had nearly lost control over something so trivial had Rasp's blood pumping hot again. If he couldn't handle this with his magic, then that left only one other option. "Can you distract him long enough for me to get close?"

"Little bird, whatever you are considering doing, I would not recommend—"

"Don't worry. I'm long past the considering part!" Rasp sprang to his feet and sought the wall, brushing his fingers against the damaged stone as he tripped and stumbled at a clumsy run.

A flash of blue lit the alleyway. The energy caster took Whisper's bait and slung another energy blast in their direction. Green flared against blue and, for the briefest of moments, the conflicting colors lit the passage as bright as day. Rasp was only steps from his quarry before the witch realized their game. The caster turned, hands glowing with energy, but it was already too late.

Rasp's foot planted into the witch's gut, sending them sprawling across the debris-littered ground. He launched himself onto them, fists swinging as he landed blow after blow. With the last of their strength, the witch lifted his hand and a surge of magic struck Rasp directly in the face.

It hit like a kick in the teeth. The concentration of the force was so strong it sent him careening. Daggers of red-hot pain radiated through his jaw and up his forehead. Rasp cursed as he held a hand to his mouth. His fingers came away wet. The taste of iron pooled across his tongue and bubbled over his lower lip, spilling down his open mouth. Amid the agony, he felt something hard rolling around his mouth.

Rasp spat into his hand, realizing it was a tooth. An exploratory search of his mouth confirmed that several others had been knocked free from the blast as well.

"I gonna fucking kill him!"

"No need, little bird." Whisper's voice came from near the energy caster. "That was the last of his energy. He's already succumbed to his injuries."

Rasp considered personally ensuring that the damned witch wouldn't come back a third time, but he didn't think he had the strength. Besides, he needed to find the rest of his teeth. Bent over the ground with hot blood spilling from his mouth, frantically searching the broken cobblestone for his broken teeth, a familiar sound stopped him dead in his search. Rasp's heart skipped a beat as the hard clack of hoofs against cobbled stone drew nearer.

It couldn't be, could it? No, he was dreaming, surely. Forget dreaming, it was probably a hallucination brought on by the extensive blood loss. Despite the slew of rapid-fire excuses rattling around his muddled brain, the footsteps kept coming. Fuck reason, it was happening. It was finally happening! His best friend in the entire world had tracked him down and found him.

Rasp rose shakily to his feet. "Faris?"

It was a raven that answered him. *Croak!*

With his head spinning, Rasp didn't register Father's words. "You did this, Dad? You found Faris?"

There was so much Rasp wanted to say and do. He didn't know whether to laugh or cry. This was the happiest he'd been in months. Rasp staggered toward the approaching faun, arms flung wide. He managed a single step before his body gave out. His legs crumpled as he sagged toward the ground. A strong pair of hands grabbed him, preventing him from hitting the upturned cobblestone and losing any more teeth.

"Rasp?" Faris's voice sounded strangely far away. And not much like Faris either, to be honest. "Good gods, why does it look like someone kicked you in the face?"

Rasp slumped against him, eyes fluttering shut. "Everything's all right now that you're here."

"You've lost a lot of blood. I'm going to get you out of here, alright? Please refrain from biting me."

Rasp wanted to protest that he could never do such a thing to Faris. Before, maybe, sure. But not now, after having been reunited at long last. Words were getting increasingly harder to form, however. Despite his best efforts, the only thing Rasp managed to get out was a gargled, ". . . 'Kay."

He was picked up and slung over Faris's shoulder. Rasp didn't remember Faris being this tall. Or strong enough to lift him on his own either. But those were trivial details. His best friend was back and that's all that mattered. The rest of the journey passed in a confusing blur as more blood steadily trickled from his splintered mouth.

CHAPTER TEN

Unhinged

Daana's scream bounced from one stone wall to the next, filling the cramped cell with what sounded like multiple shrieking banshees.

"Oh! I'm so sorry, miss." The sweet voice did not match the towering frame of its owner. The prisoner pulled Daana against her chest and roughly stroked the top of her hair in what was probably meant to be a comforting gesture. With her face smashed against the rough fabric of a musty-smelling shift, Daana found the gesture neither comforting nor comfortable. The sudden squeezing did manage to smother her panicked screams, though.

"There, there. You're all right," the rumbling voice crooned. "I mistook you for one of the new inmates. They give me extra yard time if I scare the piss out of them on the first day. Keeps things quiet around here."

Through her tears and the ragged, raspy pants for air, Daana forced herself to look up. The pained face of an orc shifted into clarity. The shape and color of her eyes, the blunt nose, all the way down to the strong cut of her jaw, were all eerily familiar. Oralia, basically—but with different scars, a few faded tattoos peeking out from under the shift along her collarbone, and a very eye-catching septum ring.

Daana's voice was barely a squeak. "Ashwyn?"

"What was that?"

"You're Ashwyn, aren't you?"

"Nobody here by that name, miss." The orc released Daana from her crushing embrace and ventured a polite step backward. The space between them was not nearly far enough for comfort.

Daana took a giant gasp of air, allowing her lungs to fully inflate for what felt like the first time in many hours. Although she was relieved to no longer have the damned hood over her face, her current surroundings weren't much of an improvement. The cell was small and windowless. The only source of semi-fresh air wafted in from the barred door. There was a stiff cot bolted to the wall in the corner. A small stone ledge protruded from the wall beside it, pulling double duty as both a shelf and desk. The orc's meager belongings included a toothbrush, several books, and piles of neatly stacked parchment.

With her visual sweep of the room complete, and the regular in-out-in-out rhythm of her breath restored, Daana summoned the courage to speak. "I know who you are. I'm friends with your sister, Oralia." The fact that Oralia tolerated her didn't actually make them friends, but Daana couldn't think of a word that accurately described their acquaintanceship while simultaneously conveying trust. "You look just like her."

"Oh, you sweet thing. I squeezed you too hard, didn't I? Must have popped something in your head."

"I'm Daana." She tried again, hoping against all odds that a familiar name would lower Ashwyn's guard. "I'm told you knew my mother, Larkspur."

The silence that followed was neither cold nor hostile, but strangely warm. In any other circumstance, Daana might have shied away from the unfamiliar orc that drew closer, but she didn't. She remained still as Ashwyn reached for her. There was something about the orc's soft movements that conveyed no harm was intended. "My goddess, as I live and breathe." Ashwyn's flint-colored eyes grew wide as she cupped Daana's chin in her calloused palms. "Yes, of course. How could I have missed it before? You're the spitting image of her."

An unexpected whimper bubbled up from Daana's throat. "Really?"

The warmth vanished and Ashwyn rolled her head back, laughing. The harsh cackle filled the cramped chamber, echoing against the ancient stone until it sounded as if the building itself was mocking her. What started as a gentle touch turned into an iron grip, preventing Daana from pulling away. Ashwyn's glistening eyes narrowed. "Does he really think I'm this stupid? What was the plan here? Get on my good side? Convince me to tell you all about the great Larkspur Denari? The poor lass is dead. Let her stay that way."

Daana stood paralyzed by terror. "Let go. You're hurting me."

Ashwyn's thick lips pursed as she twisted Daana's head this way and that, studying her features. "Geralt did his homework. I'll give the little runt that. To say there isn't some resemblance would be a lie. How much did he pay you?"

"It's not a trick!" Daana attempted to slap Ashwyn's hands away without success. She realized only after having done so that it was a poor decision. Not only was she still stuck in Ashwyn's iron grasp, but she was utterly defenseless in the event the much stronger orc decided to retaliate.

Ashwyn released her. She moved toward the other side of the cramped cell with a chuckle. "Well, you certainly have her temper, at least. A pity about the brains."

Daana dropped her voice and glanced in the direction of the door. "Look, I don't have time for this. Is the guard still nearby?"

"Who? You mean Pauly? Nah, he's probably back at the guard shack by now. He and Winston like to play a few rounds before the evening cell count." Ashwyn pulled the solitary chair from beneath the ledge and twisted it around. She sat backward, utilizing the stiff backing as a convenient place on which to rest her brawny arms. While smaller in stature than her infamous sister, Ashwyn was equally as imposing. She looked as if someone had smuggled a statue of the orc goddess of war from the temple and slapped a loose tangle of hair and an ill-fitting garment over the top in the hopes that no one would notice. Her lean, sinewy muscles were so sharply defined, they may as well have been cut from stone.

Daana reached for her collar with an unsteady hand. "Would you mind turning around for just a moment?"

Ashwyn's single, raised eyebrow communicated that she minded very much.

Looks like I'll be doing this with an audience then. Great . . .

Biting her lower lip, Daana unbuttoned the upper portion of her dress and shimmied it down her shoulders. She reached both hands behind her back and worked the girdle hooks free. While the palace guards had removed her weapons, they hadn't bothered to give her a change of clothes. She and Snag had stayed up all night stitching the iron tools into the support strips of her undergarments by candlelight.

"Oh, goddess." Ashwyn grimaced, tilting her chin toward the low ceiling with a groan. "Before you pop those knickers off too, just know, I find the seduction angle rather insulting. Just because I'm partial to a nice pair of tits doesn't mean I'm going to fall for every elf he throws in here."

With the girdle unlatched, Daana whipped it free, grateful for the sudden ability to breathe unhindered once more. She hastily rebuttoned everything back into place, scrunching her eyebrows together as she did so. "Made an exception for your wife then? Ellisar will be the first to tell you she's as flat as a washboard."

"Back to name-dropping, are we?"

"Believe me, I wish I weren't familiar with that name. And, for the record, I'm not trying to seduce you, either." Daana laid out the individual pieces of her pick set by the door, attempting to recall the parts of her training that did not involve name-calling. She selected two tools and threaded her arms through the bars, working the pieces into the lock.

"What in the chaos are you doing?"

"Breaking you out." Picking locks, it turned out, was much easier when one could see what they were doing. With her face pressed against the rough metal bars, Daana was forced to arrange her tools by feel. It was going about as well as expected.

"Breaking me out? Really?" Ashwyn rested her chin against her arms. "And when will that be? Next year, perhaps? You've got that pick in upside down, Peaches."

With a groan, Daana peeled herself away from the bars and extended the implements in Ashwyn's direction. "In all fairness, your wife was a horrible instructor. She spent most of the lesson belittling my efforts."

"I can see why."

Daana winced. Ellisar had warned that if all else failed, Daana would have to use the code. She would have utilized it from the start had Ellisar not also warned that Ashwyn's reaction would go one of two ways. Either Ashwyn would accept that her deeply untrusting wife had trusted someone enough to give them the code, or she would believe that it had been forced out of Ellisar through torture. The first option would end well. The second would just end. For Daana, anyway.

Snapping her eyes shut, Daana raised her voice, attempting to keep her tone from fluttering the same way as her insides. "Use that tone with me again, miss, and I'm afraid I will have to get very cross with you!"

The wooden chair legs squeaked as Ashwyn moved to her feet. Slow, cautious steps started in Daana's direction. "What did you just say?"

Daana forced her fear back down with a difficult swallow. "You heard me."

For a few torturous seconds nothing happened. When Daana opened her eyes again, she found Ashwyn crouched in front of her. The orc's dark eyes bored into Daana like twin, black holes. Ashwyn leaned closer, whispering, "Got anything else to add to that, miss? Or are you satisfied with those being your last words?"

Daana scrambled backward until her shoulders struck the door. "No, I'm with her! I swea—"

"Ha, kidding!" With a lighthearted punch to Daana's arm—which felt more hearted than it did light—Ashwyn took the lock kit from Daana's trembling hands. A pearly smile split between her lips. "Sorry, Peaches. I couldn't help myself."

Daana nearly melted onto the floor. The anger that bloomed across her face in hot patches was quelled somewhat by the small pinprick of relief that came with knowing she wasn't about to die. Not relieved enough to keep silent, though. "You are the worst! Honestly, I should have expected this. There's no way in the seven realms of chaos that a sane person would have entered a committed relationship with Ellisar willingly!"

"That's it. Let all that anger out. Expressing yourself is supposed to be very beneficial for mental health, you know."

Emotional whiplash was nothing new to Daana. It was par for the course when you traveled months on end with the dregs of society. And yet, this version felt unfamiliar to her. Usually it was one person causing the pain, while another smoothed it over. Ashwyn was somehow filling both roles simultaneously.

"You just keep venting away while I take care of this pesky lock here. Ha, look at us! Practically a team already." Ashwyn took the hook pick in one hand and worked it through the bars. Once the pick was slid into the lock, she wriggled the next implement in place beside it. While the lock picking itself appeared to be going rather smoothly, Ashwyn was clearly having difficulty navigating her muscular arms through the narrow gaps between the bars.

Her cheery voice strained with effort. "Is Ellie here, by chance? Call me old-fashioned, but I always pictured her kicking down the door and sweeping me off my feet. It's not nearly as romantic doing all the heavy lifting myself."

"Nearby." Daana decided against pointing out the obvious flaw in Ashwyn's fantasy. "The plan was for me to get thrown into the dungeon with you and for them to follow." That was the problem with secret dungeons. It was common practice *not* to advertise their location to the general public. There was also the issue that the heads of the realm kept multiple dungeons at any given time. Although Ellisar knew a few of the most common locations, it would have been tedious to check all of them without getting caught along the way.

"Them? Who's them?" Ashwyn glanced at Daana out of the corner of her eye. "Don't tell me Ra Ra is here, too?"

"I don't know who that is."

"O-ra-li-a." Ashwyn's teasing smile widened as she returned her full concentration to her work. "You should try calling her that sometime. She loves it."

Daana peered hard at her. "Are you sure you two are related? She's, well, you know . . . and you're . . ."

"Fun?" Ashwyn ventured.

"Different," was the word Daana settled on. Calling the orc unhinged seemed not only impolite, but rather stupid too. Especially with the door still securely locked.

During Daana's practice session, it had taken her nearly twenty minutes to pop a single lock. It had been a simple one too. According to Ellisar, anyway. Ashwyn seemed more versed in the art of breaking and entering. After several minutes of jamming, twisting, and rearranging the slender metal pieces in the keyhole, the heavy iron mechanism within the door gave way with a rusty *click-clunk-clank*.

"Alright, Peaches. Ready to go?"

"Why Peaches?" Daana said. While it was marginally better than what the others called her, it didn't exactly inspire fear either.

"Because you remind me of a peach. Sweet but soft, particularly in the head."

"Rude!"

Ashwyn rolled the implements back into the grease-stained cloth and offered it to Daana, along with another pearly grin. "You don't by chance have any weapons stashed in that girdle of yours too, do you?"

Admittedly, it was hard to stay mad at that brimming smile. "Afraid not."

"Right, we'll make do with what we got then." Ashwyn moved swiftly across the room and hobbled her chair by snapping three of the wooden legs free. She passed one to Daana and kept the other two for herself. "Stay behind me. If we come across any unfriendlies, let me do the talking, alright?"

CHAPTER ELEVEN

A Romantic Reencounter

Ashwyn put her shoulder to the bars and eased the door open as quietly as possible. Tilting her head for Daana to follow, the orc slid soundlessly out into the empty hallway. Daana tiptoed close behind, attempting to mimic Ashwyn's confident movements. Truth be told, having Ashwyn assume the lead was something of a relief, actually. Daana knew they were supposed to be traveling downward, utilizing the same staircase that brought her to this floor, probably. The problem was she didn't know where to find it.

Ashwyn padded on ahead with the confidence of someone who had either done this hundreds of times before, or was simply very, very good at faking it. Several empty lantern hooks hung above the dark passageway as they passed row after row of empty cells. They were nearing the bend that Daana suspected housed the stairwell when Ashwyn held out her palm and pressed flat against the wall.

Daana tried, without success, to make herself one with the wall as the sounds of slapping feet moved up the stairwell in their direction.

The footsteps stopped shy of the entrance. After a moment of unease, a familiar voice rang out from around the corner. "Daana, if that's you, you'd better say something, else I'm gonna clear that hallway with a powder charge!"

"It's me, Snag!" She pushed free of the wall, waving her arms. "I've got Ashwyn with me."

The footsteps started up again, faster than before. Snag's voice called out ahead of them. "In that case, I suggest you move before you get trampled."

A willowy shadow burst from the dim stairwell and doubled its speed in their direction. Daana threw herself flat against the wall and out of Ellisar's path. The elf leapt the remaining distance, sailed through the air, and landed like a fully sprung net trap. Her arms and legs latched around Ashwyn's body, knocking the orc a step backward. Realizing it was not a matter of what, but who had hit her, Ashwyn dropped her chair legs and pulled her wife in for an uncomfortably passionate kiss.

Ashwyn pulled away seconds later, sputtering, "Your breath! Dear goddess, Ellie. Why does it taste like you ate a raw onion for lunch?"

"An onion *and* a bulb of garlic." A devious smile cut across Ellisar's normally expressionless features. It was somehow more unnerving than her glare. "Word of advice, don't bet against Snag when you've run out of money. He gets rather creative."

"You could have at least brought a mint. Brushed your teeth beforehand, maybe?"

Ellisar snaked her arms behind Ashwyn's head and pulled her closer. "Less talking. More tongue."

Daana averted her eyes, watching as Snag moved toward them at an unhurried pace. His left leg still dragged a little, but if it bothered him, he never mentioned it. Unless he was trying to get out of work, of course. And then suddenly they were lucky he'd survived his injury at all.

"Oi!" Snag hissed. "Can you two keep it in your pants until we're free of the creepy crawly dungeon?"

Fighting the elf's pawing hands, Ashwyn dropped Ellisar back onto the ground and proffered a winning smile. "You must be Snag."

"And you must be the sane half to"—his clawed fingers gestured vaguely in Ellisar's direction—"this."

Ha! As much as Daana wanted to correct him, she decided it would be best to let Snag draw his own conclusions on the matter.

"I know we haven't officially met, but I feel like we're family already. Ellie writes all about you in her letters." Ashwyn caught the repulsion that crossed Snag's grizzled face and lifted her palms into the air innocently. "The clean parts, I mean."

Snag's glistening eyes shifted from Ashwyn to Ellisar as a needled smile split across his face. "That's not very fair. The dirty parts are the only bits I get to hear. I think that entitles me to some embarrassing stories. Tonight, preferably. When we're miles from this wretched place."

"Sounds like a date."

Ellisar followed Snag toward the stairwell. She twisted around, mouthing "over my dead body."

They descended the spiraling staircase with Ellisar leading, Snag and Daana in the middle, and Ashwyn bringing up the rear. Ellisar was slinking down the final few steps when a bolt struck the wall behind her and ricocheted across the room.

She retreated behind the protective curve of the wall with a snarl. "I thought you got them all!"

"No, I said I got all the ones at the *front*," Snag hissed back. "You were supposed to sweep the corridors!"

"Drop your weapons!" a shaky voice called from beyond the stairwell. "That's the only way out. Try to run and I'll pick the lot of you off."

Ellisar looked over her shoulder at Daana. "Sounds like it's time to deploy our fire starter."

"Are you trying to get us all killed?" Snag said. "No! We agreed never again. Using Daana is not an option."

"When did you become an old stick-in-the-mud, Snag? You used to be fun."

"You want a repeat of Alkurth? Because this is how you get a repeat of Alkurth!"

Ashwyn's tall form leaned over Daana's shoulder, whispering, "I think I may have underestimated you, Peaches. You got some sort of specialty I'm not aware of?"

"Oh, uh, not really," Daana stammered. Briefly, she recalled the smell of smoke as red and orange embers danced on the wind, illuminating the night sky above as the city burned below. She blinked the image from her eyes, forcing the memory back into the dark, unvisited recesses of her mind. "It was an accident, actually. I don't think they're ever going to let me live it down."

Daana returned to Snag and Ellisar's conversation in time to hear the tail end of Snag's plan. "That bolt came from a crossbow. Which means the fucker's got to waste time to reload. You throw a little distraction his way and I'll clear the room with a charge, yeah?"

The edges of Ellisar's mouth pulled downward. "You're already leading in points. If I'm the bait, then you get the kill."

"Should have swept the corridors then, hmm?"

"Hold on, you two." Ashwyn squeezed past Daana, placing her hand on Ellisar's shoulder as she navigated the cramped stairwell. "Stay here. Let me take care of this."

"Armed with what, exactly?" Snag demanded.

"Admittedly, it's been a while since I've done this. Might be a little rusty." Ashwyn spoke as though she hadn't heard Snag's question. She looked to Ellisar, who merely imparted an impassive shrug. With her spouse's seal of approval, Ashwyn whispered to Snag, "How many did you take care of at the guard shack when you came in?"

"Three." He glanced worriedly between them. "Am I missing something? What is the plan here? You can't just stroll down there and—"

"It's fine, Snag," Ellisar replied. "Let her do her thing."

"Oh, good. She's as mad as you. Glad we established that early on. I'll adjust my expectations for survival accordingly."

Ruffling Ellisar's hair as she slipped past, Ashwyn started down the stairs with her shoulders pressed to the stone. Her voice reverberated off of the grime-covered walls below. "Winston, love, I know it's only you down there. You can talk a big game all you want, but no one rang the alarm. The next shift isn't due to come in for another three hours. Help isn't coming, mate. But that doesn't mean this has to end in blood. You've always treated me fair and I'd like to return the favor."

She was near the bottom step now, still pressed flat to the wall. "You've got three babies at home and a fourth on the way. I'm not intending to rob those rascals of their father, but you're going to have to work with me here. First things first, I need you to understand these people don't mess around. You fire off another bolt and I won't be able to talk them out of making your wife a widow."

"I c-can't let you leave. If they find everyone else dead and not me, they'll—"

"Which is why I'm going to knock you unconscious." With her palms raised, Ashwyn stepped out of the protection of the stairwell. "You remember when Big Brutis took a swipe at you in the yard? Who was it who dropped him with a nerve pinch? And he came back around with all his faculties, didn't he? It'll be just like that. Except that when you're out, I'm going to break your arm to make it more believable."

"*What?*"

Ashwyn didn't flinch at his response. She edged farther into the room until she was lost from sight altogether. "I'll do it clean, promise. I've got a healer with me back on the stairs. He'll give you something so you won't wake up in agony, alright? At the end of all this, you still get to go home to a wife and the little ones and the boss is going to be none the wiser. You're just the lucky sap who got a bump on the head during a jailbreak and lived to tell about it."

Daana strained to catch the soft words of the guard, but was unable to make sense of his reply. Her gaze jumped to Ellisar. "She can't be serious. For the gods' sakes, she's not even armed!"

"Enchanting, isn't it?" A smile hovered over Ellisar's lips. There was a dreamy, far-off look in her eyes that made Daana want to shy away in terror. "This one time we got held up on the road by bandits. We were outnumbered four to one and they were looking for an excuse to draw blood. By the time Ashwyn was done with them, the whole gang was ugly crying as they took turns writing letters to their mothers apologizing for the way they turned out."

After a moment of quiet deliberation, Daana turned away, shaking her head in disbelief. "I can never tell when you're fucking with me."

Ashwyn's voice called from below. "He's down!"

Daana skittered down the remaining steps behind the other two. True to her word, Ashwyn stood with her hands locked on her hips, peering down at a still guard. "Snag, I might need your professional opinion here. Where's the best place to snap an arm so it'll heal straight?"

"You're . . . not just going to kill him?" The goblin sidled closer, wringing his clawed hands.

"I meant what I said. It's the only way the whole convincing thing works."

"Is it a form of magic?" Daana asked. She hadn't sensed any, but she hadn't exactly been looking for it, either.

"Nothing like that, no." Ashwyn dismissed the idea with a wave of her broad hand. "In the end, all most people want is to make it through one more day. I'm just giving them the option, is all. It's how I won Ellie over."

"You abducted me!"

"Arrested you," Ashwyn corrected with a dreamy smile. "I still get the flutters thinking of you hogtied and thrown over the back of my horse."

A sudden sense of awe filled Daana. What she had originally mistook as yet another violent lunatic was shaping into something else entirely. Nothing about her new life came easily, but the realization that she could navigate the path ahead of her without needless death was an opportunity too good to pass. "Can you teach me?"

"Oh, sweet Peaches, there's nothing to it."

"Really?"

"You just ensure their hands and feet are tied real tight first. The horse does most of the work, honestly."

CHAPTER TWELVE

Seven Pages of Unadulterated Smut

Fairguard was New Adderwood Republic's southernmost settlement. It was a small, fully enclosed outpost, whose sole reason for existence was the Copperstone Inn. Once the pinnacle of stately travel destinations, the inn's high-end clientele had ranged from the top-ranking members of court, to wealthy merchants, and anyone with a ludicrous amount of coin to spare. But, like the brightest-burning stars, the momentum eventually fizzled out. Newer, faster coach roads gradually siphoned away the better-paying crowds. Without steady income, both Fairguard and its famous inn fell into disrepair.

War changed that. The heads of the newly formed New Adderwood Republic seized Fairguard and resurrected it to its former glory, utilizing the Copperstone Inn as its temporary headquarters.

The inn's reception area was pleasantly empty when Oralia entered. The usual mix of officers and civilian volunteers had left to greet the returning party at the front gates, no doubt. Oralia and her small personal company rode hard to arrive ahead of the main force. A small sum paid to the guards at the west gate ensured that her arrival would go unmarked for at least a little while. It wasn't so much that she minded the cheering crowds, it was the expectation for her to drop everything for an emergency debriefing immediately after that bothered her. She had needs, after all. Attending another tedious meeting smelling fresher than a horse ranked high on the list—among other things.

Oralia strode across the frayed rose-colored carpet to the front service desk. She slapped a piece of silver onto the counter as she passed. "You saw nothing. I have not yet arrived."

The unenthusiastic attendant was perched on his stool with his long nose stuck in a book. He was an elf of indeterminate age, with greasy, slicked-back hair and multiple piercings threaded through his ears and nostrils. While his attempt to encapsulate the nonconformist vibe was commendable, he would have looked rather ordinary next to her goblin soldier, Snaglebrag.

The *real* one. Not the stand-in.

The elf merely licked his fingertip and turned the page. "That'll be two, please."

"Two?"

"My fees have doubled in your absence."

"On what grounds?"

"Command is growing concerned with the rate at which I *don't* see you. They've scheduled an eye exam."

With a click of her tusks, Oralia dug into her pocket and retrieved a second silver coin. Despite the urge to slam it with all of her might, she deposited it delicately onto the desk as though it were made of glass.

The attendant drew back the faded red curtain that obstructed the small doorway behind him, managing to do so without lifting his gaze from the page. "Blast. Once more, your highly anticipated arrival has slipped my notice, madam. My superiors will be most displeased."

"You have my thanks."

"And you have two hours before my vision miraculously recovers."

Oralia traveled the dim staff corridor for several twists and turns until it deposited her into the kitchen. The hazy air was balmy and so heavy with the scent of stewed cabbage, it nearly took her out at the knees. Ignoring the sudden lurch in her stomach, Oralia braced herself against the doorframe as she peered inside, searching for a familiar shape.

"It's about damn time!" A plump, frizzy-haired human woman was leading the fight against that morning's dishes near the sink well. She waved her scouring brush as if it were a sword in Oralia's direction. "If you had delayed your return any longer, I would have had to put the poor wretch out of his misery myself. He nearly took off his thumb dicing the last of the onions this morning. And when I finally got him calmed down enough to stop shaking, he nearly did it again!"

A pitiful twinge dropped in Oralia's chest. The long hours and treacherous excursions had taken their toll on everyone, including those left behind. It normally took a few days of being back before Sascha's nerves straightened themselves out again. "Do you know where I might find him? I assumed he would be here."

Nuri gestured over her shoulder with the soapy brush. "Out back taking a smoke break."

Oralia started across the worn kitchen tile toward the delivery entrance. "Sascha does not smoke."

"Well he does when you're away! It's his third one today."

Oralia swung open the rickety wood thatch door and stepped out into the uneven cobblestone courtyard that butted up to the back of the inn. Her lover's hulking frame stopped pacing when the door swung shut with a clatter. He swiveled his head in her direction and the harsh lines around his eyes and mouth softened. Oralia started to move in his direction, but there was no need. Grinding the cigarette stub under his heel, Sascha was across the uneven ground in three swift strides and pulling her into his arms.

The smell of tobacco smoke hung heavy on his clothes. It didn't churn her stomach like the cabbage. It had the opposite reaction, in fact, and Oralia found herself craving more. Aside from the few times Ellisar had coaxed her into smoking with her—a substance which was most definitely *not* tobacco—Oralia never saw the appeal. Gods, every day it felt like more and more of her old self was slipping.

She pressed into him, listening to the rampant drum of his heartbeat. "I came back in one piece, just like I promised."

"Gods, I swore I wouldn't cry." Sascha's deep voice cracked and he rested his chin against the top of her head as fat, salty tears rolled down his face and wetted her hair. "I heard about the ambush and the fighting and I was so worried. If anything happened to you, I'd—"

Oralia tilted her head so she could look up to him. Tears traveled along the deep worry lines etched across Sascha's face like the marred channels of a weathered ravine. The wrinkles used to disappear by the day's end, but as of late, they seemed to have taken up permanent residence. "I know you do not like it when I am delayed," Oralia said, brushing a stray tear from his cheek with her thumb. "But I did send a letter."

"Yes." His tusks clicked against his upper teeth as some of the softness fled from his face. "We're going to have to have a frank talk about that letter."

A prickle shot up her spine and she stood straighter. "It was supposed to ease your fretting."

"It said 'Ran into trouble. Don't worry. She's going to be fine. Back home later than expected.' I don't know who dictates your messages, but could you tell them to be a little more specific next time? I didn't sleep the last three nights because I kept wondering what it was I wasn't supposed to be worrying about!"

"You did not like it any better when I left Rali in charge of relaying the messages."

"She was sending thinly veiled ransom notes!"

"To be fair, a case of garlic pickles and two bottles of rum was a very affordable ransom. And you paid so quickly, too." A smile tugged at her mouth as Oralia rose onto her toes and kissed him. "For which I am forever grateful. I missed you." The familiar scents of fresh mint and cloves engulfed her as her lips pressed against his. She tasted the smokey hint of tobacco and leaned into him harder, wanting more.

Sascha's mouth was tight-lipped and unyielding. Although he still held her, his hands were locked tight, refusing to explore her body with their usual inquisitive touch. From his frigid demeanor, she suspected he was attempting to hold strong against her affection to prove a point. It probably wasn't meant as a challenge, but Oralia accepted it as one anyway. She pulled his head closer, nipped his earlobe between her teeth, and growled.

"That's not going to work, Moonflower," he said. "Not this time."

Her other hand, having threaded past the front of his apron to steadily work away at the clasp of his belt, hesitated. "Are you telling me to stop? Or was that an invitation to change your mind? I want to be one hundred percent certain before I rip your trousers down the front."

An unexpected blush swept across his nose and cheeks. Snapping his teeth, Sascha groaned, "By the gods, woman. For days on end, you cause me nothing but anguish. And then the moment you return, after I've rearranged the same lecture in my head for the past week, getting every point perfect, you say something like that and I suddenly can't recall a damn word of it!"

"A lecture? For me?" Her hand released his belt and went to her hip instead. "All of this because a letter was too vague for your liking? I have had the misfortune of hearing the love notes Ellisar writes to Ashwyn. And not by choice, either. She once insisted on reading one aloud to get my thoughts. It was seven pages of unadulterated smut. Is that what you would prefer? An overly detailed breakdown of every filthy act I intend to do to you upon my return?"

For a moment, he only stared. And then, at last, a sinister smile split across his tusked face. "Forget the lecture. That sounds like a far better solution. I'm so glad we were able to see eye to eye on this, Moonflower."

Oh dear gods.

". . . I do not think I have the imagination to fill seven pages. How do you feel about a well-structured paragraph? I could include bullet points, if necessary."

Sascha nuzzled his face into her with a laugh, planting soft kisses along her neck as his strong hands worked down the small of her back. "Seven pages, no less. But I could give you a little inspiration, if you think it would help."

CHAPTER THIRTEEN

Bird Business

In retrospect, Oralia should have seized Sascha by the hand and whisked him away to somewhere more private the moment she laid eyes on him. There was always someone looking for her these days and no amount of bribery kept her pursuers away for long. She flinched when she heard the rear kitchen door open and shut with a clatter.

A set of confident footsteps clomped down the stone steps and approached, absolutely undeterred. "Ha! Knew I'd find you out here."

Oralia flinched twice as hard at the nasal voice. "Lingon?"

The harsh clack of boot heels against cobblestone stopped just shy of her. Lingon's reply dripped with sticky-sweet insincerity. "Yes, Moonflower?"

"Do you recall the talk we had about not interrupting?" Oralia rested her forehead against Sascha's broad chest, ignoring the impulse to slam her skull against something more solid. Repeatedly.

"Of course. But here's the thing, you didn't like it any better when I stood off to the side and politely waited for you to finish last time, either."

Sascha buried his face into Oralia's shoulder to muffle his snorts of laughter. With an exasperated huff, Oralia replied, "No, you are correct. That was substantially worse." Reluctantly, she untangled her arms from around Sascha's neck and turned about to face the intruder. "My point is, can this wait? With you somewhere else, preferably?"

Lingon stood with his arms crossed and feet firmly set a shoulder width apart. It might have been intimidating had the human been more substantial in size. Alas, barely surpassing five and a half feet, with long, feathered hair, little muscle tone, and a face that would have been attractive if it were not for the unruly mouth to which it was attached, Lingon was more visually confusing than he was terrifying.

"Well, I suppose it could wait," he said with a shrug. "Although it might get awkward for everyone involved, considering there's about to be a supply wagon and gaggle of soldiers rounding the corner here any minute now. Just got word that the main force has reached the gate. Thought it'd be polite to give you a heads up, seein' as there's gonna be people looking for you soon. But hey, you two do you. Or, you know, each other. Don't mind the unsuspecting soldiers. I'm sure the horrors of war have dulled them past the point of caring anyway."

Sascha's ears perked at the news. "We have supplies coming?"

"Damn right. That's what happens when you send the super-secret infiltration team ahead of the main force," Lingon said with a proud puff of his scrawny chest.

A harsh croak cut through the air as a raven circling overhead suddenly dipped lower.

Lingon continued his recount of the raid undeterred. "We reached the storeroom before those fleeing fuckers got a chance to set the whole place aflame. They had enough supplies squirreled away to keep an army for nearly a year! And I mean good stuff too, not just beets an' those slabs of rock you all mistakenly refer to as biscuits."

"Hardtack," Oralia clarified, gaze fixed on the circling bird.

The raven abandoned trying to gain Lingon's attention from afar and settled on a more blatant strategy. It landed on the cobblestone beside him and pecked at his boot with a shrill screech.

"Yeah, that shit." Lingon shuffled his feet to avoid the bird's frenzied pecking.

"Is that all?" Oralia gestured to the bird hopping in little circles around his feet. "Because it seems like you may have business elsewhere."

Lingon peered down at the raven for only a split second, as if noticing it for the first time, before snapping his gaze back to her. "Nah, that's nothing."

"It does not sound like nothing."

The raven agreed with a ruffle of its feathers and another peck to Lingon's foot.

"Not now," Lingon hissed as he encouraged the bird away with a gentle nudge of his boot.

"Are we done here?" Oralia asked, forcing an unfriendly smile.

"Don't you give me that look. You were in such a hurry that you neglected to collect your spoils of war. I took it upon myself to track you down and deliver it in person. So yeah, you're welcome." Lingon swung his pack around to his front and rooted through it, explaining to Sascha, "Bossy britches here had me fetch a present for you while I was raiding the kitchen. She said to get a jar of allspice."

Oralia caught Sascha staring at her. His eyes were big and his lower lip looked to be on the verge of quivering. She had heard a saying once, detailing that the quickest way to someone's heart was through their stomach. And while she had initially misunderstood the implications of the sentiment—horrifically—the intended meaning was surprisingly accurate. Except, in this case, the quickest way to Sascha's heart was not a meal, but through a well-stocked spice cabinet.

"Ta-da!" Lingon produced a glass jar from his pack with unnecessary flare.

"Oh." Some of the smile slipped from Sascha's broad face. "You combined every spice into the same container."

"All of them. As requested."

Oralia planted her face in her hands with a groan, forced to watch Sascha's soul slowly die between the gaps in her fingers.

Sascha accepted the gift and forced a smile. His words were spoken with care, as if to remove every ounce of disappointment from his voice. "That was very . . . thoughtful of you, Lingon. Thank you."

"Yeah, yeah, yeah, save the mushiness for bossy britches. If you'll excuse me, I'm in need of a stiff drink, a hot bath, and a lover with questionable judgment." He trotted away, calling over his shoulder, "Don't wait up!"

The raven fluttered after him in a flurry of feathers and harsh croaks.

Sascha waited until Lingon's lithe shape disappeared back through the kitchen door before allowing his stoic shoulders to slump. "Remind me again why he and the other one haven't returned home yet?"

"They do not know where home is." No one had expected to survive the previous battle on Mount Hook. As such, the Stoneclaw brothers, Lingon and Mul, never bothered to ask where their clan was evacuating. Lacking direction in both the physical and authoritative sense, the pair had simply hung around until Oralia had no other choice but to grudgingly accept them into her ranks. It wasn't all bad. With Ellisar and Snag gone, the brothers had helped make up for the sudden drop in manpower.

Oralia's gaze shifted to the jar of mixed spices and her frown deepened. "I am sorry about your gift. I mistakenly assumed it was a task even he could handle." While merciless fighters, Mul and Lingon's royal upbringing meant their ability to perform any other form of vital life skill was severely lacking.

Unless it involved killing, fucking, or lighting things on fire, the brothers were largely helpless.

"I appreciate the gesture."

"I must admit, a small part of me feared he would find a way to blunder it." Oralia unfastened the pocket along the front of her jerkin and withdrew a small, carefully packed vial. "I took the liberty of passing through the kitchens on my way out just in case."

He held the prize up to his face, wide-eyed and unable to tear his gaze from the collection of thin, red, twig-like structures that nestled together on the inside. "Saffron?"

She didn't know why she felt suddenly vulnerable. She had never actively sought anyone's approval before and yet, the thought of disappointing him was a hit she was not prepared to bear. Personal relationships were strange that way. Having only been in a dedicated partnership for several months, Oralia still struggled with putting words to the racing thoughts that rampaged across her mind each time he was near.

If she were more composed, she might have said: "Is it enough? Does it communicate to you the feelings that I am yet incapable of finding the words to convey?" In the end, past the flowery language, at the very heart of the matter, perhaps it boiled down to a simple: "Am I as good to you as you have been to me?"

She was trying her damnedest to be worthy of his love. But it was difficult. Things had changed since the mountain. How was she expected to share herself with another person when she no longer knew who she was? For two hundred years it had been simple. She was Oralia Dawnsight, Protector of the Realm. Straightforward, no nonsense, easy to define. Now, her title fluctuated between traitor and rebel based on present company.

Sascha threw himself forward and held her to his chest. "Gods, I love you." He leaned into her ear, whispering, "No one else has seen us yet. There's still time for us to duck around the corner before that wagon gets here."

A flicker of excitement pushed some of the dread from her mind. That was one thing that hadn't changed. Her loving, endearing, positively fuckable fuckmate was still the same tender soul as before. And, judging from his mischievous smile, he was more than ready to indulge her regardless of whatever her current status happened to be. Swallowing the little squeak that caught in her throat, Oralia seized his hand and hurried around the corner of the building with Sascha in tow.

CHAPTER FOURTEEN

EVIL LAW

Alright, listen up you swabbies! For the next hour, this bathhouse has been reserved for the meeting of the Emotionally Vulnerable Insight for the Lads and Lasses Affected by War. Now, I'm not saying any of you lovely people need to vacate, nay, quite the contrary actually. We welcome you to join us as we bare our souls to one another free of judgment. A fair warning for the squeamish, though. There will be lots of crying involved. And I don't mean the pretty kind, either; we're talking snot dripping down our noses, uncontrollable wailing, hysterics, all the good stuff." Rali steepled her hands together beneath her chin as she stood in the center of the doorway, wrapped in an oversized bath towel with steam wafting around her ankles. "With that said, who among you is ready to break down some emotional barriers?"

Oralia lingered outside of the archway as the bathers jostled behind one another in their haste to not be the last person left in the water. Waiting until the last elf skirted past, still struggling to tie his towel across his waist, Oralia pushed off from the wall and stepped inside. "That is only going to work so many times, you know. One of these days someone is going to take you up on that offer."

"You deeply underestimate my ability to make people uncomfortable. Worst case scenario, I'll just start talking in depth about menstruation or diarrhea." Rali padded over to the wooden bench set alongside the stone wall and rifled through a gunny sack she'd co-opted as her "everything" bag. "I raided the toiletry closet while you were taking your sweet time getting here. Check it out, new soaps still wrapped in their little papers. Didn't know what scent you might fancy, so I nabbed us an olfactory smorgasbord."

Oralia held one of the bars to her nose. "It smells like cardamom and pears."

"Fancy, right?"

". . . I have an unexplainable urge to put this in my mouth."

"Alrighty then." Rali promptly relieved her of the soap. "No fruit fragrances for the hormonally charged orcess. Maybe you'd be better suited for something with a more floral bouquet. That is unless you're finding yourself compelled to eat flowers, too. Not gonna lie, I'm going to be a little worried if that's the case."

"Anything that does not smell of horse will do fine, thank you."

"Jasmine it is."

Checking to be sure the bathhouse was empty, Oralia let her robe drop to her ankles and stepped gingerly into the warm waters. Although she wore a thin undershirt and undergarments, the top showed a certain amount of skin that would undoubtedly draw attention. And not the lustful kind, either.

The Copperstone Inn had been built over the top of a natural hot spring. While this meant the dingy air continually smelled of rotten eggs, the hot, mineral-tinted bathwater more than made up for this downside. As the bathhouse was a communal space, getting into the water alone had been something of an impossibility at first. A problem remedied by Ralizak and her formation of the Emotionally Vulnerable Insight for the Lads and Lasses Affected by War.

A series of blue and white tiled steps led Oralia deeper until the water level reached past her navel. She sought the stone lip situated along the edge, hovering halfway below the surface, that served as seating. Oralia sank to her shoulders and rolled her head back, savoring the way the water worked at the overworked muscles in her lower back. There was an unceremonious splash across from her. Rali surfaced near the middle of the pool several breaths later.

Rali glided through the water and came to a rest alongside Oralia, flipping the wet, black hair from her face. "I assume from your very lengthy absence, you had a visit with your fuckmate?"

"You assume correctly."

"Good, good." Rali allowed an unusual moment of silence to pass between them before adding, "And you put your big girl britches on and finally told him that those markings of yours are getting worse, right?"

Submerged beneath the bubbling waters, the dark spiderweb of veins branching from the center of Oralia's sternum was still woefully visible. An invisible weight dropped within her chest and she sank lower in the water, unwilling to answer.

"*Right?*"

"He already knows about the markings."

"Yeah, but does he know they're spreading? You know, that thing you promised you were going to get around to telling him?"

Oralia wondered, briefly, if the interrogation would stop if she were to slip completely beneath the water. Unlikely, given the way Rali was going at it. With her luck, the dwarf would fish her out and continue to berate her between chest compressions.

Rali threw her hands over her head, flinging warm droplets of water as she did so. "How is that even possible? Sascha's got eyes, doesn't he? There can only be so many times you blindfold the big fella before he starts to catch on."

"If you absolutely must know, I keep my top on."

"And you plan to, what? Just do that indefinitely?" When Oralia made no immediate answer, Rali locked eyes with her. "It's a miracle you've gone this long without him discovering it, Oralia. You can deny its existence all you like, but you won't be able to hide it forever. Sascha's going to notice sooner or later."

"I keep hoping that if I ignore it, it will just go away." Wishful thinking, she knew. But at the moment, it was easier to indulge in the fantastical rather than turn the only constant in her life upside down.

"That's a terrible idea!"

"I know," Oralia groaned. "But he already worries enough as it is. And with everything up in the air right now, I would rather wait until I have answers."

Specifically, whether or not the dark veins would prove fatal. So far, all of the medical professionals consulted regarding the matter had been utterly stumped. They'd advised her to seek the help of a healer in the magical field. A grand idea that was made all the more grand by the fact that healers were next to impossible to find. Not due to scarcity, but because they were a commodity often hoarded by those in power. Any healers not under contract would have gone underground at the first whisper of war.

"You already know what I'm going to tell you," Rali said, "because it's the same thing I've been telling you for the past several months now. For the love of the gods, tell Sascha soon, please. I don't like secrets!"

"You love secrets," Oralia countered.

"I love uncovering other people's secrets and using that information against them as blackmail, yes. What I don't like is having to keep secrets. Especially when it's for people I care about. The truth is eating me up inside,

Oralia. Do something about it!" Rali settled deeper into the water with a huff. "When Ellisar gets back, she's going to take one look at me and know I'm hiding something. And then she's going to pull out every dirty trick in the book to get me to spill the tea and, frankly, I don't think I can stomach watching her cry again. That last time just didn't sit right."

"I will tell him soon, I promise."

Rali opened her mouth to respond, but paused, tilting her head curiously to the side. "Do you hear that?"

"Someone running." The loud slap of feet against tile echoed from farther down the passage as the sound drew steadily closer. "Barefoot."

Rali looked to the entrance and her brown eyes grew wide. "Ah, fuck."

A burly, tanned blur of a man hurtled through the archway and leapt out over the pool, tucking his body into a ball before crashing into the water. A wave rolled across the surface in his wake, lapping loudly against the stone steps. Mul's head surfaced seconds later, throwing his luxurious hair back behind him in a spray of green-tinted water droplets.

"This is a private meeting!" Rali said.

Mul slid through the water toward her, grinning. "As a founding member of the Emotionally Vulnerable Insight for the Lads and Lasses Affected by War, it is my right to be here." He settled onto the underwater bench beside her, resting one muscular arm against the edge of the pool in an overly comfortable gesture. "Besides, Pickle, how else could I possibly expect you to open up to me if I don't bare my sweet, tender soul first?"

Rali sank so low, her chin dipped beneath the water. "You should know that I am currently menstruating."

Mul thumped his fist to his chest. "Then my heart bleeds with sympathy for you, my love."

"Did I, uh, mention the horrific diarrhea?"

"Who among us hasn't had a bad case of the shits before?" Mul edged closer, fishing her limp hand from the water and clasping it in his own. "I am here for you, Quartzey. Whatever you need, you only have to ask."

"You could start with going the fuck away? And stop calling me Quartzey or they're going to start calling you the Eunuch."

He leaned forward, whispering into her ear in a manner that might have had a more enthused recipient swooning. "As you wish." Mul pushed off from the edge of the pool and surged backward in the water, holding his finger in the air above him. "Just remember, love as pure as ours isn't something to run from. When you're ready to face your feelings for me, I'll be waiting!"

"I knew I should have brought my bathing knife." Rali's dark eyes darted in Oralia's direction, noticing the way she was biting her tongue to constrain her laughter. "It's not funny!"

Oralia disagreed, covering her mouth as the small snorts of laughter slipped free. "After years of tormenting everyone around you, I never thought I would see the day you met your equal."

"He's not my equal! I just haven't found his weakness yet."

A nervous throat clearing echoed across the cavernous bathhouse, drawing their attention to the front archway. Captain Bernstein stood in the entrance looking remarkably bashful for someone still fully clothed. "I apologize for interrupting the meeting, but—"

"Stay back, Almas!" Mul stood to his full height near the steps, allowing the warm water to rush down his tangle of back hair. The waterline, fortunately, was high enough to leave some things to the imagination. He lowered his voice to a loud whisper. "Quartzey's got the menstruation shits."

Rali's expression turned to ash as she sank so low in the water, she nearly disappeared beneath the steaming green surface.

"Captain Bernstein," Oralia greeted. From his position by the doorway, she was confident he could not see the black veins branching from her sternum. She folded her arms over her chest for additional cover nonetheless.

Captain Bernstein spoke as though he had rehearsed the speech several times in his head on the way over. "As a show of gratitude for helping Adderwood secure our independence, the council has invited you and your team to attend a celebratory banquet tonight in the great hall."

Oh gods, no. Oralia could handle the endless traveling, the many cold nights spent under the stars, and the occasional skirmish or two, but not this. She no longer had the stomach for feigned niceties and politics. All she wanted to do now was run from her problems and stab things. Was that too much to ask?

"I do not suppose there is any flexibility with the date?" Oralia had already planned to spend most of her evening unconscious in a soft bed. If she was able to convince the council to move the dinner to a later date, there was a good chance she could keep finding convenient excuses to put it off indefinitely. Like skipping town, for instance. "As you can understand, we have only just arrived. My team is weary and requires time to rest."

"The council were quite insistent," Captain Bernstein assured her.

She bit back the agonized groan that nearly escaped her lips. Not one for subtlety, Rali openly stated what Oralia was thinking. "Cappy, with all due respect, you can tell them where to shove it."

"Wait, what?" Mul glanced over his shoulder at Oralia, somehow managing to make his eyes big and puppylike. "But it's a banquet. The kind with all the free food and fancy drinks, right? Why wouldn't we go?"

"Food and drink does not make the torture any less torturous," Rali explained.

"Oh." His broad shoulders shrank, managing to look almost pitiful for someone who Oralia wanted to strangle almost daily. "It's just me an' Lingon have never been to one of those before. Was hoping to check that one off the bucket list before we inevitably die a gruesome death for a cause that's really more yours than it is ours."

"Or you could just go home," Rali countered.

Oralia swore the man summoned tears to his eyes. "What home? You mean the one you destroyed with that poorly planned plot of yours?" He bit his knuckle, turning away as his voice cracked. "I still get worked up thinking about it. If only there was a way to forget. Like, I don't know, maybe a really nice banquet or something."

Rali turned to Oralia, whispering, "We could send the dingleberries in our place."

"We are trying to avoid a dinner party, not start an open war."

"Kinda late for that, boss. We already started a—"

Oralia decided that instead of acknowledging Rali's reply, she would simply speak over the top of it instead. "Thank you for delivering the message, Captain Bernstein. You can tell the council to expect our attendance." Although her reputation allowed her some leeway, she no longer had the status necessary to flat-out ditch social obligations. Meaning, of course, that if she wished to remain in the favor of Adderwood's new leaders, she would have to indulge their silly theatrics.

Captain Bernstein expressed his gratitude before quickly excusing himself, managing to do so without staring too blatantly at Rali. The dwarf in question was still slouched in the warm water, glowering at the prospect of having to put on pants for the occasion. "I thought we were past all this," she grumbled. "What's the point of being an outlaw if I've still got to do the song and dance?"

"Because even outlaws need allies."

CHAPTER FIFTEEN

Misery

Rasp didn't know how long he'd been seated in the same position: reclined, head back, with a block wedged between his molars, and drool rolling down his chin. At first he'd tried to watch, but the blazing white light overhead was nauseatingly bright and all he could pick out was the blurry shadow standing over him. Occasionally, the metal tool being used to rip apart the inside of his mouth would be traded out for another torture implement, reflecting the light from the glowing orb above as it passed from hand to tray with a soft clatter.

The night of the Hanover Harvest Festival was still something of a muddled blur. Rasp remembered the incident at the fountain and then being pursued, but the events afterward tangled together into a knot that was simply too painful to unravel. For some inexplicable reason, when he awoke days later, sore in places he didn't know existed and missing a good number of his teeth, he'd expected to find Faris at his side. But, like everything else in his miserable life, it had simply been too good to be true.

In his state of delirium, he'd mistaken Hop, the third and final member of their small traveling party, for Faris. Truth be told, it wasn't a hard mistake to make. They were both fauns, their cloven feet went *click-clack* wherever they went, and both seemed inexplicably committed to keeping him alive. There were differences between the two, of course. But Rasp was simply too miserable to even think about the many, many ways in which Faris was infinitely better.

Unfortunately, trying to will his overactive mind into a state of blank emptiness was having the reverse effect. The pang of loneliness came crashing down, filling his insides with the insatiable urge to peel off his clothes and run as fast and as far as his legs would carry him. Rasp would have, too, if it were not for the fact that he was currently laid up with his jaw pried wide open, getting the remnants of his splintered teeth ripped from his mouth.

"Try not to move," Hop's voice said from above him.

Stifling the instincts screaming at him to either fight or take flight, Rasp settled on the only other option available to him: be as annoying as possible. Some days, it was the only part of his personality that remained. He clung to it for all he was worth, afraid if he didn't, it too might slip away.

"Are 'ou un 'et?" he managed around the wood block wedged firmly between his molars. His tongue, numb from the gel, navigated his mouth like an inebriated slug, idly pushing frothy spittle up and over his bottom lip without regard for how stupid it made the rest of him look.

"No. And again, please refrain from speaking while I have my fingers in your mouth."

Rasp sputtered for breath, nearly choking on the excess saliva that pooled around the edges of his sluggish tongue. Hop, bless his big, naive heart, had yet to grasp the nuance of phrasing. Even after months on the road together, the poor sap still couldn't wrap his head around why the word "masticate" sent Rasp into a fit of giggles.

The dark, blurred shape hovering over him drew back with a sigh. "I suppose I walked into that one, didn't I? I mean it, though. If you move your tongue during this next part, you stand to lose it."

It was a good thing Whisper was out, otherwise Rasp was certain his mentor would have interjected something about the lack of tongue being an improvement.

Coughing the last of the spit from his throat, Rasp sank his head farther back into the cushion propped behind him. The tooth extraction process did not hurt nearly as much as he expected it to, thanks largely to Hop's numbing gel. It was the tedious sitting for hours on end unable to shift and fidget or, more importantly, complain, that was getting to him. Not to mention the boredom.

Bored, bored, bored . . . definitely not sad that Faris isn't here, but bored . . . bored . . .

Immobile, unable to speak, curse, or otherwise fight, Rasp was helpless against the internal demons steadily clawing to the forefront of his mind. The pressure built behind his eyes until, eventually, he had no other choice but to acknowledge the truth of the matter—this was the most miserable he'd ever been. Everything hurt, inside and out. A cloud of constant lingering dread weighed over him. It served as a cruel reminder that this was what life had become. And no matter how hard he tried, Rasp couldn't shake the feeling it wasn't going to get any better.

Mother would have known exactly what to say to pull him out of his slump. But she was gone too. Separated not just by distance, but existence itself. Rasp missed her most of all. The thought of her death caused an involuntary twinge so strong, he flinched to avoid it.

"Sorry," Hop said, mistaking Rasp's flinch for a different kind of pain. "That last root was being stubborn. The good news is they're all out now. Ready for the next part?"

Rasp offered him a halfhearted thumbs up. Any pain Hop was capable of inflicting paled in comparison to the self-imposed torture taking place within his mind.

"You sure you don't want a break first?"

"N'uh. 'Ust 'o it."

While the words themselves sounded nothing like Rasp meant, Hop understood the overall sentiment. There was a soft, metallic clatter as he traded his current torture implements for another. "Alright. We'll move on to placing the implants then."

"Tal' me th'o it."

"What?"

Rasp repeated the same line with limited success. His hand gestures weren't any better, but he tried anyway. He lifted his left hand and mimicked the movement of a mouth using only his fingers and thumb.

"You want me to talk?"

He nodded.

"You, who insist I blabber your ear off on a daily basis, suddenly want to hear me ramble on about nothing? Do I have that right, Rasp?"

Rasp offered his best *I'm an asshole, pity me anyway* look.

"My gods, you must be desperate." Hop's blurry shape drew closer once more. "I suppose if it will help you get through this without stabbing me, it's the least I could do."

Oh, yes. This was far superior than being stuck inside the downward spiral of emotions whipping about his head. Hop had that boring, droning kind of voice that was easy to get lost in. Rasp breathed a small sigh of relief as he relaxed into the chair, ready and willing to leave all of his pesky thoughts to sort themselves out. Hop's hand moved back to Rasp's upper jaw. Seconds later, Rasp felt pressure as something blunt pressed into the tender gum line.

The flesh of his mouth put up a fight, briefly, before the object slid neatly into place.

"You're going to feel a little heat, but it shouldn't hurt. And whatever demented thing you're about to say, don't. Stay still."

Something blue glowed just below Rasp's line of sight, not that he would have been able to tell what it was anyway. A warmth pulsated across his palate, the source of which was centered around the base of the false tooth. Just as the heat was beginning to grow uncomfortable, it stopped, and Hop withdrew his hands from Rasp's open mouth. True to his word, the faun kept Rasp's mind occupied by going over in great detail how each false tooth had carefully been crafted from blah, blah, blah substance, hardened through a science-y sounding process, and finished with blabber, blabber, blabber powder. Rasp assumed it was all top-notch work, as he understood absolutely none of it.

The next three implants went similarly and it was not long after that the wedge block was removed completely. Sadly, the torture was far from over. Once the implants were set, Hop checked and rechecked the alignment several times, grinding and filing each individual implant as needed to ensure a proper bite. Rasp was nearly ready to call it quits and make a break for the door—regardless of whether or not he knew where the damn thing was— when Hop finally declared his handiwork complete.

"There, finished." There was an audible *click* as Hop extinguished the glowing headlamp nestled over the curl of his horns. As fascinating as the lamp was, it barely scratched the surface compared to the other tools the faun kept in his leather satchel. During the slower evenings, Hop would go through them with Rasp, explaining each item's purpose and how it worked. In the end, all explanations basically boiled down to the same common denominator: magic.

Not Rasp's kind of magic, either. Hop was an artificer, someone who used a combination of magic and science to manipulate common materials and substances into acting *uncommon*. Or at least that's how Rasp understood it. There was probably a lot more to it, but that required actually paying attention to Hop's long-winded explanations.

"How do they feel?" Hop asked.

First, he had to make sure his jaw still worked. After a few experimental stretches, Rasp attempted to run the tip of his tongue along the edge of his teeth. All he succeeded in doing was pushing a dribble of saliva up and over his bottom lip. ". . . Uh?"

"That will wear off soon."

He wiped the spit from his face and then traced the outline of his new teeth with the pad of his thumb. The implants certainly felt better, not splintered in jagged little pieces or missing altogether. This was going to make eating so much easier. Biting, too! Seeing as he couldn't yet verbalize his gratitude, Rasp threw his arms around Hop's neck into a hug instead, nearly pulling the startled faun into the chair on top of him.

"Not the face!" Hop squirmed to get away before coming to the swift conclusion that Rasp's intentions were not violent in nature. "Sorry. Little jumpy. I'm never sure if you're going to hug me or hit me."

Faris would have known.

The thought caught him by surprise. Well, it would have, if it were not such a recurrent one. Rasp often thought of his best friend, and where he was, and what he was doing, and why the fuck he wasn't here yet. Hop was a decent substitute, but he would never be the real thing, no matter how many times Rasp absentmindedly called him by the wrong name.

"You're welcome, Rasp." Hop patted Rasp's arm nervously, adding, "Do you think you could let me go now?"

Hop stood and it was not long before Rasp heard the metallic clink of his tools being gathered and taken across the room for cleaning. "I put a charm on the new teeth," Hop called from wherever he was, undoubtedly sanitizing his equipment very, very meticulously. "It's going to take real force for one of those to pop out. And that's not a challenge, so don't try too hard, okay?"

There was a knock on the door in a familiar, rapid pattern. Hop's clacking hoof steps hurried to unlock it. "Oh dear," he said, sounding crestfallen the moment it drew open with a creak. "You have that look on your face. It's time to move already, isn't it?"

"We have to depart immediately," a new voice said.

Rasp saw the telltale silhouette of a person framed against the light pouring in from the doorway. They moved swiftly inside, which made tracking their movement by sight difficult as their muddled form blended in with the rest of the cabin's blurred interior. It did not take brilliance to know it was Whisper employing yet another of their many mortal disguises. The fae often changed their look from one place to the next to keep their pursuers in a constant state of confusion.

"I knew this place was too well-kept to be abandoned," Hop said with a sigh. "Are we expecting another angry homeowner?"

"No," Whisper said. "I was not the only stranger in town. No one approached me outright, but they were certainly watching. We need to put as much distance between us and this place as possible in the event they try to follow."

Rasp felt another small tinge of sadness. It had been kind of nice having a roof over his head, even if it was only for a few days. Such was life on the run, however. They never stayed anywhere for long. Rasp pushed from the chair onto his feet, his question directed at Whisper. "See'thers?"

"What?" Whisper said.

Right. That's still not working.

"Seekers," Hop translated as he scurried about the cabin, gathering their sparse belongings.

"Ah. I do not know, little bird. But a number of them were magical in nature." After a pertinent pause, Whisper addressed Hop. "Why is he speaking like that?"

"I paralyzed his tongue during the dental work."

"It's a marked improvement. You should consider making it permanent."

Rasp extended his middle finger in Whisper's approximate direction. "Fu'k ew."

"I see you got some of the fight back in you," Whisper said. "Good. We may need it."

That sounded like the opposite of good, actually. Rasp may have had the will to fight, but his magic hadn't fully recuperated yet. It was a small miracle he was even standing at this point.

"Worry about it on the way, little bird. We must leave, now."

CHAPTER SIXTEEN

The Inconsolable Lump

Rasp shifted in the stiff saddle as the surrounding light grew dimmer, obscured by the thick treetops overhead. The earthy fragrance of sweet pine and forest rot clouded the air so thickly, he nearly choked on it. Other than the occasional warble of a bird in the distance, the only sounds he could hear were the steady footfalls of the mule below him.

Rasp had protested the idea of traveling via mule while the others were allowed to walk—loudly and vigorously, as often as possible, regardless of whether or not anyone cared. He was a Stoneclaw, after all, and riding a beast of burden came as naturally to him as a fish took to long, romantic walks on the beach. Rasp was so adamantly opposed to the idea that he chose to stumble along beside the mule in protest instead. He made it an entire day and a half before conceding that perhaps riding *might* decrease the number of times he tripped and nearly broke his neck. Riddled with tree roots and unseen tripping hazards, the forest floor was simply too precarious for a blind man to navigate on foot with any efficiency.

Thus, the mule stayed. Rasp even awarded her the loving name of Bonecrusher, on account of how many times she nearly broke his foot stepping on it. Hop tried to convince him to give her a more pleasant name, but Rasp refused. He would be damned before he, a mighty and formidable Stoneclaw warrior, the former Iron Devil himself, would be caught dead riding a Buttercup into battle, or through the forest, or wherever the fuck they were currently headed.

Come to think of it, that was probably something worth knowing. Rasp opened his mouth and his tongue flopped uselessly over his lower teeth, producing a babbled string of nonsense. "Where 'e 'oin'?"

"That's lasting longer than I anticipated," Hop said, failing to fully disguise his snort of laughter.

It was a shame the faun's tall, blurry outline was just out of kicking range. For this exact reason, probably. Rasp was considering jumping from the saddle and tackling him when Whisper disrupted his poorly plotted revenge.

"We are headed east, little bird."

As if that answered anything other than what direction they happened to be traveling. Hop, fortunately, could always be counted on to press Whisper for additional details. "What's east?" he said. "Do you have an actual destination in mind or is this another case of 'we'll know it when we see it'?"

"Supposedly there's an old realm settlement out that way."

"Supposedly?" Hop's tone shifted from inquisitive to disheartened in the span of a single word. "This isn't going to be like your last lead, is it? Fruitlessly wandering the wilderness for weeks on end to no avail?"

Rasp fought the smile that pulled the corner of his lips. It was nice having someone else pester Whisper for a change. Unlike Rasp, Hop was also capable of getting his point across without relying strictly on copious amounts of profanity. A method that often left Whisper with no other alternative but to actually address said concerns.

Whisper grunted in response. It was the sort of sound that was equal parts frustrated and annoyed. "According to the villagers I spoke to, there's been a surplus of realm activity in the area as of late. A large caravan passed through some months ago, headed east, in the same direction as the old settlement."

"That's all they told you? No names, no places, no 'stop when you see the secret fortress, if you hit the river, you've gone too far'?"

"That's it."

"East it is then," Hop said with a resigned sigh.

To no one's shock, Rasp's "surprise relocation" was not for the sole purpose of apprenticeship after all. In addition to forcing Rasp to actually learn to use his gods-awful powers, Whisper was dragging him along on what was swiftly becoming the magical equivalent of a wild goose chase. With iron poisoning slowly sapping their lifeforce, the fae was in a race against time to recover a lost magical item—insisting it alone possessed the power to make everything right again.

Whisper believed their item had been bought and placed in a collection possessed by none other than the infamous Geralt Lazuli himself. For years, the fae searched the capital high and low without success. Geralt kept his secret treasure trove well hidden, however. Whisper may not have ever found it had it not been for the recent uprising. With rebellion breaking out across the United Territories, and the threat of an attack on the capital looming in the distance, rumor was Geralt had moved his collection to a safer location.

For the past four months, Rasp and Whisper had been chasing down every two-bit lead without success. They'd met resistance along the way. Their attackers ranged from common bandits to realm patrols, seekers, and a few unnamed magical groups that, for whatever reason, all thought it was a grand idea to take their chances against a highly powerful fae and a half-trained witch with anger issues.

That's how they encountered Hop, actually. He'd been traveling with a party from the Division of Divination. Whisper seemed to have a soft spot for those forced into a situation not of their choosing and had let the faun go. Free of the division's control, and without a home to return to, Hop just sort of stuck around. Rasp hadn't minded that part, actually. Whisper was, by all accounts, as conversational as a cactus. It was nice having someone else around who understood the merits of companionship. Plus, as it turned out, the prospect of raiding a super-secret, magically guarded stronghold would be infinitely easier with someone who possessed functioning vision.

"Little bird?"

Rasp flinched at the use of his nickname. It was better than "fuck for brains," he supposed, but not by much. A part of him wondered if the title would change as his abilities improved. Would he eventually graduate to large bird? Was there a middle bird? A mediocre bird? Increasingly disappointing bird? The possibilities seemed endless.

The wind picked up, blustering the hood from Rasp's head as a burst of magic filled the air. Seconds later, he felt the familiar pain of tiny, clawed paws scrambling up his leg and over his back, nestling into the fur-lined hood of his cloak. **You seem in better spirits today.**

In other words, "You're no longer an inconsolable lump refusing to get out of bed. What changed?"

You spend half your days as an inconsolable lump, Whisper said. **That is nothing new. Is the new potion working?**

Hop had been experimenting with various potions in an attempt to stop the spread of the dark magic burrowed within Rasp's veins. It was a kind yet futile effort. Rasp didn't have the heart to mention that he'd managed one sip of the most recent concoction before pouring the vile substance into the chamber pot.

The potions might work better if you actually ingested them.

Gods dammit. It wasn't fair having a mentor who could read his every thought on a whim. Rasp groaned, concentrating inward as he composed his internal monologue into a coherent reply. *You know it's a lost cause. No amount of witch's brew is going to un-curse me.*

Have you told him that?

What kind of asshole do you take me for? Taking care of me is the only reason Hop gets out of bed.

And here I thought it was because you enjoy being doted on. Now that you no longer have your best friend to depend upon, you've gone out of your way to replace hi—

No, I haven't! And you can stop right there because we're not talking about it.

Fine. Whisper's heavy sigh rippled through Rasp's mind. **May we discuss that other thing you've been avoiding then?**

Rasp sank lower in the saddle, dread pooling in his stomach. Naively, he'd hope to avoid this conversation. As if not talking about what happened the night of the Hanover Harvest Festival would make the event itself cease to exist. Unlike his memories, Whisper could not simply be pushed into the back of his mind and forgotten about. Rasp reached up and scratched the base of his neck with a trembling hand. The skin itself didn't feel any different. And yet, the way everyone had been treating him with kiddie gloves lately spoke of a different story.

He supposed there wasn't any use avoiding the inevitable. *How bad is it?*

The branching has spread considerably. It now stretches from the top of your neck past your ribcage.

After months of training, it had taken but one moment of weakness to shatter his illusions of control. Rasp gritted his teeth, hands clenching uncomfortably tightly around the reins. *Fan-fucking-tastic.*

I will continue searching for a cure, as promised. In the meantime, as disappointing as it is, you cannot allow one minor setback to—

Dread transformed to rage, its blistering heat swelling inside of him. *Can we skip the niceties and you just get to the part where you yell at me for being a complete fuckup? You haven't mentioned it once in the last three days. It's probably eating you up inside.*

Eating *me* up inside? Even in thought, Whisper somehow managed to impart this with the verbal equivalent of an eye roll. **Why would I need to? Seems like you are doing a far better job of tearing yourself apart all on your own.**

Great. Good talk. Glad we finally did this.

I could yell at you if you think it would help, but that is not the point I wanted to speak about. I was there, little bird. I saw what happened. You touched on powers you did not know existed.

A fragmented memory flashed before his eyes. Rasp recalled how effortlessly the magic had bent to his will, as if the ability had been there all along, buried deep out of sight. There was something else, too—a moment Rasp swore he had been able to see the magical auras of the witches around him. What came next was harder to explain. It wasn't so much an ability as it was a feeling. An insatiable hunger that damn near overtook him.

Rasp snapped his eyes back open, scattering the memory back to the far corners of his mind. *Those powers weren't mine.*

How do you know?

I wanted to eat you, Whisper. I'm all kinds of fucked up, but even I have hard limits.

The hunger was not your own, no. But the powers were.

Rasp wasn't sure whether or not to feel relieved by that.

Don't you see? This is what I have been pushing for. I've known what you were capable of from the first day we met. You've barely scratched the surface of your potential and the only thing holding you back is yourself. You are on the cusp of a breakthrough. As I said before, you cannot allow one setback to destroy all of the progress you've made.

A setback? Rasp fired back. *Is that what we're calling it now? It nearly took control. I was on the verge of caving the whole city in! If you hadn't been there, I would have . . .* His thoughts trailed, unwilling to finish what they'd started.

You might have done something horrendous, I know. That is the whole point of training, little bird. You were woefully unprepared for that situation. You were never supposed to be there. I told you to stay with the bags, remember? You ignored my instructions and put yourself in danger.

There it was, the inevitable tongue-lashing. The last few days Rasp had felt trapped in a bizarre state of limbo, trying to avoid the impending lecture while seemingly doing everything in his power to provoke it. He had hoped getting it out of the way would make him feel better. It didn't, though. Instead of the sweet kiss of relief, he had the sudden urge to tip over the side of his mule and become one with the forest floor.

He yelped when a set of needled jaws nipped at the back of his neck. **Fall off of the mule after I have finished.**

That's what she said.

Oh good. Apparently some parts of his personality were still functioning normally. They didn't do anything to make him feel better, but at least they were still there.

Once certain they were not about to suffer a traumatic fall, Whisper rearranged themself into a more comfortable position and went still. **As I was saying, the blame does not fall entirely on you. Pushing you to resolve the situation when you weren't ready was shortsighted of me. Hopefully what happened will serve as a reminder to both of us to finish your training before attempting something like that again.**

Rasp didn't know what to say to that. Unfortunately, his indecision allowed the thoughts to slip out unobstructed. *I'm sorry.*

Figures, Whisper muttered.

What?

The one time you muster an apology just happens to be the one time you don't have a working tongue.

Is my repentance not good enough for you?

I suppose. But gleaning it from your thoughts is not nearly as impactful as hearing it said aloud.

It probably wasn't meant as a challenge, but Rasp took it as one anyway. He released the reins, throwing his hands out from his sides as he sucked in a lungful of dingy forest air. "Whith'per, I'm th'orry!"

"How unexpected," Hop murmured from somewhere alongside the mule. "Is what I would have said only two months ago. Oh, how traveling with you two has changed me."

Right. There were other people capable of hearing him. He'd sort of forgotten about that. Rasp's smiled sheepishly. "Th'orry 'op."

"Truth be told, I was starting to feel a bit like a third wheel. I can tell you two are having one of your secret conversations. And here I am, stuck on the outside, no way of knowing whether or not it's me you're talking about."

Rasp hooked his right foot in the stirrup to ensure his balance as he leaned out over the left side of the mule, just far enough to pat the faun's shoulder. He certainly hoped it was the shoulder anyway. "Tha's all we 'alk abou'."

"I knew it."

CHAPTER SEVENTEEN

A Meal Fit For Birds

The dark canopy stretched overhead in an endless expanse of rustling leaves and creaking branches. Rasp's limited vision picked up occasional shafts of sunlight that trickled down through the dense treetops here and there, but the majority of the journey was carried out in what amounted to absolute darkness. Unable to track the position of the sun, his sense of time was turned on its head. He didn't know how long they'd been traveling since leaving the cabin, but the fact that they weren't stopping meant it had only been a few hours. A bit of a shame, considering his ass had gone numb ages ago. No matter how he shifted in the saddle, he could not rid himself of the pins and needles feeling working its way down his leaden legs.

Whisper spent the journey nestled in his hood, going on and on about magic this and potential that. The words flowed in one ear and out the other. There was a trick to fooling Whisper into thinking he was paying attention, Rasp found. All he had to do was keep his thoughts open, mindlessly mirroring what his mentor said without actually absorbing any of the information.

. . . Which is why the obvious course of action will be to throw you over the next cliffside, Whisper's voice carried on in the background.

The next cliffside, Rasp mindlessly agreed.

Into a pit of sharpened stakes.

Oh, yes. The sharpest.

Full of snakes.

Full of snakes.

I know you're not listening.

Not listening, yep, yep. Got it.

Raspberry Stoneclaw!

His name shot like a lance of lightning down his spine. Rasp sat straight in the saddle, gritting his teeth as the echo of Whisper's voice bounced along the inside of his aching skull. *Gods dammit! Will you stop doing that?* Rasp released the reins, using his forefingers to massage the sudden throb from his temples. *It fucking hurts.*

If you were paying attention, I wouldn't have to.

Rasp rolled his head back with a groan. *But it's so boring.*

You don't even know what I was talking about.

Of course I do. Magic, training, how I'm not listening.

For a few blissful seconds, Rasp's mind was free of Whisper's voice. Naturally, it did not last. **Lucky guess.**

Please, it's the only thing we ever talk about. I need a break. My mind's not a sponge, it doesn't just absorb these things. Your lessons need time to ferment before they stick.

I will leave you to it then. Whisper sighed. **Before I do, however, I have one final question.**

Rasp could feel his eyes rolling into the back of his head.

Have you given any more thought to what it is you want?

And just like that, his mind went blank, void of all intelligible thought as it struggled to piece together what the question even meant.

You do not have to provide an answer right away. *Ferment* on it.

Rasp stared straight ahead, face slack in puzzlement, as Whisper's thoughts detangled from his own. The question echoed within his mind. *What is it you want?*

What an odd thing to ask. Not the question itself, really, but the fact that anyone cared what he wanted. Rasp's entire life had been a matter of other people telling him what they expected of him and he, in turn, doing everything in his power to carry out the exact opposite. His training wasn't supposed to last forever. After he finished his apprenticeship, he would be free to do as he wanted.

The problem was he didn't know what he wanted. He didn't have a home, no family, no purpose. He was blind, possessed unimaginable power, had no desire to use said unimaginable power, oh, and literally cursed on top of everything else. By all accounts, he was destined to spend the rest of his life on the run, avoiding any people who wished to use him for their own means. Which, apparently, was nearly all of them.

The happiest time in his life had subsequently been the shortest. He found himself looking back on the six months he'd spent with the Belfast family more and more, kicking himself for not realizing what he had had while it was in front of him. He could go back to Lonebrook, he supposed. But doing so would be placing the very people he loved in the line of danger.

In the end, when he got to the root of it, what he really wanted was to be someone else. The type of person who only dreamed of going on fantastical adventures but never actually broke from their dull life. Someone destined to live out their existence in quiet monotony, surrounded by friends and a warm bed and lots and lots of food. No more stringy onions and bitter dandelion greens, but bread, and meat pies, and mountains of mashed potatoes swimming in butter.

On second thought, maybe he was just hungry. He tended to drift into overdramatic territory when his stomach was nearing empty. "Hop?" Rasp spoke without thinking, surprised to find some of the life had returned his tongue.

"Still here, Rasp. Haven't gone anywhere," the faun replied from somewhere to the left of Rasp's mule.

A false sense of contentment eased the storm brewing within his thoughts as Rasp realized he finally had an answer to Whisper's daunting question. "I want a sandwich."

"Can't help you there, I'm afraid."

"I would get it myself, but you don't let me near the rations," Rasp reminded him. "Ergo, you are the food provider. Chop, chop now. You have no one to blame but yourself." Safeguarding their food was a rather selfish act on Hop's part, Rasp felt. As if he couldn't be trusted not to scarf down their entire supply the moment Hop's back was turned. The absolute lack of trust was completely unwarranted. After all, he'd only done it once so far and it had only been half the rations, not all of them!

"It's more complicated than that," Hop said. "Do you remember the night we were in the city?"

More than he desired to, unfortunately. "Yes."

"While you were left with the bags and Whisper was off doing whatever it is Whisper does, my task was to replenish our food supplies."

Already, Rasp did not like where this was going. Partly because Hop always took forever to get around to his eventual point, touching on as many needless details as possible before circling back around to his answer. The other, much larger piece of Rasp's discomfort stemmed from the fact that the sudden lack of food was probably his doing somehow.

Hop carried on, oblivious to Rasp's internal woes. "Having finished my other errands, I was on my way to get the food when I was interrupted by a very persistent raven. I followed him and, instead of replenishing the supplies as planned, I wound up carrying you out of the city in a burlap sack slung over my shoulder."

Crap. He hated it when the consequences of his actions came back to bite him in the ass. "We don't have *any* food leftover?"

"Some. The point of rationing, however, is to make it last."

"Didn't Whisper just visit a village? They didn't pick something up on the way back?"

Hop hesitated. "Are they, um, asleep? Whisper, I mean."

"Why are you whispering?"

"Because I've read about far too many fae encounters to knowingly insult one to their face."

Rasp didn't see what insults had to do with food, but for the sake of filling his grumbling stomach sooner than later, he dutifully checked. He drew into himself, opening his mind, and waited for the uncomfortable moment the obnoxious voice in his head went from one to two. When the moment never came, Rasp concluded that his mentor had likely fallen into a deep sleep—an occurrence that was becoming increasingly more common these days.

"They're asleep."

For whatever reason, Hop still felt the need to keep his voice annoyingly low. "I don't know if you have noticed, Rasp, but Whisper does not eat. Not in the same sense as you or I."

"So?"

"So to answer your question, yes, they did bring food from the village. Specifically, several bags of dried corn feed."

"That's good, right? I like corn."

"The kind you feed to chickens."

"Oh." Rasp's sudden hopes for a decent meal deflated, much like his empty stomach, which was quite insistent it would start cannibalizing itself if he didn't fill it soon. That was one of the quirks about depending upon a fae for survival. Although Whisper had spent many eons living among humankind, they still didn't have a good grasp on what constituted edible. For example, there were a number of wild mushrooms not meant for human consumption. After the second accidental poisoning, Rasp had insisted on doing most of the foraging himself. Hop's unexpected enlistment into their troop had come with many added benefits, including a surplus of meals that Rasp didn't have to question whether or not would be his last.

"If you're insistent on eating something right now, there are several edible food sources around us. White clover, dandelions, a nice strip of birch bark to chew on, perhaps?"

Before Rasp could comment how he would have preferred chicken feed to any of those, the feathery snap of wings filled the air near his head. Pain erupted across his right shoulder moments later as Father landed, talons digging into his cloak and, consequently, the tender flesh beneath for stability.

Rasp tilted his head toward the raven. "You've been notably absent. Where have you—"

With a muffled croak, Father shoved something into Rasp's open mouth.

It was cold, bloated, and covered in a slick layer of watery mucus. Rasp panicked. Instead of spitting it out, he swallowed, feeling it start to liquefy on its way down. "Oh my gods," he croaked, mortified by what he'd just done. "That . . . that . . . was a worm. Did you just feed me a worm? Tell me you didn't just feed me a worm!"

Father confirmed Rasp's suspicion with an approving click of his beak.

Rasp frantically wiped his tongue against his sleeve. His efforts succeeded only in adding an extra layer of filth to his soil-flavored mouth. "Why was it mushy?"

Father's answer was as simple as it was stupid.

"Because you found it in a puddle?" That certainly explained the texture and lack of wriggling. "So not only did you feed me a worm, you gave me a dead and bloated one you found in a puddle?"

Croak?

"No, I don't want another one!"

Father ruffled his feathers with an angry gurgle before going still.

Rasp hung his head with a groan. "Seriously?"

"Oh good," Hop muttered. "Another conversation I can't be a part of."

He spoke with his head down, chin resting against his bony chest. "Father said he has imperative information, but now he's not going to share it because I don't appreciate how he provides for me."

"Try giving the worm back to him. I hear birds like that sort of thing."

As lovely as it sounded to regurgitate the contents of his stomach and offer it to the raven perched on his shoulder, the last thing Rasp needed was to drive the wedge between him and his father deeper. "Oh!" He snapped his fingers at Hop. "Give me some of the chicken feed."

"You're missing something," Hop said.

"Look, I know he's not a chicken. But he'll literally eat anything. Come on, I'll show you."

The faun issued a weary sigh. "I meant please."

"Oh my gods, give me some of the chicken feed, Hop, *please*."

With an irritated flap of his ears, Hop's blurry shape moved out of Rasp's peripheral vision. Rasp could hear him rustling around in one of the saddlebags behind him. Hop returned, moments later, thrusting a handful of dried corn into Rasp's outstretched hand. "You're welcome."

"Thank you." Rasp lifted the offering to the sulking raven. "I'm sorry for not appreciating your worm, Dad. Please accept this gift as a token of apology."

Father pretended to not notice for several seconds before gluttony got the better of him.

"Be gentle!" Rasp flinched as the raven's beak stabbed into his palm, gobbling up the offering as quickly as he could. Rasp waited until he'd had his fill before asking, "About that imperative information?"

Father garbled his reply around a mouthful of dried corn.

"He says there are five travelers following us," Rasp translated.

Thus far, his father was the only raven from the flock to have found him. Whether the others were actually searching or not, Rasp didn't know. Despite their oftentimes volatile relationship, they were trying to make it work. One upside was that Father operated as an additional set of eyes and ears. With the raven watching from the skies, the trio had thus far managed to keep one step ahead of their many, many pursuers.

"Are they the same ones Whisper saw at the village?" Hop asked.

"How would he know that, Hop?"

"Fair point," the faun conceded. "What about uniforms? Were they wearing any sort of identifiable symbols or clothing? Robes, maybe?"

Croak, croak, croak.

Rasp popped the rest of the chicken feed into his mouth, detailing Father's report around increasingly desperate attempts to grind the dried corn to pulp with his molars. "He says they didn't look like they were from the division. They're carrying weapons and at least two had plated armor. Whatever trick Whisper used to disguise their trail has them turned around for the moment, but he thinks they'll find the cabin by nightfall."

"That's, admittedly, not good. But for the love of gods, stop eating the poultry feed!" Hop cried. "I just fixed your teeth!"

"How else do you expect me to test them out?" The implants were working remarkably well so far. Unlike the petrified corn, which, even when ground into more manageable sizes, was akin to swallowing broken shards of river rock. Rasp was committed to ridding his mouth of the vile worm flavor and persisted in spite of the pain.

Father normally would have put up a bigger stink about being deprived of a hard-earned meal. From his smug cackle, he seemed to be enjoying Rasp's self-inflicted torture.

"For the record, I blame you," Rasp told him.

Croak?

"Well, yeah, partly for the worm but also the lack of thinking things through. I definitely didn't inherit that from Mom."

CHAPTER EIGHTEEN

Flirting with Murder

The week following the jailbreak came and went in a noxious blur. The party traveled during the night, utilizing the dark to cloak their movements, while hunkering down during the day when the realm patrols were most active. Daana caught only short bursts of sleep between stops and rotating watch shifts. When she awoke, for what might have been the third time that day, she was surprised to find the sun was already setting beyond the horizon. Its final rays filtered in through the dense trees, coating the moss-riddled ground in eerie patches of waning pink and orange light.

Easing upright, Daana took stock of her surroundings as the hazy visions of sleep slowly faded from her waking mind. Snag was gone, as was Wormy, the goblin's trustworthy horse. Ellisar's pack was on the ground beside her saddle and the only things that looked to be missing were her bow and quiver. Off hunting, probably. Ashwyn was seated on the trampled dirt near the center of camp, working a needle in and out of a cut of cloth.

Daana had seen Oralia do similar work around the campfire before. The notable difference was that Oralia made it look soothing. From the way Ashwyn muttered and cursed her way through, pausing every few stitches to suck the sting of a needle prick from her fingertip, it was not an activity she enjoyed.

Stifling a yawn, Daana moved forward in an awkward shuffle. Her sore legs and hips protested any and all movement. Her knees buckled and Daana went down with them, managing to make her descent look more like an intentional sit and less like a full-bodied flop. Ideally, she would have worked the ache from her unruly limbs through stretches, but with the threat of another torturous ride looming in the near future, she was going to take advantage of the stillness for as long as possible.

Daana's dazed stare moved to the large cut of cloth clenched in Ashwyn's hands. "Making a blanket?"

The orc's dominant hand jerked to an abrupt halt. "A tunic, actually."

"That was going to be my second guess."

"The flattery is not necessary, Peaches. I know dog shit when I see it." Ashwyn stretched the garment between her hands and held it aloft, examining the sloppy line of stitches with a scowl. "I wanted something that didn't scream 'I'm wearing my bigger sister's secondhand britches' quite as loudly as what I've got on now. Thought I could fashion something myself. I think I'd be better off with a potato sack at this point."

Daana nodded along, too preoccupied with the nervous fluttering in her stomach to offer anything more than a smile. She'd waited all week for the opportunity to approach Ashwyn alone, and now that she finally had it, she couldn't summon the courage to turn her thoughts into words. They all just jumbled together in a useless string of nonsense that clogged the inside of her throat, making it impossible to say anything.

"Got something on your mind?" Ashwyn offered a knowing wink before Daana could sputter out an excuse. "Looks like you're about ready to ask me to the winter solstice ball with the way you're blushing."

Her skin burned hot against the cool evening air as her embarrassment crept from her face to her ears. "There is, actually," Daana said, still fighting the stubborn lump caught in her throat. "I know there wasn't time back in the cell, but do you think you could, well, tell me about my mother now? What she was like?"

Ashwyn's eyebrows pressed together as her unsteady hand slipped the needle in and out of the garment once more. "Did I know her?"

"Larkspur, remember?"

"You meant that?" The orc's gray-blue head swiveled around in surprise. "You're Lark's kid, for real? Did she have more children or . . ."

"I was the one put on the boat headed for the flatlands. I didn't know until recently, but Ellisar said you would be able to give me answers."

"Me? Ellisar was the one with ties to your mother, not me. I barely knew her."

"She was?"

Ashwyn hesitated. "They were a couple, formerly. Long before Ellie and I met. That's the entire reason Larkspur reached out to us for assistance in the first place."

"*What?*"

Ashwyn dropped her work into her lap and rolled back her head with a groan. "Of course Ellisar didn't tell you."

"No, she didn't!"

"Look, from what I understand, their relationship was very . . . volatile. Ellisar didn't want anything to do with your mother afterward. When Larkspur reached out after the division had taken her captive, it was me who convinced Ellie to help."

Ashwyn looked like she wanted to say more, but did not yet know how. Slowly, she reached out and rested the flat of her hand on Daana's knee. "May I ask why you're not with your mother now? If learning about her was your goal, this seems like a very convoluted way of accomplishing that."

"Because she's dead?"

The orc's gray eyes grew wide. "Larkspur *died*? When did that happen?"

A nagging idea pulled at the back of Daana's mind. Something about their stories wasn't aligning and she couldn't shake the feeling that somehow, some way, it was all intentional. "Of course she's dead. Your sister killed her!" Daana gestured with her hands as she spoke. "Why am I even explaining this to you? You were there, weren't you? Shouldn't you know all of this?"

Ashwyn's painfully blank face said far more than words could have.

Daana attempted to jog her memory with a brief history lesson. "It was a pivotal moment following the Night of Stolen Lives. The Protector of the Realm, your sister, chased those responsible across the territories, cornered them in a tiny town in the middle of nowhere, and slew the main instigator, Larkspur Denari. It's in all the history books."

"That's the funny thing about history, Peaches. Tends to change depending on who's telling it."

Daana dropped her hands into her lap in defeat, shoulders slumping. "So what are you telling me? It didn't go down that way? Because Ellisar said otherwise. Warned me not to tell Oralia who I was because she was the one who killed my mother. Implied she'd kill me too if she found out."

"That's . . . not right."

For what felt like an eternity, Ashwyn said nothing else, silently stewing in whatever thoughts were slowly unraveling within her head. Finally, with a hard glint in her eye, the orc lifted her fingers to her mouth and blew a series of sharp sounds that were remarkably similar to birdsong. Daana had heard Snag and Ellisar use similar calls to communicate with one another over distance. She could differentiate the "danger" whistle from the "all clear" and was even starting to get a grasp on Ellisar's infamous "fuck off" warning, but this sound was new to her.

"There's no point in you and me trying to figure this puzzle out on our own if we're missing half the pieces," Ashwyn explained. "We may as well consult the source."

It was not long before Ellisar's tall shadow slipped from between the dark trees with a pair of rabbits thrown casually over her shoulder. "I hope you have a good reason for interrupting me," she grumbled as she made her way toward them. "You scared off a nice fat one."

"We need to talk," Ashwyn managed between clenched teeth.

The elf huntress stopped near her saddle, a good three-meter stretch from where Daana and Ashwyn sat. Ellisar's golden eyes swept between the pair, silently gleaning unspoken bits of information from their varied expressions while keeping her own strategically blank. Whatever eventual conclusion Ellisar reached, she kept to herself. She tapped her foot impatiently at Ashwyn and said, "You interrupted my hunting to have a conversation? Surely you're not serious."

"I am." Ashwyn accentuated her next statement with a stern finger pointing. "And you are not going to do that thing you do. I am focused."

Ellisar tilted her head to the side curiously. "What thing I do?"

"Where you try to distract me by—gah! See? You're already doing it. Not today, miss. Walk yourself over here and take a seat."

Wordlessly, Ellisar slid the rabbits and quiver that hung from her shoulder to the ground in a single, fluid motion. Reaching back, she unfastened her waist-length hair from its tie, flipping the straw-colored mane from her face with a casual whip of her head. When the cascade of hair settled, her face had changed. Softer somehow, and lacking its usual steely coldness. With her primping finished, Ellisar approached, adding a subtle sway to her hips as she strode confidently toward them.

Daana sat utterly petrified. The hairs on her neck stood on end as she found herself wondering when exactly Ellisar had developed hips. The technique wasn't bad. Quite the opposite, actually. Which by itself was alarming enough to make Daana consider darting into the trees and ducking under a shrub to wait out whatever chaos was about to take place.

Ashwyn patiently awaited Ellisar's seductive approach. An unamused scowl pulled at the corners of her mouth. "You are really outdoing yourself here."

Ellisar reached Ashwyn and extended her hand downward, cradling the orc's chin in the center of her open palm. Her voice was nearly as soft as the uncharacteristic lift in her eyebrows. "I knew our time apart would come with changes. Mostly for you, a few for me, but the malnourishment was a real shock. Even now, I hardly recognize you."

"This is not the conversation we are having."

"You're right. Because I should be out fetching your dinner right now. That dungeon left you skin and bones. If I'm going to get you back to your original strength, I can't waste prime hunting hours on silly conversations."

Ashwyn's formerly fixed expression started to slip as her eyes wandered down Ellisar's lean figure. "I'm the skin and bones in this scenario? Me? The one who had nothing to do but lift heavy things over my head and eat two regular meals a day for the better part of a century?"

"I didn't want to say anything before, but I think I might actually be able to take you."

"My arms are bigger than your head!"

Ellisar slid her arms around her lover's shoulders and collapsed against her back, nuzzling her head into the crook of Ashwyn's neck. "Hush now," she whispered, with a sympathetic pat to the top of the orc's head. "That's the delirium speaking. You'll come around once we get a few rabbits in you."

"If your master plan is to fatten me up so I can't catch you, think again, miss. I'll have you facedown in the dirt before you can say uncle."

The flicker of excitement that lit in Ellisar's golden eyes caused Daana's stomach to churn. "Hold up!" Daana injected before Ellisar was given the opportunity to incite a chase. "What in the name of chaos is happening right now?"

Ashwyn flipped Ellisar over her shoulder and into her lap. "You never seen flirting before, Peaches?"

"I have. This is not that."

"Says the unbedded one." Ellisar was a melted puddle within her lover's arms. Daana had seen enemies cut down for merely looking at Ellisar wrong and yet, suddenly, the blasted elf was as docile as a kitten.

"First of all, that's not true. Secondly"—Daana addressed Ashwyn, attempting to rekindle some of her previous fire—"I thought you called her here to set the record straight?"

Ashwyn's brow furrowed. "Did I?"

"Yes!" Daana slapped her open palm to her forehead, groaning, "Our stories don't align, remember? I was led to believe that your sister killed my mother and that seemed like news to you."

"Seven realms, Ellisar!" In a single swoop, the orc lifted the elf from her lap and deposited her onto the patchy ground beside her. "You shameless cad! It's cheating to butter me up with your sultry little hip waggle and you know it."

"As it happens, I have some butter on hand. I was saving it for later." The elf leaned closer, long hair cascading over her face as she whispered, "But if you want it now, simply say the word. I'll have you slick and glistening like a roast duck fresh out of the oven."

Daana choked on the vomit that was desperately trying to evacuate the inside of her throat. "Dear gods, make it stop."

Ashwyn struck the flat of her hand against the ground. "Ellisar Winifred Farrow, for the love of goddess, stop trying to seduce me and start talking. Starting with, why does Daana think her mother is dead?"

In the span of a single heartbeat, Ellisar's sultry pout disappeared. Her mask of indifference returned with twice its normal severity. "Was I supposed to tell her something different? I thought the point of a good cover story was to keep our lies consistent."

There was a definite edge to Ashwyn's voice now. "Did you let Daana think her mother was dead this entire time?"

"This really shouldn't surprise you."

Ashwyn lifted her hand and held all four fingers and thumb splayed for Ellisar to see. If it was meant to be a threat, all it did was coax a half smile from its recipient. Ashwyn closed her hand into a fist and lowered it, gritting out through clenched teeth, "I don't understand. Why would you not have told her? You could have alleviated years of heartbreak at no cost to yourself."

"There was a cost," Ellisar disagreed. "Daana would have dropped every-thing to go find her mother. Goddess knows Oralia would have bent over backward to help if she found out. Obviously I couldn't let that happen. I needed Daana to get you out."

"You could have found another way, I'm sure."

"That's the catch though. If all else failed, I planned to make a trade with Geralt. Daana for you."

It was Daana's turn to raise her voice. "You were going to do *what?*"

"I don't know why any of this surprises you, kid. Don't ever trust people who take an interest in you. It's rarely for your benefit."

Ashwyn caught Ellisar's stare and the two appeared to battle one another with only their eyes. Finally, after coming to some form of conclusion, Ashwyn turned back to Daana. "As my wife clearly has not been forthright with the truth, I will. Your mother is alive, Daana. My sister never killed her, that was simply a cover story. Larkspur took her escaped followers, fled the realm, and took up residence in the flatlands. She has dedicated herself to helping other witches escape the control of the Division of Divination. It is my understanding that she is still there, amassing a sort of magical resistance."

Ashwyn allowed the weight of this to sink in a moment before asking, "Would you like to meet her?"

Daana's head snapped upright. The sting of betrayal was lessened by the sudden joy bubbling up inside of her like an uncorked bottle of fizzy spirits. She was so excited she wanted to scream and yet, her words were uttered barely above a whisper. "More than anything."

"Then I'll be happy to take you to her."

CHAPTER NINETEEN

The Lost Cause

The cold evening air stung the tip of her nose and each pointed ear. Daana hardly noticed. Not with the radiating warmth that spread from her chest to each fingertip and toe, filling her with a happiness she had never known before. Her mother was alive. What's more, Daana was being taken to her. She blinked away the swelling tears that threatened to fall, all while wondering if this was just another cruel dream and, any moment now, she would awaken to find herself lost and alone in the world once more.

The ruckus coming from the lithe figure who paced back and forth, kicking up the dirt on the edge of her peripheral vision, was, admittedly, making the scenario a little less dreamlike. "No!" Ellisar thundered, accentuating each word with a dramatic foot stomp. "No, no, no, no!"

Ashwyn's offer to reunite Daana with her mother had flipped the conversation on its head, reversing her and Ellisar's given roles. The orc remained seated on the ground, her once rigid shoulders now noticeably relaxed—the cool, calm antithesis to Ellisar's fiery rage. A faint smile played on Ashwyn's lips as she watched her partner's increasingly desperate antics. "This is not your most compelling argument so far, dear."

"You want an argument?" Ellisar whirled around, loose hair whipping over her shoulder as she threw her hands out from her sides. "I'll give you a fucking argument. Starting with, are you out of your fucking mind?"

"I think that qualifies as a question."

"I broke you out so we could retire. The last thing we need is for you to get us roped into another bloody war!"

"Returning Daana to her mother is not getting involved," Ashwyn replied matter-of-factly. "It is repaying a debt. One that you incurred by lying and manipulating her in the first place."

"That's what I do!"

"I know, and you're so good at it. Just like I'm good at volunteering our services for lost causes. We balance each other out."

"This is not a lost cause. It's suicide!" Ellisar said. "We already have Geralt and half the realm tearing apart the countryside looking for us. We don't need to take on any more trouble right now."

The radiating warmth stirring within Daana's rapidly beating chest started to dissolve. Her wide-eyed gaze darted back toward the trees as she considered—for what would not be the first, nor last time that evening— whether or not it was too late to extract herself from the heated conversation as quickly as her feet could carry her. Although she had never had the privilege of witnessing a parental argument, she was certain this was what it must have felt like. Ashwyn and Ellisar argued back and forth in front of her, *about* her, speaking as if she weren't even there!

"Whether or not we help Daana doesn't change the fact that we're wanted fugitives, Ellie." Ashwyn collected the cloth from her lap and resumed the process of stitching it into something that loosely resembled clothing. "We're still going to have a bounty on our heads either way."

"Yes, and do you know what makes wanted fugitives easier to catch? Stupid shit like trying to smuggle a palace brat across war-stricken territories to another fucking continent! Larkspur is all the way out in the flatlands, remember?"

"I would argue that leaving the territories in which we are wanted fugitives might actually be a good thing, no?"

Ellisar was back to pacing, stopping every few steps to punt any stone she happened upon as far into the trees as physically possible. "The flatlands are not a simple hop, skip, and jump away. Getting there will take weeks."

"Months, even. Depending on the route and how vigorously Geralt is patrolling the borders." Ashwyn passed the needle through the cloth and pulled the thread taut as her eyes roved upward, considering alternatives to their predicament. "Passage by sea would be faster. That would require finding a vessel traveling in that direction and bribing our way onboard, of course."

Ashwyn tilted her head at Ellisar curiously. "Remind me, how much money do you have on hand again, dear?"

"None!"

The orc resumed her stitching with a hapless shrug. "By horseback it is then."

"Fine!" Ellisar accentuated this with her most powerful kick yet, sending a fist-sized stone hurtling into the woods at lethal speed. A thunderous *crack* rang out the moment the projectile struck a tree trunk beyond their line of sight. "I'll return Daana myself then. You just stay out of it. I'll hole you up in a cave somewhere and come back for you when I'm finished."

"For Daana's sake, I think I will be seeing this one through."

Daana narrowed her eyes at Ellisar. "You were planning on ditching me, weren't you?"

"Yeah." Ellisar's stare was as cold as ice. "That's what I was planning. Definitely not something more permanent involving a rock, some rope, and a fast-moving river."

"You big flirt," Ashwyn said with a snort.

Ellisar approached the argument from a new angle. "You don't know the way."

"True." The orc nodded, no longer able to disguise the mischievous smile that pulled across her tusked face. Despite the inescapable tension hanging over their heads, there was clearly a game afoot of which Daana neither understood the rules, nor wanted to. Ashwyn carried on, as chipper as ever. "Never fear, love. I'm certain Daana and I can make do without you."

"That could take months!"

"Years, even. What with my tendency to treat directions like suggestions and all."

Ellisar's rigid shoulders slumped. "We're not even going to talk about this?"

"Oh, now you want to talk? Funny how that only happens when the situation is an inconvenience to you." Ashwyn kept her eyes on her work, moving the needle in and out of the cloth with not a practiced hand, but a determined one. The previously light, cheery playfulness left her voice, leaving in its stead a tone that had more weight to it than an iron anvil. "Of course we're going to talk about this more. Later, preferably. When there isn't an impressionable elfling present."

Ellisar's reply came in the form of an unintelligible growl.

"So feisty tonight." Ashwyn waved her off with a chuckle. "I'll have to remember that while we practice our counting later."

Ellisar's pinched expression held strong for several heartbeats before it gave in, transforming into something that looked merely annoyed, and no longer teetering on the edge of committing a murder spree. With a disgusted shake of her head, the elf collected her bow and quiver and slung them back over her shoulder. "You make it very hard to stay angry at you when you say things like that."

"Love you too," Ashwyn replied sweetly.

Ellisar's harsh stare dropped to the pair of dead rabbits before shifting to Daana. "Make yourself useful and clean these while I'm gone." And then, in a manner that was as unnatural as it was unexpected, the corner of Ellisar's upper lip lifted and a single, pained word emitted from between her tightly clenched teeth. "Please."

Now Daana *really* wanted to run.

Wordlessly, Ellisar tugged her hood back over her head and strode back into the trees, disappearing without a sound.

". . . What just happened?" Daana asked feebly.

"Sorry. Didn't mean for you to see all that, Peaches. It was nothing really. Just your typical marital spat."

Daana was one hundred percent certain none of what she had just witnessed could be classified as typical—particularly the "please" part. Deciding it was best if she didn't understand, Daana grudgingly stood and went and collected the rabbits. She tried not to notice the way they stared up at her with wide, vacant eyes. Ellisar had already performed a quick field dressing, slicing the rabbits from chest to tail on the underside and removing their entrails. She'd graciously left the skin and heads intact for Daana to deal with on her own.

"It builds character" was Ellisar's customary response when Daana objected to such indelicate work. Stifling a sigh, she rolled her sleeves to the elbow and slipped a folding knife from her trousers. Daana selected the larger rabbit and set about slicing a pocket into the hide along the back, trying not to look the poor thing in the eyes as she did so.

"Can't believe you're Lark's kid," Ashwyn said.

Daana hooked her first two fingers on each hand into the pocket and pulled, separating the hide from the meat with a series of strained tugs. Talking helped keep her mind off the fact that the pelt was not tearing away as neatly as she would have preferred. "I'm still wrapping my head around it, too."

"You some kind of witch then? Like your mother?"

There had been a time in her life, not too long ago, that Daana would have sold her soul to become a witch. As of late, those dreams had turned to nightmares and Daana had done everything in her power to bury them. Such information didn't make for polite conversation so she grunted a simple no instead.

"You cursed then?"

Her eyebrows knit together. "What?"

"Your arms, Peaches. You've either got very interesting taste in body modification, or something else is going on. And I mean this in the nicest way, but you don't seem like the type to sit through a tattoo, much less whatever *that* is."

"Oh."

Shit. She'd forgotten how well orcs could see in the dark. Suddenly self-conscious of her exposed arms, Daana fought the urge to tug her sleeves back over the black veins. Not a good idea at the moment, considering her hands were slick with rabbit juices. "Maybe?" she said, separating the last stubborn strip of hide from the meat with an ungentle tug. "Hard to say, really. No one's been able to provide any answers so far. All I know is that it acts squirrelly around magic."

The use of her powers seemed to exacerbate the spread as well. While Daana could not rid herself of the infection itself, abstaining from magic was helping slow the transmission. And, as if that wasn't reason enough, there was also that other unfortunate side effect the dark magic had each time she activated her powers. On cue, her vision filled with the memory of crackling yellow and orange tongues of flame licking the dark night sky. She could suddenly feel the scorching heat against her face as the screams grew fainter in the distance.

"Daana?"

Daana cleared the haunting images from her mind with a violent shake of her head, only vaguely aware that Ashwyn had said something. "I'm sorry, what was that?"

The orc narrowed one eye at her suspiciously. "Is it going to be a problem, I said."

"No, not at all." So long as Daana forwent the use of magic, everything would be just peachy. "Not to you anyway. Might kill me though."

"Sorry to hear that." To Ashwyn's credit, she managed to impart this while sounding believable. "All the more reason to go see your mother, I imagine. If anyone knows how to fix it, it'll be her."

"Was she nice?" Daana resisted the sudden urge to kick herself. Of all the questions she could have blurted out, why did she pick that one? It was better than *did she love me?*, Daana supposed. Or *did she regret abandoning me? Will I finally have the family I so desperately want?*

"Was she nice?" Ashwyn repeated, seemingly stumped by the question.

"My mother. Ellisar says she was a bitch."

"Ah well, if it helps, Ellie calls almost everyone that."

"I want to know what she was like." Daana reached for the second rabbit. "You know, if we're going to get along or if she's just going to end up tolerating me like everyone else does."

"Oh." From Ashwyn's startled expression, she was thinking something along the lines of *I am woefully unprepared for a conversation of this magnitude.* After a moment of pained deliberation, she offered something that helped ease some of the growing anxiety rolling around Daana's empty gut. "You've got to remember, I met her in a very desperate time. We were on the run with half the realm at our backs. Nice wasn't something any of us cared about. She was determined, though. And fierce. Goddess, your mother didn't back down for anyone or anything."

That was something, wasn't it? Daana lifted her head, feeling her spirits do the same. "Yeah?"

"Put it this way, most days I was just relieved she and I were fighting on the same side."

CHAPTER TWENTY

Revenge Box

It was past sunset when Ellisar returned from her hunt with a third rabbit slung over her shoulder. She cleaned and skewered it herself this time, placing the rabbit over Daana's crackling fire alongside the other two. Alas, not even the mouthwatering aroma of roasted meat was enough to lift the mood. No one spoke, not even after the food was broken down and portioned out. Seated near the fire, gnawing every edible scrap from a piping hot hind leg, Daana racked her brain for some way to ease the apprehension that hung over their heads. Each attempt to start a conversation, however, was met with single word answers, serving only to thicken the mounting tension.

Daana practically jumped to her feet with relief when Wormy's shaggy shape materialized from between the dark trees.

"By the gods, it took me nearly all day, but I did it! I finally found it!" Snag slid from the saddle and sauntered toward them with an uncharacteristic spring in his step. Some of the glee bled from his smile when he noticed Ashwyn and Ellisar glowering across the dwindling coals at one another. "What, honeymoon over already? You two sure work fast."

"Just having a moment," Ashwyn assured him. Her easy smile returned, even if it didn't quite reach her eyes. "You're awful chipper. What's it you found?"

"That is for me to know and you to find out. The sooner, the better. Now hurry up and get off your butts, let's go."

Daana extended half a skewer of roasted rabbit in Snag's direction. "Don't you want to eat first? We saved you some."

"Do I look like I need mothering to you?" Snag snatched the stick from her hand and swung it at her for daring to be considerate of his needs.

Daana ducked the hunk of charred rabbit that whizzed past her face. "Ha!" she said. "You missed."

The goblin lifted the skewer to his mouth and ripped away a charred mouthful, chewing as he spoke. "You're getting faster."

"Funny. I was just about to accuse you of getting slower."

"Yes, yes, pick on the old slow goblin, why don't you? Never mind that he's been away all day scouring the countryside all by his lonesome. No food, no water, no rest." Snag met Daana's scowl with his widest smile yet, displaying every needled tooth in his jagged mouth. "Go saddle your damn horse already. We've got places to do and things to be."

And with that, the campfire was extinguished, the horses saddled, and they were plodding off into the dark wilderness. Ashwyn and Ellisar trailed behind them, trading hushed whispers. At least they were speaking again, Daana supposed. Even if it didn't look like a particularly productive dialogue.

"What's with the shovels?" she said, noting the two new, suspicious additions strapped across Wormy's saddle.

Snag glanced at her from the corner of his eye, using a rabbit bone to dig out the stringy bits of dinner still caught in his teeth. "Are you confused what a shovel is for? Or what I plan to be doing with 'em? Not that it matters, really. The answer's the same."

"I know what a shovel is for." Daana rolled her eyes.

Daana's persistent questioning came up woefully empty. Snag insisted their destination was a surprise, and he wanted to keep it that way. Had this meager statement come from Ellisar, Daana might have turned and ridden as fast and as far as she could in the opposite direction. But Snag was infinitely more trustworthy and, despite his insistence otherwise, had too much of a conscience to lure anyone out into the dark woods to make them dig their own grave.

After nearly an hour of travel, the towering pines started to thin, revealing a wooded area that had been cleared of trees once upon a time. A *long* once upon a time ago, judging from the random scattering of saplings that grew in the shadows of their ancient brethren.

Snag wasted no time with explanations. He slid from the saddle and flung a shovel in Daana's direction. "Look alive!"

Daana caught it, nearly spilling from the horse in the process. She dismounted and tied her mare to a tree before picking her way across the fern-carpeted ground after him. A glance over her shoulder confirmed that Ellisar and Ashwyn were hanging back, both with their arms crossed, looking prepared to launch into a fight the moment their companions were out of earshot.

A chill wind blustered through the surrounding trees, carrying with it the familiar scents of decayed autumn leaves and damp toadstools. Daana shivered, drawing her cloak tighter over her shoulders. She could just make out the decayed ruins of a former stone cottage ahead. At least that's what it might have been. After decades of neglect, the surrounding wilderness had simply grown over the top of it.

"What is this place?"

Snag came to a stop several yards from the site. "Home. One of 'em anyway."

"Oh." Daana looked up and down the rotted plot of land, racking her brain for something nice to say. "I like what you've done with the place."

"After I returned you, I used the reward money to open an apothecary," Snag explained. "The nearby villagers weren't a fan of my kind, turns out. So they burned it to the ground. I rebuilt, a little farther from town just to be safe. And they burned that one, too. The third and final testament to my obstinate nature was this little rundown hovel way out in the middle of the woods where only the truly desperate would care to find me. Business was slow, but steady. It wasn't much, but it was mine at least."

"This is going to be another sad story, isn't it?"

He wrinkled his upturned nose at her in a teasing manner. "Did the rotted pile of house give it away?"

Nothing seemed to go right for Snag. She supposed she could let him tell the story without interrupting at least. "Go on then. What happened to this one?"

"It was all going surprisingly well, actually. And then one day this crazy elf comes knocking down my door. Says she's looking for a doctor. Before I could get two words in, an orc barges in and drops an injured dwarf on my worktable. All three of 'em were covered in blood and armed to the teeth. I just shut up and did what I could to stop the bleeding. Turns out, they'd been sent in to take care of a nuisance dragon problem. What they didn't tell me was that the beast was still alive. It tracked them back to my shop and—can you guess what it did?"

Daana covered her mouth. "It didn't."

"The next thing I know, the roof is up in flames!" Snag threw his hands over his head for effect. "They got their friend out in time, but there was no saving the place. I got so mad I blacked out. I don't remember what happened, but when I came around again, I was covered in dragon guts and the other three were looking at me like I was foaming at the mouth. Apparently I'd made some mixture, popped it into the beast's mouth, and stood in front of it waiting for it to blow fire at me. It did just that, except instead of incinerating me, whatever I'd thrown down its gullet caught fire first and blew the damn thing's head off. The orc was real quick to compensate me for all the damages after that. She paid in full, too. No questions asked. Didn't even try to haggle the price down—which was a stroke of luck considering I'd quoted her double.

"And then the unthinkable happened." Snag lowered his arms and hugged them to his chest as his gaze swept across the reclaimed hovel. "She offered me a job. Said she could use someone with my skills on her team."

"And you accepted?"

"To be fair, I had no idea who she was. There was still a bit of a language barrier at the time. But she had coin and obviously wasn't shy about dishing it out. I figured I'd join up and fleece her blind for a couple months before going off on my merry way." Snag's smile lessened. "I eventually figured out who she was and realized swindling the Protector of the Realm probably wasn't the best idea."

"But you stayed."

"My salary was never stiffed and no matter where we went, there would be chaos to pay if someone refused me service. I was planning to leave, just never got around to it."

"Aw," Daana said. For a Snag story, this one didn't seem to end as miserably as most. For that reason, she hoped it didn't have a part two. "Did you bring us all the way out here just to tell me that?"

"I wanted to rub it in Ellisar's face one last time before I leave this wretched place forever. For that, I'm gonna need money." Snag walked to the large, bent willow tree growing on the left side of the destroyed cottage. He studied the trunk briefly before picking a direction and walking heel-to-toe, counting softly to himself.

"Don't trust banks?" Daana called to him. "Why am I not surprised?"

"Find me a single bank in Sunstorn that'll open an account to a goblin and I'll show you a two-faced liar." Finished counting, he marked the ground with the largest claw on his foot and turned to her expectantly. "Got your shovel ready?"

"Nice try. You're not conning me into doing your grunt work."

"Ah!" The goblin took a step and winced as imaginary pain coursed across his body. He dropped to the fern-carpeted ground, drawing one knee to his chest dramatically. "Curse this wretched leg! Sometimes I wonder if it would have been better if the mountain took me."

"Not buying it."

Snag writhed helplessly among the weeds for several more awkward seconds.

"Still not buying it."

"I really thought the pity card was going to work on you." Snag sat upright and fiddled with the ring strung through his lip. "Think it'll work on Ashwyn?"

"Think what'll work on Ashwyn?" The orc in question strolled into the clearing and joined them. There was a sort of bounce to her step when she walked, giving the deceptive perception that she was lighter than she looked. She stopped alongside Daana and folded her arms over her chest as she eyed the crumbled cottage skeptically.

"He brought us all the way out here so someone could to do his dirty work for him." Daana leaned on the shovel as she spoke. "Usually I'm the sap that gets suckered into it, but the last thing I need is any more blisters on my hands."

"Ah, that's why Ellie calls you princess. Makes sense now."

"Hey!"

Before Daana could protest further, Ashwyn snatched the shovel out from under her, nearly causing her to fall. "Peaches, those scrawny arms are never going to be more than twigs if you don't break a sweat now and then. If I'm going to spend the next few months in your company, we're going to have to work on your survival skills."

Snag offered Daana his shovel, along with a bright, beaming smile. Daana took the shovel from his claws, grumbling, "Since when is digging a hole considered a survival skill?"

"How else are you going to bury the bodies and your loot?" Ashwyn already had a sizable hole underway. Her gaze shifted to Snag as she tossed another shovelful of dirt to the side. "Poor thing doesn't even have a grasp on the basics. What have the two of you been teaching her?"

"She was nobility before this, you know. We had to start from the ground up. Lying, thieving, cheating, the works."

"You'd think those would come natural to a noble."

"Right? Figures we get caught up with the one morally decent person from the capital."

Daana struck the blade of her shovel into the ground. "I am not morally decent!"

"Of course not, Peaches. You're as crooked as they come. We'd be foolish to think otherwise," Ashwyn said. "I, however, feel personally obligated to help speed your downward spiral along. I have a reputation to uphold, after all. As such, we'll need to polish out your hand-to-hand combat skills, knife work, those sorts of things."

She was going to receive training? Actual training from Ashwyn Pride, the former scourge of the glass seas? A mercenary, notorious cutthroat, and slightly less successful revolutionist? A strange combination of dread and excitement stirred to life within Daana's belly. If she was going to survive her new life, it only made sense to learn from one of the best. With her pride temporarily inflated by the prospect, Daana threw her whole concentration into digging the best and fastest hole possible.

"How the fuck do you do that?" Snag said.

Daana was so consumed with making the best impression, she failed to notice that Ashwyn had retreated out of the way and was now resting against the shovel beside Snag, watching her progress with a satisfied smirk.

The orc lifted one shoulder, shrugging. "I told you, just gotta make them think it's their idea."

Before Daana could come to terms with the fact that she'd been duped into doing the majority of the work, her shovel struck something solid with a metal *clang!*

"Out of the way! I've got it from here." Snag leapt down into the dirt and used his hands to uncover the buried object. Daana climbed out of the hole to give him room to work. A cloud of loose dust bloomed into the air as the goblin made short work of the digging. Moments later, Snag heaved a small chest over the side of the hole. He scrambled out after it, wiping the filth from his clothes.

"You want to do the honors with that latch there?" He looked to Ashwyn expectantly. "Seems to have rusted shut."

Ashwyn slammed the shovel across the iron latch. The rusted iron held strong, unlike the warped wood sidings, which gave away in a burst of rotted splinters and dirt. The orc's brow pressed into a firm line as she used the spade to sort through the strange collection of belongings. "Did you, uh, invest all your money in women's silken undergarments? No judgment. Sorry they didn't hold up all that well."

Snag's ears flattened against the back of his head as he stared at the rotted pile of nightgowns. "Decoy box. This one's sort of a revenge thing, actually."

"Ah."

Ellisar came trudging out of the tree line to join them. She stood along the edge of the pit, surveying the unusual collection. "That's where all my silkies went. And here I thought it was Rali stealing them all these years. Snag, you perv."

Snag disappeared back into the hole. "I thought maybe all the loud sex would stop if I took her nighties. Joke's on me, though. She just paraded around without 'em."

CHAPTER TWENTY-ONE

Melancholic Toad

Fireflies flickered about, illuminating the gloom like miniature paper lanterns. Miniature paper lanterns that had not only gained sentience, but now possessed the insatiable need to procreate on his face. Stupid sentient horny lantern bugs. Snag sat on the edge of the dirt pit, flicking his ears at the humming cloud of insects that refused to bugger off. There was a second, empty wooden chest beside him—its contents now evenly distributed in the various saddlebags hanging from Wormy.

Snag held a weathered sack no larger than a sock in one gnarled hand. It might have been a sock at one point, given the pungent mildew stench emitting from its rotted exterior. The years of being buried underground had taken their toll, wearing the fabric so thin, the bag looked to be on the verge of disintegrating. A second smell, peppermint, wafted on the breeze toward him. It clawed its way up his nasal cavities, singeing the individual nose hairs as it burned away any lingering odor of old sock.

Snag's reluctant gaze moved from the bag in his hand to the source of the peppermint smell.

Ellisar lounged in the grass, snatching unsuspecting bugs from the air and popping them into her mouth. He hadn't ever met an elf that did that before. Eating bugs was something reserved only for the lowest of the low—sad, despicable creatures like him. Gods, there were times he swore she was more goblin than him. Maybe that explained why his next move felt so wrong. He wasn't a grubby, good-for-nothin' gobby anymore. Somewhere along the way, he'd turned into something else. Something unrecognizable even to himself.

Stop being a melancholic toad and just get it over with!

"Here." Snag extended the sack in Ellisar's direction, avoiding direct eye contact. Such unwarranted generosity would have been a cause for concern with the others. Both Oralia and Rali would have suspected ulterior motives and demanded an explanation, keeping at it until he broke. But Ellisar was different. Unlike the other two, she seemed to know that sometimes the best thing to say was nothing at all.

Too bad this wasn't one of those times.

"What's this?" From the corner of his eye, Snag watched as her brow pressed into a flat line. Cautiously, the elf accepted his strange offering. Some of the distrust softened from her face when she drew back the opening and peeked inside. "Are you paying me up-front so I don't rob you later? Honestly, Snaggy, I was only planning to skim a few gold pieces when you weren't looking, anyway."

"Just take it, alright?"

Ellisar held the sack next to her ear and gave it an experimental shake, listening as the contents clinked together. The fact that the rotted sock held strong was a small marvel on its own. "Did you hide something in here? Is it going to burst into flames the moment I reach my hand inside? No, on second thought, you're craftier than that. I bet you coated the coins in poison, that way my death couldn't be traced back to you."

"Since when do you question anything? It's a free sack of money!"

"Since when do you hand out free sacks of money?" she countered with one silvery eyebrow raised higher than the other.

Drat. It looked like he had some explaining to do, after all. But why? Why couldn't she just blindly accept the gift? It was money, not one of the many beverages he'd offered her laced with his own spit. Ellisar never questioned those. Not even after he told her what was in them.

"It's not mine. I'd kept all the bet money I ever won from . . ." The name died on his tongue. With a shake of his head, Snag adjusted his posture and looked away. Nope, nope, nope. He was going to keep it together. No more of this tearing up over circumstances he couldn't change crap. "I planned to give it to Curly as a leg up for when we got disbanded. Not a lot of good it's going to do anyone lying buried under the ground out here."

"Oh . . ."

"Yeah."

"Well fuck. How am I supposed to spend it knowing where it came from?"

The pressure of tears built behind Snag's eyes. Nope, nope, nope! *Keep it together, you limp pussy willow. You're supposed to be a mean, scary goblin. Start actin' like it!*

Try as he might, his voice still came out rather pathetic. "Because it's what he would have wanted."

Ellisar tilted her head in the direction of Daana and Ashwyn. Snag's gaze followed. The orc appeared to be attempting to teach Daana some sort of game that involved keeping a little baggie of sand from hitting the ground using only her foot. Daana was, as expected, not very good at it. It didn't seem to deter her, though. She kept at it, laughing each time she missed a kick by an embarrassing lead.

Ellisar said, "What Curly would have wanted was to blow it all on that little elf princess over there."

A fleeting smile pulled at his mouth as some of the pressure in his eyes receded. "Gods, it would have been gone in a fortnight. He was far too generous for own good. Don't know where he learned it."

"Says the goblin giving me a sack of money."

"Just take it!" Snag added, shrinking back down, "Please."

Ellisar stared at the money bag for longer than any proper thief should have. "I know you're planning to ditch us. Probably the whole reason you dragged me out here. Thought you could make me feel bad one last time. But it ain't happening. I'm not taking your money unless you agree to come with us."

This managed to distract him from shoving the feelings back down inside of himself. Snag's nose scrunched in disdain, left ear twitching as if it had a will of its own. "You want me to retire with you and your wife? What, do I get a little bed shoved in a cupboard somewhere? My own water dish? Some old parchment put down in the corner, maybe?"

Did you just make a pet joke? Horror gripped Snag at the realization. *The maggot would be pickled pink if he'd heard you right now. No, wait. Pickled is not the right word. Tortured! Yeah, tortured pink sounds right. Gonna torture Rasp pink next time I see him for teaching me all these idioms backward.*

Overhead, the sparse treetops rattled together. Patches of star-speckled skyscape peeked through the bare branches, like a living tapestry. The earthy stink of forest rot and sprouted fungi carried on the cool breeze, intermixing with the aromas of peppermint and wet sock in a way that didn't make his current situation any easier to stomach.

"We're not retiring," Ellisar grumbled. "Not yet, anyway. The wife volunteered us to deliver the palace brat back to her mother."

"But you said Daana's mother was de—" Snag whipped his head at her, earrings jangling together like windchimes in a gusty breeze. "You dickhead! I should have known you were lying through your teeth this whole time."

"It wasn't all a lie. That's how you make it convincing. You sprinkle a little truth over the fib sandwich."

"And what part of it was true then, huh?"

"I told you who her mother was, didn't I? Mentioned she was a bitch. That was all true."

Snag narrowed his eyes at her, attempting to peer past her jaded exterior. There was more Ellisar wasn't saying. Try as she might, she couldn't quite hide the extent of her discomfort. It showed in the lines around her eyes and the way she held her mouth locked tight, not even bothering to make one of her deeply disturbing innuendos to keep him off her scent.

"You and the mother have got history, don't you?"

"Obviously. If it weren't for her stupid revolution, Ashwyn and I would be retired by now. Feet kicked up on some beach somewhere, basking in the sunset, licking mushroom powder off the flavor-of-the-day's naked skin."

Ah, there it was—the innuendo. A rather weak one as far Ellisar went. Snag didn't even feel the usual urge to throw up. Whatever had El off her game tonight was eating away at her like maggots on putrid flesh. "Nah, not that. I meant like history-history." Snag tilted his head at her, squinting harder than before, as if this would help bring the missing details into focus. Just made everything kind of blurry though. "You running from something, El?"

"How in chaos did you get that from—" Ellisar snapped the words back into her mouth before she revealed too much. She willed her face back to its natural blankness. "We've spent entirely too much time together. I shouldn't be this transparent to anybody."

"All the more reason to part ways, don't you think? Gonna be hard to keep lying to yourself if I'm there to call you on your bullshit."

"I mean, if that's the worst you're throwing my way, I'd still rather have you."

Snag's mouth snapped shut as something on the inside of his chest did an obnoxious little tumble.

"Come on, Snaggy." Ellisar bumped him with her shoulder in a manner not nearly hard enough to knock him into the pit. "Tag along with us. You barely scraped by the last time you tried to go it alone. And don't mistake this for a pity invitation, either. I need you. This group needs your chaotic neutral balance, else the two goody-two-shoes are going to drive me over the fucking edge."

As much as Snag detested the idea of waltzing willfully into the open jaws of danger, the feeling of being wanted was an addiction unmatched by any other. Not that he was going to admit that. Still, a nice feeling all the same. "You got a destination in mind?"

"Flatlands."

"Oh. The other place where there's an active bounty for my head. Lovely."

"I also kind of need a guide. I know the waterways around the area, but the land itself is a bit fuzzy. The few times I went ashore, I was usually high out of my gourd with a crew to steer me in the right direction."

There it was. The real reason she wanted him to tag along. Ellisar didn't want one last adventure with a friend, she needed a schmuck who was familiar with the territory. Story of his fucking life. Snag's ears flattened against the back of his head as he decided against calling her out for being such a predictable asshole. "How are you even alive right now? Like, seriously? With the amount of time you spend as an intoxicated puddle, you should have walked off a cliff by now! Or been sold out to the enemy. Or-or drowned in a big vat of, I don't know, your own juices or something."

"Am I ham? Why am I secreting enough juices to fill a vat?"

"I don't know! Just like I don't know how you've managed to live this long!"

"I don't know either, Snag. Just do what I do, chalk it up to one of the great mysteries of the universe and move on."

Snag was now so thoroughly confused he couldn't remember what it was he was mad about. Hams, maybe? That didn't seem right. He racked his brain for the answer, but it was no use. The fire in his belly was gone, already replaced by a sinking sensation that threatened to swallow him whole. He blamed it on the rabbit, of course. Concluding that Daana's dinner must have gone rancid in his stomach.

Ellisar drew a crude map into the upturned soil with her finger. "If we keep riding south, we'll cross the Castle Bay border into Hallowbac by tomorrow evening. The ports up there aren't as closely monitored. I should be able to barter our way onto a ship."

"You're going by sea?" He felt the lovely green color drain from his face.

"Since when are you afraid of water?"

"First of all, it's not the water I'm afraid of. It's what happens when the boat runs out of water and hits the reef along the coast that I'm not comfortable with. Secondly, trapped in a small, enclosed space without any chance of escape is essentially the culmination of my worst nightmares. So, thanks, but no thanks. You'll have to make do without me."

Ellisar considered this a moment. Having reached a verdict, she raised her left shoulder in a cavalier shrug. "If that's your decision."

He narrowed his eyes at her suspiciously. "It is."

"And it's a good one. I'm not trying to talk you out of it."

"Good."

"Good," she agreed, standing. Ellisar stretched her long limbs high over her head before starting off toward the others. "I want to find us somewhere a little more comfortable to bed down before dawn. If we're parting ways, be sure you say your goodbyes to the princess while you still have the chance."

"I will, because I'm not an asshole who up and leaves without any thought to how it affects anyone else." He pulled his arms tighter over his chest. "Including you, by the way. So don't you even think about riding off into the trees before I've had a chance to smack you upside the head one last time."

"Oh, please. You're destined to run into me and Ashwyn again eventually."

"And what makes you think I won't see Daana again?"

Ellisar looked over her shoulder and smiled. It was an awful, terrifying look that sent panic rocketing to the pit of his stomach.

Snag's ears flared as he considered the many different ways Ellisar's words could be interpreted. And then realization struck and he shot upright, scrambling after her. "What the fuck, El! Do you mean goodbye or final goodbye? It's the second one, isn't it? Seven realms, you're a sick fuck!"

CHAPTER TWENTY-TWO

A Sweet Moment

For the other diners gathered in the great hall, the evening meal was a welcomed reprieve from watered-down cabbage soup and expired trail rations. For Oralia, it was an overpowering cacophony of competing smells. The rich aroma of the meat and gravy pies battled for supremacy against the sulfuric punch of the garlic-roasted brussels sprouts. Every now and then, she caught a whiff of the honey-glazed yams from the far side of the table. All three overpowering notes paired together in the same way week-old fish complemented rotten banana peels at the bottom of the waste bin.

To make matters worse, Sascha was being extra attentive. Food was his passion and he insisted on sharing it with those he cared about. Oralia had lost track of the number of times he'd served a small portion of something onto her plate, insisting she try it with a pinch of this, or a drizzle of that. Caught up in his excitement, he'd attempted to feed her from his own fork on more than one occasion. A firmly set brow was all that was necessary to remind him that she was perfectly capable of handling the task herself.

Unfortunately, tonight her lover appeared to be suffering from a short-term memory dysfunction. From the corner of her eye, Oralia saw a food-laden fork start to edge in her direction. It took damn near all of her willpower not to grab it and stab the offending utensil into the tabletop. "Sweetheart." The word was laced with equal parts sticky-sweet adoration and venom. "If that fork comes any nearer, it is going across the room."

Oralia's expression added, *and I might send you with it.*

"But you've barely touched your plate. Is something the matter?"

"Just tired." Ignoring the sideways glance from Rali, Oralia retrieved the dinner fork from the long line of meticulously arranged silverware and used it to stir the food on her plate into an unrecognizable pile of slop. There. It was touched. After all, Sascha had said nothing about it being eaten. And no, in this situation she was definitely not being a petulant child. This was a perfectly mature response to a situation she had no desire to partake in.

Oralia's fingertips drummed against the linen tablecloth as she eyed the sealed double doors, debating whether to sit and suffer in silence or attempt a hasty getaway. Leaving the table early would be rude, undoubtedly, but it wasn't like she had anything to lose. Her participation in New Adderwood had been strictly volunteer-based. They couldn't withhold her pay if they weren't paying her anything to begin with.

Yes. It was decided. She was doing it.

Oralia jumped when a heavy hand settled on her leg from beneath the table. Sascha gave a gentle squeeze, managing to do so without breaking from the argument he was having with the Stoneclaw brothers regarding the rules of whatever drinking game they were attempting to rope him into. Oralia did not miss the fleeting smile that curled over his mouth as he watched her from the corner of his eye.

The fucker was on to her! This was the trouble with having a partner. She and Sascha were on even footing now. She couldn't simply do as she pleased anymore, including ditching the dinner party thrown in her honor.

Perhaps this was why she had always surrounded herself with the derelicts of society. Their constant swirl of chaos had made her own uncouth tendencies appear reasonable in comparison. Her faithful four also wouldn't have objected to her cutting out early. Seven realms, they would have thought of it first, prompting her to follow under the excuse that she needed to address the behavior in private. Gods, what she would give for one of their elaborate heists right now.

A smile flickered across her face as she recalled the midsummer eve disaster. The palace had spared no expense. There were tables upon tables of exquisite foods, hundreds of guests dressed in their finest. Oralia had tucked herself in the corner, trading words with some windbag in red and gold tights, when a disturbance from the servant's entrance allowed her a convenient excuse to cut the conversation short. She'd navigated her way through the thickest part of the crowd in time to see Ellisar race across the dance floor, struggling to see around the seven-layer cake she'd lifted from the kitchen. Rali and Curly had not been far behind, lugging a crate of alcohol each. Even reluctant Snag had been talked into serving as the lookout. He had the side entrance opened and shut behind them before the nobles could start up about the deterioration of society.

It was the last time the realm figureheads insisted Oralia's team make a public appearance. When she found her faithful four again, they'd lit a bonfire in one of the back gardens and had a chair and a generous slice of cake waiting for her. They did not succeed in getting her drunk, nor changing her mind about the copious amounts of public service each would be serving the following morning. But for the remainder of the night, bathed in firelight beneath the stars, she'd let her mask slip, allowing herself to enjoy their company not as their commander, but as an equally complicit member of the team.

The hand resting just above Oralia's knee squeezed again. Around her, the dancing fire and star-speckled sky faded away. Oralia found herself in a drab, musty-smelling banquet hall once more. Her heart suddenly weighed twice what it had before. Her hand slipped under the table and threaded her fingers through Sascha's as the heaviness threatened to bubble over. The warmth of his hand reminded her that no matter what, she would get through the evening in one piece. And then, after it was all said and done, she could drift asleep in the crook of his arm while he lamented over how badly Mul and Lingon cheated at drinking games.

Gesticulating movement from the other end of the table caught her wandering attention. An elf, slender with blonde, feathered hair, waved a breadstick in the air. With one foot planted in her chair, she struck a heroic pose, enrapturing the rest of the gathering with an impractical tale of heroism. The logical inaccuracies of her account were wasted on the Adderwood attendees, who sat forward in their seats, hanging on each word like dogs begging for scraps.

"—I'm outnumbered ten to one, but I can smell the fear wafting from their scurvy hides. So I says, 'take another step at me, buckos, an' the lot of ya will be walking the plank!'"

Oralia leaned closer to Rali. "Why is the Ellisar stand-in talking like a pirate?"

Rali pushed a chunk of steamed carrot back and forth through a pool of congealed gravy with a sigh. "I thought it would make me feel better."

Oralia's heart sank a little more. The stand-ins for Ellisar and Snag had been a matter of practicality. So long as Geralt continued to receive reports that her faithful were working alongside her, he would have no reason to be looking for them in his own territory. Unlike Snag's stand-in, the elf selected for Ellisar was practically identical in appearance. So much so, Oralia had begun to question if Ellisar had conveniently forgotten to mention the daughter she'd abandoned at birth.

An actress by trade, Kalihn was enthralling to watch as she dazzled starry-eyed audiences with far-fetched yarns. Rali insisted she was entirely too likable to pass for the real thing.

Oralia asked Rali, "Did it?"

"Did it what?"

"Did it make you feel better?"

"No!" Rali dropped her fork with a muffled clatter, gesturing with her hands while fighting to keep her voice above a harsh whisper. "It's like they don't even notice. Look at 'em. They're all fawning over her like she's some la-di-da dandyess. It's unnatural. Ellisar's supposed to be off-putting. That's her whole thing!"

Oralia debated whether or not to reach over and pat the top of the dwarf's head in the most patronizing manner possible. It would lead to an altercation, possibly even missing fingers, but that seemed just the sort of distraction they both desperately needed. Before Oralia could lift her hand, Sascha leaned over her, murmuring, "Does anyone else notice the captain staring rather intently in our direction?"

Oralia's stare darted across the clustered table, inadvertently locking eyes with Captain Bernstein. The dwarf captain hastily dropped his gaze into his cup, shoulders shrinking as his heavily bearded face reddened with embarrassment.

"I think he was looking at you, Rali," Sascha said.

"Like chaos he was!" This disturbance came from the other side of Sascha. Oralia heard the telltale squeak of wooden chair legs as Mul leapt to his feet, slamming his fist to the table. "You ogling my Pickle, boyo?"

"I-uh," Captain Bernstein stammered into his cup.

"What? You think she's just some fine strip of meat you can rub your eyeballs all up and down without any respect for her say in the matter?"

"Dear gods, no. Of course not."

"No?" Mul cocked his shaggy head to the side. "Why? My Pickle not pretty enough for you? I'll have you know Rali's as beautiful as a fresh-picked daisy in moonlight. You do not merely ogle her beauty, you worship it! You fall on your knees and thank it for gracing your otherwise dim, colorless life with even a glimpse of perfection."

"Mulberry Stoneclaw," Oralia groaned, "sit down. You are drunk."

"I'm drunk on love, boss," he slurred, slumping back into his chair. "It can't be helped. I'm not a man who bottles his feelings, you know."

"A light stabbing might help with that!" Rali called from between the pair of hands she was desperately trying to disappear behind.

The whole table lurched as Mul leaned out across it, waggling his bushy eyebrows at her suggestively. "You can give me the ol' thrust and jab whenever you like, Pickle. I'm no prude. Not like the Cap'n here."

Rali was suddenly not the only dwarf at the table burying their face into their hands. Poor Captain Bernstein looked to be slowly melting lower and lower into his chair. At this rate, he'd be puddled across the floor by dessert.

Rali thundered, "You're about to be a corpse, bucko!"

"Then you'd make me the happiest corpse alive!"

"You'd be dead!"

"Exactly. I'd die happy."

It may not have been as grand as the summer solstice cake heist, but it was something. Oralia sat back and allowed the chaos to unfold as her team threw increasingly disturbing sentiments back and forth at one another. She watched the rest of the gathering, fighting the pleased smile that threatened to cross her carefully guarded face. Judging from the council's horrified expressions, she and her team would not be asked to stay on after this. Such a shame.

Caught up in her euphoria, Oralia even accepted a bite from Sascha's fork without thinking. The honey-glazed yams melted on her tongue as she came to terms with the fact that it was quite possibly the best thing she had ever tasted. A sweet bite for a sweet moment, because without a doubt, this would be the last time she was ever asked to suffer through another honorary feast again.

CHAPTER TWENTY-THREE

Negotiation Knife

Remarkably, Rali and Mul's increasingly nonsensical back-and-forth yelling match failed to get either ejected from the feast prematurely. The pair continued their passionate exchange well into dessert. One slung heartfelt longings while the other settled for simply slinging whatever foodstuff could be used as projectiles. Finally, the wine got the better of Mul, at which point the object of his adoration switched from Rali to the generous slice of almond cake piled on his plate.

It wasn't until Adderwood's new head of agriculture passed out face-first in his dessert that the dinner officially came to a close. A pair of attendees shuffled past, ushering their drunk companion toward the double doorway. The soused fellow still had bits of clotted cream clinging to his beard like fluffy snow. A ruddy-faced council member stood at the far end of the table and called for the attention of those gathered. After thanking all for their attendance, he wished a goodnight to anyone not asked to stay for the impromptu council meeting afterward.

Dirty snakes, Oralia thought. The councilor's closing statement confirmed what she had suspected from the start. The honorary dinner had been a ruse all along—an unclever way to strongarm Oralia into attending another one of their dull meetings without having to hunt her down first. Unfortunately for them, she had come prepared with a decision in hand. The only downside was that she had to deliver it in person.

Rali nudged Oralia from beneath the table with her knee. "Are you sure you want to do this? We could just run and skip town. Say the word, and I'll have the horses saddled and ready."

"It is one council meeting," Oralia replied. "I have survived many before it. Just as I will this one."

"No offense, but it's not the surviving part that's got me worried, boss. It's the part where they talk you into staying long-term."

"That has never happened before."

"Yeah, 'cause of me." Rali's cheeky grin widened at Oralia's resulting glare. "We both know full well I'm the only reason we've ever walked away from the negotiation table unscathed."

"Then you will be relieved to hear that this is not a negotiation. I have my answer and I will not be swayed from it."

"Alright, alright, fine. At least take my negotiation knife in case you run into trouble."

Oralia looked at the ceiling as she massaged the persistent ache from her temples. "The fact that you have a negotiation knife says everything I do not need to."

"What it's saying is 'gee, thank gods my second-in-command is here to cover my ill-prepared ass.'" The dwarf drew back her jacket, revealing an ornamental dagger strapped to her hip. "Come on now, admit it. You want my little lovely here. Better yet, you want me *and* the knife. A little added insurance that you don't accidentally sell our souls to another well-meaning empire can't hurt, you know."

The audacity of her former lieutenant. It was as if Rali held no confidence in Oralia's ability to say no whatsoever. There was an immediate way to prove the dwarf wrong on that account. "Thank you, but no," Oralia said. "There is no need for you to die of boredom for my sake."

"That's what the knife was for, boss. Thought I'd make things interesting."

Oralia's gaze shifted from Rali to Sascha, who seemed to be having some difficulty keeping his balance. The fact that he had a Stoneclaw brother on either side of him pulling in opposite directions was not helping. "Walk Sascha home for me instead?" Oralia asked. "I think Mul and Lingon finally succeeded in drinking him under the table."

"That's 'cause they're dirty, rotten cheaters!" Sascha slurred, trying to shrug off the pair of giggling parasites currently latched to either arm.

"Don't worry, boss, we got this! We'll get him home and tuck him in bed nice n' cozy for you," Lingon called, trying to drag Sascha out the door with him. The slender man succeeded only in walking in place as the worn tread of his boots slipped uselessly against the polished wood for traction.

"See?" Rali shrugged. "The dingleberries have it handled."

"The last time Sascha was left drunk in their care, the brothers took turns playing horsy in the courtyard." Oralia still didn't know how they'd gotten the saddle on Sascha without losing an arm in the process, but it was a sight that haunted her memory more often than she cared to admit. Sascha had been so far gone he had no memory of the incident. She insisted on keeping it that way, threatening all manner of bodily harm any time either Mul or Lingon so much as whinnied in her presence.

"Lightweight," Rali scoffed.

They traded equally severe looks until Oralia was forced to concede the effort was a losing battle. She dropped her scowl in favor of something more beseeching, possibly even pitiful. If Oralia's vulnerability didn't appeal to Rali's soft side, it would at the very least make her want to crawl out of her skin. "For me? Please? As a friend?"

The noise Rali uttered bordered on feral.

"I will not be long," Oralia said. "I promise."

"Damn you and those puppy-dog eyes." With a huff, Rali stood and whirled about, seizing charge of the deteriorating situation with a deafening clap of her hands. "Alright, buckos, we're out of here. I want to see some gusto, hup-two-three-four, hup-two-three-four, on my mark, go!"

The team stumbled out into the adjoining hallways after slurring their goodbyes. The last of the plates were whisked from the table, the double doors closed, and Oralia found herself surrounded by a host of mildly drunk, exuberant faces. One of the older dwarfs cleared his throat and looked expectantly in her direction. He steepled his hands onto the table and flashed what he mistook for an inviting smile. "Madam Protector—"

"Oralia," she corrected. "And, if I may, Counselor, I would like to precede your meeting with an announcement."

They appeared genuinely surprised by this, but no one objected. Oralia's gaze dropped to the table, realizing the reason may have been due to the ornamental dagger resting where her plate had been.

It may not have been the best look, but it was far too late to backpedal now. Oralia placed her hand over the knife and casually swept it into her lap. "As you all are aware, my team and I have spent the last two months helping your forces uproot the previous realm's stranglehold from your territory. It is my pleasure to announce that yesterday's settlement was also the last. With the exception of a few remaining stragglers along the border, the realm no longer has an active presence in your territory."

Had there been a chalice in front of her, this was the moment Oralia would have lifted it in celebration. Unfortunately the only immediate item at her disposal was the damn dagger and brandishing a blade above her head would send the wrong message. Thus, she settled for a forced smile. "Let me be the first to congratulate New Adderwood on its independence."

The dingy room burst to life with a round of cheers as the more unruly members of the council stomped the floor and pounded the wood table with their fists. Oralia waited for the excited murmurs to die down before moving on to her actual announcement, swiftly so, in the event one of the others tried to wrangle the floor out from under her. "As you all know, my position here was strictly on a volunteer basis. You needed a familiar name to unite your cause and I lent you mine. Now that New Adderwood's independence is secured, it is time for me to step down and move on."

This did not land quite as well as her congratulatory line about independence. The cheering and hearty pats on the back faded as the gathering slowly came to grips with the fact that their senior military consultant had wasted no time issuing her official resignation. It was their own blasted fault, Oralia told herself. Had they not pushed so persistently for a council meeting immediately upon her arrival, she would have at least given them a few days to enjoy their independence before crushing their hopes of keeping her on permanently.

Several council members clustered together at one end of the table, whispering fervently among themselves. It was Captain Almas Bernstein who broke the stunned silence, appearing even more dejected than he had during dinner. "You're leaving so soon?"

"I am."

"And your team?"

"Free to do as they wish, as always," Oralia replied. Unfortunately for him, there was a good chance the team member Captain Bernstein was particularly interested in had already climbed the city gate and was striking out on her own, swearing off friends and lovers alike for good. At least until Rali remembered traveling was much easier via pony and grudgingly returned to retrieve it.

The dwarf captain sat straighter in his chair. "Would it be out of line of me to offer a position to certain members of—"

"Enough, Almas," a senior member of the council groaned. "Give someone else a turn."

One of the others piped up with, "Have you given any thought to what you plan to do next, Madam, er, Oralia?"

Did planning to sneak away into the night the moment the meeting was over count? While Oralia was certain it did, it was also not the answer they wanted to hear. "Not as of yet, no."

She regretted her poor choice of words immediately as the faces gathered around the table brightened at the prospect. The ruddy-cheeked dwarf at the far end of the table designated himself the unofficial spokesperson for the table once more. "This council is more than ready to offer you a full-time position."

"As I stated before, my presence here is only to help straighten some of the upset caused by my untimely withdrawal from the United Territories." Untimely withdrawal sounded so much better than treason. They were both technically correct, but Oralia preferred the former for obvious reasons.

It had taken only a matter of weeks after the battle on Mount Hook for the tales of her treachery to reach the capital. Geralt had done his best to paint her as the villain, but he'd underestimated the consequences it would have on the country. The outer territories had been in turmoil even before Oralia changed sides. For decades, the Division of Divination had been raiding their communities, tearing apart families, and stepping all over the local government's toes.

Oralia's desertion was all it took for the outer territories to follow her lead, declaring their independence from the current regime. Adderwood was the first to descend into open rebellion. Hallowbac soon followed and there were whispers that Mossborn was not far behind. Suddenly lacking an experienced military head, the realm was openly struggling to keep its remaining pieces intact.

Oralia had not intended to get caught up in another war, but she did feel partially responsible. And, anyway, it offered her the chance to forget about her own personal predicament. It really said something about her situation that she'd opted to throw herself into a rebellion as a means of distraction. Permanent employment by the newly formed independent territory, however, was a step too far, even for her. With New Adderwood's independence temporarily secured, it was time to move on.

Where exactly, she had no idea. Well, that wasn't entirely true. She at least knew where she *didn't* want to be. "Council members," Oralia said, interrupting what was probably meant to be an irresistible offer of which she conveniently heard not a single word, "thank you for the lovely evening, but it is well past time for me to retire. My decision on the matter is final. Goodnight."

With that said, she stood and strode for the entrance, wondering if she'd meant retire for the night or from her current life path completely. It was a wondrous, terrifying thought. One that fortunately could wait until the morrow when she didn't have a splitting headache.

CHAPTER TWENTY-FOUR

Into the Fire

The worn floorboards creaked underfoot as Oralia navigated the long hallway of the Copperstone Inn. She glimpsed the dark night sky from a passing window as she turned the final corner toward her room. It was well past midnight, judging from the position of the stars. The inn was blessedly quiet, with the majority of its guests having fallen asleep hours ago. The tantalizing visions of a soft bed and warm fire drifted through her mind as she reached the last room at the end of the long hall.

The tarnished handle turned when she gripped it, but the door itself refused to budge. Oralia tried again to no avail. So much for sneaking in quietly. Stifling a roar, she put her shoulder to the wood and shoved with all her might. The stubborn, paint-chipped door swung open with a groaning protest. Rubbing the soreness from her shoulder, Oralia trudged inside, depositing her jacket onto the powder-blue, high-back chair as she passed.

Her current living quarters constituted a generously sized suite, complete with a cozy breakfast nook, sitting area, fireplace, and a private bathroom that housed its own, woefully undersized copper tub. Currently, her quarters smelled strongly of cedar embers and smoke. There was an additional scent as well—strong, like pine, but with faint undertones of stale beer. While the aroma was familiar to her, it did not belong in the privacy of her bedroom.

"Ralizak?" Oralia scoured the room for the source of the scent. The candles were unlit, but the smoldering fire highlighted the apartment in a warm, red-orange glow.

"The conquering orc hath returned!" Rali's drowsy voice hailed from one of the overstuffed chairs in the sitting area.

"Why are you still here?" Oralia hadn't meant it to sound rude, but it came out that way regardless. At the moment, all she wanted to do was leave her trousers in a pile on the floor and pull Sascha into bed with her. And while this was certainly doable with Rali in the room, she feared she wouldn't find it nearly as restful with the dwarf watching.

"And stay awake all night tossing and turning, wondering what sort of trouble you got us talked into? Nah." Rali popped up over the back of the chair situated strategically in front of the glowing embers. The dwarf rested her chin in her hands and smiled. "Besides, someone had to stay and keep an eye on your fuckmate. Make sure no one tried to sneak in and take him for a nice gallop around the courtyard."

Sascha was sprawled across the couch catty-corner to Rali. There was a book resting over his face. His voice emitted from beneath the pages at a weak groan. "I am not a child. I need no watching."

"You held a twenty-minute conversation with the coatrack, bucko."

"Need no watching," he reiterated with a low rumble.

"Hush, you're supposed to be napping." Some of the smile slipped from Rali's face as her attention switched back to Oralia. "Well, don't leave me waiting in suspense forever. How'd the war council go?"

Oralia's stare shifted to the small breakfast table, noticing the ominous stack of loose papers awaiting her. "I would not know. I am not involved in any wars."

"Yeah, yeah, we've all heard your spiel," Rali said. "Let's skip to the part that involves us. How many more realm nests did you agree to flush out before we can call our volunteer work here done for good?"

Oralia dropped into the wooden chair beside the table and slumped uncomfortably low. She pressed her fingertips against her forehead and massaged the aching flesh with slow, deep circles. "Yesterday's settlement was the last. There are no more nests to be flushed."

"That's it then? Our part's done?" The open book spilled from Sascha's face when he shot upright. His sable eyes were large and rimmed in white, looking nearly as hopeful as he sounded. "We can actually retire now?"

"Ha! Don't be so naive. You know they offered her a position," Rali said. "The real question is whether or not it was good enough to get her to bite."

Even now, after everything they'd accomplished together, Rali seemed to believe Oralia was incapable of putting her foot down when she wanted to. Ordinarily Oralia would have turned the overt lack of faith into an argument, but she was simply too exhausted to put up a fight. She sank lower in the chair, sighing, "They did. I refused."

Sascha rolled his head back and thundered, "We're finished. Finally!"

Oralia winced as the surrounding walls protested Sascha's volume with a rattle. "There is still the matter of deciding *where* we go from here, but yes. We are finished."

The rest of Rali's smile drained from her weary face. It wasn't merely exhaustion that had sapped her of her usual charm and wit. Oralia saw worry weighing heavy within her dark eyes. "You know I'm not one to volunteer us for more work," the dwarf said. "But before we make any life-altering decisions, you might want to have a look at those papers first."

"If it is another call to arms from Larkspur, I am not reading it."

"Worse than that, I'm afraid."

Oralia reluctantly reached for the yellowed pages. Wanted posters, she realized as she leafed through the stack. Each page consisted of a brief description, a crudely inked portrait of the outlaw in question, and the promised amount for their eventual capture. The face on the third page caused Oralia's steady hand to falter. Blinking back the hurt, she separated Curly's poster from the others and placed it facedown, away from her.

Surely the realm already knew of his death. Oralia wondered if they kept printing his likeness simply as a means to torment her.

Rali's dark eyes moved from the lone sheet back to Oralia, explaining, "Captain Bernstein gave me the stack before dinner. A patrol found them posted along the border near Mossborn. He thought they'd make good souvenirs."

"Are you upset that they depicted you with a monobrow? Or that Ellisar's bounty is worth more than yours?"

"Both, actually. Thanks for noticing. Not why I showed them to you, though. Take a gander at the last page."

Oralia flipped through once more to the end. She studied the portrait as confusion wrinkled her brow. "They put out a bounty for Faris?"

"Reward, not bounty. Apparently we kidnapped the little sprout and held him against his will. The money is to ensure he's found and freed of our oppression," Rali paraphrased from memory. "Check the amount. He's worth twice what they're willing to fork over for the rest of us. With the stipulation that he's returned to the capital alive."

"We did not abduct Faris. He went home."

"Well obviously we know that."

Oralia sat quiet for a moment as she considered what this was supposed to be telling her. A thought flickered in the back of her overworked brain and she shuffled back through the stack of posters. A second and third check confirmed her suspicions. "There's no bounty on Rasp. Not even an honorary mention. Why would they go to the effort to list his brothers but not him? He is the one they really want."

In the four months since the battle on Mount Hook, the stories of what took place had grown more far-fetched and fantastical with each retelling. The cursed mountain folk heir, Rasp Stoneclaw, was rumored to have obliterated an entire realm army, his own people, sometimes a dragon, and—according to the latest version of the tale—the undead army of the seventh realm of chaos itself. Virtually overnight, Rasp had unwittingly become the most wanted witch on the entire continent. Geralt Lazuli and the Division of Divination had exhausted their combined resources tearing the realm apart looking for him. Oralia herself had not heard from either Rasp or Whisper. The lack of communication was intentional, she suspected. If no one, not even their allies, knew of their whereabouts, the pair could weather the oncoming storm undisturbed.

"Geralt's figured out what the rest of us already knew," Rali explained. "If there's one person capable of drawing Rasp out of hiding, it's Faris. I think this is Geralt's attempt to find him before we caught on."

"Has there been any communication from Faris?" Oralia knew he had returned home to Lonebrook, but that was the extent of her knowledge on the matter.

"Not a peep, actually."

The page crumpled in Oralia's tightly clenched hand as her mind raced with possibilities. Here she thought she'd been the one distracting Geralt Lazuli but, as usual, the snake had been working his own angle. Geralt didn't want her, nor her people, not as badly as he wanted Rasp. Oralia's head amounted to little more than a trophy to be mounted on a stake. She was a nuisance, yes, but incapable of leveling an entire city without an army. Rasp was the real prize. And, somehow, someway, Geralt had discovered the key to getting exactly what he wanted.

"Faris's last known whereabouts was Lonebrook," Oralia said. Home would have been the first place Geralt went looking for him. The evidence of the posters, however, suggested Faris was no longer there. The question then became: where had he gone?

"Have we received any news from the area?" Oralia asked. "The village maybe? His family?"

"The territory's been flooded with realm forces trying to keep it from going belly-up like Adderwood. As far as the village itself, it's been eerily quiet. Nothing in, nothing out. I assumed the Belfast family was staying low, trying to ride out the impending rebellion unnoticed, but I'm starting to think their silence might be something more sinister."

"Sinister how?" Oralia sensed she already knew the answer but hoped, secretly, that Rali would prove her hunch wrong.

The dwarf outlined her thought process with an idle flick of her hand. "If I were Geralt, I wouldn't waste my time hunting Faris down. Not when I know he's got a family and whole village of people he cares about. I'd take them hostage instead. Lure the rat back to the nest, so to speak."

Hope sank in Oralia's chest. "I was afraid you were going to say that."

"If we were to get involved, completely hypothetically speaking, of course, we would have quite a dilemma on our hands." Rali's gaze swept aimlessly across the sparsely lit apartment as she spoke, purposely avoiding eye contact. "Our main objective would be to find Faris before Geralt does, obviously. But, in order to do so, we'd have to go talk to the people most likely to know where he's hiding. Those same people are probably under heavy surveillance right now."

"Lonebrook would be crawling with soldiers," Oralia said. "Going any-where near there would be walking right into Geralt's trap."

"Not if we use our heads. The surrounding area is dense forest. Wouldn't be too hard to smuggle a small team over the border and investigate from a distance."

It was possible, Oralia conceded. Unfortunately, this realization only served to make her decision more difficult. Had the plan been unfeasible from the start, there would have been no obligation to try. ". . . Are we actually considering this?"

Sascha's head lifted, the hope slowly draining from his expression.

Rali pretended to be more nonchalant over the matter. "I mean, hypo-thetically, sure."

"Ralizak, we cannot hypothetically get involved. We either do or we do not." Oralia paused, almost reluctant to say her next words. Here she had thought they were finally retiring and, already, she could feel the dream slipping from her grasp. "I thought we wanted to be done with the fighting."

"It's not the fighting I object to, boss. It's the damn politics that muddy the waters. I'll hack and slash with you any day of the week."

Gods dammit. Rali was normally more combative than this. She could always be counted on to provide an extensive list as to why they didn't need to volunteer for more unpaid charity. "Are you saying you *want* to do this?"

"I don't know what I want, alright?" Rali threw her hands into the air as she sank lower in the chair until only the top of her head was visible. "It just feels, I don't know, kind of bad? We should have been keeping a better watch on Faris. And now he's gone missing, with gods know how many people looking for him. His village is probably being overrun right now, and here we are none the wiser, looking like complete assholes who don't give a shit! He may not be family, but he's damn close, and you don't abandon family."

"That's what's eating at you?" Sascha was unable to contain his thoughts on the matter any longer. "Not the part where Geralt is going to use Faris to lure Rasp right into his trap? The rumors have gotten out of hand, no question, but we all saw what the boy could do."

This was not the sort of objection Oralia was hoping for.

"Don't get me wrong," Sascha continued, "the last thing I want to do is get involved in another cause, but keeping Rasp out of enemy hands seems like a disaster worth preventing. Frankly, I'm just relieved the two of you are involving me in this conversion for a change."

"Your fuckmate strikes an excellent point, Oralia," Rali said, voice muffled slightly due to the fact she had her face buried in the back of the overstuffed chair. "We need to do this, not for ourselves, for the betterment of the people or whatever."

"That is not what I said."

"Plain as day, big fella. We all heard you. Your argument is rock solid, too. I could squabble all night as to why getting involved is a shit idea, but I know when I'm beaten. You win. It's decided. We've got to find Faris and spare the world of the impending Rasp disaster."

Sascha crossed his burly arms and scowled. "I don't like that you're pinning this on me."

"Fine." Rali's hand popped up from over the back of the chair, gesturing vaguely in Oralia's direction. "We'll pin it on her then. She makes a good scapegoat."

"I have not yet decided anything," Oralia reminded them with an irritated click of her tusks.

Sascha stood, catching himself against the back of the couch as he lumbered toward the breakfast table. "In that case, I may as well start drafting a supply list."

"We are simply thinking out loud." Oralia's glare settled on the back of Rali's chair, attempting to bore holes through it with her eyes. "Some of us are merely speaking with more confidence than they rightfully should."

"Oh, Moonflower." Sascha caressed the top of her head as he stumbled past. "There's no use pretending you haven't already reached a decision. Everyone here knows your personal mantra by now: straight out of the frying pan into the fire. Seeing as our work here is done, it's high time we find you another fire."

Oralia's jaw dropped in disbelief. "Excuse me? The two of you devised this plan. I will not be blamed for this decision."

"Such a bleeding heart," Sascha crooned.

"It's impossible to tell you no when you get like this," Rali added.

This was no longer a battle or words, but an all-out massacre. What's worse, Oralia found herself on the losing side. "If you must know, yes, I think locating Faris and keeping him from Geralt is the right thing to do. But there is no reason to act rash in the matter. I maintain we should sit on the decision for a few days, truly consider our options, weigh the consequences, and, when the time is right—"

"Yep, sounds great." Rali slid from the chair and swaggered toward the door with her thumbs hooked in her belt loops. "You do that, boss. I'm going to get some shut-eye before our grand departure tomorrow."

"No one said we are leaving tomorrow!"

"You hear that sizzling sound, Sascha?" Rali called over her shoulder as she drew open the creaky door with a strong tug.

"Indeed. Just about ready for the flames, I'd say."

Oralia crossed her arms with a huff. "I refuse to engage when the two of you gang up on me like this."

"You drive a hard bargain, Moonflower. But dammit if you aren't convincing." Rali's voice echoed from the hallway as she disappeared from sight. "Say the word and we'll follow you all the way to the gates of chaos and back!"

CHAPTER TWENTY-FIVE

Motivational Corn Cakes

The wind rattled the blurry yellow and orange treetops overhead. From the crunch of leaves underfoot and the pungent stench of decaying foliage, autumn was quickly taking hold of the land. Rasp sat wrapped in a warm blanket, enjoying a rare patch of sunshine filtering down from the intertwined boughs above. The moment would have been more enjoyable if he weren't expected to be doing something else right now.

"Are you ready?" The echo of Whisper's voice indicated they were a reasonable distance away. On the edge of their makeshift camp, likely.

Rasp rolled his head back, muttering under his breath. "As much as I ever will be."

"So, not at all then?"

"Precisely."

"If we could move your self-loathing along a tad faster, little bird," Whisper said, "there are other things I wish to do today."

Rasp supposed there was no harm in getting it over with. Maybe he'd get lucky and Whisper would call it quits after a few failed tries, allowing him to spend the rest of the afternoon basking in the sun like the lazy, well-fed housecat he sorely wished to be. "As long as you've accepted that it's not going to work, then fine. I'm ready."

After traveling throughout the night, they finally called it quits around dawn. Rasp slept soundly for several uninterrupted hours and awoke to a hot meal of ground corn cakes and dandelion tea. All things considered, it was a rather pleasant start to his day. It was a shame Whisper had to go ruin it with training. And not the easy stuff either, like lift this rock into the air, make the wind blow, stop setting the trees on fire. Nope, long gone were the days of the easy-peasy shit. After finally glimpsing Rasp's untapped potential, Whisper insisted it was high time they explored the depths of his magic sensitivity.

Considering what'd happened the last time he did so, Rasp was perfectly content to keep scratching the surface. Which was probably why, other than languidly raising his hand, he didn't put much effort into the exercise.

"Anything?" Whisper asked from afar.

"Nope."

The wind blustered overhead with more intensity than before, stirring dried leaves into the crisp air around him. It was Whisper's doing undoubtedly, employing one of their lesser spells to try to spark Rasp's magic sensitivity. Of course he didn't need to rely on his powers to know that.

"How about now?" his mentor said.

"The hairs on my arm lifted." That could just as easily have been attributed to the frigid wind as it could the presence of magic, but who was he to look an *it's something* horse in the mouth?

"Dig deeper, little bird. You manifested magical auras once before. You can do it again."

Manifestation was the official term for it, according to Hop's longwinded explanation. Essentially, Rasp's powers had adapted to compensate for his impaired vision. His mind was taking the information gathered from his magic sensitivity and projecting it over the top of his otherwise hazy world, creating a form of phantom vision. It applied only to magic, however—the reason Rasp was not in any particular hurry to master his new talent. That, and also because the last time he had done so, he'd had the sudden, irresistible urge to eat everyone.

He wasn't eager to make that mistake twice.

"Try again," Whisper called.

Rasp waved his hand back and forth to emphasize that he was definitely trying very, very hard.

"I understand the hesitation," his mentor said, "but I assure you, you're not going to awaken the darkness. Conditions are ideal. You're fed, rested, no one is actively trying to kill you, and I am here in the event something goes wrong. I am not expecting you to get it right straight away. I am simply asking that you try."

"You see my hand, don't you?" Rasp waved it more vigorously.

Whisper issued a long, dreary sigh before reconsidering tactics. "I'll give you another corn cake."

Finally some motivation he could get behind! Naturally, he couldn't simply accept Whisper's offer without trying to sweeten the pot first. "Two."

"One," Whisper countered.

"One and a half."

"Half."

"Now you're going the wrong way!"

"A fistful of pine needles."

Rasp threw his hands into the air. "Nobody wants that!"

"Worm jam spread over a single corn cake."

"Are you saying 'warm' or 'worm'?"

Although he could not see his mentor's expression, Rasp was one hundred percent certain Whisper had a predatory smile stretched across their scaled face. "Excellent question, little bird. Are you daring enough to find out?"

"No," Rasp grumbled. "You're a terrible negotiator, by the way."

"I believe this qualifies me as an excellent negotiator, actually. One corn cake, final offer."

It was better than a fistful of dried pine needles, Rasp supposed. "Deal."

With the promise of a slightly less empty belly looming tantalizingly closer, he sat straight and focused his breathing. Next, Rasp filled his lungs with air and held it. The drum of his heartbeat slowed as he released the breath. He repeated the process three times before his surroundings shifted. It was a slight change, barely noticeable at first. He could still feel the crisp breeze on his bare skin; his nose identified the smells of smoldering coals and forest rot; and the ever-quaking rustle of the treetops never ceased. But each sense was fainter now, as if the world around him was situated on the other side of a thick glass window.

Guided by instinct, he opened his eyes to find the same blurry world from before. Only now there was a new addition. It started as a faint blue glow, flickering far beyond the usual constraints of his poor vision. The more he focused on it, the brighter the light became, until it grew three times in size, like a beacon, pulsing with a life of its own. Rasp blinked the strain from his eyes and was surprised to find the phantom aura still there when he opened them again.

"... I see ... blue?"

"Where?"

Rasp pointed in the appropriate direction. The pulsing light shifted smaller and then zipped into the air. It moved so swiftly Rasp nearly lost track of it. His finger followed the phantom glow as it flittered overhead several seconds before touching back down again and returning to its previous size.

"You were big, and then you were small, and then flying all over the place and . . ." Rasp attempted to make sense of what he'd just witnessed. "That was you shifting forms, wasn't it?"

"It was. Regardless of what shape I take, you should always be able to track my magical signature."

Well that could come in handy. For what, Rasp had no idea. The important thing was that he hadn't fucked it up. He'd manifested Whisper's magic aura as plain as day and his mouth hadn't even salivated once with the insatiable desire to eat his mentor.

Wait, what? Why did he just think that?

The wayward thought caused Rasp's concentration to slip. Whisper's dazzling blue glow faded, shrinking in size as the shadowy dark closed in around it. "Shit!" Rasp clenched his hands, scrambling to regain control. "Sorry! I didn't mean that. I'm not going to eat anybody. That's just what happened last time and . . ."

The more he spoke, the more the phantom image slipped like water from between tightly clenched fingers. Across from him, the blurry dark descended, snuffing out the last spark of glowing light.

"Dammit!" Rasp threw his head back with a groan. "I had it. I fucking had it!"

Whisper's soft footsteps crunched across a sea of dry leaves toward him. "There is no reason to be upset, little bird. You were able to glimpse my aura on your first try. That should be reason to celebrate."

Molten acid slithered up Rasp's throat and flooded his mouth. He stewed in his disappointment for a few annoyed seconds, allowing his temper to simmer, before swallowing it back down. "Celebrate?" he said, after a deep breath ensured his vitriol would not bubble over into his words. "Like with more corn cakes?"

Whisper stood before him, nothing more than a vague, pokey-looking shadow. "If only all of mortal-kind was so easily influenced by their stomachs as you."

"Sounds like a 'yes, Rasp. Stuff your face with as many corn cakes as you like' to me."

"You get one."

"Fine." Rasp extended his hand expectantly. "Pay up."

"*After* you have completed your lesson in full."

Life, yet again, proved to Rasp how utterly unfair it was. He slumped onto the leafy ground and spread out, slowly, like cold syrup across the breakfast table.

"It's going to be one of these days, I see," Whisper muttered. "Fortunately for me, my portion of this lesson is concluded."

Rasp lifted his head from the ground. "You're leaving?"

"Yes. I will be spending the rest of the afternoon scouting the area for the settlement. Your father will be accompanying me so that we may cover twice the ground."

Whisper and Dad were leaving? Together? With no one left to keep him from napping the rest of the day away? It seemed Rasp's luck had turned. Fate had finally looked down upon him and smiled.

"You will stay here and resume the rest of your training with the artificer." Whisper did nothing to hide the amusement in their voice. "You will be relieved to hear that he was positively enthusiastic to be given the opportunity. Already has an entire lesson planned and went on and on in profuse detail about plans for future assignments."

And just like that, Rasp's visions of a relaxing afternoon turned to dust. "Why can't I go with you instead? Don't you need me to translate Dad for you?"

"Your father's mind is not an easy one to meld with, but I'm making progress. You will be more useful to me here, working on your training."

Rasp groaned.

"There, there." Whisper patted the top of Rasp's head. The fact that Rasp was still facedown in the dirt meant the fae had either stooped to his level or, the more likely scenario, was using their foot. "I think you may actually get something out of this one."

"A headache doesn't count!"

"You're forgetting the corn cake."

The original luster of the promised corn cake had started to lose some of its shine. "I would feel better if it was two."

"I would feel better if you would stop acting like you were two, but here we are." Whisper's soft footsteps padded away in the distance as they called over their shoulder. "I expect a glowing report upon my return."

CHAPTER TWENTY-SIX

Fittingly Pretentious

Rasp never understood the practice of meditation. For one, reining in the unconscious squirms and fidgets his body made all on its own was damn near impossible. He was a natural squirmer, after all. And even then, his head presented a greater challenge. It was rarely quiet, churning out a constant stream of miscellaneous thoughts incapable of being calmed nor quelled. The effort to get both his body and his mind to behave themselves at the same time was simply too great of a challenge to even try.

At least until something less desirable came along, of course. And then Rasp was suddenly all about meditation. Like training, for example. Instead of participating in his lesson, Rasp was envisioning himself as a flower, who existed only to take in the sun and sway listlessly in the crisp autumn breeze.

A strong hand gripped the top of his knee, shaking him from his plant-life bliss. Judging from his tone, Hop did not sound nearly as ecstatic that Rasp had achieved his afternoon-long dream of becoming one with the universe. "Are you even listening?"

Rasp kept his palms pressed together, not because it helped with his concentration, but because it seemed fittingly pretentious for someone using meditation as a means to procrastinate. "Flowers do not need to listen. They simply exist."

"What are you talking about?"

"Shh." Rasp smashed his finger against the faun's nose in a poor attempt to find his lips. "We're meditating."

"There is a world of difference between true meditation and ignoring someone because you don't want to roll up your sleeves and get to work. I think we both know which category you fall into."

Rasp tentatively opened one eye and squinted accusingly at Hop's blurry shape. "Flowers do not have sleeves."

"They don't have mouths either. Which, in case you have forgotten, are necessary to eat with."

"Back to talking about mastication already? So predictable, Hopalong." It was adorable how terrible Hop was at keeping him on task. Honestly, Rasp didn't know what Whisper had been thinking. Leaving him and Hop alone, together? With the expectation that Rasp actually learn something? Ha! The only one learning a valuable lesson would be Hop—specifically, to never accept another assignment from Whisper ever again.

Rasp's only regret was that his temporary instructor hadn't yet realized the futility of the undertaking. He tried to ease Hop into reluctant acceptance with a patronizing pat to the arm. "Come, leave behind your endless wanting and be a flower with me."

"I don't want to be a flower. I want to do the lesson," Hop said miserably. "Come on, Rasp, please? I never get to test any of my ideas. I planned an entire lesson around it and everything."

Guilt gnawed at Rasp's resolve. Whereas most people relied on bribery or threats to strong-arm him into compliance, Hop wasn't employing either of these tried and true tactics. It was as if he expected sheer pity alone to work in his favor. The idea was laughable. Almost as much as the fact that it was working. *Almost.* Rasp, luckily, was equipped with a fickle moral compass and an arsenal of distractions at the ready for keeping the guilt-riddled feelings buried deep down out of sight.

"Oh, that reminds me! I have a new joke for you." Rasp nudged the dismal faun with his shoulder, grinning. "What do you call a debate about mastication?"

"Nothing. Because that's not a thing."

Rasp's devious smile grew wider. "A mas-debation."

The joke earned both an ear flap and an irritated snort, scoring it a solid two out of three on the Annoyed Faun Scale. Alas, Hop had no appreciation for the humorous things in life and refused to acknowledge Rasp's overwhelming creativity. "Whisper warned that I might have to get firm with you."

"Oh, Hoppy. You know I can't resist when you talk dirty."

"If you're not interested in participating, then maybe you'd prefer some light reading? We could start with my favorite volume on the frequencies of magic and move on to the heavier subjects once we've gone through it beginning to end."

So much for not resorting to threats.

Rasp performed a full body slump in protest. Despite his many brilliant and hilarious attempts, the damned faun would simply not be deterred from his lesson plan. "Why are you being so insistent about this? Whisper's not even here. It's not a requirement to dedicate every spare second to training, you know. Too much learning is bad for the brain."

"I can't believe this," Hop huffed. "You may be the single most magical person I have ever encountered, and you have not a single curious bone in your body."

Rasp lifted his finger over his head pedantically. "That's not true. I have a very curious-looking bone. You've said so yourself."

"Where is your sense of wonder?" Hop refused to break from his tirade to point out that the body part Rasp was referring to didn't qualify as a bone. Not even to reassert the part where he wished to never see it again. "We're testing magical theories that have never been touched on before. A witch that can manipulate two separate elements at the same time? Possibly more? This could be the breakthrough of the century!"

That all sounded like work. A concept Rasp typically avoided at all costs, oftentimes at the expense of creating *more* work down the road. But that was Future Rasp's problem. Present Rasp merely wanted to enjoy the sunshine a little bit longer before Whisper and Father returned and he had to climb back onto the damn mule.

Hop knew he'd won their battle of wills. "I've arranged three objects in front of you. Like before, each one represents a different element. I've added a twist this time, but we'll get to that. Begin with water. Relying solely on your magic, locate the water and use your powers to manipulate it."

Ever since learning about Rasp's newfound ability to influence multiple elements at once, Hop had been abuzz with all sorts of lofty ideas on how to apply it to his current training regimen. Rasp was not so keen. Manipulating one element by itself without it blowing up in his face was hard. Two at the same time seemed like a recipe for disaster. Making it rain, for example, was good. Making it rain fire was, arguably, less good.

"But—"

"It's either this or the book."

Realizing his options had run out at last, Rasp thrust his hand out in front of him with a groan. At least they were starting with water. He liked water. It was relatively straightforward and, in small quantities, harmless. Unlike fire, which hurt like a bitch when he got it wrong. Magic coursed down his arm and gathered in his fingertips. Clearing his mind of distractions, Rasp closed his eyes and drew into himself. He felt the magic lift from his skin and twist and curl in the air, seeking its intended source. The light in his mind flared blue as it made contact with the element he sought.

A wry smirk pulled at his mouth as Rasp flicked his fingers. He was rewarded with a splash and a startled yelp from Hop.

"While dumping water on my head constitutes manipulation, it is not what I meant," the faun gruffed.

"I think it earned a corn cake, no?"

"No."

"You're no fun." This time Rasp spread his fingers apart, widening the scope of his magic as he searched for the next element. The second object was proving more difficult than the first. Despite Hop's insistence otherwise, Rasp could not find the earth element with his magic. After the umpteenth time, he dropped his hand into his lap with a resigned sigh. "Can I give up now, please? I can't find the stupid rock."

"Earth is made up of more than just rocks, Rasp."

"Great. Don't care."

"Here." Hop uncurled Rasp's fingers and placed something cold into his hand. "Don't think about it, just *feel* it." After a few seconds of awkward silence, the faun clarified. "With your magic."

Too late. Rasp's fingers were all that were necessary to identify it. "I think you're the first person to ever give me a knife willingly."

Sensing Rasp needed less of a push in the right direction and something more akin to a full body-slam, Hop explained, "One of the main components of that blade is iron. Iron is a mineral mined from the earth. Given that you grew up in an area with an abundance of iron, I suspect you may be more sensitive to it than you realize. Being able to seek iron with your magic and manipulate it could be a serious advantage to you."

Rasp twiddled the blade absentmindedly between his fingers. "How so?"

"Use your magic to find the iron object in front of you and I'll tell you."

Biting back the groan that lodged in his throat, Rasp gripped the blade in one hand and stretched the other out in front of him. Once more, he sent tendrils of magic into the air like runners from a vine. Using the iron in his hand as a reference, he checked the energy signals of the objects closest to him, searching for one that matched. At last, he found it. The object glowed in his mind's eye a dull red.

"Ha!" Hop exclaimed. "You've got it, good. Now hold your concentration. We're going to introduce our last element."

Rasp heard a match strike and then the gentle burn of flame. The fact that it didn't go out after a few seconds told him Hop had used it to light their lantern.

"Oh good," Rasp sighed. "We're adding fire. This usually ends well."

It was too bad he'd already dumped the water.

"The iron object is a pan. I want you to use the energy from the fire to manipulate the iron."

"This feels like an overly complicated ploy for me to make dinner. You could've just asked."

The excitement in Hop's voice was somewhat endearing, actually. At least one of them was getting something out of the stupid training. "Harness the heat from the fire," Hop instructed. "And apply it to the pan."

Rasp slipped the knife into his pocket and lifted his free hand in the direction of Hop's voice and, consequently, the lantern. With one half of his concentration focused on the iron pan and the other on the flame, he melded them together within his mind. The dull red glow behind his eyes flickered before it turned a brilliant crimson.

"You did it!"

Rasp hesitated before asking. "And you're sure it's not on fire?"

"No, you transferred just the heat energy. Well done!"

Being praised was not something he was used to. Hop meant it in a genuine way, but that didn't stop Rasp from having the sudden urge to crawl deep into a hole and roll in the dirt until the itchy feeling subsided. "Can I stop now? My palms are starting to burn."

With the go-ahead from Hop, he snapped his magic back into his body and allowed the noise of his thoughts to refill the void. Many different voices shouted in his head at once. Most of them complained about the throbbing sensation coming from his fingers. A few wanted a nap. Someone in the back protested that, despite the many, many promises of food, no one had yet delivered a corn cake into his mouth.

Wringing the last stings of pain from his fingers, Rasp asked. "So what's the advantage of that?"

Short of heating the kettle when they were out of firewood, he didn't see the point. That was probably his biggest gripe with magic. It required so much effort for a payoff that could've been secured by simpler means. Added steps with little practicality. All the magic users in the world seemed so consumed with the how, they never bothered with the why.

"It's limitless, really." Hop sounded like he was preparing to launch into one of his excited ravings where he produced lots of words and little sense, when he stopped and considered his audience. "Say you were to get cornered by soldiers."

"Like that ever happens," Rasp scoffed.

"You're already at a disadvantage. One, you can't see them and two, it would drain your magic to fight them all at once. If you were to apply the heat from fire to their swords, for instance, the metal would grow too hot to handle and they would be forced to drop their weapons. Suddenly, you're no longer the one at a disadvantage."

"Except for the archers."

"Yes, Rasp. Except for the archers," Hop agreed, adding, "Although I've heard you're fairly decent at lighting bows on fire."

"Oh. My. Gods." Rasp's jaw lowered as a burst of excitement worked its way up from his core. "That was a dig! Your first one, too. Undeniable proof that I am rubbing off on you!"

A pregnant pause followed as he waited for Hop to say something clever in return. Rasp waited, nearly ten painful seconds in total, before he was forced to concede the matter with a pitiful shake of his head. "I know you're new to this, but that was your cue to give me shit back. I left a very open window of opportunity for you."

"I noticed. No, thank you."

"What? Suddenly don't want to get firm with me?"

"I will give you two corn cakes to never bring that up again."

As much as Rasp wanted the extra food, the perpetual need to have the last word won out as usual. "You drive a real *hard* bargain."

"That's it." Hop stood. "I'm getting the book."

CHAPTER TWENTY-SEVEN

Babies of Defiance

Now this is the kind of magic I can get behind." Rasp spoke around the mouthful of food tucked into the corner of his cheek. He still didn't fully grasp how Hop had turned something as horribly inedible as dried chicken feed into a denser version of a biscuit. The food was rustic, lacking just a touch of sweetness to combat the stale mealiness of the aged corn, but it sure as chaos beat trying to chew a mouthful of rocks.

"That's not magic, Rasp." Hop sat beside him, his attention torn between their riveting conversation and whatever new thingamabob he was currently tinkering with. "It's basic food preparation. Believe me, I've made do with worse."

"Worse than a bloated worm?"

"Ever heard of a dirt cookie?" the faun grunted, voice audibly strained as he tightened a bolt, or screw, or something into submission. At least that's what Rasp hoped was taking place. There were only a handful of other activities worthy of such strenuous grunting. And, frankly, he didn't want to consider those. Especially since he had not been invited to partake.

"Is that anything like a mud pie?" Not that Rasp ever ate those, willingly anyway. Alas, having five older brothers often meant he was the recipient of many, many terrible pranks growing up. Mud was preferable to donkey shit, at least. How he'd come to know such information was not something Rasp cared to admit.

"Similar concept," Hop said. "The taste is terrible, but you're so desperate to fill your stomach, you hardly notice the grit it leaves between your teeth."

It was not often Rasp met someone whose childhood was as grim as his own. His mouthful of soggy corn cake was suddenly difficult to swallow. "You ate it by choice?"

"When it's the dead of winter and the ground's frozen solid, you make do with what you can find."

Rasp's attention dropped to the last bit of food nestled within the palm of his hand. It wasn't much, a bite at most. He'd done his best to eat his cake slowly, savoring every nibble. All of a sudden it felt wrong to finish it. He lifted his hand in Hop's direction. "You want this?"

"You just spent the last two hours hounding me for a second helping."

"That was before I felt sorry for you."

"For what? Having to put up with you?"

"My company is a perk of the job, not a drawback, so no. I meant the depressing shit you try to pass off as normal." Rasp's hand closed around the morsel as sadness pooled within his stomach. "I swear, sometimes you say something so pitiful it makes me want to leave you on the doorstep of the next happy family we come across."

"After all the trouble you went through to kidnap me, you're just going to turn around and abandon me?"

"Abducted, Hop." Rasp patted his arm sympathetically. "You're not a child. Taking you against your will would have constituted abduction, not kidnapping." And it wasn't like they'd technically abducted him, either. Yes, he and Whisper *might* have destroyed the rest of Hop's team and ended his employment with the Division of Divination, but in a bigger, more important way, they'd liberated him as well. It wasn't their fault Hop had nowhere else to go afterward.

"I feel so much better already."

"Good, I knew you would."

"I'm certainly not biding my time, secretly waiting for a better opportunity to come along."

Better opportunity? What could possibly be better than life on the run? Never knowing where your next meal would come from, or who was out to kill you, or how many teeth you'd wake up missing after a night out on the town? Actually, come to think of it, Rasp wanted the answers to these questions as well. Who knew, maybe he'd invite himself along and see just how much better these other opportunities truly were.

"What'cha got in mind, Hopalong?"

The faun thought on it as he tinkered away on whatever was taking up the other half of his concentration. His answer was delivered slowly, as if considering the validity of each word as he spoke it. "Well, I've always wanted to find a little village to call my own. Settle down. Build a proper workshop."

"Get yourself a wife and kids?" Rasp was certain he could find a few of those lying around the next village they came across. Of course, *that* probably did constitute kidnapping.

". . . Some of those things, perhaps." Hop switched the subject before Rasp could double down on his idea to illegally procure the missing members needed to make his happy family complete. "Honestly, when you talk about Lonebrook, you make it seem like paradise. I think I'd like to go someplace like that."

"Lonebrook?" Rasp frowned, not sure how he felt about sharing *his* happy family. "Did you miss the part where I mentioned the son of the local judge made me fight for money? He used to pay me in buttons."

"I've seen you fight over buttons before, Rasp," Hop ever-so-helpfully reminded him. "I realize nowhere is going to be without flaw, but almost anything will be better than life at the beck and call of the Division of Divination."

Hop's story, the bits and pieces Rasp could wrangle out of him over the past two months, was rather sad. To start, he was born to exceptionally cruel parents—the fact that they named him Hopalong Humphry was, unfortunately, only the first of many ways they'd set Hop up for a life of misery. The eldest of three siblings, Hop was left in charge of raising his brother and sister, often going to extremes to meet their basic needs. This arrangement came to an end the moment Hop started to show magical talent. Instead of fostering their son's budding talent, Mister and Missus Humphry promptly sold him off to the Division of Divination for a handful of silver.

Ripped from everything he knew, Hop poured his heart into becoming a successful artificer, determined to return home and rescue his brother and sister from the life they'd been dealt. The Division of Divination had other plans. Immediately following his graduation, the academy insisted Hop repay his debt to the institute by accepting a lowly position as a traveling artificer instead. Resolute, Hop sent any spare money home, only to later learn there was no one left to receive it. His family had moved on without him, leaving him alone in a world that intended to wring him dry.

Rasp remembered the day they'd met and how, after he and Whisper had laid waste to the rest of the party, Hop hadn't even bothered to run, content to wait his turn to die. Since then, Rasp had made it his personal mission to rekindle the faun's former passion—there could only be one grief-stricken husk in the group, after all, and he wasn't about to share his hard-earned title! Thus, amid copious amounts of complaining and feet dragging, Rasp selflessly put up with the extracurricular training sessions solely for Hop's benefit.

And definitely not just because Whisper told him to. It was all one hundred percent Rasp's idea. Who was utterly selfless, and absolutely deserved to finish eating the piece of corn cake slowly turning to soup within his sweat-soaked palm.

"There you go again, making me feel sorry for you." Rasp shoved the soggy morsel into his mouth, trying his utmost not to sputter crumbs as he spoke. "Tell you what, I'll take you to Lonebrook when all of this finally blows over. I'll introduce you to the Belfasts and whatever happens afterward, happens. Who knows, maybe they'll agree to adopt a third son."

"Third son?" Hop stopped his incessant tinkering for the briefest of moments. "I thought Faris was their only son?"

"They just tell him that so he doesn't get jealous."

"I see." There was another thoughtful pause before Hop asked, "And are the Belfasts aware they adopted you?"

"Not yet. It works best as a surprise, I think. Just spring it on them without warning, that way they can't say no."

"I will forever be envious of your confidence, Rasp. Imagine what I could accomplish had I not felt the need to ask permi . . ." Hop's voice trailed, leaving the rest of his backhanded compliment unsaid.

Rasp opened his mouth, a halfhearted protest already curled on his tongue, when Hop's hand clamped down onto his shoulder and squeezed. Rasp fell silent, straining to catch whatever had his companion on the alert. In the distance, through the rustling of the wind and a squirrel angrily chattering several trees away, he heard the ominous *snap* of a twig underfoot. Rasp instinctively slipped the folding knife from his pocket. He had an actual sword, but it was all the way across camp, stashed under his saddle. A lot of good it did him now.

"There's more than one," Hop whispered. "They're starting to close in. I think they have us surrounded."

Old Rasp would have opted to stay and stand his ground. That Rasp, however, had possessed a working sense of vision. It was much easier justifying such reckless behavior when you were capable of seeing who or what was trying to kill you. He still preferred fists over magic, of course. But he also preferred those fights to be a little less one-sided. "Can we leg it?"

"I don't—"

"Good afternoon, gents!" an overly friendly voice called as someone extracted themselves from the undergrowth across from them. "We have had quite the night deciphering that trail you left us. Now"—there was a notable pause, as though the speaker was looking for something—"where might that third one of you be?"

"Hello, creepy stranger!" Rasp returned the greeting, mirroring the threatening warmth of the newcomer's voice. He gestured his hand from the blurry outline of the intruder to the vague, brownish mule-shaped one currently grazing off to the side. "Here she is, right here. We call her Bonecrusher. Get any closer and you'll find out why."

Hop slammed Rasp with his shoulder, hard.

Okay, so maybe there was still some Old Rasp hanging around in his brain somewhere. He liked to come out at the most inopportune times too. Naughty little devil.

"Oh, boy," the newcomer said. "We've got ourselves a comedian."

Before Hop could mitigate the damage, Rasp opened his big mouth once more and made things substantially worse. "Can we skip the banter and get to the part where you tell us who you are and what you want?"

"Delighted you asked, friend. I am Irvan and we are proud members of the Stolen Uprising, the Sons and Daughters of Defiance, the citizens' answer to the crimes committed by the—"

Dear gods, they were going to be here a while. One of the key selling points to a successful revolution was uniting the cause under a single name. The moment you started throwing in the extra titles was the moment things got too confusing to keep track. Rasp leaned closer in Hop's direction, murmuring, "Are these the resistance fighters that have been giving the Division of Divination the runaround?"

"Looks to be. I think it would be best for me to handle—"

Too late. "Hey, Toddlers of Defiance, good news! We're not with the division, either. So you can just go on your merry way and find someone else to fuck with, alright? Alright. Thank you, bye-bye."

Irvan's hazy shape swaggered a little closer. Rasp could not tell what species he was. Some type of smudgy cloud according to his poor vision. "I'm afraid you misunderstand," Irvan tutted. "You see . . ."

"Good gods, he's still talking." Rasp hung his head, whispering under his breath to Hop, "Can you pinpoint where the others are?" If these were the same idiots that'd been following them since the last village, then that meant there were four more members hanging back, using the trees as cover most likely.

Rasp half expected Hop to tell him to give his phantom aura vision another try. Thankfully, the faun could read the fucking room, and sensed now was not the time for another surprise magic lesson. "I hear four others," he said. "Two behind, two flanking."

Irvan, the self-appointed spokesperson for the Babies of Defiance, carried on as though he enjoyed the sound of his voice. Which, to be fair, was a very nice-sounding voice. Rasp was particularly interested in hearing the way it gasped with his hands cutting off its air supply. "We were sent into the territories to recruit like-minded individuals of the, how shall we say, magical persuasion? We haven't had much success in that regard, but we do keep hearing tales of a particular witch that has thwarted the Division of Divination at every turn so far. As you can imagine, we are very interested in making their acquaintance."

"Tell you what, if we come across any witches, we'll let you know." It was daring, Rasp realized, but the little devil stomping around the back of his brain was done with talking. He stood, nodding for Hop to follow. "Come on, I've heard enough of this. Let's go."

The four hidden members rushed forward, snapping every blasted twig between them and the edge of camp, as they moved in to cut off Rasp's escape.

"Not yet, stand down," Irvan called off his companions. "Forgive my men, good sirs. They've been put through a lot lately. As you can see, there's no need for this to end in violence. We're not like the division. We do not force anyone into working for our cause. All that our leader asks is that you accept her invitation to speak with her face-to-face."

Rasp, once more, spoke so only Hop would hear. "What kind of weapons are we dealing with here?"

"Two fighters in full body armor with swords, two others with walking staffs—looks to be the magical kind. Their spokesperson is the archer, but he's using his hands to talk." Hop leaned closer. "I vote we play along and wait for Whisper to find us again."

"What's the point of teaching me magic if you're too scared to let me use it?"

"At least two of these people are witches as well, Rasp. There's no telling what they can do. Best not to risk a confrontation until we know who we are dealing with."

Rasp spoke to Irvan. "Your leader, is she here?"

"It's a bit of a journey, I'm afraid. If we leave now, we can make decent headway by nightfall."

Yeah, that wasn't happening.

"Lantern," Rasp hissed, flexing his fingers. He bowed his head and tightened his grip on the iron blade within his hand. His surroundings shifted in the span of a single breath, so fast it made the inside of his head spin.

Hop's muffled voice sounded farther away. "What?"

"Light the damn lantern!"

Several voices rang out, shouting all manner of warnings he did not bother to decipher. There was movement, too. Fast footsteps and the clatter of swords being drawn from wooden scabbards, but Rasp kept his focus. Magic lifted from his body and, like a moth to flame, found the sources he sought. Once more, the iron pulsed with a dull red glow within his mind. With his targets locked in, Rasp pulled the heat from the flame and amplified it. Power coursed through his veins and shot forth. The dull red glow burned hotter, hotter, hotter.

The muffled voices turned to screams.

Lights flashed within his head, warning that the strain was too much. His practice session had been conducted with a pan—an item that was both relatively small and incapable of moving on its own. Rasp's current targets were larger, on the move, and pulling far too much of his magic too quickly. Already, he could feel his concentration starting to slip. His surroundings melded together in a chaotic haze of shifting light and dampened shrieks.

"Rasp!" Finally, a voice broke through. Rasp's consciousness resurfaced, vaguely aware that Hop was shaking him. "Stop, please!"

With a wave of his sore fingers, Rasp severed the connection between his magic and the iron and fire elements. The sudden drop nearly took him out at the knees. He blinked the last of the flickering lights from his eyes, leaning heavily against Hop as he waited for his other senses to play catch up. His nose, in particular, was not adjusting well. The only smell it picked up was that of burnt hair.

"Fuck, my hands hurt." Rasp paused, realizing the surrounding forest had gone eerily quiet. "Why aren't they attacking us? Was that really all it took to make them run?"

"Yeah," Hop gulped. "It definitely was."

Something about the faun's tone made his stomach drop. "I fucked it up, didn't I?"

"It's my fault, actually. I was so enraptured by the idea, I overlooked several glaring details." After a moment, Hop steadied his breath and clarified, "Plated armor is made of iron. Helms, too."

". . . Oh." Rasp's knees buckled beneath his weight. He struck the ground as the lurch in his stomach rolled upward, clogging his throat with hot corn and bile. The smell. Oh gods, the smell was going to be burned into his memory forever.

"If it helps, the three not wearing armor got away."

"That doesn't help!"

"It's not your fault, Rasp. You didn't know." And then, for whatever reason, Hop kept talking. "Well, I mean, it is your fault. But I realize you didn't intend to cook the soldiers alive in their armor."

Yep. That mental image was going to haunt the dark corners of his mind every sleepless night for the rest of his life. Rasp forced the lump of vomit back down with a difficult swallow. "How are you so calm? Why aren't you panicking?"

"Shock, probably."

"I'm going to be sick." Rasp sank farther into the dry leaves.

Hop yanked Rasp to his feet with a firm tug. "No time for that. We should get moving."

CHAPTER TWENTY-EIGHT

The *Ducky Luck*

It took two days for Daana's party to smuggle themselves across the border into Hallowbac territory, avoiding swaths of realm and resistance fighters alike. Another three days were spent canvassing a small wharf town before Ellisar secured passage on what she insisted was a reputable sailing vessel. The fact that the captain was willing to take a bribe should have been Daana's first tip-off that her and Ellisar's definitions of "reputable" were not the same. Daana's second tip-off came the moment she set eyes on the ship in question.

The *Ducky Luck* was on the smaller side, with patched sails, paint-chipped sides, and held together by a combination of pitch, barnacles, and sheer tenacity. A narrow plank stretched across the lapping waters, serving as the bridge between the rickety pier and the equally rickety boat. The gang-plank wobbled in the middle, a good twenty-foot drop over the churning sea. Daana tested its sturdiness with her foot. The fact that it didn't immediately snap in half was not a good enough reason to edge farther out onto it.

Snag stood bent beside her, the ends of his black-and-gold coattails flapping haphazardly in the wind. Due to his measurements, the suit had been purchased, not stolen. As Hallowbac bordered the neighboring swamp territories and had a thriving goblin population, finding a tailor had not been difficult. Convincing Snag to fork over two gold pieces for clothing he deemed "prissy," however, was an entirely different story.

He looked the part though, Daana had to give him that. Unlike in other realm territories, here goblins made up a large percentage of the head mer-chants. You could pick out the more important ones from the crowd based on attire alone—that and the line of comically muscular bodyguards trailing in their wake. Snag had known exactly the image he wanted to project and selected a black doublet with red embroidered details, a pair of ankle-banded trousers, and a sharp overcoat. His clothes advertised that he was a mid-level merchant, well-off enough to afford a bodyguard, but not so much that it would be worth the hassle to jump him in the streets.

With the territory in open rebellion, the noble and merchant class were fleeing the area to ride out the oncoming storm in calmer waters. Daana's small group would be indiscernible from all the others rushing to buy passage farther up the coast.

Although Snag did not enjoy the change in attire, he certainly wielded his newfound sense of status with gleeful vigor. "Secretary." He tapped the butt of his cane against the pier. "Are you going to cross or not? I grow weary of your indecision."

Daana's nervous gaze shifted from him to the rickety gangplank and then all the way down to the frothing waters below. Her stomach clenched in protest. Daana shuffled to the side, gesturing for Snag to take the lead. "My apologies, sir. After you."

Or, better yet, they could ditch the boat altogether and travel on land as Daana had been vehemently insisting from the start. So what if the sea was faster? It was also a lot deadlier. Considering the travel arrangements were Ellisar's doing, this was probably just another ploy to get Daana to give up.

It was a shame that it was working.

Snag peered cautiously over the side of the pier into the heaving waters below. His ears flattened against the back of his head as he slunk away from the edge. "Maybe we should send someone bigger. Make sure the gangplank's got structural integrity and whatnot."

"We could send Wormy," Daana agreed.

He raised his cane at her. "Mind your tongue, you worthless girl!"

Whereas the other horses had been sold off to net a little extra coin before their voyage, Snag had insisted on keeping Wormy. It had taken a small fortune and Ashwyn's sweet-but-scary negotiation skills to get the captain to agree.

"Today, ya lubbers!" A harsh voice rang out from farther down the pier.

Daana glanced over her shoulder at the odd pair awaiting their turn to board. Somewhere in the past two days, Ellisar's speech mannerisms had slowly reverted back to the seafaring type. And yet, this was not the strangest of her transformations. The posh, neatly dressed elf with finely combed hair and a touch of makeup looked every inch like Snag's wealthy business partner, and not a wanted criminal with the dwindling patience of a cranky toddler. The most alarming part was that, visually speaking, Ellisar was pulling it off.

The moment she opened her mouth was, alas, the same moment the cover stopped working.

Ashwyn's hair had been cut and greased to resemble a man's. Her freshly procured uniform of worn leather and wool all but screamed *working muscle*. The addition of a few convincing blood stains probably helped sell the package, too. Unlike Ellisar, Ashwyn had a better handle on her role and kept having to remind her wife to stop carrying the bags.

Wrangling the pack from her wife's stubborn hands, Ashwyn turned in their direction and broke into an easy smile. "What's the holdup, boss? Not afraid of heights, are you?"

Snag twiddled his lip ring nervously. "Shipwreck, actually. Seen a few too many of those to board one of these with confidence."

"And you, miss?"

Daana gazed down at the choppy waters wide-eyed. "All of it. Heights, dark water, shipwreck, this little measly board that no person in their right mind would ever consider crossing."

"Oh, sweet Peaches, it's a gangplank, not a tightrope. There's nothing to it." To demonstrate, Ashwyn strolled out onto the makeshift bridge with practiced ease. She stopped near the middle, seemingly unperturbed with how the wood sagged beneath her weight. "See? Perfectly safe."

Snag covered his eyes with a moan. "Please stop bouncing."

"What's the matter, Daana? Having second thoughts already? There's still time to back out, you know." Without Ashwyn to interfere, Ellisar had slunk up from behind. She kept her voice low and free of the fire that burned in her eyes. "A lot can go wrong at sea. Swept overboard, a nasty fall from the rigging, sick to your stomach so bad you vomit your own organs."

"That last one's anatomically impossible," Snag said with his eyes still covered.

"You're right. I made it up to sound scary." Ellisar took Wormy by the lead and moved out across the gangplank without any concern for the dark, frothy waters below. "Spewing blood and stomach acid 'til you choke to death didn't sound nearly as ominous."

Ashwyn intercepted Ellisar at the top of the wobbly gangplank. A look of exasperation danced across the orc's firmly set eyebrows as she extended her broad hand in the elf's direction. "My lady, please allow me to take that horse from your delicate hands. Such work is unbefitting a person of your status."

"Shove off, ya peasant!"

What followed could only be described as a sort of childish standoff. Ashwyn remained at the top of the gangplank, blocking the path as she waited for her wife to surrender the lead to the horse. Ellisar simply stopped midway across, content to run her wife's patience into the ground instead.

"What does it mean when Ashwyn does that thing with her hand?" Daana leaned closer to Snag, unable to tear her gaze from the signal the orc was holding aloft. "The number of fingers changes, but there doesn't seem to be any pattern to it."

"Awarding demerits," Snag replied, sounding slightly amused.

Daana considered this before realizing she had more questions. All of the questions, in fact. "I know what demerits are, but I don't understand how they apply in this context."

Snag snorted into his sleeve. "It's probably better if you don't."

"That's not fair. An explanation like that only makes it more intriguing."

"I suppose you'll just have to ask Ellisar then."

The elf in question whipped her golden head around, scowling at them. "You've realized this is a lost cause by now, right? If you can't even get on the bloody boat without issue, there's no way you'll survive two weeks at sea. Do us all a favor and call it quits."

"She might be able to board easier if someone wasn't blocking the damn bridge." Ashwyn lurched forward and seized the braided rope from Ellisar's hands, leading Wormy all the way up the gangplank and onto the ship.

With Wormy plodding up the gangplank behind her, Ellisar had no choice but to move with him. Ellisar threw her hands out from her sides as she was forcibly ushered up onto the ship. "What is with you and your insatiable need to pick lost causes? I already offered to get you a damn puppy!"

Something about Ellisar wanting her to fail lit a fire in Daana's belly. Giving up now was exactly what she wanted. Daana would be damned if she proved the stupid elf right. Resolute, she grabbed Snag by the wrist and started out across the gangplank. Gaze focused on the ship and not the churning sea below, Daana managed one careful step in front of the other.

Snag slunk along behind her, muttering, "Daana, I like you, but if you start to pull me overboard, I'm severing your hand."

As she was committed to staying in character and, therefore, could not call Snag the childish name that curled on her tongue, Daana demonstrated her irritation by tightening her grip on his wrist instead. "Hush now, sir. We're almost there."

"We're barely three steps across the rickety plank!"

"Almost there," Daana repeated. "We'll be on the boat before you know it."

"Boat? I don't see no boat! This here's a leaky bathtub. Barely fit to stay afloat above watery depths teeming with sea beasties all hungry for fresh gobby meat."

In a small, practically nonexistent way, it was a relief not being the one in the middle of a full-blown panic for once. Snag's antics were making it easier to ignore the pooling sense of dread currently turning Daana's legs to leaden weights. She kept her line of sight on the nearing ship, ignoring the way the lapping tide caused the board to undulate beneath her.

"Look, I know Ellisar can be an asshole, but she has a point," Snag said. "We don't actually have to do this. We can turn back and find another way."

Daana tuned out the rest of Snag's bellyaching. Not due to annoyance, but because he was talking sense. By some miracle, the rickety gangplank maintained enough structural integrity for them to complete the crossing without falling to their watery deaths. Daana stepped over onto the ship, pulling Snag with her. She resisted the urge to drop to her knees and kiss the wooden deck.

Ha! Take that, Ellisar. Daana, one. Gangplank, zero.

The sudden rolling sensation beneath Daana's feet caused her to stumble backward into the taffrail. Her stomach churned in protest, threatening to upend that morning's breakfast all over her shoes. Oh gods. What was this? Seasick, already? Seven realms, they hadn't even left the harbor yet! And this was only the bay! The open waters beyond the sheltered alcove would be substantially worse.

Suddenly, the idea of asphyxiating to death on blood and stomach acid didn't seem so far-fetched.

Daana's panicked gaze swept across the bustling deck. The vessel was even smaller than it had looked from the dock, packed from bow to stern with the crustiest crew she'd ever laid eyes upon. A particularly malnourished-looking individual accepted Wormy's braided lead from Ashwyn with a grunt. He led the scruffy horse toward the crowd working the pulley system, lowering the rest of the livestock into the animal pens below deck.

The crewmember's one glazed eye looked Daana up and down as he passed, uttering something under his breath about the sudden surplus of fresh, young meat.

"That's it." Daana whirled back around, heat rushing to her ears. "I changed my mind. We're walking!"

So what if the journey took a few extra weeks? She'd already survived one shipwreck and that had been enough for a lifetime. And anyway, Snag was right. Out on the open sea, there wouldn't be anywhere to run in the event of trouble. As formidable as her party was, they were heavily outnumbered and no match for an entire crew. Daana didn't know why she'd agreed to this stupid plan in the first place. Walking was obviously the more practical option.

Her plan to scuttle back down the rickety gangplank was thwarted by Ashwyn. The orc reached out and caught her under the arm, pulling a desperately struggling Daana with her whether she wanted to or not. "Oh miss, you can't let your fears get to you like that. We've already made the arrangements and the money's been spent. There's no sense in letting all that go to waste."

"Let go! I don't want to do this anymore. I want to live!"

CHAPTER TWENTY-NINE

Symbol of Power

The breezy air was heavy with the funk of salt and sunbaked bird shit. Overhead, the harsh cries of seagulls and cormorants intermixed with the roar of the waves crashing along the rock jetty sheltering the bay from the might of the open ocean. Daana noticed none of this as she twisted and pulled, attempting to break free of Ashwyn's viselike grip.

"Unhand me!"

"Oh sweet goddess, child. You are one for the dramatics today. What has gotten into you?" Ashwyn grumbled as she tugged Daana along behind her. Their progress would have been swifter had Daana not planted both feet firmly against the worn wood deck and actively pushed in the opposite direction. It wasn't working as effectively as she intended, but at the very least, it was slowing them down.

"I'm not a child!" Despite her best efforts, the worn tread of her boots was no match for the orc's raw strength. Daana's feet slid out from under her and she landed hard on her ass. To her dismay, the undignified pulling didn't stop and she was dragged, with the seat of her pants catching every snag and splinter along the way.

"And it's sense, by the way," Daana added. "Sense has gotten into me and I don't want to do this anymore!"

Her rescue came from the most unlikely of sources. Ellisar stepped forward, blocking Ashwyn's path. Her arms were locked tight across her posh green-and-silver-embroidered frock coat. "Hold up. It's Daana's call, isn't it? If she wants off the boat, let her."

"Yes, thank you, Ellisar! Let's do that!" Daana had never imagined these particular words to spill forth from her mouth, but here she was. Intentional ploy to derail the trip aside, it was nice that she and Ellisar were finally seeing eye to eye on something. Who knew, perhaps Daana would buy the elf a drink afterward. Together, blessedly intoxicated and with their feet planted firmly on sweet, sweet dry land, they could commiserate over whoever's stupid idea it was to go by boat.

Unfortunately, the person responsible for said idea was not so easily swayed. "Normally, I would agree." Ashwyn lifted Daana by the arm and set her back onto her feet. "But she's clearly not thinking with her smart brain at the moment. Poor thing's gone floppy. Some food and a little rest should have her right as rain in no time."

More words passed between the pair, but Daana couldn't decipher them over the sounds of her own mounting panic. Her heartbeat hammered in her ears like a war drum. Despite the frosty, salt-laced wind, the skin on her face burned to the touch. The only other sound she could hear was the crashing waves as they struck the jetty from across the bay. Slam, crash, boom. Slam, crash, boom—it grew louder, and louder, and louder.

She had to get away, now, before her panic overwhelmed her completely. And yet, no matter how she tried, she couldn't wrench free of Ashwyn's grip.

There is one way.

The thought caught her by surprise. Although she hadn't had much use for them since the incident on the mountain, Daana had kept the armlets that'd made her the most infamous seeker back at the Division of Divination. Corrupt or not, you didn't just part with something that powerful on a whim. There was even a little bit of magic left in the stones. Not a lot, but enough in case of emergencies. And this certainly felt like an emergency.

Daana swung her pack around and fought to open it with a single hand, sweat gathering along her brow as she concentrated on her work, hoping Ashwyn was too preoccupied to notice. Daana's hand plunged through her tightly packed belongings until she reached the bottom. She spread her fingers, groping along the strange assortment of personal possessions until her fingertips touched the small bundle she kept tucked away in the corner. Gripping the wadded sock, she wrenched it free with a single pull, grateful she didn't empty the contents of her bag as she did so.

Ashwyn and Ellisar were still arguing, which was fortunate because it meant they hadn't noticed what Daana was doing. Alas, this also meant Ashwyn's hand was still locked around Daana's left arm, leaving her with the awkward challenge of trying to unravel the sock one-handed. In the end, it didn't matter. The power stored within the stones sprang to life, reaching out to Daana with the sweetest of songs as it wormed its way through the material and up her arm. The familiar warmth of magic lit a fire within her bones that had been long extinguished.

The sweat on Daana's brow was slick and beginning to drip down her nose. She ignored it, consumed with the raging heat building within her core. *Get out. Get free.* The words echoed across her mind as the icy panic running rampant through her veins melted away.

Was this the way, though? Was she sure? After all, she'd sworn off magic. Ever since she'd helped banish the dark spirit on the mountain, her powers hadn't operated the same. No matter how slow she took things or tried to ease back in with a simple spell, something inside her would lose control. A simple flame spell had turned downright disastrous a few months back. What if it happened again?

Get out. Get free. Use it and no one will be able to hurt you again.

"Daana?"

She nearly jumped out of her skin when a clammy, leathery hand touched her own. Shaking the thoughts from her head, Daana realized she'd forgotten all about Snag. He stood beside her, gazing up with wide, yellow eyes rimmed in worry. "I didn't mean for my fretting to get in your head," he said. "It's going to be fine. Ships make the crossing all the time. We've survived a lot worse than this, you an' me."

Daana barely recognized her own whispered voice. "I can't do this."

"Give yourself some credit, girl. You've done far scarier shit than this."

"Yeah," Ellisar agreed, breaking from her conversation to contribute her thoughts on the matter. "Like what you did in Alkurth. Who could forget that?"

The empty pit churning within Daana's stomach felt as though it were going to open up and swallow her whole. There wasn't any need to round on Ellisar as Snag was doing a good enough job of it on his own. "Knock it off, El! We agreed we weren't going to bring that up anymore."

Ashwyn, still gripping Daana's arm like a vise, leaned closer to Ellisar and murmured, "What happened in Alkurth?"

"She burnt the city to the ground."

"What?" The orc's grasp lessened for a split second before she recommitted, perhaps just a touch rougher than before. Ashwyn's dark eyes roved back and forth across the crowded deck, assessing whether it was safe to make her inquiries here or save it for somewhere more private. The busy crew paid them no mind as they hustled about preparing the vessel for launch, allowing Ashwyn's curiosity to get the better of her. "You mean with, like, torches, right?"

"She's the daughter of she-who-will-not-be-named," Ellisar replied flatly. "If it involved torches, do you think I would be mentioning it right now?"

"But I thought Daana wasn't capable of . . . you-know-what."

"Oh definitely capable. Maybe a little too much at times."

"Which is why she swore off it for good." Snag stepped forward, still glaring daggers at Ellisar for spilling what they had all previously agreed to take to their graves. He fiddled with the black-and-gold cane in his hand, seemingly torn between whapping the elf across the knees with it or slamming the metal tip against the deck.

"Only 'cause you made a stink about it," Ellisar said. "I maintain that Daana should have stuck with the cursed magic. That kind of power is sure to come in handy, you know."

"It was killing her!"

"That wouldn't have stopped her, Snag."

"Yes, it would have! Not everyone is a chaos monster like you!" Fury won out at last and Snag's cane struck the deck with a resounding slam.

"Then explain why she's got her armlets in her hand." Ellisar tilted her head at Daana. The wind tore at her neatly brushed hair, undoing hours of tedious plaiting. "That's right. I went through your bag a ways back. You never got rid of those like you said."

Some of the fury dissolved from Snag's curled expression. He whipped his head to look at Daana, hurt tugging along the edges of his jagged mouth. "Daana?"

Daana's panicked gaze shifted from him to the bundle clenched in her hand. The bubbling heat within her chest fizzled out as quickly as it had come. Oh gods, what was she doing? This wasn't the way. She'd let fear get the best of her and nearly allowed herself to lose control. "I, uh, was just . . ."

"About to blast the ship to pieces," Ellisar helpfully finished the rest of her sentence for her.

Snag wasn't taking the news nearly as well as Ellisar. "Seven realms, Daana! You tryin' to kill us? Why would you even keep those?"

"I didn't want to be helpless, okay? I'm not like you. I don't have the means to defend myself. I just wanted to—"

Snag's left eye twitched as he thrust his clawed finger in the direction of the water. "Do like you should have done two months ago and throw those damned things overboard!"

"Sweet goddess, Snag." Ellisar rolled her head back with a groan. "It's an empty gesture and you know it. They're a symbol of her power, not the real thing. You want to get rid of the cursed magic? You've got to throw her overboard, too."

Snag appeared furious enough to try.

Ashwyn unlocked Daana's arm and placed a reassuring hand on her shoulder instead. "I'm obviously a little lost here. What's with the sock?"

Wordlessly, Daana peeled back the wool fabric, revealing the pair of leather armlets with matching amethyst stones.

Ashwyn's brow furrowed. "That's not making this any clearer. Someone tell me what I'm looking at here?"

Snag obliged her. "Daana used the magic stored in those stones to burn down Alkurth."

"Accidentally!" Why was everyone glossing over that? It wasn't like she'd meant to! "And it wasn't the whole city, either. It was just the city watch building!"

Alright, a handful of shops near the city watch might have caught flame as well. And then a few stables and whatever structures butted up alongside them. All in all, it had been *maybe* a city block, at most. Which, again, had been a complete accident—Daana's part in starting the fire, anyway. As much as she would love to point fingers at Ellisar for making the night in question substantially worse, it was best just to leave the whole ordeal behind them and never speak of it again.

"Ah," Ashwyn said. "And why are we not throwing the jewelry in the ocean? Seems like a pretty straightforward plan."

"Thank you!" Snag said.

Ellisar disagreed, widening her defiant stance. "Because it's the only thing that makes her useful."

"May I propose a compromise then?" the orc offered. "How about instead of allowing Daana to carry them, the stones are entrusted into my care for the meantime? Boat doesn't get burned to a crisp, we make the journey safe and sound, everyone lives, but we have the option to use the magic if necessary? How's that sound?"

Daana perked at the idea. "Really?"

"Sure." Ashwyn outstretched her hand and Daana placed them into her hand. The pair shared a warm smile. It was a beautiful, trusting moment that was over in the time it took Ashwyn to coil her arm behind her and lob the bundle as far out over the water as she could. The sock sailed a ways before disappearing beneath the undulating surface with an inaudible splash.

Ellisar cupped her hands to her mouth. "Boo!"

"Glad we got that taken care of." Once more, Ashwyn's hand encircled Daana's arm as she moved toward the cabin area. The journey went much smoother without Daana resisting. She didn't dare this time. "Now let's get to our lodging. I suspect there's a lot more you three aren't telling me and this Alkurth business is just the tip of the iceberg."

Daana glanced behind her and regretted it. Snag was still glaring at her, teeth clenched so hard he looked to be on the verge of drawing blood. She turned around again, stomach dropping lower as the cabin neared. Alas, despite her vigilant attempts to keep the infamous Alkurth incident locked away in her memory forever, it had an annoying habit of resurfacing at the most inconvenient of times.

Daana's fingers twitched as an insatiable itch clawed up her hand. Clenching her fist, she tucked the unruly appendage into her coat pocket before anyone took notice. The dread pooling in her chest doubled as she walked. The magic, as brief as its contact had been, had stirred the monster lurking beneath her skin.

CHAPTER THIRTY

What Happens in Alkurth . . .

Their cabin, the room equivalent of a musty shoebox, normally functioned as the first officer's private quarters. Ellisar convinced him to rent the cabin to them in exchange for a generous handful of coins—freshly picked from someone else's pocket, no doubt. The cabin was located on the quarterdeck and consisted of four timber walls, a grease-stained floor, and a small table with chairs. A single bed was shoved against the aft-facing wall, above which hung the cabin's only window.

Daana shuffled to the back wall as she took in the full scope of what would be home for the next two weeks. Normally she would've been more perturbed by the single bed, but she was presently more concerned with whether or not the rounded window nestled above it actually opened. With the way Snag was glaring at her, she felt suddenly inspired to jump through it.

Snag was seated at the table in the middle of the room. Ellisar was beside him, leaning uncomfortably close to the first officer, who seemed to be having some trouble remembering the correct method for counting to thirty. After double-checking his fee had not been shorted, the man swept the loose money into a bag and stuffed it into his pocket. He stood, casting a final suspicious look at his cabin's new occupants before hiking up his sagging breeches and sauntering toward the open door.

"Will you be needing anything else?" he said.

Daana suspected it wasn't so much an offer for further assistance as it was a declaration that their business was concluded and if they wanted anything else, it would come at a cost. Snag was still too preoccupied with glaring at Daana to respond, leaving the honor to his less-than-enthusiastic business partner.

Ellisar waved the man with a disinterested flick of her hand. "No, be gone."

Clasping one hand firmly to his now bulging pocket, the first officer ducked out of the open doorway and scurried off to go stash his treasure elsewhere.

"Lowly servant," Ellisar called to Ashwyn, "shut the door. It's letting in a draft."

Ashwyn stood tucked alongside the entrance. Having resumed her role of the strong-but-silent bodyguard for the duration of the transaction, she hadn't spoken a word since, resigned to a hostile silence that could be felt from all the way across the room. Her scowl deepened as she swung the door shut with a slam and started toward the table.

"And the lock," Ellisar reminded her.

Clenching her teeth, Ashwyn backtracked several steps and fitted the wooden drawbar into place. With the room's main source of fresh air now gone, the pungent smell of water-damaged timber clouded the air so thick, it bordered on smothering. Darkness permeated the cabin. Daana blinked as her eyes slowly adjusted to the gloom, vaguely aware that the twitch in her hand had started anew.

"You know, this plan of yours isn't all bad. I do enjoy ordering you around for a change." Ellisar paused, allowing a rare smirk to pull at the corner of her sharp mouth. "We could make a game of it."

Snag grimaced at her words. "Seriously?"

"What?"

"How can you possibly be thinking about anything else after what just happened out on the deck?"

"You mean all of my coy flirting?"

Snag finally broke his unrelenting eye contact with Daana to whip his head around at Ellisar, earrings jingling. "How high are you right now? Because I was out on that deck just the same as you, and flirting was the last thing that was going on!"

Ellisar tracked Ashwyn's movements, watching as the orc trudged across the small cabin and dropped into the open chair to her left. "For you maybe," the elf said. "I've been trying to work the missus into an angry rumpy-pumpy session all morning. With all this blasted boat business, my needs have gone to the wayside."

"You did it last night!"

"Only once, though. And barely a cuddle this morning. I lash out when I feel neglected." Ellisar slid her hand across the table and placed it over Ashwyn's, watching the orc's expression for tells as she did so.

Wordlessly, Ashwyn removed her hand from the table and placed it in her lap, out of reach.

"Think you might have pushed too far," Snag remarked. His yellow eyes darted back in Daana's direction and narrowed. "Seems to be a common theme today."

The sting of humiliation crept across Daana's nose. Although the crushing weight of her panic had settled some upon entering the cabin, she still could not shake the urge to run. Doubly so now that Snag had remembered she existed and was back to watching her every move. Daana placed her hand against the cold glass of the window, cursing it for being far too small to jump through.

Clunk!

The table lurched behind her, drawing Daana's attention back to the center of the cabin. Ashwyn was scowling down at Ellisar, whose own pinched expression appeared to be caught somewhere between pain and ecstasy. "Alright, footsies are off the table," Ellisar wheezed around the breath caught in her throat. "Message received loud and clear."

"You're not getting a lick of attention until you've explained what the fuck is going on." Ashwyn's clenched fist struck the table with a slam. "Starting with why in goddess's name you didn't tell me we've had an unstable witch in our midst this entire time!"

Ellisar drew her leg up into the chair and cradled her smarting foot. "Witch is generous, but I see your point."

"No wonder you fought the stupid boat idea so hard! I should have known something was fishy when you—you, who fucking loves being on the open water—wanted nothing to do with it. I thought you were dragging your feet because of the ex, not because Daana's been burning her way through the realm!"

"Is now a good time to point out that the ex is still my main reason for being difficult?" The resulting glare from Ashwyn forced Ellisar to reconsider her strategy. A strategy blatantly void of groveling or even the slightest form of apology, of course. "Alright, yes. We probably should have mentioned Alkurth before. But we've been through so much fucked-up shit in the last six months, it all starts to blur. Nothing sticks out as extraordinary anymore. There was everything that went down on the mountain, a battle with magic flying everywhere, a dragon, a flood. Honestly, Daana burning a city to the ground felt like small potatoes in comparison."

"For the last time, it wasn't the whole city!" To her horror, Daana realized her unruly mouth had betrayed her once more. Seeing as she already had everyone's attention, she supposed it wouldn't hurt to correct Ashwyn's other highly incorrect assumption. "And, again, as I have pointed out numerous times, I am *not* a witch."

There was a fourth, empty wooden chair tucked beneath the rickety table. Ashwyn kicked it out from under the table in an unspoken invitation to join the conversation.

Daana's gaze darted past them toward the barred doorway, debating whether it was even worth the effort to reiterate what everyone obviously already knew—that she was a fuckup and that agreeing to deliver her to her mother had been a cursed promise from the start. She could hear the bustling crew scuttling across the deck beyond the cabin. The *Ducky Luck* had yet to launch, meaning she could simply waltz back down the deck and disappear if she truly wanted.

Ultimately, it was Snag's expression that gave her pause. Daana was convinced he hadn't blinked in nearly ten minutes. Stifling a sigh, she moved to the table and sank into the chair.

"You were saying?" Ashwyn prompted.

Staying had only been half the battle. Regretfully, that still left the talking part to muddle through.

Daana slumped lower. "I'm sort of a dysfunctional half step between a witch and a magic-sensitive person. I don't have magic of my own, but I can use the magic of others under the right circumstances. Those stones you threw overboard were a means for me to store magic when there wasn't a readily available supply nearby."

"Sounds an awful lot like a witch to me," Ashwyn grumbled. "So what's the deal? Is your control shit or something?"

Daana stiffened at the insult. "It's not shit!"

Ellisar snickered, but it was the low growl from Snag that wilted any remaining argument from Daana's tongue.

"It's just that my powers weren't this strong before. I used to be able to control them without any issue, but after, well, this"—Daana pulled her sleeve back to expose the branching veins on her wrist—"it hasn't been the same. Something from that mountain latched on to me and ever since, it feels like my powers have been supercharged. A simple push spell levels a city wall and no matter how hard I try, I can't seem to get a handle on it."

"And each time you do, it causes the infection to spread." Snag's tiny fist struck the tabletop, causing the ancient wood to tremble in protest. "Which is why we agreed you would retire from magic!"

Behind the anger, Daana sensed a deep disappointment. Regret pooled in her chest as she stared down at the chipped tabletop, unable to meet his gaze without flinching. "I'm sorry, Snag."

"Don't be. Keeping the stones was the first badass thing you've done." Ellisar added with a shrug, "Besides the fire, of course. Gonna be hard to top that."

"You!" Snag wagged his claw at Ellisar, shoulders bristled for a fight. "Stop encouraging this! You understand her carelessness not only puts her life at stake, but ours as well, right? We're gambling with death each time she taps into her power."

"Meh."

"Meh? She's putting our lives at risk and that's all you can say? Meh!" A second shrug from Ellisar caused Snag to throw his scrawny arms into the air above his head. "Why do I even bother trying to talk sense into you? You're perfectly content to watch the world burn, with us right in the thick of it!"

Ashwyn pinched the bridge of her nose with a heavy sigh. "You know, it would be a lot easier knowing how pissed I'm supposed to be if someone told me what actually happened."

Daana supposed it would be better if the explanation came from her, if only to prevent Ellisar from including some of the more colorful details that really had no impact on the story whatsoever. "It was an innocent mistake, honest. Ellisar and I got pulled in by the city watch and thrown into a holding cell for the night. We were both a little plastered and—"

Ashwyn held up her hand. "For what?"

Daana didn't know whether the lurch in her stomach was due to the question or the shifting of the waves beneath her. "Come again?"

"You got pulled in by the city watch for what?"

"Prostitution." Ellisar held the palms of her hands in the air to mockingly ward off Daana's glare. "Sorry, *attempted* prostitution without a license. Ya happy?"

"No, actually," Daana said. "I'm not. Because I never asked for your involvement in the matter to begin with. You took it upon yourself to find me a lover and got us both thrown in jail because of it!"

"Admittedly, offering money to an off-duty officer was not my best idea. In my defense, he wasn't wearing a uniform and I was drunk off my ass. You'd been so uptight, I thought a good romp would make you more tolerable."

Daana desperately wanted to sink into the floor. Alas, the cat was out of the bag now and there would be no shoving it back in. She opted to move the retelling along to the part that actually mattered. "While in the cell, Ellisar said to create a distraction while she popped the lock. I only meant to start a small desk fire, but things quickly got out of hand."

"The important thing is I got us out." Ellisar tilted the chair back on two legs and folded her hands behind her head. "Even had time to stop and retrieve our belongings before the entire building was engulfed in flames. All in all, one of our better getaways, I'd wager."

Daana desperately wanted to kick Ellisar's chair off-balance. She stretched her right leg as far as it would go, coming to the dismaying conclusion that she'd have to be under the table to reach. "I think it's only fair to mention that, while I might have started the initial fire, the destruction wasn't purely my doing. Snag's powder charges played a part, as did the certain someone *throwing* them."

"You're right," Ellisar agreed. "Our *best* getaway ever."

For some uncanny reason, Ellisar's words sparked a twinge of pride within Daana's sinking soul. The feeling was fleeting, however, and Daana's momentary elation was immediately brought back down by the presence of the scowling goblin beside her. Wordless, Snag's curled expression spoke volumes on its own, something to the tune of: "We do not seek validation from Ellisar."

Ashwyn drummed her fingertips against the table in thought. "Daana, you said your powers only work if you have access to a magical source, yeah?"

"Yes."

"And now that I tossed your pretty little stones overboard, you no longer have access to said magical source?"

"Yes." She could pull from witches too, but that seemed redundant to bring up at this point. Daana hadn't felt any source of magic since boarding the ship. Rich merchant and war ships had uses for magic, certainly, but cargo vessels such as this simply could not afford to keep a witch on the payroll. For the better, probably, in Daana's case. Although the twitching in her fingers had eased, the irresistible itch crawling beneath her skin was still alive and well. Perhaps a few weeks at sea, free of magical temptation, was just what she needed to get it out of her system.

Ashwyn was busy talking herself through a rundown of everything she'd just learned. "So you're not a witch, but you can use magic—poorly, from the sounds of it. Which is why after burning *parts* of Alkurth to the ground, you swore off magic completely. Right up until just a few moments ago." Ashwyn's understanding hit a dead end, prompting the orc to tilt her head at Daana quizzically. "I'm still not sure how that ties in. Remind me again, what possessed you to drag out your shiny stones of destruction back there on the deck?"

Daana rubbed the edge of her elbow as she tried to explain her reasoning without sounding unhinged. "I just have a thing with ships and water. I panicked and . . ."

"Almost blew us to smithereens," Ellisar contributed.

The table lurched a second time as someone's foot nearly sent Ellisar spilling to the floor. Ashwyn kept her focus on Daana, pretending as though she had no idea where the kick had come from. "Because you felt helpless?"

She hated how easily her overreaction could be summed up in a matter of words. What's worse, they were stupid words. Stupid words for a stupid problem, all befitting the equally stupid girl to whom they were directed. Daana's response tasted bitter on her tongue. "Yes."

"Well the solution seems simple, then." Daana didn't like the sudden calm, confident tone Ashwyn had switched to. She didn't dare question it, though, and sat silent instead, dreading what sort of resolution the orc was about to present. "We teach you to fight. That way I get to kick your ass on the regular, you learn not to be so helpless, and start to actually pull your weight for a change—a real win-win all around."

That didn't actually sound too bad. Unfortunately, her confounded mouth had to go and open, allowing the first thought in her head to come tumbling out. "That's it?"

"It?" Ellisar repeated. "What, were you expecting more? Sweet goddess, Daana, she's not your mother. Keep your weird power fantasies to yourself. Ashwyn's already got more than she can handle with me."

"Excuse me? I am well-versed at handling you, miss. Right side up, upside down, sideways sometimes."

"Stop, you're making me all steamy." Ellisar was up and out of her chair in the blink of an eye. She slumped over the back of Ashwyn, draping her lanky arms over the orc's shoulders and down her front, while whispering in her ear at a volume that was, regrettably, impossible not to overhear. "Are you finished playing scary orc interrogator yet? Because it gave me some ideas."

While Ashwyn's scowl remained stubbornly fixed in place, the harsh glint within her eyes softened. "Now?" was the only thing she said.

"Yes, now." Ellisar nuzzled her face against the orc's neck. "You look fit to burst and I've been begging for your undivided attention all day."

"You realize we share a cabin, don't you?"

Ellisar hooked her arm through Ashwyn's and made a rather futile attempt to pull her from the chair. It didn't stop her from trying, however. Remarkably, she managed to drag both the orc and the chair several inches closer to the barred doorway. "Come on. I saw a dark, secluded little nook on the way in. If you can keep from drawing blood when you bite, nobody will even know we're there. Besides," Ellisar said, glancing over her shoulder at the table's remaining occupants, "Snag looks like he's got something to say and believe me, you do not want to be around when he pops off."

Against her better judgment, Daana stole a glance at Snag from the corner of her eye. The state of his face made Daana suddenly wish she'd been invited to tag along. She didn't even have the opportunity to stand before Ashwyn and Ellisar were up and out the door, slamming it shut behind them.

The silence that followed was suffocatingly thick. Daana drew a breath, managing a single word. "I . . ."

"Don't talk," he snapped.

"But—"

"I've heard enough out of you already. You want to convince me you're no longer a stupid little girl?" Snag stood, shoving away from the table. "Then start acting like it."

CHAPTER THIRTY-ONE

The Dirty Rotten Role Reversal

Oralia's clothes clung to her skin uncomfortably tightly. To her annoyance, no amount of tugging kept her linen undershirt from riding up past her stomach. The stubborn garment moved with a mind of its own, bunching beneath her leather jerkin despite how many times she yanked it back down. The only reason the infernal shirt hadn't navigated all the way up to her neck was on account of her chest, which was currently serving as an unwitting barricade. Those, too, were being unreasonably annoying. As of late, no manner of binding seemed to keep the pair under control. Her flesh was heavy, and ached—and gods forbid she complain about it without someone commenting about it being her time of the month!

Oralia clicked her tusks at the thought. If she received one more offhand remark about her body's cursed reproductive cycle, she would ensure the speaker wouldn't live to see another month again.

"You doing alright there, boss?" Rali said.

Oralia stopped fidgeting with her clothing, painfully aware once more that she was in public. "I will be substantially better once we are on the road."

"Told you we should have slipped out before dawn."

"That you did," Oralia sighed, opting to keep the addition of "and I regret not listening to you" to herself.

Her irritated gaze swept across the bustling streetway. There was a crowd gathered at the city gates twice the size of the last one to see Oralia's team on their way. A makeshift platform had been erected alongside the wall. Some official dressed in a garish tunic and tights was atop it, pouring their soul into a heartfelt speech, tears and all. Oralia would have preferred to sneak out unnoticed, but their need for supplies had slowed her departure by several days, giving the city time to amass a going-away party.

Included among the theatrics was a token of honor that, from Oralia's position as far away from the platform as she could manage, looked to be a repurposed brass medallion on a ribbon necklace. She wondered if the words "first place for half-yard sprint" were still etched into the metal or if they'd managed to get it buffed out in time. As she had no desire to partake in the political theater, she'd sent Ellisar's body double in her place instead. Kalihn beamed bright, enjoying every moment of the attention as she accepted the award with far too much grace to be believable.

Shifting her gaze, Oralia spied Captain Bernstein several persons down from where she and Rali lingered at the back of the crowd. He was doing his best to keep his composure, but every time he looked in Rali's direction, his proud shoulders drooped just a little farther. If Oralia's team lingered at the gates any longer, someone would have to scrape the poor captain off the cobblestones afterward. It wasn't helping that each time he worked up the nerve to approach, one of the Stoneclaw brothers would hook their arm through his and drag him away, insistent on knowing the history of some mundane piece of architecture.

Judging from Rali's stiff posture, it was highly likely that she had orchestrated the interference herself. A means to avoid hearing whatever was on the captain's mind, no doubt.

While it didn't solve the issue with her clothing, a little teasing would, at the very least, provide a momentary distraction from her growing list of bodily discomforts. Oralia leaned closer, whispering to Rali, "Is that the captain's jacket you are wearing?"

"What?" The dwarf's brown eyes bulged, nearly doubling in size. "No!"

"It is. I can smell it. He wears a very unique cologne." Sandstone and cypress, if her nose was to be believed.

Rali's lower jaw opened and shut. Strangely, no words fell out.

"I do not know how you manage, Ralizak. It was only a few hours before dawn when you staggered out of my apartment this morning." Oralia watched from the corner of her eye as Rali's face went from pale to beet red. "Did you get any sleep?"

"As a matter of fact, I did."

"Ah, must have been between rounds then. Good for you."

Rali whirled around, wagging her finger at Oralia as she hissed between her teeth, "I know you think you're funny, switching the roles around on me so that you're the one giving me shit about my romantic life for once, but I'll have you know it's not working."

"Clearly."

"I just wanted a little company, is all. There's nothing wrong with that!"

"As I said, good for you."

"And so what if I'm wearing his jacket? I left mine at your place and I was cold. I'm only borrowing it. It doesn't mean anything. Stop reading into it!"

Having had her fun, Oralia paced her hand on Rali's shoulder and smiled. "It is a good look on you."

Rali's rigid shoulders deflated beneath Oralia's touch. The dwarf's listless gaze slowly swept across the gathering, as though seeing, but not taking any of it in. "I think he's going to ask me to stay."

"Gods, Rali." It was Oralia's turn to go ashen in the face. "It was only one night!"

Rali's wilting expression begged to differ.

"No?" It wasn't so much a question as it was a statement of utter disbelief. "How long has this been going on?"

"A few weeks . . ." The dwarf's voice trailed, before adding, "After we arrived here in Fairguard."

"You have been in a secret relationship for two months?" The signs had been there all along, Oralia supposed. The coy glances, the smiles, the way Rali often threw things at the back of the captain's head and then ran. Oralia hadn't realized what had been taking place between the two constituted flirting but, then again, she had never been well-versed in the art of flirtation to begin with. The only reason she'd ever caught on that Sascha had feelings for her was because he said so, to her face, repeatedly.

"Alright, hold it right there, miss." Rali went back to throwing her fingers into the air. "One, it's not a relationship. You know I don't get involved with those. It's like, I dunno, a fling, I guess? And, two—"

"Does the captain know it is only a fling?" Oralia interrupted. Again, while not well-versed in the courting practices of dwarfs by any means, it seemed unlikely that a mere "fling" would invite the other half to live with them afterward. Unless, of course, Oralia was misinterpreting what "stay" meant. That one seemed rather straightforward, though.

Rali ignored Oralia's question in favor of powering right on through to her next point. "Secondly, just because you didn't know doesn't mean it was a secret."

The revelation stung more than she expected it to. Oralia's jaw dropped in disbelief. "You told someone else before me?"

Rali's arms fell to her sides. "Well, no, not exactly. I intended to keep it a secret, but then Mul went and barged into my room without knocking and saw more than he bargained for. The little shit still hasn't let me live it down. This whole stupid courting me thing was his misguided attempt at blackmail. Was, anyway. Now he does it just because he thinks it's funny."

That was a lot of information to process. Amid the deluge of tiny revelations, Oralia noted the suspicious lack of details concerning the captain and his would-be proposal. "Rali, are you . . ." She paused, unsure if she even wanted an answer on the subject. "Considering staying?"

Rali's eyebrows merged together, forming a very angry caterpillar. "What the fuck did you just say?"

"It is all right if you are. You are allowed to make your own—"

"Are you out of your blooming mind? How dare you!"

Rolling her eyes, Oralia resigned herself to silence, allowing Rali's outrage to run its loud and, inevitably, short course.

"No! We've got schemes in the works! And we both know you can't get shit done without me."

That much was true. And as dearly as it pained Oralia to break up whatever was or was not going on between them, she needed Rali by her side for the trials to come. It seemed only fair considering their current scheme was *mostly* Rali's idea, after all. Although Oralia agreed on the principle of the mission, she still didn't see why she had to spearhead the damn thing. Let someone else save mortal-kind for once! She was old. She was tired. Her feet hurt. Risking life and limb was a young person's game.

The last one, she vowed to herself, full well knowing even she didn't believe it. It was a nice thought, though.

A startled cry caused Oralia to turn her head. She watched as the Stoneclaw brothers dragged Captain Bernstein farther away once more, talking loudly over his weak protests. "I have never seen Mul and Lingon quite so enamored with the captain before," Oralia remarked. "I shudder to think how much it cost you, Ralizak."

"Who said I had anything to do with that?"

"Your face."

"Ugh. Do you know how much booze I had to fork over to get those two numbskulls to do what they normally do for free any other day of the week? Too much!" Rali crossed her arms with a scowl. "Mul offered to do it for a kiss, of course. I countered with my fist instead and then, after some posturing, we settled on a compromise that didn't involve me strangling him."

They exchanged knowing glances.

Rali pursed her lips, allowing Oralia's unspoken question to hang in the air over their heads for several seconds, before clarifying the matter. "The strangulation was his idea. Not my thing."

A faint smile pulled at Oralia's lips. "And you accuse me of going to great lengths to avoid my feelings."

"Don't know what you're talking about, boss," Rali said, tugging the ends of her new jacket with a sniff. "All I really wanted was this here fancy new jacket. You know how hard it is for me to find stuff that fits in the shoulders."

A deafening round of applause broke out as the main speaker stepped away from the makeshift platform and shook hands with Kalihn, signifying the theatrics had come to a close at last.

"Shall I do the honors?" Rali asked.

"Please, before someone starts another round of speeches."

The dwarf's baritone voice rang out, reverberating off of the surrounding stone walls. "Look alive, ye swabbies! We're heading out. Move it or lose it."

Their departure would have been much swifter had they mounted the horses and taken off at a gallop. Alas, that would have meant leaving Sascha behind as he dared not sit on any animal smaller than an elephant. Kalihn probably would have fallen out of the saddle just outside of the gates—calling into question how the notorious Sergeant Farrow had managed to forget how to ride since her time on the mountain. Thus, they were forced to proceed at a painful walk. Rali was ensuring it was a fast walk, at the very least.

They were through the gates, down the winding dirt road, and into the trees in record time. Behind them, the cheering faded. Oralia kept a watchful eye on the gates in the event the people were cheering because she and her company were finally gone from their city. To her surprise, the gates did not slam shut behind them.

"Yoohoo! Rali, hold up." Kalihn trotted to the front of the procession, where Rali and Oralia strolled together. "Captain Bernstein asked that I give this to you."

Rali stared at the sealed envelope in Kalihn's hand for longer than nec-essary. Finally, eyes darting back and forth to be sure no one else saw, she took the letter and quickly stowed it in the confines of her jacket. "You saw nothing."

"Well, that's not true. Almas handed me the letter personally and asked that I—"

"Nothing," Rali reiterated with a hiss.

Kalihn held up her palms innocently. "Sure, sure. Whatever you say."

"And what happened to speaking like a pirate, bucko?"

Kalihn managed an unenthusiastic, "Aye, aye. Whatever you say, Cap'n."

"That's better. Now, let's discuss this serious lack of commitment to your character. I feel like you still haven't embraced the true essence of Ellisar."

"For the last time, I'm not eating slugs."

"You are doing a marvelous job, Kalihn," Oralia congratulated. "As I mentioned before, now that Fairguard is behind us, there is no reason for you to keep playing the part. You are free to be yourself."

With her part in securing New Adderwood's independence complete, Oralia no longer had a need for stand-ins for Ellisar and Snag. Soldiers, however, were a different story. Dewpetal was already proving well worth the money and Oralia was inclined to keep paying the goblin for as long as there were funds to do so. Kalihn was . . . less useful.

Oralia had done her best to let her off gently, but the elf wouldn't hear of it. Kalihn insisted she stay on, if not for money, then to make a name for herself. She swore to learn the ropes, insisting that by the end of the ongoing strife, everyone on the whole continent would be familiar with the name Kalihn Whatever-Her-Surname-Was. Kalihn's assertation probably would have been more impactful had Oralia bothered to remember the elf's full name.

"Really?" Kalihn's long, golden hair cascaded off her shoulder as she perked up at the idea. "Does that mean Dewpetal and I can stop holding hands now?"

"Holding what?" Oralia turned, but Rali was already scuttling away, stifling snorts of laughter with her hands.

CHAPTER THIRTY-TWO

PDA: Public Displays of Awkwardness

Instructing Kalihn to be herself was a grave mistake. The elf was like a cicada, capable of chirping away for hours on end about absolutely nothing. What's worse, she'd singled out Oralia as the unwilling audience to her endless babble. From theater, to literature, to her favorite color, Oralia was certain Kalihn had somehow touched on every topic in existence without imparting anything of actual substance.

Gentle hints were not working. Nor blatant ones. Oralia even attempted to switch from the head of the procession to the back, but Kalihn followed at her heels, yapping away like an unruly lap dog. Rali—who was not only unopposed to causing ripples in interpersonal relationships, but delighted in the opportunity—normally would have interjected on Oralia's behalf by now. Not today, unfortunately. From the dwarf's smug smile, the retribution for Oralia's teasing had unfolded all on its own.

"Kalihn." Oralia kept her voice low. "We are nearing the Mossborn border. Speak only when necessary."

"You got it, boss," Kalihn whispered back. "It's remarkable how you can tell we're near the border without any signs or fences or anything."

"Truly," Oralia agreed.

"Just looks like trees to me. Brown ones, gray ones, white speckled ones with—"

"I see the trees, Kahlin. You do not have to describe them to me."

"Oh, right. Sorry. I tend to blab when I'm nervous."

Oralia bit back her reply of "I noticed," hopeful that if she demonstrated how to keep one's mouth shut, the elf would follow suit.

"My friends used to refer to it as flux of the mouth. 'Oh there goes Kalihn again,' they'd say. 'Jabber-jawing away as usual.'"

Oralia tilted her head skyward, cursing the gods above for having such a cruel sense of ironic humor. Talked to death by Ellisar's stand-in. If Oralia's demise could not be committed by Ellisar's hand, it seemed only fitting that it be carried out by her body double.

Other than Kalihn's fervent whispering, the serene forest around them was still. A light breeze rippled through the orange and yellow treetops, sending cascades of spent leaves drifting downward, destined to join the thousands of others spread across the mossy woodland floor. The air was cold and crisp, laden with the pungent stench of autumn decay.

A single dirt road connected New Adderwood territory to Mossborn. Oralia had kept to the beaten path for as long as she dared. Traveling along an established route, one free of fallen trees and unlevel ground, was undeniably faster. With Mossborn's border looming in the distance, and their chances of running across a realm patrol increasing with each step, Oralia reluctantly gave the order to move into the trees sometime around midafternoon. The going went much slower after that. Painfully slow, in fact. At their going rate, they would be lucky to cross the border by nightfall.

Not that she would be telling Kalihn *that*.

"It's so quiet," the elf remarked nonchalantly, as if unaware her mouth was moving again. "Like eerie quiet."

Not quiet enough.

Scanning the dense forest ahead of her, Oralia's eyes caught the telltale shape of a man stealthily picking his way toward them. Her sense of smell assured her that the approaching scout was one of her own. Mul stepped out from behind a towering poplar, its green and yellow leaves shivering in the breeze. He leaned against the trunk of the narrow tree, waiting for the laggers to catch up as he chewed on the root end of a flowering plant.

"Find something?" Oralia asked once she was within a reasonable distance that did not require her to shout.

"Lots of activity in the area," he said around whatever in the gods' names it was he was eating. It had a delicate, floral smell that did little to combat his personal aroma of sweat and mud. "I came across an old encampment. Whoever made it left about a week ago, I'd say."

Oralia merely nodded along to Mul's report. In addition to realm patrols, they had roving bands of bandits to contend with as well. Adderwood and Mossborn were both expansive sprawls of uninhabited territory, with few towns, a single road, and not enough law enforcement to safeguard either. Oralia knew the bandits would be staying close to the roadway, tucked out of sight, awaiting the opportunity to ambush any unsuspecting victims who happened to pass by. Even with a handful of competent warriors at her side, she did not intend to give the bandits the opportunity.

"Any suitable areas to bed down for the night?" Oralia asked.

Mul scratched his stomach as he spoke. "I'm good to bed down with you here if you're in that much of a hurry. Might get a bit awkward for your beau, though."

"What happened to wooing Rali?"

"There's enough of me for everyone."

Oralia's resulting glare did nothing to discourage the cheeky smile split across Mul's heavily bearded face. It did, at the very least, earn her an actual answer. "There's an ideal camp spot not too far from here."

While Oralia did not relish Mul's impudent nature, she had nothing but respect for his prowess in the field. He was a proficient tracker, capable of reading the signs of the forest and following a trail with the persistence of a bloodhound. It was uncanny how someone so obnoxiously loud could make the switch to silent, stealthy hunter without triggering an identity crisis. It was the Stoneclaw way, Mul insisted, going on to claim that he'd be dead before any would-be bandits caught him "ass out in a blizzard."

Questionable idioms aside, Mul's expertise meant Oralia did not have to double-check whether or not his proposed campsite was well covered, away from the road, and near a source of clean, running water. Mul had undoubtedly taken all of this into consideration, and bringing it up would earn her nothing short of mockery.

"Excellent," Oralia congratulated. "We will follow your lead."

"Finally starting to acknowledge my stellar leadership skills, eh? It's about fucking time."

Considering Mul equated leadership with a genitalia-measuring contest, Oralia sincerely doubted he possessed any skills to speak of. Reminding him of this, however, would require more mental energy than she currently had. In a move born from pure desperation, Oralia guided Kahlin forward with a strong push of her hand. "There is more to being a leader than being followed, Mul. A good leader must also be a teacher."

"Counterpoint," he replied, navigating the chewed root stem to the corner of his mouth. "A good leader *recruits* good teachers."

"Congratulations, consider yourself recruited."

His pale green eyes roved between Oralia and Kalihn, gathering bits of information from Oralia's body language as he devised a way to use what he found against her. "And rob you of this young lady's gripping conversation skills? I couldn't possibly, boss. It'd be cruel of me."

The true cruelty was that Oralia was still having this conversation. "I insist."

"Uh . . ." Kalihn said, digging her heels into the ground in an attempt to stop whatever was happening.

The elf's pushback was no match for Oralia's strength. She propelled her toward Mul with a gentle push. "Kalihn here has expressed a desire to learn."

"Have I?" Kalihn said. "I mean, yes, I said that. But I meant from you."

"Mul is one of my most competent scouts. It would be a disservice to you, Kalihn, to learn from anyone but the best."

"And what exactly am I getting out of this?" Mul demanded.

"You are learning to be a leader."

"Forget it." He spit the nibbled plant to the ground and crossed his arms. "Changed my mind. I don't wanna lead no more."

"It would be good practice for your own people," Oralia reminded him. A part of her hated how easily the words flowed from her mouth. Fortunately, the part of her that was desperate for peace and quiet was overriding her conscience. "Eventually, one of your siblings will have to assume the Stoneclaw throne. Having leadership experience under your belt could serve you well."

Neither Mul nor Kalihn appeared convinced.

One of the perks of actually being in charge meant Oralia could have her way. Sometimes. "In case I was not clear, I am not asking in this instance. I am telling. Mul, take Kalihn with you and start her on the basics of scouting." Oralia shot a look over the top of the elf's head at Mul that all but shouted "without making your pupil cry."

"This is the last time I ever do a good job of anything," Mul grumbled under his breath as he shuffled ahead with Kalihn tentatively following.

Blessed silence returned. And yet, it was not as serene as Oralia had hoped. Without Kalihn's incessant whispering around to grate on her nerves, the mounting complaints from her own body swiftly assumed the vacancy. The hours of walking had worked up a sweat and yet, the bones in her hips felt cold and achy. It wouldn't be long, she feared, before they started to creak with every burdensome step.

Additionally, her linen undershirt was riding up again.

Oralia stood off to the side, allowing the others to pass as she fought the sweat-soaked fabric back into position. From the corner of her eye, she saw a hulking shape come to a standstill paces from her. Oralia lifted her head, trying to decipher whether Sascha's expression was more amused or concerned. There was a healthy dose of both present, but the fact that he wasn't cracking a joke probably meant it swung more toward the latter.

"I am fine," Oralia assured him, smoothing her outer clothes back into place.

Three pack mules stood behind him. Each beast was tethered to the one in front of it, with the guiding lead clasped firmly in Sascha's right hand. He raised his eyebrows skeptically. "Would you tell me if you weren't?"

"It is this blasted under cloth!" The words leapt from her mouth as if they had a mind of their own. "It keeps riding up, and no amount of adjusting it is helping. I am about to tear the damn thing off and be done with it."

"I have no objection to that plan." A wry smirk split across Sascha's face. He gestured for her to join him with a sweep of his free hand. "You should walk with me once you're finished. I promise I won't talk your ear off."

A few irritating wardrobe adjustments later, Oralia stomped to his side and, together, they walked on. She and Sascha made up the tail end of the procession, which was fine by her, as it meant the others were less likely to overhear her childish complaints. "For the record, I blame you."

"Mhm."

He didn't even ask what she was blaming him for. Best not to leave him guessing. "I have never had a competent cook in my company before. We took turns, got by the best we could, but dinner was more of a chore than something to be enjoyed. You and your three solid meals a day are having an impact on my waistline."

"Obviously. That was my grand scheme all along," Sascha replied. "It's easier for me to keep up this way."

His free hand hung at his side, swaying in time with each step. Oralia stared at it for longer than she should have. She'd never been one for public displays of affection, but understood that, for some gods-awful reason, it was something others enjoyed. Trying not to make a face, she timed the movement of Sascha's hand and caught it upon the backswing.

She stared straight ahead and kept walking, ignoring the impulse to yank her hand free when his strong fingers interlaced with her own. Sascha didn't draw attention to it, which, after several prolonged seconds of silence, seemed somewhat suspicious. Fearing she'd misjudged him and that he was simply holding her hand out of a misplaced sense of duty, Oralia glanced his way.

The big lug was practically beaming. There was a giddy smile curled on his face that reached well beyond his sable eyes. Sascha's normally blue-gray cheeks had a touch of color, too. His expression eased some of her discomfort. In fact, it would have been an entirely pure moment if it were not for the slick layer of sweat collecting between their warm palms.

That was going to take some getting used to.

"Are you going to startle if I say something?" he asked.

Startle? She considered, briefly, whether or not she'd just been compared to an untrained horse. "Why would I do that?"

"Because it looks like you're one teasing remark away from running for the hills."

"I am not," she scoffed. Running would have been murder on her stiff joints. A swift walk was all that was needed to stay ahead of Sascha.

"And you're not going to let go of my hand if I do?"

It was times like this that Oralia found him so utterly adorable, she had to stifle the impulse to say something disgustingly mushy. "I want to eat you up" was an expression she'd overheard on several occasions. That seemed to send mixed signals, however. Particularly when it came from a hungry orc. She opted to lift a single eyebrow slightly higher than the other instead, challenging Sascha to test his luck.

Sascha rarely backed down from a challenge and today was no exception. "Honestly, I can't tell if you're sick, or if this is you feeling better."

Truth be told, Oralia wasn't so sure of that herself.

"But I like it." Sascha gave her hand a reassuring squeeze. "And if this is what happens when you finally let me carry that cursed stone of yours for the day, then I might just keep it."

It was a nice change of pace not having the burden of the powerstone weighing her down. Oralia was reluctant to entrust it to another, which was the reason only Sascha and Rali were allowed to transport it from time to time. Normally it took a bit of convincing but, with a long journey ahead of her—with a body that already felt stretched too thin—Oralia had surrendered the stone without a fight.

"Over my dead body," Oralia said. "I may not know what to do with it yet, but I can assure you, it will not be staying in your care." Just because she hadn't put up a fight earlier didn't mean she was ready and willing to give up being a stubborn curmudgeon altogether. She had a reputation to maintain.

Growing soft was not something that happened overnight. It was all about the baby steps.

"And why's that?" Sascha said.

Oralia's gaze dropped to their hands. Hers was practically engulfed within his, creating a small reservoir of sweat between the two of them.

Sascha's wry smile pulled into a full smile, teeth and all. "Because you *love* me?"

"Ugh," was the only reply worth mustering.

"And because, against my better judgment, I love you?" He leaned into her, bumping her with his shoulder playfully.

She considered releasing his hand to prove her point. The fact that she didn't probably spoke far more than any silly words could have.

"Mhm." He gave a definitive bob of his head. "Thought so."

"Hush. We are nearing the border."

"I don't think that works on anyone, love."

CHAPTER THIRTY-THREE

The Hunter and the Walnut Head

Figures he'd be the one to get stuck with the blabbering elf. *Go hunt for some rabbits, Lingon. Ensure we all have full bellies, Lingon. Never mind that we've got bagfuls of food already.*

Lingon stealthily picked his way through the overgrown landscape, mindful of his footing as he slunk along, stewing in his thoughts. *Oh, by the way, why don't you take the gal who can't shut her gab to save her damn life with you? What's that? She'll scare all the game away? Nah, nah, don't worry about it. While she might be severely lacking in the wilderness survival skill area, who better to teach her than you?*

The party's progress through the deep forests that connected the Adderwood and Mossborn territories was slowed by their valiant leader's refusal to use the road systems. Oralia's reasoning had something to do with roving hordes of bandits plaguing the roadways or whatnot. Not that Lingon particularly cared. Stoneclaws were used to picking their way through trees and over rocks and brambles. While rife with wickedly dense thickets and nasty blackberry vines, the terrain was flat and relatively easy for an experienced woodsman to navigate. This, alas, did not apply to his tagalong.

"Elf," Lingon hissed, glaring over his shoulder at the nervous lady-elf who trailed behind him at a snail's pace. From the start, he'd refused to refer to Kalihn as Ellisar. It was an insult to the real thing—a temperamental, cutthroat, absolutely enchanting warrior who would've been mortified to learn she shared an alias with this walnut head. Even now, with the go-ahead to use Kalihn's real name, Lingon decided it simply wasn't worth the effort.

"Pick up your damn feet already," Lingon said. "Boss said I ain't allowed to lose you."

Their party reached where they were going to bed down for the night just as the sun was beginning to set. Lingon had barely gotten his bedroll situated when Oralia tasked him and Dewpetal with hunting duties. While he didn't agree with the assignment, considering they had plenty of food from the city, Lingon at least understood her reasoning. He and Dewpetal were the best bowmen, after all. He knew it, the boss knew it, practically everyone but Mul acknowledged their superiority. What didn't make sense was the boss's flimsy excuse for why it was absolutely necessary for her best bowmen to drag Kalihn along and "teach her the ropes."

"I'm going as fast as I can." Kalihn held her puny arms to her chest like a squirrel cradling its last acorn. "Please don't leave me in the woods to die."

"Don't make it so easy then."

Originally, Lingon had tried to pawn their tagalong off on Dewpetal, but the blasted goblin was a step ahead of him. One moment she'd been alongside them and the next she was gone, like a damn shadow or whatever else could come and go without detection. Ghost maybe? Who knew. Lingon left the metaphorical imagery to the more imaginative types.

Lingon cursed Dewpetal under his breath. "Sneaky little devil."

"Pardon?" Kalihn froze, one boot still lifted midair, seemingly unaware of the bramble vine tangled around her ankle. Another few steps without correcting it, and she'd be flat on her face.

Could be worthwhile to stick around long enough to see that, Lingon supposed.

"Were you referring to me?" Kalihn whispered.

"Did I say 'stupid elf'? If not, assume it's not about you." Lingon watched as his whimpering companion ventured another step before noticing the vine wrapped around her ankle. She shook it loose, simultaneously dashing Lingon's hopes for a good show. He turned, annoyed. "Hurry up. I'd like to find some decent grub before we lose all the light."

A dark shape flittered down from the treetops above and landed on a lower branch with a gargled croak. Lingon's spine stiffened at the sight of the raven. Damn things had been following them for weeks now. Persistently, he might add. No matter how many rocks he threw at them.

He wagged his finger at the raven. "I already told you to fuck off. Whatever you've got to say, I don't wanna hear it."

Croak.

Lingon flinched at the harsh sound. He wasn't like his baby brother, Rasp, who claimed he could understand what the flock said. It all just sounded like obnoxious noise to Lingon. Still, the bird's intent was clear. Almost as clear as his resolve to get rid of the damn thing. "Go away."

Croak!

"Get out of here. Go on, get," Lingon hissed before turning his back to the pesky messenger. "You're gonna scare off all the game carrying on like that."

From the startled look on Kalihn's face, she undoubtedly had questions. She was smart enough to keep them to herself. At least the ones pertaining to the raven. "What about these mushrooms?" The elf indicated a small circle of white-and-brown-capped mushrooms nestled around their feet between the ferns. "They're not meat, but they are something."

Lingon sucked his teeth as he considered this option. Mushrooms were finicky things. The kind that went great in stew looked practically identical to the ones capable of causing a man to shit himself to death. That didn't sound like a particularly fun way to go. "You know anything about mushroom identification, elf?"

"Not really."

"Me neither," Lingon said with a sniff. "Tell you what, collect a few and we can take 'em back with us and the big guy can decide if they're safe or not."

With a look sharp enough to kill, Kalihn crouched down into the dirt and gingerly collected several handfuls of mushrooms and dumped them into her pockets. "We have names, you know. We're not just 'big guy' and 'elf.'"

"Good for you. Don't care." Lingon watched the raven from the corner of his eye. It hadn't moved from its perch. Lingon didn't understand why it was being so persistent. He had already made his decision. He wasn't going to change his mind just because his older brother couldn't take no for an answer.

"Is it really because you don't care?" Kalihn carried on. "Or is it because you're uncomfortable being amicable around so many other species for the first time in your life?"

"Nah. Me an' Dewpetal get on just fine. You should try taking a page out of her book. Like actually being good at shit." He didn't bother to listen to the elf's muttered response. Adjusting the bow slung over his shoulder, Lingon started off without her. He knew Kalihn would follow regardless of whether or not she wanted to. The alternative was trying to find her way back to camp on her own, which probably wouldn't go over so well.

The raven hung back, out of sight. Lingon could feel it watching him, even from a distance.

The waning light grew dimmer as Lingon ventured deeper into the trees. It wasn't too long before he found a nice game trail twisting along the forest floor, half-obscured by fallen leaves and sagging ferns. The day-old droppings that littered the dirt path told him deer frequented the area. Bagging an entire doe would be quite the boon. Especially now that he had an extra pair of hands to help drag the carcass back. Maybe he'd even pull the whole *gotta eat the heart to honor the beast* thing they did when hunting with newbies.

"Lingon," Kalihn whispered from behind him.

Lingon rose back onto his feet with an exaggerated eye roll. "What?"

The elf wasn't watching him. Kalihn's wide-eyed stare was focused on a spot in the trees due east of their position. "Something's headed this way."

By the gods, while the elf had proved to be a general disappointment to her species thus far, at least her darn ears worked. Lingon couldn't hear any sort of commotion himself, but after growing up in a cave system with five brothers, his sense of hearing wasn't the greatest to begin with. "Alright then. Let's see what kind of food we're bringing home tonight. Go on. Find somewhere to hide, quick now."

He moved swiftly away from the trail and led Kalihn to a nice hidden spot between a thicket of silverberry bushes. Lingon held a finger to his lips in the universally understood sign of *you make a fucking sound and I'm leaving your ass here.*

Kalihn demonstrated her agreement with a nervous bob of her head.

Lingon slid the bow from his shoulder and loosely nocked an arrow. Animals often took their sweet time making an entrance. There was no sense straining his arm waiting for the creature to mosey on into a clean shot. Twigs snapped and cracked underfoot as the beast approached, unafraid. A bit careless for a deer, Lingon noted. Then again, this was the middle of fucking nowhere. Maybe the game in these parts hadn't learned to be wary of hunters.

Unfortunately, this theory was immediately disproven by the presence of a voice. *Voices*, actually. Two of them, from the sounds of it.

"We've been walking for hours, Grettie. Are you sure you're not turned around?"

"Shut up! I know where I'm going."

"Do you, though? Because you've said that several times now and none of this looks familiar."

Out of the corner of his eye, Lingon saw Kalihn start to move. He grabbed her roughly by the arm and pulled her back down. He didn't want to take his eyes off of the approaching strangers, but he felt a well-placed glare was needed in order to keep the elf from bolting and giving away their cover. It seemed to work, too. Like a dog with its tail between its legs, Kalihn shrank down in a fearful cower.

The craggy voice identified as Grettie pulled Lingon's attention back in its direction. "What do you mean this doesn't look familiar? It's all bloody trees, Hank. They all look familiar!"

"So you admit it then," Hank wailed. "We are lost."

A disheveled pair tromped into view, dressed from head to toe in mismatching garments of questionable size and equally questionable origins. Grettie was a human woman. Admittedly, it was hard to tell given that her body was hidden beneath a ragged cloak meant for someone substantially larger. She had a crossbow slung over her back and a dagger dangling from her hip. It was her companion, however, who gave Lingon pause. Hank was an orc. And although he wasn't much of a big one, he probably still outweighed Lingon three to one. Hank was apparently a fan of stereotypes, as his primary weapon appeared to be a well-battered club.

Ordinarily, Lingon would not have hesitated to drop both with a handful of arrows, but bandits rarely traveled alone. Even if he managed to finish off these two without anyone overhearing, it'd only be a matter of time before their friends went looking for them. The last thing he needed was to have a search party stumble across his own group in the dead of the night.

Thus, fighting the hot warrior blood that surged through his proud Stoneclaw veins, Lingon settled back, watching silently as the pair trudged past none the wiser. Perhaps it was good he'd been saddled with the elf, after all. Kalihn excelled at doing nothing. Had Mul come along, Lingon was certain his idiot brother would've rendered the situation into a bloodbath by now.

Lingon and Kalihn remained hunkered down in the bushes until well after the bandit pair were out of sight. And then they waited some more for good measure. Fortunately, the one named Grettie refused to admit defeat and, after ten minutes of tedious waiting, Lingon and Kalihn appeared to be in the clear.

Lingon stood, arching his back. "So much for dinner then."

"Please tell me we're not going to follow them," Kalihn said.

"Psh, of course not. We're going to leg it back to camp and let the others know we're not alone here in the woods. Also probably means we'll pack up and move on, put some distance between us. No more fires for a while, either."

That was the part that would ail him the most. The cold didn't bother him so much. Lingon hailed from the great Iron Ridge, after all. The type of cold the lower regions experienced was almost laughable in comparison. No, he'd miss the fire for the piping hot food. And boy could the gentle giant Sascha cook. It didn't seem to matter what sort of vittles he had on hand; it all tasted like a slice of heaven. Practically bordered on witchcraft, but Lingon enjoyed it far too much to say anything on that front.

Still dreaming of tender, spit-roasted venison and crispy potatoes, Lingon nearly jumped out of his own skin when Kalihn seized him by the arm. Lingon whirled around, mouth curled open, ready to volley a mouthful of spite, when the elf's terrified expression gave him pause.

"I hear something again," Kalihn whispered.

Lingon was about to dive for cover when a scraggly figure slipped out of the bracken beside them. Kalihn's hand shot to her chest, gripping her frilly shirt as she nearly fell over backward with fright. "Gods, Dewpetal! Warn us before you pop up like that next time. You nearly startled me to death."

The goblin had a pheasant hanging limp from her shoulder. She regarded Kalihn briefly before deciding an apology wasn't worth the effort. Dewpetal's steely gaze swept back to Lingon as she rattled off a hushed response in the Yolcavisch tongue.

Lingon wasn't an expert by any means, but he could piece together most of what the goblin said. It probably helped that Dewpetal was using small words, speaking to him in the same manner one would a toddler. Now wasn't the time to be offended by that. "Two fellers?" he said, holding up a pair of fingers.

Dewpetal nodded, long ears bobbing.

"Yeah, we saw 'em too." After several clumsy attempts, Lingon was fairly certain he'd managed to convey his thoughts to Dewpetal in the goblin's mother tongue. Again, Lingon knew he wasn't an expert by any means. But he and Dewpetal seemed to reach a mutual understanding regardless. With a final nod of her head, Dewpetal turned and started back toward camp.

Kalihn dutifully fell in line, her blonde head sagging miserably. "We're not going to get any rest tonight, are we?"

"No hot food, either." Lingon eyed Dewpetal's successful catch mournfully. Pheasant wasn't as finicky as rabbit. With the temperatures dipping in the anticipation of winter, the meat wouldn't spoil by the time they got around to plucking it. Still, day-old pheasant was still day-old pheasant. He was pretty sure not even Sascha could dress that up enough to drown out the gamey taste.

The last of the light was fading around them when both Dewpetal and Kalihn froze in place ahead of him. Lingon stopped as well. He didn't know why. It just seemed like the sensible thing to do. And then he heard it. The sounds of loud footsteps coming from the same direction the bandits had gone. Wordlessly, the three of them traded concerned looks before picking up the pace.

Behind them, the sounds of a heated argument rang out as the bandits trampled through the undergrowth, retracing their steps.

CHAPTER THIRTY-FOUR

Thriving like a Fish on Dry Land

Rasp hoped that as the day progressed, and he traveled farther and farther from the carnage, the heavy weight in the bottom of his stomach would lift. But, as the hours passed and the shock of the events faded, the heaviness doubled. Lying facedown with his arms pulled over his head, Rasp heard the crunch of the brittle, curled leaves as someone settled onto the cold ground beside him. The flat of their hand hovered against his shoulder, as if unsure whether a familiar touch would help or hurt the situation.

"You had a difficult day." Whisper stated this not as a question, but an irrefutable fact.

Rasp couldn't tell whether his mentor's purposely blank tone was meant to disguise their pity or disgust but, at the moment, he wanted neither. Rasp pulled his arms tighter over his head. "It wouldn't have happened if you'd been there."

"The outcome would've been the same had I been there."

Minus the part about the spontaneous soldier barbecue. "Not helping."

"You made a mistake, little bird. The most you can do is learn from it and move on."

Rasp rolled over and glared at the fae's hazy shape. "That's your advice? Seriously? The only thing I learned was to never trust my magic again!"

Whisper's sigh was deep and heavy. "This is not the first time you have taken a life. I daresay, you're quite experienced at it. Why was this incident any different than the others?"

"Because I cooked two people alive in their armor!"

"You did," Whisper agreed. "And what are you going to do about it?"

". . . Not do it again?"

"Might be a useful skill to harness."

"No!"

"Mortals," Whisper muttered. "I have lived among you for thousands of years and your loose sense of morality is still a mystery. Why is one method of taking a life acceptable over another? The outcome is the same, no?"

"It just is, okay? I don't make the rules."

"You don't follow the rules either."

"Can we change the subject, please?" Rasp gathered his blanket and heaved himself upright. The dimming light suggested the hour was near twilight. A frigid breeze rattled the sprawl of juniper bushes surrounding their makeshift campsite. There would be no fire tonight. The thought made his shivering worse.

Rasp adjusted his tone to something that sounded *almost* like he cared. "How was your day? Did you find what you were looking for?"

"I found the settlement. Whether or not the item I seek is being stored inside is yet to be discovered."

"Good for you."

A stretch of silence passed between them that heavily implied Whisper was trying to murder him with their eyes. Rasp continued to stare into the distance, entirely unaffected.

"We have been traveling for several months together," Whisper said.

"Mhm."

"And not once have you asked *what* it is I'm looking for."

That would require caring. Something Rasp found himself in short supply as of late. "Picked up on that, did you?"

"It is the entire reason I am training you."

While he would've preferred to dance around the subject for the rest of time, some minuscule part of Rasp's brain signaled him to sit straighter. Ever since the events on the mountain, his life had felt aimless. Adrift on an ebbing tide without a purpose other than to do as he was told—go here, do this, stop putting that in your mouth. This information was probably something he needed to know. He hated to admit it, but an even tinier part of him *wanted* to know.

"Is this where you impart a bunch of vague nonsense disguised as wisdom and I just nod my head and act like I know what it means?" Rasp jumped when one of Whisper's quills scraped along his ribcage. What? Just because he wanted to know didn't mean he had to act like it.

"I chose you as my apprentice for a very specific reason, little bird. But in order to understand how it correlates to the item I seek, you must first understand that I am not like you."

The fact that Whisper had quills, didn't eat food, and never had to stop for a piss were all reasons Rasp already knew this to be true. Probably not what his mentor meant though.

"My kind is not brought into existence the same way as yours," Whisper explained. "Fae are not born, but awakened. An excess of magic is required for a youngling to be stirred from stasis. It required the help of three or more fae—an impossible amount of magic by mortal standards, but for us, it was attainable. In order to breathe life into the new, the old had to surrender a piece of themself. The more magic that was given, the stronger the next generation would be."

"Seven realms." Rasp cursed as realization dawned within his hazy thoughts. "This item of yours, it's not an item at all, is it? You're searching for an unborn of your kind."

"Yes. I was away when the mortals declared war on my people. I returned to find my ancestral city ransacked and in ruins. What they didn't take, they destroyed. There was a stasis chamber where the elders kept the unawakened, and when I found it, the door had been ripped away, taking the future of my kind with it. Hidden among the ruins, I found a single unawakened youngling."

Rasp wrinkled his nose. He recalled the day the winds were so strong they knocked the sparrow nests from the trees. That was the first time he'd ever seen an unhatched chick splattered on the ground. The mental image made his stomach churn. "Like, out in the open? All gooey and with no bones?"

"What? No! I told you, it doesn't happen the same. To you, an unawakened would look like a blue pearl."

That was definitely a lot easier on the imagination. "To me, they probably wouldn't look like anything."

"Are you done being a smartass?"

"We both know the answer to that."

There was a soft rattle of quills as Whisper shook their head in futility. "I took the unawakened and carried it with me, hoping one day to reunite with others of my kind and bring about the new generation. Alas, I eventually realized there were no others. I was the last."

Rasp was probably supposed to feel sad about that, which, to be fair, he did. But things were starting to come into focus now and he dared not deviate from his current line of thought for fear of losing it completely. "So you need magic to awaken your egg?"

"Not an egg, but yes."

"Like, a lot of magic."

"Yes, little bird. A lot of magic."

"That's why I'm here!" Rasp said. "You're going to use my magic to help wake up your egg."

"It's not an egg!"

Rasp made a mental note to keep referring to it as an egg whenever possible. "How do you know it's going to work?"

"I don't," Whisper replied grimly. "But you proved yourself capable of awakening magical beings before, as you did with the entity on the mountain. My hope is that with enough time and training, you can learn to do it again."

For the first time in many days, weeks, months even, Rasp's spirit lifted from the depths of its internal tomb. Like the almighty phoenix, from death born anew, his hopes reared to life, lighting a flame within his soul that Rasp had feared he would never feel again. A giddy smile pulled across his clammy lips. "If I give your egg my magic, that means it goes away, right? Doesn't regenerate? No take-backsies?"

No more running for the rest of his life? No more training until his fingertips were raw and blistered? Or accidental soldier barbecue? Oh, how bright the future suddenly looked.

"Little bird, you misunderstand," Whisper said softly. "I will not be taking all of your magic."

Damn it. "Why not?"

"Because you have lived with it your entire life. Whether you like it or not, you have never gone a day without your magic. Taking all of it would be like tossing a fish onto dry land and expecting it to thrive."

"Oh." Rasp's soaring spirits dipped back down, dashing his hopes for the future against the proverbial rocks of reality.

"I see that disappoints you."

"But you can still take some of it, right?" Enough to take the edge off at least? Maybe it wouldn't stop Rasp from being able to light things on fire, but it could downgrade his powers from raging wildfire to controlled burn.

"Yes."

Better than nothing, Rasp supposed.

"So where is it, this unborn egg thingy of yours?" Rasp said, deciding he wasn't going to fixate on the cloud of darkness steadily closing back in around his shriveling soul. He had all night to toss and turn and wallow in self-pity, after all. No sense in starting early. Especially not with Whisper being uncharacteristically forthcoming for a change.

"That is what I am attempting to discover. With any luck, it will be in the settlement."

"Ah," Rasp said, as if he understood. "So you lost it."

"I didn't lose it!"

"Can't find something that's not lost," he countered. "Not to point fingers here, but that was very irresponsible of you. You really should take better care of your babies."

From Whisper's notable silence, Rasp assumed they were debating between hitting him or giving up on the conversation as a whole. He offered a placating smile as a truce. "Alright, I'm done being a smartass. You may continue."

"I told you how I was captured by a powerful witch and forced into servitude?"

Rasp nodded. Even he didn't dare take a jab at that subject. It was Whisper's original master who bound the fae to a powerstone and used it as a means to extort their magic.

"I had the unawakened on me when I was first caught. In that moment, I was left with a difficult choice. I could fight capture with everything I had, knowing that if I failed, it would render my kind extinct. The alternative was to use the last of my strength to disguise the youngling as something innocuous. I chose the latter. Even with the glamour spell, it still produced a faint magical frequency and wound up in a collection headed for the capital."

Great. Now Rasp felt bad for teasing. He rubbed the tip of his elbow to ease some of the queasiness rumbling around the inside of his gut. "Sorry."

"There is no need to apologize. It was long before your time, little bird."

A question gnawed at the edge of Rasp's mind. "This whole time you knew how I felt about my magic, and had a way to rid me of it for good. Why didn't you tell me all of this before?"

"I tried to tell you many times. You didn't listen." Whisper said, "Losing your magic is not something to be taken lightly. Had I offered to remove it sooner, you would have given it without question. I wanted to give you time to learn to use it, to wield it, in case you changed your mind."

"Nope. Still hate it."

"That may change."

Had his attitude toward magic changed? Sure. Rasp now realized the existence of power did not inherently make something good or bad. Good or bad depended on the intentions of the person wielding it. He also recognized that the type of person wielding magic should, by all accounts, not be *him*. Reckless, impulsive, and emotionally unstable were not the cornerstones of a hero, but a monster. Getting rid of his power sounded much easier than having to relearn everything that had gotten him this far.

"What about the infection? It's attached to my magic, isn't it?" Rasp asked. If Whisper used his power to release the unawakened, was it possible that the darkness would infect the youngling as well? What happened when an inexperienced fae, gifted unimaginable power, touched the darkness? Would the evil spirit consume it too, as the entity had its previous victims?

Shit. Had Rasp staved off one apocalypse just to start another?

"The infection will have to be addressed prior to the ritual. You are right to be fearful of what would happen if one of my kind succumbs to evil. But that is a worry for another time. Our first step is to find the unawakened, and then we can seek out how to rid you of the infection."

Whisper's answer was about as comforting as a blanket made from thistles. Suppressing the groan that built in the back of his throat, Rasp dropped face-first into his bedding. He drew the cover over his head and burrowed deeper. He couldn't do anything about the darkness in his veins, or the gnawing guilt that ate at him from the inside. He couldn't even bury the feelings inside of him. Thus, the only logical conclusion was to bury himself deep into his blankets until the warm, dingy air lulled him into a restless sleep.

Once more, Whisper's hand touched his shoulder. "I'm afraid that is not a possibility at the moment. The revolutionists you encountered earlier are not the only ones in the area. They will come looking for us again. And now that they have some idea what they are up against, they will use whatever means possible to capture you alive."

"More running." Rasp's voice came out muffled by the surrounding blankets. "Yay."

CHAPTER THIRTY-FIVE

Ghost Town

A fierce wind howled overhead, rocking the towering forest giants from side to side in a rhythmic sway. Rasp shuddered as he wrapped his cloak tighter over his shivering shoulders and focused on not falling from the mule. Resigned to the saddle, unable to move, his leaden legs had gone numb hours ago. If it weren't for the occasional sharp, stabbing tingle in his toes, he would've sworn his lower limbs had fallen from his body and were slowly rotting away among the ferns some miles back.

Whisper was the only one of the three equipped with night vision. With Bonecrusher's lead in hand, the small fae led the mule through the dark forest, forgoing the use of lanterns entirely. The dark was intentional, as light would have advertised their location to every unsavory group patrolling the area. Thus, they moved among the shadows, creeping along at a pace that would have made the world's slowest snail shed tears of sympathy.

Whisper walked on undeterred. In fact, for someone who was currently on the run, slowly dying from iron poisoning, the fae demonstrated an unusual abundance of energy. Whisper rarely traveled in their true form anymore, opting to spend the time curled in Rasp's hood to preserve their dwindling strength instead. Had Rasp possessed the willpower to turn his sluggish thoughts into comprehensible words, he might have asked about this marked change in behavior.

As he could do little more than cling to the mule swaying beneath him with the remaining strength in his numb hands, he kept the questions to himself. Rasp satiated his growing curiosity in the knowledge that, in due time, the answer would reveal itself. What he wasn't expecting was for the answer to come so soon.

"I do have more energy than normal, little bird," Whisper called from ahead of the mule. "The reason for which I am eager to show you."

Rasp narrowed his eyes in the direction of Whisper's voice. He had no idea whether or not he was glaring at the back of the fae's head, but surely it was the thought that counted. *Stop reading my thoughts. One of these days you're going to come across something real nasty, and I won't be held accountable for it.*

Hop's heavy footsteps slogged alongside Rasp's mule. "I thought the whole point of traveling in the dead of night was to outrun the people following us."

"Our midnight travels can serve multiple purposes," Whisper replied. "We're still moving in the direction of the realm settlement in search of my item, ahead of our new pursuers, as planned. It just happens that I discovered something of great interest earlier, and I wish to share it with you."

Croak. Father's groggy call rang out from above, lacking its usual ear-splitting potency.

"Dad says he found it," Rasp corrected.

Rasp uncurled his stiff left hand from its white-knuckled grip on the saddle and raised it to his shoulder, adjusting his cloak to make room for a feathery passenger. "Come on, old man." He patted his shoulder invitingly. "You've been going all day. Can't have you falling out of any trees from exhaustion."

The mere suggestion of taking a break would ordinarily have caused a fight. Proud Stoneclaw leaders did not take slights to their machoism very lightly, after all. Which meant Father was either growing as a bird-person or, the more likely option, was too worn down to draw blood. His feathers rustled softly as he swooped down from the treetops and landed on Rasp's shoulder.

Rasp grimaced as the raven shifted its weight, talons gripping cloth and flesh alike, until Father achieved a secure roosting position. "Comfortable?" Rasp managed between clenched teeth, making a mental note to trim the bird's damned claws once he regained the full functioning use of his frozen hands.

Croak.

Rasp ignored Father's demand for silence. "Good, good. Now that you're all nice and cozy, showered in my overwhelming filial love, mind telling me where Whisper's taking us?"

"Don't tell him anything," Whisper called from ahead of them. "I want it to be a surprise."

Not that it would have mattered anyway. From the bird's still movements, Rasp was almost certain Father had already fallen asleep. He dared not test his theory by poking the winged beast perched so precariously close to his unprotected face.

Hop issued a full-body sigh. "Could we save the surprise field trip for when we're *not* trying to outrun an enemy?"

"What he said," Rasp agreed.

There was an unmistakable edge of amusement to Whisper's melodic voice. "Neither of you even know where we're going."

It took effort not to scream his next words. "Because you won't tell us!"

"Which, not going to lie, I do find slightly worrisome," Hop added, mumbling under his breath about having read too many stories of wayward travelers being lured into the woods by an overly cheerful fae, never to be seen again.

Whisper cackled with delight, too enthralled with their new game to give up any pesky details—such as where they were going or why, in the seven realms of chaos, they chose now of all times for a surprise detour.

The only way to obtain the information Whisper was currently dangling over their heads would be to play the fae's favorite game of *keep asking questions and maybe I'll get around to an answer eventually*. Rasp was not a fan of this particular pastime, but supposed it would be best to jump right in and get it over with. "Alright, fine, I'll bite. If you're not going to tell us, then at least give me a hint so I can guess."

"Somewhere off the beaten path."

The fact that they were currently traveling through an overgrown forest, woefully lacking any paths to speak of, rendered this clue absolutely useless. Knowing Whisper and their love for equivocation, their vague answer was entirely intentional.

"Straight from the tomes of history, one could say," Whisper continued in a manner that made Rasp want to spur the mule forward with his heels. "Metaphorically speaking, of course. You would be hard-pressed to find very many books on the subject."

Rasp's eyes rolled so far back in his skull that, had he possessed functioning vision, he was certain he would have made eye contact with the inner ghoul responsible for all of his poor life decisions. He imagined the ghoul was rolling their eyes as well. "Whisper," Rasp gritted out, "so help me."

"Exactly, little bird. This short detour is meant to *help* you."

"You know what, just for this, when your little spiky baby is awakened, I'm naming it Egbert."

Whisper prattled off another unhelpful explanation, not deterred, but seemingly fueled by Rasp's growing irritation. "You may not be aware, little bird, but this territory did not always belong to the realm. The people who resided here had their own culture and way of life, some of which was heavily dependent on magic. Unfortunately, the United Territories of the Realm has a long history of cannibalizing other nations, and those who lived here originally fell to its power long ago. All that remains are the ruins of their former cities."

Hop, unlike Rasp, anticipated where Whisper's long-winded explanation was going several steps ahead of schedule. "So you found a ruined city and you're taking us to it, is that what you're getting at?"

"It was more of a village, but yes," Whisper agreed with a grumble, notably perturbed that their fun had run its course so quickly.

Gods help him. As if being dragged along in the middle of the night unable to feel his numb ass in a saddle wasn't torture enough. Afraid he might upset his sleeping passenger, Rasp resisted the urge to throw his hands out from his sides in exasperation. "You're taking us sightseeing?"

"Consider it a history lesson. Learning the past is as important to your training as the rest of it is."

Oh good. Rasp's worries that they were sightseeing just for funsies were immediately put to rest. Learning while taking in sights he literally could not see was *so* much better. "Whisper, in case you've forgotten, we're being followed, remember? This seems like a good way to get caught."

"Not to mention all the ruins out here are supposedly haunted," Hop added.

"Thank you, Hop," Rasp said, struggling to keep his own volume at a level that wouldn't garner unwanted attention. Traveling in pitch darkness, after all, would be for naught if he gave in to the urge to start screaming at the top of his lungs. "I was concerned this random detour couldn't possibly get any worse."

"On the contrary," Whisper replied, still slowly plodding away, leading Bonecrusher along in their wake. "The haunting works in our favor. The ruins are not far from the realm settlement. Between the superstition surrounding the village and the outpost swarming with realm soldiers, our pursuers will be reluctant to follow us into such obvious danger."

So not only was Whisper planning to move them closer to the military settlement crawling with realm soldiers, they intended to stop off at a haunted village along the way. What a perfectly reasonable plan. Not crazy at all. Rasp was so utterly delighted to be under the wing of a perfectly sane mentor.

"So dramatic." Whisper tutted. "You well know a sane mentor would have never taken you on."

"Stay out of my head!"

"For the record," Hop cut in, steering the conversation back on track with an exasperated snort, "I think this is a terrible plan."

"The worst," Rasp agreed.

"We might as well light the lanterns and put bells on at this point."

"Yeah, and take our clothes off while we're at it."

There was a contemplative pause before Hop revealed his thoughts regarding Rasp's contribution to the plan. "That might actually keep unwanted company away."

"So you're in agreement then? Let's do it."

"It's freezing out."

"I thought the whole point was coming up with ways to make Whisper's stupid plan stupider."

"It's not stupid," Whisper insisted with a rattle of their quills. "We are using the enemy's superstition to our advantage by going to a place they will be reluctant to follow."

"Because it's haunted." Rasp didn't exactly believe in ghosts, but it did seem like an important detail to keep bringing up.

"Supposedly haunted," Whisper said. "I can assure you, whatever shadows lurk within the abandoned village pale in comparison to the enemy hot on our trail. You were lucky the resistance members you encountered earlier were so easily caught off guard. That is not a mistake their leader will permit them to make a second time. If they catch up again, they will throw everything they have at us."

Welp, so much for his fun. Along with the reminder of *who* they were running from came the memory of *why* they were running. Rasp shook his head to clear the sudden smell of burnt flesh and hair that clawed up the inside of his nose. In his haste to bury the carnage he'd caused that afternoon deep, deep down out of sight forever, Rasp realized he hadn't bothered to ask about the people currently hunting them.

"You sound like you're familiar with the idiots chasing us, Whisper." Rasp paused, attempting to recall the group's ridiculously overcomplicated name. "They called themselves something really obnoxious. Girls and Boys of Revenge or something."

"The Sons and Daughters of Resistance," Hop corrected.

They had said the same thing, as far as Rasp was concerned.

"I am familiar," Whisper said in the sort of tone that implied it was not an ecstatic familiarity. "They are the magical group formed in opposition to the abuses committed by the Division of Divination on the behalf of the realm. Their leader has been operating within the flatlands for over half a century, waiting for exactly this moment to move in."

Rasp was following so far. "So they're here to dismantle the realm, right?"

"One would assume."

"Wouldn't that make them on our side then? You know, the whole 'the enemy of my enemy makes good bedfellows' or whatever?" Such prevailing wisdom had never applied to Stoneclaws in any meaningful way. Rasp's people took great delight in creating as many enemies as possible and fighting them all at once. Rasp would've thought that Whisper, of all people, would have realized this was a losing strategy. "Because for someone who shares a common enemy, you don't seem all that keen to make their acquaintance."

Granted, cooking two of their members in their armor could very well have been Whisper's sole reason for avoiding the group as a whole, but Rasp wasn't about to bring that up again.

"While the resistance's cause may seem noble on the surface, their end goal is no different, little bird. The Sons and Daughters of Resistance want the same thing the division does—absolute power."

"Oh." It was becoming clearer now. Or so he thought. Maybe it was just the sleep deprivation finally catching up to him.

Whisper's melodic voice carried on the bitter breeze, intermingling with the crisp smells of wet needles and pine sap. "No matter the cause, we would be but tools to those that capture us. Used until there was nothing left to take. Our best course of action is not to get involved at all."

Ah, running from their problems, Rasp concluded, feeling the weight of sleep pull at his heavy eyelids. Finally, a solution he and Whisper agreed upon.

In the distance, muffled by the rattling, rhythmic sway of the forest giants, the faint screech of a raven sounded in the night. Had Rasp not been drifting off to sleep, he might have noticed the way Father's head snapped to attention. Father's feet shifted, tightening his grip on Rasp's shoulder with his sharp talons as he tilted his head, listening for the familiar call.

CHAPTER THIRTY-SIX

Needlessly Dramatic: A Love Language

Rasp drifted in and out of consciousness, jerking alert to catch himself each time his body listed dangerously over one side of the mule. The dark forest canopy blocked out any natural light provided by the moon or stars, obscuring his already finicky sense of time. Rasp didn't know how many hours passed before Bonecrusher's plodding steps came to a stop; he was merely grateful that they'd reached their destination while he still possessed feeling in some of his fingers.

Father stirred to life on Rasp's shoulder with a shake of his feathery head. He stretched his wings, smacking Rasp across the face as he did so, before fluttering away in search of a perch that smelled less like an amalgamation of mule musk and swampy armpits.

Rasp was preparing to slide from the saddle when Hop's steady hand braced against his shoulder. "I think it would be best if you let me assist with this part."

The insult struck like a limp-handed slap. Fresh heat flushed across Rasp's frostbitten face, stinging the tip of his nose. He swatted Hop's hand away with a scoff. "In case you didn't notice, I'm a big boy now. I can dismount all by myself, *Mom.*"

"I only meant—"

"Stand aside, please." Rasp struck a dramatic pose. He held his left hand clenched to his chest and the other outstretched in Hop's direction, keeping the faun at a distance. "Just because I'm blind does not mean I'm helpless."

Hop mustered a halfhearted ear flick, so light Rasp barely heard its leathery snap. "Of course. My apologies. By all means, have at it."

Gripping the saddle with both hands, Rasp swung his right leg over, intending to let gravity do the rest of the work. Unfortunately, this tactic relied on fully functioning legs, and not the gelatinous noodle bits that now constituted his lower extremities. Rasp's numb feet struck the ground and folded uselessly beneath him. He went down with a startled yelp in a flurry of flailing arms, stirring a cloud of frost-encrusted leaves into the air.

"As I was saying," Hop continued pleasantly, "it was your legs, not your vision, I was concerned about. Particularly whether or not the lack of circulation had caused temporary paresthesia. I suppose I have my answer now."

Croak, croak, croak. Father's harsh laughter echoed around them, bouncing between tree and stone.

"Oh, shut up, Dad," Rasp snarled, definitely not embarrassed at all by his sudden and most unexpected reunion with the ground. "You always take Mom's side!"

"If you don't mind, I'm going to ignore everything you're saying and just pick you up now," Hop said as his cloven feet dragged closer, disturbing the piles of curled leaves heaped across the woodland floor. His hand caught Rasp beneath the arm and lifted him from the ground with far more care than he rightfully deserved.

Rasp inhaled sharply as blood rushed to his legs in a surge of pins and needles. "I take it all back, Hopalong," he said between short gasps of breath, clinging to Hop like a helpless baby possum to its mother. "You're an excellent mother. I shouldn't have acted the way I did. I'm sorry."

"Must you make everything so weird?"

"There, there. Compliments are hard to take, I know." Rasp found the side of the faun's face with his hand and gave it a sympathetic pat. "Anyway, now that my pride's been buried, I'm ready to be carried now."

"I'm not carrying you."

Some tender face fondling would be sure to change the stubborn faun's mind, Rasp was certain of it. "Lil horsey-back ride?"

"No."

"Fauney-back ride?"

"Not a thing," Hop assured him as he started to pull, intending for Rasp to fall into step beside him.

"A light dragging it is then." Rasp slid his arm free from the crook of Hop's elbow, willing his body to assume its natural slug form once more. His wobbly knees took their cue and buckled on command, spilling him back toward the ground.

"Rasp." Hop caught him before he got halfway, groaning, "We've been walking all day. I'm exhausted. Do you think we could just get to where we're going without the theatrics for a change?"

"How dare you, sir. You know my love language is needlessly dramatic."

"And here I thought it was because you didn't want to step foot near the haunted ruins of a dead civilization."

Was that the cause for his sudden bout of *I don't want to do this and you can't make me*? How insightful. It was a shame this knowledge didn't do anything to stop the creepy crawly sensation currently skittering up and down his spine. With a plaintive sigh, Rasp reluctantly stood and threaded his arm back through Hop's. "Can't fault me for trying."

"To your credit, it did delay our inevitable deaths by a few minutes." Leading the mule with one hand and with Rasp hanging on to the other, Hop started them off with slow, painstaking steps.

The spongy forest floor gradually shifted to something more solid. Not completely solid, Rasp noted, as his left foot sank ankle-deep into a swampy layer of decomposing foliage. He pulled his tattered boot free with a grunt as he attempted to keep pace with Hop. The rhythmic rustle of the treetops grew faint as the smells of wet stone and moss enveloped them from all sides.

"Is there a reason this is taking so long?" Whisper's voice rang out from up ahead.

"What? Afraid the ancient ruins are going somewhere, Whisper?" Rasp snapped back. Judging from the cavernous echo, he assumed they were near stone structures of some sort. He swiveled his head this way and that, unable to identify anything among the unrelenting darkness. "Alright, give it to me straight," he whispered to Hop. "How haunted is this place?"

"Honestly, I can't see much at all."

"Welcome to my world."

"However, there is . . ." Hop's voice trailed, giving him time to reconsider whatever terrible thing he was about to say. "You know what, never mind. It's fine. We're fine."

The hairs on the back of Rasp's neck stood on end as the crawling beneath his skin doubled. "Um, no. Not never mind. We're in this together, Hoppy. You tell me everything, the good, the bad, and the nightmare fuel."

Their voices echoed as they passed beneath what might have been a stone arc. The musty air was thick with the smell of wet stone and decayed vegetation. "It's just, I've read about places like this before. Kalikose, specifically." Hop anticipated Rasp's next question before he had the chance to put his confusion to words. "Kalikose is another ruined city, the most famous probably, located deep in Yubak territory. Similar circumstances: ancient magic city, supposedly haunted, etcetera. My point is, every journal entry detailed the same strange phenomenon. A feeling, if you will, that everyone who ever visited felt before entering."

"You mean the feeling like something is seriously off and, despite no obvious signs of danger, every muscle in your body is screaming at you to run?" Rasp ventured.

"Precisely."

Rasp clung to Hop's burly forearm as the pair exited the stone arch back out into open air. Dark shadows rose up on either side of them, obscured by the unrelenting dark. He was used to not being able to see anything; that wasn't anything new. What Rasp found truly unnerving was the lack of sound. Forests were rarely silent. The rustle of the wind in the trees, birds, the incessant buzz of insects—all were eerily absent.

"Alright, Whisper," Rasp said. "You've strung us along long enough. What's so special about this place?"

"You can feel it just as strongly as can I, little bird. That tremble beneath your skin? The static in the air? It's downright intoxicating."

"Yeah, not how I'd describe what I'm feeling."

"We are standing in what used to be the village center," Whisper explained. "Look around you. Isn't it marvelous?"

"You know I can't see shit."

"Because you are using the wrong set of eyes. In order to understand why I brought you here, you must rely on your sixth sense. Do as we practiced."

Gods, he was too tired for this shit. Holding back his lashing tongue, Rasp closed his eyes and drew inward for the simple fact that complying was easier than protesting. The shift between planes was subtle. So much so, that when Rasp opened his eyes again, convinced he would see the same unrelenting world of shades and shadows, he nearly keeled over with fright.

Veins of pale white light weaved across the ground in concentric circles, casting the crumbling walls in a ghoulish glow. The shapes moved together as one, coalescing in the middle of the ruined courtyard. A single stone pillar rose up at its epicenter, its chipped exterior carved with intricate runes. The symbols glowed, pulsing in time to the vibration crawling beneath Rasp's skin.

Tearing his gaze from the pillar, Rasp realized his phantom vision was casting the magical auras of his companions as well. Hop's was a dull violet, towering close to six feet in height beside him. Whisper's blue aura was farther away, glowing brighter than Rasp had seen it before. Faint waves of light pulsed from the center pillar, curling into the air and enveloping Whisper's body like wisps of smoke, as though naturally drawn to the fae.

Rasp studied his open palm, fascinated by the yellow glow highlighting his individual fingers. He reached for a passing wisp of magic. It curled around his hand, prickling his skin as it dissipated between his fingers and re-formed its shape, continuing its path back toward the pillar.

"You seeing any of this, Hop?"

"Not a thing."

"The place is crawling with magic." Rasp explained what he was seeing the best he could. He tried to be articulate, but it still came off like a toddler explaining scientific theory to a learned adult. "But it's different looking. Fainter, I guess? Like a ghost magic. Oh, and symbols. Lots of those. They're carved into the ground and seem to be channeling all of the ghost magic toward that pillar in the middle there."

"You're describing a harmony stone." To his credit, Hop actually sounded impressed. Probably with the stone itself and not Rasp's super-descriptive explanation, though. "Most were destroyed during the Great Expansion. It's rare to find one still standing."

Rasp was forever amazed how, even though he and Hop spoke a shared language, he only understood about half of what the faun was saying at any given time.

Whisper, fortunately, could be counted on to help fill the gaps in Rasp's understanding. "The harmony stone is a shrine, constructed using a combination of fae and mortal magic. It served as a representation of the amity that once existed between the two."

Amid the ghoulish white glow, Rasp saw Whisper's silhouette approach the stone. The carved runes sparked blue when Whisper placed their hand to the pillar. "Once upon a time, you could find a harmony stone in every mortal village. The shrines were charmed with healing properties and served as an unspoken invitation for any fae seeking shelter to stop and stay. Helping a weary fae was thought to bring favor to the village."

Rasp turned his head, studying the eerie light that weaved across what remained of the village. Squinting, he could just barely make out a ring of broken stone walls shrouded in moss. "What kind of favor?"

"Plentiful times of harvest, fertility, protection, to name but a few."

"Huh," Rasp said. "Doesn't look like it worked."

"I'm not with him!" Hop stepped backward, allowing for an adequate smiting buffer between him and Rasp. "Just in case anyone or thing listening might care."

"He says, still holding my hand," Rasp remarked flatly.

"Attempting to reconcile that."

"It's too late, Hop. The ghosts already saw. They know we're together."

"I really wish you would be more mindful of phrasing." Despite the faun's commendable attempts, he was unable to shake off Rasp's iron grip. "Seven realms! Why are you only this strong when you're actively trying to endanger my life?"

"Active endangerment is your love language."

"The little bird is not wrong about the effectiveness of the harmony stone." Whisper's shifting blue aura moved away from the glowing pillar toward them, intent on concluding the history lesson regardless of Rasp's lack of participation. "The fate of the mortals who once lived here were intertwined with that of the fae. When my people disappeared, so too did their blessings. For the first time in eons, villages such as this found themselves susceptible to a rapidly changing world. They may have wanted harmony, but their neighbors wanted power. One by one, they fell to the greed of mortal-kind."

Rasp didn't know whether the sudden drop in his spirits was due to the overextension of his magic, his overwhelming weariness, or the lesson itself. Feeling the last dregs of his energy slipping away, he closed his eyes and extinguished his aural vision with a flick of his fingers. "Are all of your history lessons going to be this depressing?"

"It wasn't all depressing," Hop countered. "The part about the harmony stone was interesting."

"Yeah, right up until everyone died for putting their trust in a hunk of rock."

"We have barely scratched the surface," Whisper assured Rasp. "One day, when you are ready, I will tell you of the original gift of magic and how spectacularly that failed."

The mere thought made his knees wobble in protest. There was only so much depressing history one could cram inside their aching skull before bedtime. "Not tonight though, right? Haunted or not, the ground is starting to look awful comfy."

"Yes, yes. Make your bed. We will camp here tonight."

"Yay," Hop murmured weakly under his breath as he turned to unsaddle the mule standing dutifully behind them. "Haunted sleepover."

CHAPTER THIRTY-SEVEN

The Gift of Magic

Rasp was having the loveliest dream of charred snake on a stick, with skin so crispy it shattered in his mouth. There was hot capsicum dipping sauce and serpent bones so tender they disintegrated to gelatinous goop after the third chew. Rasp was preparing to sink his teeth into another when the snake reared back and struck its fangs into his face. He screamed, throwing up his hands to ward it off as a second and third strike rained down upon his unprotected head.

Croak!

A fourth strike came with the realization that it was not a serpent attacking him. Rasp rolled away from his feathery assailant, pulling his blanket over his head. "Oh come on, old man! I hadn't gotten to the dessert yet."

Father yanked Rasp's covers away, tsking his irritation.

"Yes, I'm awake," Rasp assured him, heavy eyelids already drooping.

The large raven spoke in hushed gurgles and clicks, upsetting the loose piles of curled leaves heaped around them between nervous hops and flutters.

Rasp nodded along, absentmindedly, as his consciousness slipped back into another confusing dream. A harsh peck to the scalp startled him awake again. "Ah!" He clutched the top of his head, grateful he didn't feel the warm trickle of blood. "Will you stop that? There was a noise in the night and you're going to go investigate, I heard you."

Father was an independent spirit. He didn't normally share such details unless they were pertinent. Try as he might, Rasp simply couldn't muster the tone that demonstrated both his appreciation and attentiveness to the seriousness at hand. The trouble with relying too heavily on sarcasm was that, after a certain point, his responses all started to sound the same, regardless of his better intentions. "Yeah, I get it. It's important. I doubt you would have stabbed me awake if it wasn't."

Coming off like an asshole here, buddy.

Rasp dropped his head with a sigh. Unfortunately, the only alternative to sarcasm he could come up with was to speak slowly, with great, methodical care. To Rasp's annoyance, his efforts sounded somehow more sarcastic. "Thank you for telling me this super important information so early in the morning, Father. Go. Do what you must. I will eagerly await your return."

Father snapped his beak, unamused.

"Try not to get eaten by a bear while you're at it, alright?"

With an exasperated croak, Father's clawed feet pitter-pattered against the cold ground as he hopped away.

"I was being serious!" Rasp rose into a sitting position, rubbing his weary eyelids with the back of his hand. As usual, the most important sentiments to say were also the most difficult to put words to. "You're the last family I have. I never thought I'd say this, but I think I might actually be sad if something happened to you."

Unlike that time Rasp accidentally killed him. No sense in dredging up the past, of course.

With the raven equivalent of a gag, Father took to the crisp air with several mighty flaps of his powerful wings. Naturally, the bastard waited to screech his heartfelt goodbyes until he was soaring off between the trees, already at a distance too far to catch Rasp's ensuing response, had he chosen to make one.

Stupid, mushy bird, Rasp thought as a slow smile split across his clammy face. *The afterlife has made you soft.*

So good to see the two of you not at each other's throats for a change.

Rasp's shoulders went rigid as the smile slipped from his face. *Gods, Whisper! Were you eavesdropping on our private conversation this whole time?*

"Private" would imply you had learned the art of whispered conversation, little bird. I assure you, what I overheard was not that.

Rasp closed his eyes and challenged his concentration inward. His magic responded faster than usual. Stronger, too. A detail he attributed to the supposed healing properties of the harmony stone as he was too groggy to come up with an alternative explanation. He opened his eyes, wincing as his vision filled with the ghostly glow of the charmed rune symbols. The ripples of magic were there as they had been the night before, currently clustered around the small, hazy blue shape seated against the stone pillar at the center of the decrepit courtyard.

Perhaps it was the fae's slumped posture, or the way their words lacked their usual prickliness, but, whatever the case, Rasp found himself doing the unthinkable. Instead of flopping back down to catch a few more hours of precious sleep, he gathered his bedding and rose onto stiff, aching legs. He followed the veins of pulsing magic, feet barely lifting from the ground as he dragged them along, one in front of the other, until he reached the pillar.

It couldn't have been more than several yards at most, but he dropped down beside Whisper, grateful to not have to use his legs any more nonetheless. Rasp pressed his shoulders against the solid stone and eased his eyes shut. The phantom images disappeared from his vision as the haze of darkness assumed its customary place.

Whisper certainly had an odd way of expressing their gratitude for Rasp's generous company. "You're supposed to be resting."

"I'm not supposed to feel sorry for you, either. But you know what they say, delirium works in mysterious ways."

"No one says that. It doesn't even make sense."

"Neither does feeling sorry for you."

Whisper shuddered, quills rattling from the effort. "Spare me your misplaced sympathies."

"You know, I'm used to you being a prickly bastard." Rasp resisted the urge to jab the fae in the ribs with the tip of his elbow for fear of getting spined by Whisper's toxic quills. He settled for a shit-eating grin instead. "But you seem sadder than usual. You were all taunts last night. What changed? Did the harmony stone stop working its magic on you?"

"On the contrary, I feel better than I have in many moons." Several seconds of uninterrupted staring convinced the fae to be more forthcoming. Whisper relented with a sigh. "You were not wrong about ghosts existing in places such as this. It is memories, not spirits, however, that haunt me."

Rasp gnawed the edge of his lip as he considered Whisper's answer. "Memories of what?"

"The before." Whisper's clawed fingertips tapped against the stone, producing faint clicks. "The world has changed so much since the second generation of magic. Sometimes I barely recognize it. Time works differently in places like this. It gets trapped, straddling the line between past and present, preserving a sliver of what once was."

Rasp wondered if his mentor purposely said things he had no way of understanding as a means to get him to ask questions. Which, upon greater reflection, could not possibly have been the case. Whisper hated answering questions nearly as much as they loathed providing non-vague answers.

"The second generation of magic refers to the emergence of fae, little bird."

Rasp frowned, vowing to start picturing everyone naked if only to keep the meddlesome fae from gleaning his thoughts.

You do that already. It has yet to stop me.

"Moving on." Rasp decided it wasn't a topic either of them wanted to dwell on any longer than necessary. He trawled the limited depths of past history lessons as to why this term sounded familiar. "The second generation of magic was around the time you popped into existence then, yeah?"

"Yes."

"Gods, you're old. Like *really* old. It's got to be tough, though. I can't imagine living all those years, thousands upon thousands, just to waste the precious few you have left with me."

Whisper did the sensible thing and ignored the dig. "I'm not sure where you're going with this, but yes. I was there to witness it all. The death of the old ones, the time of fae, the emergence of mortal-kind, and the poor decisions that led to them becoming the dominant life-forms."

Rasp tucked the edges of the blanket beneath him as he slumped lower. He rested his head against the mossy stone and closed his eyes. "Tell me about it."

"Since when do you care to learn anything?"

"It's this place. Too spooky to sleep. I need something really tedious to put me out."

"In that case, I had better start at the very beginning. The birth of magic."

Rasp nodded his approval, stifling a yawn with his hand. "Perfect. I can feel the boredom setting in already."

Whisper's words flowed over Rasp's mind like water across silk. "There have been three generations since the birth of magic. The old ones, great beings of unimaginable might, were the first. When the magic of the new world dwindled, so too did the old ones, giving way to the time of fae. As our corporeal forms were smaller, we did not require as much magic to sustain life, thus allowing us to exist far longer than our predecessors.

"Mortal-kind was the third generation. But, by the time the first elves walked the land, the spark of the new world had dimmed. Mortals were cursed to live an existence without magic. For many millennia, we fae existed beside our non-magical brethren, watching as they struggled to carve out an existence built upon unimaginable hardship. My people took pity on them and bestowed the first mortal with magic. It was a gift meant to be passed down from one generation to the next."

Whisper paused before saying, "The first mortal ever gifted magic was a human. Did you know that?"

Rasp spoke with his eyes closed. "Of course. They put it in the manual we humans are issued at birth. It's right up there with the meaning of life and how to flip a bloody pancake."

"Humans were the most pitiful of all mortals."

"*Thanks.*"

"They were not strong like orcs, skilled like dwarfs, nor clever like elves. Their meager lives were short, even by mortal standards. Destined to spend the few years they had clinging to survival and barely managing that."

"Okay, now you're just being insulting."

"That's just it. I *was* insulted," Whisper said, their melodic voice taking on an unusually hollow ring. "My people were stewards of the land, gifted with abilities beyond imagination. I didn't understand why anyone would risk surrendering the most important piece of themselves to an inferior species."

Rasp waited for the eventual "but." For whatever reason, it never came. "I'm starting to get the feeling you didn't have a change of mind."

"My views on mortals may have softened since then, but I abide by my original stance. It was a fool's errand, mortal-kind would only take advantage. But my people were too blinded with their own good intentions to realize their folly. They gave anyway, selflessly, teaching the humans how to harness magic to enrich their meager lives. All was well at first. The humans were grateful for the gift they had been granted and treated it with great reverence, passing their magic on from one generation to the next. Their numbers increased, as a result, and it was not long before the human population swept across the land, spreading tales of the gift of magic as they went.

"Others species learned of the gift and grew envious of the favor bestowed upon humankind. They sought us out, asking for similar treatment. My people were accommodating, at first. But it was only a matter of time before the asking turned to demanding. Soon, what power the mortals had been granted was no longer enough. In their quest for might, the ungrateful mortals turned on the fae, stealing their magic by any means necessary."

It was Rasp's turn to voice his displeasure through the use of unintelligible sound. "Ugh."

"My thoughts exactly."

"I honestly don't know what to say to any of that."

"Then say nothing. Sit in the uncomfortability of truth, and vow to remember. There is nothing we can do to change the past. We can only strive to do better."

Rasp placed his hand on what he hoped was Whisper's shoulder, realizing he had something to contribute after all. "I vow to find a way to give you the happy ending you deserve."

And, in a mere matter of words, they were right back where they'd started. To his credit, Rasp hadn't meant to make an inappropriate joke. Words just had a funny way of coming out of his mouth and arranging themselves in the worst way possible. Worse yet, judging from the weird numbness spreading within his hand, Rasp now realized he must have accidentally pricked himself on one of Whisper's quills.

Heat flooded up his arm as his bones turned weightless. Drool dribbled from his bottom lip as he managed a single word of regret. "Shit."

"Rest well, little bird." Whisper's voice sounded far away, nearly lost to the distance. "You will undoubtedly need it."

The muscles propping Rasp up against the harmony stone went slack. Slowly, as if caught in slow motion, he listed to the side and struck the ground, too numb to feel the resulting pain. Reality disintegrated piece by piece before his mind went dark. A warmth flooded his bones, pulsing in time to the magic thrumming from the harmony stone beside him.

When his heavy eyes opened again, still steadily crossing from one plane of reality into the next, Rasp found himself slumped over a familiar table, in a familiar room, with sunlight pouring in from the kitchen window. The heavenly aroma of sweet plums, buttery crust, and thyme clouded the balmy air. Happiness erupted within his rapidly beating chest when Rasp recognized where the dream had delivered him.

An unfamiliar voice beckoned. It was tender and soft, as inviting as a mother's embrace. All of Rasp's troubles faded as the soothing words, pulsing in time to the magic from the harmony stone, rippled across his weary mind. **Hello, little one. I've waited for you for so long. Hurry now. It's not far. You're almost home.**

CHAPTER THIRTY-EIGHT

Earning Your Lumps

Daana hardly noticed the heaving ocean swell after the fourth day at sea. She'd heard the phenomenon referred to as "sea legs" before, and was secretly pleased that hers had come in rather naturally. The same could not be said for Snag, who spent most of his time bent over the railing, feeding the fishes, as Ellisar lovingly called it.

Regardless of her newfound ability to walk the ship like a seasoned sailor, Daana was still nowhere near the level of either Ashwyn or Ellisar. They took to it like ducks to water. Unfortunately, this meant that Ashwyn gave no quarter when it came to Daana's training, either. The orc didn't care about the height of the swell or the fact that there was a limited area to train her pupil; she made do no matter the circumstances.

Ashwyn convinced the captain to allow her to use a section of the top deck each afternoon for rigorous training sessions. It hadn't been so bad at first, back when the lessons were relatively easy and there wasn't an eager crowd gathered around to watch. Alas, as Daana's lessons progressed, she found herself not only challenged, but under the scrutiny of an unhelpful audience as well. Off-duty crewmembers lined the rails and rigging, eager for a show.

"Alright, Peaches. We're not finished until you've proved that you learned something. Come at me again, and I mean with gusto this time!"

Daana adjusted her grip on the shortsword in her hand and heaved her shield back into position. These were not the wooden replicas she'd seen the cadets use in training yard at Sunstorn. The sword and shield were real, dangerous, and miserably heavy. Ashwyn insisted that the best way to learn was to use the real thing. Real bruises were a heavily used portion of her training sessions, too.

With a gargled sound caught somewhere between a scream and groan, Daana rushed her trainer. She swung her blade only to have it met by a lackadaisical block from Ashwyn. Undeterred, Daana pivoted, ever mindful of her footing, and cut the air once, twice, three times, before she was swept off her feet with a simple kick. The crowd cheered, happy as always to have a show.

Daana closed her eyes and rested her head against the oiled deck. Just as she thought she was starting to get the hang of something, Ashwyn would insert something new. It was always two steps forward, one painful step backward. Over, and over, and over again.

"You weren't watching your distance." Ashwyn's cheery voice called from above her. "Come on, get up. Let's go at it again."

"That wasn't fair."

"Of course it's not fair. The next soldier you face off with, do you suppose they're going to go easy on you just because you're pretty? At least the lumps I'm giving you aren't deadly."

Daana refused to stand. What did it matter? She'd wind up back on the ground in a matter of seconds anyway. "The definition of insanity is doing the same thing over and over again, expecting different results. That's what we are doing here."

"Nonsense. I've given three different wallops today, and each time, you learned how to avoid it."

"Just to turn around and wallop me some other way!"

"And one day, Peaches, I will have run out of wallops to give you and you will be trained."

"No thank you." Daana had come to accept that, like anything, she'd be terrible at her training from the start. Truth be told, Ashwyn's wallops weren't even that bad. It was the taunting audience that discouraged her the most. "I think I'll just stay down here a bit longer."

A shadow slid down from the rigging and landed lightly on the deck between them. "Actually," Ellisar said, hands on her hips, "she has a point."

The elf's frilly dress and sharp waistcoat had been traded for the practicality of trousers and a loose fitted tunic top. Ellisar would have added a sword—multiple swords, in fact, had she gotten her way—but Snag and Ashwyn insisted it might be safer for everyone if she didn't. The salty sea air was causing her to act strangely. More strangely, at least, which seemed to have the other two worried.

"Have you been drinking saltwater again, miss?" A taunting smile drew across Ashwyn's mouth. "Since when are you in agreement with our dear secretary over, frankly, anything?"

"You're training her like she's an orc," Ellisar pointed out. "No matter how many times you wallop her, she's never going to be able to beat your size or strength. She's an elf. She needs to learn how to fight like one."

"Is this your offer to take over the training then?"

Ellisar snapped the sword from Daana's grasp and checked its balance in the palm of her hand. She approached Ashwyn, twirling the blade, unafraid. "Maybe if she sees the right way to take down a stronger opponent, she can sleep tonight with a few less broken ribs."

"It's about fucking time." Ashwyn lowered into an eager crouch. "I've been waiting all week for you to throw your weight around."

Daana scrambled to her feet and sought the railing, wedging herself between two sun-crusted sailors. Wordlessly, the human to her left offered a flask and Daana took it without question. She would have preferred water, but the warm bite of grog at least helped wash away the copper taste of blood from her mouth. Daana passed the flask back, noting the mood of the audience had changed. The off-duty crew members sat straighter, as if they too sensed they were about to witness something memorable.

Ellisar wasted no time with theatrics. A split second later, her lithe form was across the deck and inside Ashwyn's guard. The blade of the shortsword cast off glimmers of refracted sunlight as it weaved in and out with dizzying speed. Ashwyn allowed her shield to weather most of the attack as she lurched forward, pushing Ellisar into a retreat. Just as she got the elf maneuvered into a more favorable position, Ellisar was gone, having slipped from range with surefooted ease.

They went at it like this for several turns. Ellisar on the offense, forcing Ashwyn to play defense. Each time Ashwyn attempted to breach Ellisar's guard or pin her into a corner, Ellisar would move again. Gradually, Ashwyn's steady blocks grew slower. Her feet didn't shift as quickly as before and the shield started to dip.

Ellisar retreated several paces, calling to Daana without lifting her eyes from her opponent. "You will never match an orc in size or strength. The only way to gain ground is to use their weaknesses to your advantage. We may be smaller, but we're faster too. Don't waste your time trading strokes looking to land a fatal blow. Your objective is to strike over and over, in and out, dodging retaliation at every opportunity."

She lunged, dodging a swing from Ashwyn's sword, and retaliated with one of her own. Sidestepping, one foot over the other, Ellisar weaved around her opponent, managing to sneak in several strikes before retreating once more. "But speed is only half the battle. If you want to win, then you have to wear your opponent down. An angry fighter makes more mistakes. Don't be afraid to piss them off. Throw in whatever cheap shots you can get away with."

To demonstrate, Ellisar closed the gap, ducked, rolled, and came up behind her wife. A kick to the back of Ashwyn's knee sent the orc spilling forward. Ashwyn came back up snarling. She pivoted around, swung her sword in a wide arc, but found nothing but empty space. Realizing her error, Ashwyn turned and raised her shield in time to block the blow from Ellisar's sword. Little by little, the attacks ate at Ashwyn's stamina. She eventually stopped attempting blows of her own and used her sword and shield to prevent the mounting assault from hitting anything vital. Ellisar managed to send her off-balance several more times. By the fifth fall, Ashwyn conceded the fight with the tip of Ellisar's sword pressed to her exposed throat.

Through the sweat rolling from her brow, Ashwyn's dark gray eyes held Ellisar's stare without flinching. Daana didn't see anger, not even a thread of shame. If she didn't know better, she would have sworn the orc looked . . . hungry? Surely that wasn't the right word. Still, there was an unmistakable glimmer of desire etched across Ashwyn's weary face.

"It's incredible to think I used to be able to keep up with you," she panted.

"No, I was slowing down for you back then too."

"Then I guess I'm not obligated to fight fair." Quick as a viper, the orc knocked the sword from Ellisar's grasp and lunged, catching her wife around the knees. Ellisar went down with an awkward squawk. She flailed, using the points of her elbows and knees to break Ashwyn's crushing grip. They rolled to a stop, with Ashwyn on top, using her weight to pin the struggling elf beneath her.

"Get the fuck off me!"

Ashwyn leaned forward and whispered just low enough for Daana's ears to catch, "You use that language with me again, miss, and I will not hesitate to dole out your demerits right here."

Ellisar's already flushed face turned a shade pinker. Her furtive struggling ceased almost instantly.

The orc's mouth twisted to the side disapprovingly. "No? What happened to your sense of adventure?"

Ellisar's mouth parted, but before any words could escape, something solid rapped against the wooden deck, drawing every eye. Snag stood at the front of the main cabin, leaning heavily on his ornate walking stick. "Will the bodyguard please release my business partner?"

Ashwyn rolled obediently to her feet. "Yes, sir. Sorry, sir."

Most of the audience suddenly realized they had something more pressing to attend to and scattered, leaving the deck mostly empty. Snag stalked toward Daana, his left leg dragging just enough to be noticeable. He rested against the splintered railing and rolled his head backward. "Thought you were supposed to be the one getting your ass beat."

"Oh come on!" Daana protested, fists curled in exasperation. "It was just getting good. I've never seen anyone catch Ellisar off guard before."

The start of a knowing smile threatened to pull across Snag's mouth. "Don't act upset about the lesson. You just want to know what a demerit is."

CHAPTER THIRTY-NINE

Icky-Sticky Sentiments

Ellisar retired to the cabin after the training session. Ashwyn stayed on deck, attempting to stay in character or, at the very least, make it less obvious that she planned to follow and commit some form of war crime in the name of romance. The orc lounged against the splintered railing, trading friendly conversation with Snag and Daana. Despite Ashwyn's efforts, the impatient shake in her leg was giving away the fact that she wanted to be elsewhere.

Snag, having come to the same conclusion as Daana, took great pleasure in extending the orc's misery for as long as she'd let him. He asked questions, contributed enthusiastic replies consisting of more than one word and not just a harsh look, all while acting truly engaged in small talk—an activity he normally avoided like the spotted plague.

"So let me get this right." Snag didn't hide the shit-eating grin split across his weathered face. "You're saying heat *and* salinity affect an ocean's current?"

"Yep. Not just wind, like most land walkers think."

"Fascinating. Truly, truly fascinating."

A gray blanket of fog stretched around them, obscuring anything more than a few yards away. Daana couldn't remember the last time she'd glimpsed the sky. While she may have been on the open ocean, with nothing but miles of rolling waves from one horizon to the next, she felt trapped, like a porcelain figure stuck inside of a swirling snow globe. She kept waiting, days upon days, for the oppressing fog to lift, but it never did.

Ashwyn seemed utterly unfazed by the drab weather. The orc tilted her head at Snag, awarding him the mother of all side-eye glances. "Mate, no offense, but I know you don't give a rat's ass about ocean currents."

Snag's needled grin stretched wider. "You're right. I don't. But I do enjoy putting a damper in Ellisar's day from a safe distance, when I can."

Ashwyn's fingers drummed against the wooden railing. "You think enough time has passed? It won't look suspicious if I mosey on up to the cabin?"

"No, not at all. The crew would be silly to suspect something going on between my bodyguard and business partner. It's not like you two were clambering on top of each other with a deck full of sailors watching, 'bout ready to tear your clothes off."

"Sorry. I can't help it. I try to show more restraint, but when it comes to Ellie, she's like . . ." Ashwyn curled her hand into a fist as she considered the most poetic way to describe her lover. "A set of cooking tongs."

Daana lifted her eyebrow. "Cooking tongs?"

"No matter how many times you've clacked those fuckers together, the moment they're in your hand again, you're compelled to give 'em a snap. It's irresistible."

Snag nodded his understanding, long ears bobbing behind him with a jingle. "You should put that in a romantic letter. Preserve it for all of time. Women love being compared to kitchen implements, so I've heard."

"Eh, we can't all be wordsmiths. Being handsy has served me better anyways."

"Gross," Daana muttered.

Unlike Daana, Snag wasn't done poking the proverbial bear yet. "What kind of tongs, specifically, are we talking about here? Iron? Bronze? I feel like we're missing some important context."

"Alright, if you two are done having your fun, I'd like to go rejoin my missus before she starts crawling up the walls like a cat in heat."

"Double gross," Daana said. Especially considering they shared a cabin. It was better for her peace of mind if she didn't know what sort of terrible things the pair got up to during their romantic couplings.

Snag shooed Ashwyn off with a wave of his clawed hand. "Fine, go. And lock the fucking door this time, will ya? I don't think my poor eyes can handle another scarring like that last one."

"You won't mention the tongs thing to Ellie, right? It's sort of an analogy in progress." Ashwyn swaggered off at a speed that was a little too fast to be convincing. She called one last thing over her shoulder. "Oh, and don't come knocking for at least an hour. Else you are definitely going to get scarred again."

"You've got half that." Snag's yellow eyes slowly roved in Daana's direction. His tone dropped menacingly. "Should be all the time we need to get this ugly business over with."

Daana's spine straightened under the weight of his unrelenting glare. *Crap.*

The last four days had been tense between them. The few times Daana attempted to strike up a conversation with Snag, he'd give noncommittal, one-word answers. She gave up eventually, resigned to the knowledge that he would come around on his own when he was ready. In the meantime, she'd reluctantly accepted that Snag's refusal to look her in the eye was his personal way of showing she had yet to regain his favor.

Shame gnawed at her internal organs until her insides felt as though they had twisted into one giant, slippery knot. Daana tried to apologize. Many, many times, in fact, but it didn't make things better between them. Alas, all she could do was wait for Snag to come around on his own. A prospect that, until now, Daana was starting to fear would never come.

It wouldn't be long before they reached land. Another week or so after that and she'd be in the flatlands with her mother. Snag wouldn't have any reason to stick around then. Daana had held out hope that they would reconcile before his parting. After four torturous days of the silent treatment, it seemed their moment had finally come. At least she hoped so. Admittedly, a part of her feared whatever Snag was going to say next would hurt infinitely worse than silence. The thought of being disowned was a prospect that lurked along the edges of Daana's mind, steadily gnawing away at what little self-confidence she had.

"Dear gods, girl, your face. If you're going to chum, do me a favor and do it in the water." Snag shuddered. "Otherwise the smell's going to get me going too. Frankly, I don't think I have anything left in me. Not that I'm eager to test that theory."

Daana's heart raced with a runaway gallop. Here it was, her final chance to make everything right again. And, if she couldn't manage that, then at least she could get it off her chest. "Snag, I—"

"Nope. I'm doing the talking here, not you."

"Oh." Daana wasn't sure if that was a good sign or not. Regardless, she waited, for what felt like ages.

Snag wasn't in much of a hurry. He stood against the railing, bundled in several layers of clothing, looking greener in the face than someone with green skin ought to. His collar was pulled all the way up around his neck and his head was bent against the wind. The only demonstrable sign of life was his eyes, which flickered back and forth across the ship, taking in every passing detail.

"I've been thinking about you and this incessant need to use magic, and I realized something. No matter what I say, you're going to do it again."

"No," Daana objected. "I swear. I said I wouldn't. I—"

"Would you let me finish?" He held up one gnarled hand, staying the flow of words from her open mouth. Snag's gaze drifted away, unwilling to make eye contact for more than a second. "Like I said, I had time to think about it. Not only are you going to do it again, but I realized it'd be unfair to expect anything different. Don't get me wrong, keeping the armlets was still stupid. Like really stupid."

Daana winced, hoping there would be more to his words than a laundry list of all the many, many ways she was stupid.

"You may not be a witch, but magic is what you do. It's a part of what you are. And it wasn't right of me to try to force you to be something you're not. Even if I don't understand it, this whole magic nonsense is what makes you *you*."

She didn't know what to say to that. From Snag's uneasy stance, appearing as though he was considering jumping overboard, Daana decided perhaps it would be best not to say anything at all.

"It's just," Snag said as his narrow shoulders slumped lower, "be smarter about it, will you? Don't pull magic unless you absolutely have to. At least not until we get you to your mom and she can tell us how to fix it, yeah?"

Biting her lip to keep from saying something really stupid, Daana managed a nod.

"I'm sorry I acted how I did. You owned your mistake and you've been trying to make it up to me in your own weird way, but I just . . ." Words failed him. Snag took a shaky breath and held it, before releasing it as a hiss through tightly clenched teeth. "It's one thing to watch it happen outside of your control, but to see someone willfully endanger their life because they're not using their brain, it's downright maddening."

"I'm sorry."

"I know. And me too." Another stretch of silence ticked by before Snag unclenched his teeth with a sigh. "Losing Curly hurt in ways I didn't think an old toad like me was capable of feeling. I don't ever want to ever go through that again. So, if you could, maybe don't put me right back in that same situation? Don't make me watch you poison yourself piece by piece?"

A lump formed in Daana's throat. The pain she'd been ignoring since the mountain, an ever-present weight that lingered deep in the pit of her soul, flared to life once more. Memories of Curly threatened to overtake her senses.

Not the time or the place. She winced, willing the thoughts back down. *Stay focused, dammit!*

Snag's irritated stare took her in before it swept back across the foggy deck. "I prefer not to feel things. Especially not the icky-sticky sentiments your dumb face gives me."

Daana fought the urge to start running the rail-to-rail deck sprints Ashwyn made her carry out every morning. Her sore body, thankfully, protested the very idea. Thus, Daana stood stock still with her arms pulled tight to her chest instead, forced to feel all of her own icky-sticky sentiments bubbling up inside of her. Of all the ways she'd envisioned their reconciliation to go, she hadn't expected it to end so endearingly.

"Snag?" she said, once the lump in her throat had eased a little.

The goblin's response came in the form of a disgusted grunt.

Daana took it as the go-ahead to speak. "Can I hug you?"

"Absolutely fucking not."

"Then can I say something . . . vulnerable?"

"Save it for your mother, girl."

Daana said it anyway, even though she suspected that deep, deep down, Snag already knew. "If I had a father, I'd want him to be just like you."

"That's it!" Snag threw a single, clawed finger into the air as he shoved away from the splintered railing. "Where's that damned plank Ellisar's always going on about? I'm ready to walk it."

CHAPTER FORTY

Eerie Quiet

The chirps and warbles of early morning birdsong rang out around her. Oralia found the sounds of the forest soothing. Out here, the birdsong was light and harmonious, capable of blending seamlessly into the background, barely noticeable at all. Not like at the capital, where the awful screeching of palace peacocks used to rouse her from her sleep every morning.

The surrounding harmony, alas, did not apply to Rali. "And another thing," the dwarf said, throwing her forefinger into the air for what had to have been the twentieth time so far. "Don't go waltzing into obvious danger, you hear? Stay alert. Keep your eyes and ears peeled for any bandits and if you come across any, you don't fight, you run."

"Since when did you become my mother?" Oralia demanded.

"Don't you use that tone with me, young lady!"

The pair stood along the edge of their makeshift camp. Calling it a camp was actually quite generous. The surrounding patch of forest was nothing more than a bit of semi-flat ground, free of widow-makers, with enough room to throw the bedrolls down to catch a few hours of sleep. Ever since their near encounter with bandits two days before, Oralia had kept her party ready to move at a moment's notice.

Having traveled throughout the night, the group had stopped to make camp only that morning. To the dismay of the wearier members, Oralia didn't intend to linger much longer, either. The traveling party would be on the move again once everyone had had a chance to catch a few hours of sleep. In the meantime, while the second shift took their well-earned rest, there were chores to be done.

A low humming alerted Oralia to the fact that Rali was still talking. The dwarf was in full lecture mode, listing off all manner of bizarre safety concerns. "Additionally, you are forbidden from speaking to any bandits, joining any bandit gangs, frolicking with and or befriending them. Got all that, missy?"

Oralia massaged her aching temples with a sigh. "If you are this concerned for my welfare, you could take the waterskins down to the stream yourself."

"Gods no. We drew lots fair and square and you lost. I'm just doing my part to make sure you come back, is all. Sascha would be an absolute mess if anything happened to you." Rali pouted, as if the thought was simply too painful to consider. "What would I do then, Oralia? Who would cook for me? We'd all perish within the week of starvation."

"A real tragedy," Oralia agreed.

"Alright, I suppose you ought to be off if you intend to make it back by lunch. You remember the way, right?"

"If I pretend otherwise, will you hold my hand and lead me to the stream yourself?"

A merciless grin spread across Rali's face. "That's my big girl. Sassy, just like her momma. Of course you remember the way. Just straight on through the trees until you've hit water. If you don't hit water, you've gone too far. That, or you haven't gone far enough. You'll figure it out."

"You truly missed your calling as a scout, Ralizak," Oralia said as she started to turn away.

"Hold on, what about all the hugs and kisses for the road, eh?"

"Goodbye." Oralia threw the stack of empty waterskins over her shoulder and started for the trees. She almost made it all the way out of camp before a voice called after.

"Wait up, boss. I'm coming, too."

The third voice was like sandpaper to the insides of her ears. Grudgingly, Oralia glanced over her shoulder to find Kalihn scurrying after her. The elf was performing a sort of awkward, heaving scramble in order to keep pace. She carried a large iron pot, gripping the handle as though her life depended on it. Kalihn's knuckles were already white and drained of blood from the effort. To be fair, the blasted pot probably weighed nearly as much as she did.

To be less fair, she'd barely made it ten paces from the center camp.

"What are you doing?" Oralia did not bother to cloak the irritation in her tone.

"Orders from the cook," Kalihn explained. "Sascha said we needed extra water for boiling. Also, he mentioned that I shouldn't let you out of my sight for even a second."

Oralia's gaze swept past Kalihn over to Sascha's prep station. He already had a hole dug out for a fire, and was in the process of shaping the sides with stones. There was a heap of kindling and larger branches piled nearby, ready to light once the pit was finished. The low-burning fire would be ready and waiting to boil the water once Oralia and Kalihn returned from the stream.

Sascha noticed her glaring and blew a kiss in her direction, quite pleased with the trick he'd just played. *Rat bastard.*

Oralia vowed to find a creative means to get even with him. While Kalihn meant well, she talked entirely too much for even the nicest soul to tolerate for more than a few hours at a time. Oralia was not a nice soul. Her tolerance, therefore, was even shorter. Barely holding on by a thread.

Sascha's clever move was something of a two-for-one scenario. Not only had he successfully relieved himself of Kalihn's help but, by sending the elf with Oralia, he was simultaneously ensuring his precious pot returned as well. Perhaps even with water in it. The fact that the errand served to annoy his fuckmate was simply an added benefit.

Oralia's unamused stare returned to Kalihn. "Will you be able to carry that the whole way?"

"I think I'm managing all right so far." Kalihn seemed unaware that she had her tongue sticking out of one side of her mouth from the sheer exertion of walking from the firepit to the edge of camp.

"Filled with water?" Oralia asked.

"Uh . . ."

On second thought, perhaps it was best not to give Kalihn false hope that Oralia would carry the pot the moment it proved too cumbersome. The orc turned and started off into the trees. "Excellent. Glad to see you have it handled."

The surrounding forest was a mix of red alders, white oaks, and pines. Unlike the northernmost areas along the Iron Ridge, the ground covering here was thick and invasive. Even the areas of the forest untouched by sunlight were next to impossible to navigate with surefooted ease. Bramble and bracken intertwined across the woodland floor in a thick, tangled weave of thorny vines. The smell of wormwood was thick in the air as Oralia picked her way through the woods with painstaking care.

Oralia's team had been on the move for two days. Their efforts, fortunately, were proving fruitful. Lingon and Dewpetal had backtracked several times to scout for any would-be pursuers. As of yet, there were no signs that they were being followed. Still, Oralia could not afford to be caught off guard in the middle of nowhere. She resolved to keep their pace for at least one night more, putting as much distance between them and the bandits as physically possible, before switching to a less taxing speed.

She and Kalihn were nearing the stream when Oralia froze in place, holding out her hand in a silent command for Kalihn to do the same. Overhead, the birdsong had stilled to a deathly quiet. Oralia inhaled through her nose, testing the air for clues. She smelled the sharp, pungent smell of forest decay and the variety of damp fungi that thrived on its decomposing remains. There was water too, in the distance. The only other living creature of noticeable size she could detect happened to be the elf standing behind her.

Kalihn edged closer, shifting her weight from one foot to the other, clinging to the pot as if it was her most prized possession. The elf had the sense to keep her voice low. "What is it? You sense something?"

"I am not sure."

Something had caused the songbirds to go quiet. And while it could have been her and Kalihn's presence, Oralia knew better than to brazenly press forward without stopping to consider her options. She tilted her head in all directions, ears straining to catch any unfamiliar sounds. While the quiet was eerie, it also lacked any obvious signs of danger. She didn't smell anything out of place, either. The lack of evidence, however, failed to ease her growing nerves.

Unfortunately, that left her with a difficult decision. The stream was the only source of freshwater within the area. To try to locate another would not only come at the expense of time and energy, but had the potential to attract just as much attention. Especially with Kalihn in tow. Oralia took all of it into account before making her decision.

"We proceed with utmost caution." Oralia picked her way through the undergrowth, mindful to avoid the patch of devil's club that blanketed the leafy ground in tall, thorny patches. "Avoid speaking unless absolutely necessary. If you hear something, signal to me. Do not shout."

"I'm perfectly fine waiting here if you want to go on ahead without me," Kalihn ever-so-helpfully offered, going as far as to lift the pot in Oralia's direction expectantly.

A firmly pressed brow was the only motivation required to get the reluctant elf moving again. Despite Kalihn's best efforts to creep quietly, Oralia winced every time she took a step. It grew so unbearable, Oralia was forced to slow down and demonstrate how to walk without snapping every twig between them and the stream.

While painfully slow, the pair managed to reach the water's edge without alerting the entire woodland area of their presence. The stream was not large, barely spanning a few yards across. Its pebbled bottom could be seen from above, appearing no more than half a foot in depth.

Wordlessly, Oralia unslung the collection of empty waterskins from her shoulder and set them onto the bank. She could only fill one at a time, making the chore not only slow, but tedious as well. Exactly the reason why Rali had cheated at drawing lots in order to avoid being the one to carry it out.

Kalihn was not nearly as confident as Oralia. She lingered paces from the bank, her sharp eyes darting back and forth between the dark trees. Finally, having either decided the coast was clear or simply grown weary of holding the pot, the elf edged forward onto the pebbled bank. She removed her shoes, rolled up her pant legs, and stepped boldly into the icy water.

Oralia raised her eyebrows at the elf's questionable methods. "Are you trying to attract leeches?"

Kalihn's face scrunched in confusion. "Attract what now?"

"Lift your leg."

Kalihn did as instructed. As expected, there was already a small, black squiggly thing attached to her exposed skin. Before Oralia could explain the leech was perfectly harmless, Kalihn dropped the pot with a squeal. Naturally, the heavy pot then landed squarely on her other foot.

Oralia's whole body flinched at Kalihn's high-pitched scream. The boughs rustled overhead as every bird in the vicinity startled into the air. The sounds of rustling leaves and frantically flapping wings intermixed with the echo of Kalihn's scream as it bounced along the formerly still forest.

If there were any bandits nearby, they definitely knew they were not the only ones in the area now.

CHAPTER FORTY-ONE

You Finally Need Me

Oralia waited with her breath drawn, ears straining to catch any telltale sign of the enemy before they came charging from the surrounding trees, weapons drawn, out for blood. She released her breath not long after, realizing that neglecting to fill her lungs served no other purpose but to make an already difficult situation substantially more so. The minutes slowly ticked past and . . .

Nothing.

No crunch of dried leaves as they disintegrated underfoot, or snap of twigs catching on passing cloaks, or blood-curdling war cries. Around them, the birds settled back into the boughs as the woodland grew eerily silent once more. Oralia couldn't believe it. Against all odds, her and Kalihn's presence had gone unnoticed. For the moment, anyway. There wasn't any sense in sticking around longer than necessary to test the theory in full.

Kalihn clambered out of the water and hopped silently on one foot, clutching the other as tears rolled down her ashen face. Sascha's pot sat half-submerged in the fast-flowing stream, slowly sinking into the soft silt bed below.

"Gods, that hurt like a b-word." Kalihn's ragged voice was barely over a hiss. "And I know what you're going to say, boss. It was stupid, I know. But I didn't bloody mean to!"

Oralia withheld her admonishment. There wasn't any point. Kalihn was right, of course. The events leading up to the scream had been undeniably stupid *and* avoidable, but what was done was done. There was no sense in making the elf's suffering worse. Intent on getting in and out as planned, Oralia returned to filling the waterskins. When finished, she grudgingly stepped into the stream—boots on, naturally—to complete Kalihn's task as well. Oralia's annoyance paled in comparison to the wrath they'd face had they returned to camp without Sascha's favorite cast iron pot in hand.

Oralia plucked the pot from the stream and then clambered back out onto the pebbled bank. She waited for Kalihn's frantic hopping to die down before asking, "Finished?"

The elf sat on the edge of the embankment, face red and biting her lower lip. "I think it's broken."

Oralia was unable to stop the words that rolled from her tongue unhindered. "If you are referring to your pride, I am surprised it has held up this long."

"No! My foot, obviously."

"I do not think so."

Kalihn flopped back on the bank dramatically. "You'll have to carry me."

"Not happening."

"You can't just leave me here like this, boss. I'm vulnerable!"

"Be grateful I am carrying the pot on your behalf." And again, not out of pity, but because Sascha would never speak to her again if she returned without it.

With the weight of the waterskins arranged evenly across both shoulders, Oralia fitted the lid back over the iron pot and started back toward camp. She walked without her companion, pausing every so often to stop and listen as Kalihn's dragging footsteps reluctantly followed. Oralia wouldn't leave her, of course, but hoped that each time Kalihn lost sight of her, it would motivate the elf to pick up the pace.

They were making good time, already halfway through the journey, when the crunch of a twig stopped Oralia in her tracks. She froze, realizing the sound was far too close to have come from Kalihn. Oralia listened as a third set of footsteps crept up from behind, not yet aware they'd been detected. She drew air in through her nose, picking up hints of tobacco, old booze, and an overall lack of personal hygiene. Whoever was closing in on them was definitely not one of hers.

What's worse, the stranger was between her and Kalihn.

Oralia didn't dare call out a warning in case there was more than one bandit following them. Oralia counted only one set of footsteps now—Kalihn's. The stranger had gone still. Judging from their stench, Oralia could roughly pinpoint the creep's whereabouts. Unable to call out to Kalihn, Oralia reluctantly settled on another way of alerting her companion to the danger.

She closed her eyes and steadied her breath, willing a silent prayer into the universe. *Dear Sascha, forgive me.*

Dumping the water onto the ground, Oralia swung the pot in a series of fast, concentric circles to gain momentum, and then released, hurtling it high overhead. The cast iron vessel broke through the canopy, sailing higher and higher, before gravity brought it crashing back down. It plummeted, ricocheting off one tree to the next, snapping branches all the way down until, at last, slamming into the ground with a resounding *thump*!

Oralia listened as not one but three additional bodies abandoned cover and raced through the brush to find the source of the commotion.

"Uh, boss?" Kalihn's voice rang out as her slogging footsteps faltered. "Is that you?"

"Freeze, maggot!" a gruff voice shouted at her.

To her credit, Kalihn did the sensible thing and ran. Mostly sensible. The screaming wasn't doing anything except marking in which direction she was fleeing, but, at the very least, she headed back in the direction of the stream and not toward camp. When discovered, it was of the utmost importance to lead the enemy *away* from the rest of your party. You could circle back again once having lost any and all pursuers. Oralia was relieved that Kalihn possessed some tactical sense.

Alas, her thoughts spoke too soon.

Judging from Kalihn's obnoxious screaming, the elf had circled back around and, out of all the directions she could have possibly gone, was now sprinting in the one she was not supposed to be.

Oralia ordinarily would have given chase, picking off the slower runners along the way, but the smell of musty tobacco still lingered—indicating that at least one of the bandits had stayed behind to deal with her. At the moment, neither of them moved, waiting for the other to betray their position.

The stalemate stretched on for several moments before Oralia gave up waiting. She unslung the waterskins from around her neck and hung them in the nearest tree, intent on returning and fetching them when she was finished dispatching the bandit. Moving onto her toes, she crept between the trees, relying on her sense of smell to lead her to her quarry. Her opponent must have had a similar idea because several paces later, the bandit in question emerged from out of the brush in front of her.

The scrawny orc jumped in surprise, his eyes darting to the sword hanging from Oralia's hip before hastily taking in the rest of her. While the bandit was roughly the same height as her, he was thin for an orc. One better suited for running as opposed to facing down bigger opponents—which was why

Oralia wasn't going to give him the chance. She rushed the scrawny bandit, drawing her sword mid-lunge, and swung at him.

He leapt out of the way, yelping as Oralia's blade grazed along his ribs. The orc turned to run, caught his foot on an upturned tree root, and fell. In lieu of a swift getaway, the bandit found himself strewn facedown across the mossy forest floor, having nothing to show for his efforts except a badly twisted ankle. Oralia jumped the same moment the bandit flipped over. She landed with a foot planted on either side of him and brought the point of her blade down. It would be a clean run through. A quick ending, as far as untimely deaths went. Probably more than he deserved anyway.

The scrawny orc's gray face went ashen white. He threw his hands out in a futile attempt to stop the inevitable. "Please don't!"

Oralia's blade jerked to a stop, a hair's breadth from piercing her target's chest.

His eyes were clenched shut and he trembled, producing soft whimpers. The words caught in his throat, barely discernible even at such close proximity. "I want to live."

He was older than Curly would have been, thin and scrappy, with eyes all the wrong color. But logic was suddenly powerless, unable to dispel the image of her own boy cowering beneath her, begging for his life as he watched his death unfold before his eyes, unable to stop it. Pain swelled in Oralia's throat, pulling tight like a noose across her airways. She choked, gasping for breath as her knees rebelled, buckling uselessly beneath her. She caught herself before she fell, unable to tear her eyes from the orc trembling beneath her.

The name hurt to speak. "Curly?"

His eyes went wide, rimmed in white. His tusked mouth quivered open but the rampant drum of Oralia's heartbeat drowned out his response.

No, no, no. This can't be. This isn't happening. Not here. Not now.

She knew it wasn't real and yet, there was no convincing her eyes otherwise. It wasn't some scrawny bandit cowering before her but one of her own. The one she'd lost. The one she was supposed to have kept safe. The one she'd failed.

"Stop it!" Oralia roared. "Whatever this is, stop it! You're not him."

The months of pent-up grief poured from the fractures in her heart, flooding her insides until the pressure gave way behind her eyes. The birdsong and soft rustling of the wind in the trees died away as her surroundings blurred. Time shifted and when Oralia looked around again, she found the red oaks and paper birch had been replaced with a sea of dark spruce. The scents of fresh dirt and rain danced on the breeze, transforming her stomach to stone.

The noose around her neck cinched tighter when Oralia realized where her memory had taken her. She screwed her eyes shut, forcing the images back down. "No, no, not here. Not again."

Oralia knew what happened next. She knew the moment she opened her eyes again, she would relive the worst moment of her life. She'd see *him*, propped against a tree, face drained of color. His once dark eyes now dull and lifeless. She would remember the touch of his cold skin against her own as she held him one final time, begging for a forgiveness that would never come. And then, when the others finally convinced her to let go, she would see his body lowered into the dirt and how those lifeless eyes gazed back up at her with that pleading expression.

Why weren't you there? Why didn't you save me? Curly's unspoken words still haunted her each time she closed her eyes. *You were supposed to protect me.*

Hot tears streamed down Oralia's face. She wasn't even cognizant of the words spilling from her mouth. "I'm sorry. I'm so sorry."

"Grettie! Grettie, help me!"

The shrill scream snapped Oralia from her trance. She opened her eyes to find the scrawny orc desperately clawing his way out from under her. His wide eyes were fixed on the sword point still held inches from his chest cavity.

"Grettie!" he shouted.

Oralia dropped and pinned him with her knees. Abandoning her sword, she went for his throat with her hands instead. Her fingers found the delicate spot tucked along the neckline just below the ear and squeezed. She blinked the hot tears from her eyes and steadied her breath, maintaining enough pressure to ensure that, while he wouldn't die, he wouldn't be able to scream anymore either. The orc wrapped his hands around her wrist, thrashing as he attempted to break her hold. His struggle was already weakening when Oralia heard someone emerge from the undergrowth behind her. The hairs on her arm stood on end as an icy chill stirred within her veins.

Move! A surge of blistering heat burst from behind the same moment the pendant around her neck flared to life. The dark entity's silken voice rippled across her thoughts, snapping her from her stupor. **Now, orc. Now!**

Oralia threw herself to the side and rolled beneath an overgrown patch of bracken. She flipped over, scuttling backward on her hands and knees as a blaze of fire erupted across the woodland floor where she had been only a split second before. Screams lit the air as the yellow and orange flames flared brighter, reaching all the way up to the lower boughs before the fire snuffed out, filling the air with black smoke and the stench of singed flesh. The orc's screams faded as his writhing, black and charred body fell still.

"What the fuck, Hank? Why'd you get in the way like that?" A small, haggard-looking woman slunk out from between the trees. Her shrewd eyes searched for wherever Oralia had gone before settling on the overgrown bracken. Grettie's mouth pulled into a snaggle-toothed smile. "If you make me do this the hard way, you're gonna end up like ol' Hank here. Why don't you come out nice and easy like, and we talk this through like civilized folk?"

Among the myriad of voices screaming within Oralia's head, a new one added itself to the mix. **What's this? Trapped with a witch, alone and without backup? Looks like you finally need me.** Darkness stirred to life within her veins as the entity cackled with delight. **Do as I say, orc, and we may both make it out of this alive.**

CHAPTER FORTY-TWO

Unhand My Dingle

The sun was high overhead when Rasp awoke from the strangest dream. Birds sang, nested among the village ruins, their warbled chirps and whistles amplified by the surrounding stone. The cool air smelled of wet clay and moss. For the first time in months, Rasp felt rested. His back no longer ached, his knees weren't stiff and swollen, and the constant heavy cloud that hung in the back of his skull had dispersed, leaving his mind unusually clear.

And Rasp wanted none of it.

He closed his eyes and rolled over, willing his waking mind to shut the fuck up and go back to sleep. His dreams had been some of the best he'd ever had. Filled with all the foods he loved, the people he tolerated, and even a few he might have loved more than food. Faris had been there. As had Mother. And not a single person asked him to do anything. It was the closest to paradise Rasp had ever come and he was determined to drift back asleep and enjoy it for as long as he could.

The low-speaking voices conversing nearby were making the return to sleep more difficult than it should've been. Probably would have helped had he simply ignored them, but such was the nature of whispers. Any conversation you weren't meant to hear was always the most difficult not to listen to. Rasp tilted his head, noting how the surrounding walls magnified even the faintest murmur.

"I don't want to go anywhere near that settlement." Hop's voice was low and laden with both worry. "Especially if you're leaving us again."

"I can't scout the tower from the ground," Whisper replied. "And, unless you can shift into a body with wings, I can't take you with me either. If you're so concerned about going head-to-head with soldiers then stay here."

"In a haunted village? With resistance thugs on our tail?"

"I will only be gone for a few hours."

"Yeah, just like yesterday. Look how well that turned out!"

"I fail to see the issue." Unlike Hop, Whisper kept their voice calm. Almost unnaturally so. "You were ambushed and the little bird utilized his training—*your* training, specifically—to handle the situation. He was successful and the both of you walked away unscathed."

"He roasted two people alive in their armor."

"And you think me being there would have changed that?" Whisper countered. "Your attackers would have died regardless. In a different manner, granted, but dead nonetheless. All of them."

Whisper was planning another scouting mission to the nearby realm settlement from the sounds of it. Hop, meanwhile, seemed conflicted between tagging along or staying back and spending the rest of the day in the haunted village—neither option appealed to him, judging from his tone. Rasp's hopes of sleeping the rest of the afternoon away disintegrated like sandcastles among the rising tide. The sad fact of the matter was, the sooner he got up and moving, the sooner the recurrent nightmare that had become his everyday life could get better.

That's what he told himself, anyway, as the alternative wasn't an option he wanted to consider.

With a yawn, Rasp stretched his arms over his head and willed life into each toe. Sitting up had never felt so easy. "I vote we go with Whisper to the settlement."

"You do?" Hop's tone changed from surprised to accusatory without missing a beat. "Why?"

"Whisper's egg might be there, right?"

The fae's quills rattled in irritation. "Not an egg."

Rasp rubbed the sleep from his eyes as he spoke, unable to conceal the devious smile that pulled at the corner of his mouth. "I want to be nearby in case they find it. One step closer to the egg is one step closer to getting rid of some of my magic. It's only logical."

The faun disagreed with a snort. "I don't think that word applies to this situation."

"It would be useful to have a second pair of eyes on the ground," Whisper admitted, speaking slowly, as if actually considering Rasp's proposition. "The two of you could scout the area from the outside while I do so from within."

Hop, naturally, had objections. A whole list of them. What's worse, his objections were grounded in *actual* logic. "You want a blind elemental and a bumbling artificer, with no combat experience whatsoever, to scout an active realm military settlement for you? Do I have that right?"

"You forgot magically unstable," Rasp said helpfully. He steepled his hands beneath his chin, flashing a smile. "A blind, magically unstable elemental, thank you."

"Whisper, this is the plot to a tragic comedy. Not a feasible plan."

Whisper was smiling now, too. Rasp could hear it in the way the fae's singsong voice rose in pitch. "Precisely. It will be easier to snoop around the inside of the tower if the soldiers are adequately distracted."

It was rare for Rasp and Whisper to gang up on Hop together. Usually one of them, alone, was all that was necessary to persuade the faun into doing things "the stupidest way possible." "Distraction is Hop's middle name," Rasp said. "Hopalong Distraction Humphrey."

Hop and Whisper were standing not far from Rasp. He could just barely make out their shadowy forms—one tall and looming, the other short and spiky—highlighted against the sunshine filtering down from the gaps in the rustling canopy overhead. Hop's giant form shifted to face Rasp head-on, raising his voice in objection. "What happened to being depressed about yesterday? Shouldn't you be a moping puddle of self-misery right now?"

"That is odd, isn't it?" Rasp scratched at his armpit as he considered why this might be. Hop was right. Accidental acts of magically induced carnage usually took days, sometimes weeks, to get over. But ever since waking up, it was as if all his problems had been cut loose. Rasp felt set free from the iron chains that'd kept him grounded in misery.

"Blame the harmony stone," he said at last, having come up with no other logical answer. "I think it might have healed more than just my broken body, but my conscience too."

"That's not how harmony stones work."

"Not for you, apparently, Mister Grumpy Pants."

And with that, Hop's metaphorical backbone caved, giving in to the inevitable. Rasp could tell by the wearisome sigh that issued from the large faun as his reluctant steps dragged off in the opposite direction. "Why do I even try?"

"We wonder the same thing," Whisper called after him.

"Not me," Rasp said. "I'm just wondering where breakfast is."

"It's past noon, little bird."

"Fine, lunch then. Feed me. I'm hungry."

"Fortunately for me, I am your mentor, not your parent. Therefore, not my problem."

Rasp bit back his sarcastic reply, recalling how his actual parent had disappeared earlier that morning. He tilted his head this way and that, listening to the sounds of the forest. He heard the harsh screech of blue jays, the raspy chatter of magpies, and a number of songbirds. It was the one missing, however, that gave him pause. "Speaking of which, is Father back yet? He went to check on something earlier. Said it was important."

Whisper was as helpful as always. "Also not my problem."

Rasp parted the gnarled branches that scratched at his unprotected face as he followed Hop's blurry shape through the thick underbrush. After two hours of travel, they'd reached the outskirts of the old military settlement. The overgrown forest had been cut back along the wall, allowing a ten-yard clearing that kept intruders from catching the settlement by surprise. A wall couldn't keep Whisper out, of course. Shifting into bird form, the fae had flown over the top to scout the inside, leaving Hop and Rasp to check the perimeter for weaknesses.

Well, Hop got to check the perimeter. Rasp was there for . . . backup? Moral support? Delightful running commentary? His options were somewhat limited considering his vision couldn't pick up anything beyond a sea of hazy green and black shadows.

While he may have been the one to insist on tagging along to the settlement, Rasp hadn't planned on participating in the scouting part. To his dismay, Hop insisted otherwise. Apparently Rasp could no longer be trusted to sit and watch the bags after what happened last time. Which was totally unfair, considering he couldn't possibly cause mayhem if there wasn't a city within walking distance. What was he going to do? Terrorize the trees?

What a ridiculous idea, Rasp thought. He'd learned his lesson after that cedar nearly crushed him a few weeks back. Since then, he'd vowed to only terrorize things incapable of rendering him as flat as a pancake.

Hop's whispered voice drew Rasp from his thoughts. "Aside from the main gate, there appear to be two smaller points of access." The faun had gotten into the habit of narrating his findings. The information was helpful, but unnecessary. As the settlement wall was comprised of stone, Rasp could bring it down with a flick of his hand if he wanted. Might defeat the purpose of being stealthy, though.

Hop carried on, unaware of the poor ideas filtering through Rasp's head. "Once it gets dark, it wouldn't take much to sneak across the clearing and have Whisper open one of the smaller gates from the inside."

"Oh." Rasp made the mistake of voicing his inner thoughts aloud. "I guess that would make more sense than blasting the wall down."

"You . . . you weren't seriously thinking of doing that, were you?"

"What? No, of course not. That'd be reckless."

Hop stopped dead in his tracks. Rasp only noticed because he slammed into the back of the now unmoving faun, nearly toppling the both of them. A hiss from Hop kept Rasp from cursing him to the farthest reaches of the realm and back. The pair remained stock still as the grueling seconds trickled past. Rasp strained his ears, realizing the forest had grown strangely quiet. In the distance, he heard a squirrel chattering its warning call.

Rasp whispered, "Please don't tell me we're being followed again."

"No, it's something else. An animal, I think." By the way Hop's head raised higher, Rasp suspected he was testing the air. "There are other smells too, but I can't pin them down. Whatever it is, it's making quite the commotion."

"Does this mysterious creature smell hungry?"

"How would I know that, Rasp?"

"I don't know. But we did just leave two days' worth of corn cake rations next to a tethered mule alone in the forest."

"Wait, I hear something else." Hop seized Rasp by the shirt and hauled him forward until they were standing alongside one another—as if, for some reason, moving an entire two steps closer would increase Rasp's ability to hear. "That's a raven, isn't it?"

Rasp closed his eyes and listened. ". . . That's not Father."

Hop's grip on the front of Rasp's shirt lessened. "Just a regular raven then?"

"No, I just don't recognize their voice, is all. She's shouting 'quick, quick, they're gaining on us.'"

"Are you fucking with me again?"

Rasp's eyes snapped back open as he latched onto Hop's arm, preparing his weary legs for the torture they were about to endure. "Afraid not, Hoppy Boy. Fancy a run? You're going to have to get us closer."

"Or we could not do that. Stick to the plan. Stay hidden."

"You're either getting us there on foot, or I'm lifting us up with the wind again. Your choice."

"Dear gods, no." Hop stifled a whimper as he surged forward through the underbrush, dragging Rasp with him. "For the record, in case I don't live long enough to tell you so afterward, this is a terrible idea."

"You say that about all my ideas."

Instead of backtracking the way they came, Hop zigged and zagged a winding path through the trees, attempting to keep downwind from the commotion. Blurred black and green tree forms whizzed past at a dizzying rate. Rasp clung to his guide, lifting his feet higher than usual to keep from catching on every root and snag between them and the growing clamor. He was starting to suspect Hop had intentionally led them in the opposite direction when the faun ground to a halt, dragging Rasp down out of sight with him.

They were tucked behind a highbush cranberry shrub from the smell of it. Between the screech of the unfamiliar raven and the muffled shouts and roars, Rasp couldn't make heads nor tails of what was taking place. He squeezed Hop's arm, reminding him that not everyone present had the gift of sight. "What do you see?"

"It's thugs from yesterday," Hop managed between pants for air. "Looks like they've cornered a bear."

Rasp suddenly understood why they were hiding. He repeated Hop's words on the off chance he'd heard wrong, somewhat hopeful that he had. "A bear?"

"The biggest one I've ever seen."

What was a talking raven doing with a bear? Just as Rasp was beginning to question whether or not he was still dreaming, Hop sucked a breath through his teeth and offered the final piece to the puzzle. "There's a faun, too. I can't tell if the thugs are trying to help him or fight him."

"A faun?" Rasp's heart nearly leapt into the back of his throat. He gripped Hop's arm tighter. "Hooves? Horns? Furry legs?"

"Are you trying to describe a particular faun or the species in general?"

Shit. Rasp realized he had no idea what Faris actually looked like. "Short, but strong. Smells like cherry tobacco? Has a punchable face!" Fuck, this was harder than he thought. "A beard, maybe?"

"Albino?" Hop offered.

He felt suddenly stupid for forgetting that detail. To be fair, Rasp had only ever brought it up when he was in the mood for an ass kicking. The moment of shame was fleeting, gone as quickly as it had come. A mix of dread and excitement rose up in its stead. Rasp gathered his feet beneath him, heart pounding as his thoughts raced like a runaway stallion. It couldn't be, could it? There was no rhyme or reason for Faris to be all the way out here.

Bear be damned, Rasp was about to find out. "Alright, give me a quick rundown of the setup. Where are the baddies at?"

"They're positioned at twelve, three, and seven."

"What the fuck does that mean?"

"Like the number positions on a clockface?"

"Why do you assume I know what a clock looks like?"

"Oh my gods!" It was Hop's turn to seize Rasp by the arm, crushing flesh beneath his iron grip. "The bear just took one of the thugs down! It ripped open their neck and, oh shit, oh shit, oh shit, there's blood everywhere!"

There wasn't time for a strategy. Tugging his arm free, Rasp jumped upright and raced headlong through the cranberry bush, ignoring the way the branches tore at his unprotected face. Magic pooled in his hands as an unusual sense of calm flooded his veins. His heartbeat slowed, thrumming faintly within his ears, as the sounds of the scuffle faded into the background. Rasp didn't have to close his eyes this time. His phantom vision slipped soundlessly into place, overlaying his muddled surroundings with the magical signatures of his enemies.

Rasp's foot caught on a tree root and he came hurtling out of the underbrush spinning, but still on his feet. His war cry roared across the forest, bouncing from tree to tree, with the full force of a thunderclap. "Unhand my Dingle!"

CHAPTER FORTY-THREE

The Bear, the Witch, and the Audacity of this BFF

Rasp's surroundings were a shifting field of dark gray and green shadows. Three magical auras glowed against the gloom, shining like beacons in the night. The light pouring from the witches highlighted the last of the spindly poplars obstructing Rasp's path. He weaved between the trees, wincing each time a wayward branch snagged a leg or arm as he hurtled past. Rasp cleared the last of the trees and burst through the underbrush, charging out across the makeshift battlefield.

The closest magical aura also happened to be the largest. Pale green and shimmering, the aura was unnaturally big, nearly the size of a bear. Cursing under his breath, Rasp altered his breakneck course to go around it, realizing that the reason it was the size of a bear was because it *was* a bear. He'd never considered what happened to a witch's power when devoured by a large predator. As the beast itself was now glowing a lovely shade of mint green, Rasp had the displeasure of knowing both flesh and magic were being consumed at an equal rate.

Fuck that. He hadn't survived four months without his best friend just to wind up being slowly digested in the lower intestines of an apex predator.

Fortunately the bear was too preoccupied with its feast to pay any mind to the scrawny-looking witch hurtling past. Successfully skirting the carnage, Rasp set his sights on the two remaining witches. The pair were clustered together—one aura glowing dull red and the other silver—caught in a struggle with a third, non-magical shadow. Rasp recalled the unfortunate events that took place the night of the Hanover Harvest Festival. More specifically, Whisper's roundabout explanation regarding the color of one's magic and how it correlated with their abilities. Alas, as with most of his learning, the lesson had gone in one ear and out the other. With enough time and concentration, Rasp might have been able to work it out on his own but, mere paces between him and his quarry, he found himself regrettably short of both.

To the seventh realm of chaos with it! He'd never been one for strategic plans anyway. Seemed a little late to start now. Phantom tendrils of yellow magic lifted from Rasp's hands as his feet pounded against the mossy woodland floor, closing the gap. "You better fucking run if you know what's good for you!"

In hindsight, he should have waited until *after* he'd reached the enemy before engaging in shit talk. A wave of red magic tore across the ground toward him. The dirt split open, throwing a shimmering wall of rock and stone skyward. Rasp flung his hands out in front of his face, pushing back against the onslaught.

Well, shit. Red aura meant earth elemental—he remembered now. Would've been a lot more helpful had he recalled that nifty fact before getting hammered in the face with a volley of razor-edged shrapnel. Rasp kept his arms held aloft, struggling to keep the onslaught of projectiles at bay while he considered his next move, all while trying to ignore the trickle of warm blood oozing down the side of his battered face.

Preoccupied with the airborne assault, he failed to register the ground rumbling beneath his feet until it was too late. The earth tore open as shafts of rock formations shot up around him on all sides. The formations curled and twisted together, forming a makeshift cage.

Among the deafening roar of grinding, shifting stone, Rasp heard Faris call out, his voice laden with terror. "Rasp?"

"I'm coming, Dingle!"

There was a notable pause. "Are you though? Because, no offense, it looks like you just stumbled right into a trap."

"Oh shut up, Faris! It's a rescue-in-progress, alright?" Un-fucking-believable. Reunited all of thirty seconds and, already, Faris was criticizing his every move.

Gods, I missed you.

The shifting stone walls wove tighter together, closing in on him. Rasp swallowed back his growing trepidation and focused inward. He pressed the flat of his hands together and channeled power between his palms. He held it, willing it stronger, stronger, stronger. He released just as the final glimpse of daylight disappeared above him. Tendrils of yellow magic surged forth, burrowing deep into the rock, transforming the glowing red to orange. The earth elementalist's magic fought back, resisting Rasp's takeover.

In the end, the greater power proved victorious and the surrounding weave of magic shifted in color from orange to yellow. A smirk pulled at Rasp's mouth as he spread his fingers wide and then snapped them shut. His magic responded, splitting his makeshift cage into a crumbling landslide of rock and debris.

Rasp stepped free of the cloud of dust, wiping the stray particles from his eyes, just in time to have another spray of shrapnel slam into him. He deflected, hurtling the flurry of projectiles back at his opponent—making sure to throw it twice as hard.

"Stop. Making. Me." He accentuated each word with another volley of loose rock and rubble. "Look. Bad!"

As it turned out, throwing volatile spells between dramatic pauses proved both tedious and labor intensive. Weary of his own antics, Rasp ditched the separate attacks and settled for a single, concentrated wave of earth and stone. He heaved it before him, finishing his sentence with a scream: "In front of Faris!"

The yellow wave thundered across the upturned battlefield, felling entire trees in its wake of destruction. Ears still ringing, Rasp was caught by surprise when someone's back pressed against his own. "It's not fair to blame your poor performance on the other witch, Dinglehead."

Rasp's heart leapt back into his throat with a squeak.

Faris carried on unaffected. "You didn't even check to see where I was before sending that last wave of rock, by the way. I could've been crushed."

The urge to whip around and hug the daylights out of Faris was almost immediately replaced with the need to throttle him first. Alas, Rasp could do neither. A third volley of rock reminded him that they were still caught on an active battlefield and would, therefore, have to save the kissing and making up for later. "I mean this in the nicest way," Rasp grunted, forced to counter his opponent's strike once more, "but it's probably not the best idea to stand next to me right now."

"Oh, believe me, I'm aware." Positioned back-to-back, Rasp felt Faris flinch when the two magics collided together with a thunderous *crack*. "Kinda short of options at the moment, though."

"Nah, you just missed me."

"Do you think we could do this *after* you've done something about the witch attacking us?"

Rasp lifted his hands, summoning a wall of earth and stone to shield them against the magical onslaught coming from across the battle-torn field. Temporarily sheltered, he whirled around, placing his hands at his hips. "What do you think I'm doing?"

"Drawing the fight out for dramatic effect?" Faris replied. "I mean, come on. You got carried off by a dragon last I saw you. Surely Whisper taught you something in all the months you've been away."

Rasp didn't know which accusation hurt worse. The fact that he'd just been accused of being needlessly dramatic or that Faris considered his current strategy weak.

"Case in point, right now, for instance," the faun continued, unnaturally calm for someone currently insulting the very witch keeping him alive. "You just stopped mid-fight to argue with me. Coming across awfully dramatic to me, Dinglehead."

The audacity!

Rolling his head back with a groan, Rasp spread his feet shoulder-width apart and bent his knees. He closed his eyes and dug deep, searching his surroundings for an element capable of giving him the advantage he sorely needed. The breeze responded, creaking the timber boughs overhead as it whistled past. He reached out and harnessed its power, feeling the surge of fresh magic light a fire within his battered bones.

No anger, he reminded himself, remembering how spectacularly his powers had blown up in his face the last time he'd lost his temper out of frustration. A few deep breaths ensured his heartbeat was still steadily thumping along at a calm pace. *You're cool. You're calm. No dark entities stirring to life and seizing control this time.*

Rasp's voice reflected his eerie state of calm. "You want to see dramatic, Dingle?"

"Did you hear a single word I said? I asked you to *stop* being so dramatic. Not to double down on it!"

A devilish smile split across Rasp's bloodied face. With a wave of his hand, he collapsed the makeshift wall sheltering them from the enemy. His eyes swept across the sea of shifting shadows in search of the telltale glow of his opponent's magical signature. Rasp found it, partially obscured by the surrounding trees. The earth elemental was stealthily picking his way around to catch them from the flank unaware.

Rasp raised his hands high overhead and then brought them down with a dramatic flourish, sending a raging torrent of wind and rock across the ravaged ground. Leaves, dirt, and twigs hurtled past as the torrent swept the witch off the ground and flung him high over the treetops. The red blip was lost to sight almost immediately after. From the witch's fading screams, Rasp assumed his magic had done as he'd intended.

He straightened his posture, beaming with pride. "How was that?"

"Surprisingly effective, actually. Good job not killing us."

Unfortunately, dramatic shows of power came at an equally dramatic price. Rasp meant to take a step in Faris's direction, but staggered instead. Hot bile flooded his mouth as the contents of his stomach attempted to upend themselves in a single heave. Rasp swallowed, fighting to keep his breakfast down as his aura vision faded in and out. Unable to sustain the connection, Rasp's surroundings grew indistinguishable once more. While his phantom vision may have tapped out, his magic sensitivity was still holding on by a thread. The buzz rippling across his skin warned him there was still at least one, maybe two, additional sources of magic nearby.

This is what you get for showing off, the stupid voice in his head reminded him. *Now get your head back in the game and finish the job.*

Fuck, this was going to suck.

"Alright, Dingle," Rasp panted, desperately searching the makeshift battlefield for an opponent he couldn't see. "Where's the other witch?"

"You're just now wondering that?"

"Do you have to turn everything into a fight? Yes. Tell me where the other witch is!"

Faris's voice dripped with sarcasm. "You must be something real special, you know. Are all witches this polite? Patiently waiting their turn to have a go at you one-on-one?"

Alright, admittedly, Faris had a point. Rasp supposed it was a little strange the pair of resistance thugs hadn't teamed up on him together. The reason for which, he realized, was painfully obvious. "You fuck head. You already took care of the second witch, didn't you?"

"I might have hobbled him a wee bit. He went slinking off into the trees last I saw."

"You didn't kill him?"

"Look, not all of us are comfortable with spilling blood so easily, alright? If it's any consolation, I doubt he's getting very far."

"Gods dammit, Dingle. You just earned us more work, you know that, right? Now we've got to go track the fucker down before he comes back with more friends." While it ranked high on the list of shit to do, Rasp had a few other priorities to sort out first. Quick as a flash, he spun around, squishing Faris's face between his hands. "Your delightfully chubby cheeks," he gasped, still prodding the unamused faun's scruffy face. "They're gone! You're nothing but skin and bone!"

"Yeah, speaking of which—"

Faris's fist struck him in the gut with the force of a sledgehammer. All of the air left Rasp's body in a single, pained exhale. His stomach seized beyond his control, sending ripples of agony coursing through the rest of his body. Stunned, Rasp slowly sank toward the ground with a gurgled wheeze.

"—that's for making me hunt your sorry ass down for months on end without any word from you at all! Would it have killed you to send a mucking raven now and then, huh? The only reason I managed to find you was the senseless trail of destruction you left in your wake."

Rasp's legs gave out and he struck the upturned ground, gasping feebly for breath. He managed three hoarse words. ". . . Love . . . you . . . too."

"Damn right, you're sorry! Four months, Rasp! Four months of endless running with every enemy on the entire continent hot on my trail."

Unable to form proper sentences, Rasp rested his head against the upturned dirt, all the while wondering what sort of reward was in store for him, having just saved the ungrateful faun's life. While he was hoping for a hug, he wouldn't say no to a couple of cold compresses and a stiff drink.

A bone-rattling snarl cut the rest of Faris's rantings short. Rasp went rigid, suddenly remembering he'd forgotten all about the damn bear. "Shit!" He staggered to his feet, angling his hands in the direction of the oncoming beast. "Get behind me, Dingle! I'll take care of the bear."

CHAPTER FORTY-FOUR

An Enthusiastic Lack of Clothing

Crackling hot magic pooled into Rasp's hands so quickly it made his head spin. His stomach lurched as he doubled over, fighting the acidic heaves of vomit clawing its way up his throat. *Fuck.* He clenched his teeth, struggling to remain standing as wave after wave of stomach-curdling nausea flooded his insides. Sweat beaded down his forehead as the blistering heat spread across his skin like wildfire.

His incessant need to overreact had truly cost him this time. He was overspent, having depleted nearly all of his magic before the fight was even half over. Weak or not, he had to finish the bear before it finished them.

Rasp raised his trembling left hand, eyes straining to pick out the bear's blurry form from the rest of his muddled surroundings. The beast's shaggy outline drew closer, huffing and snorting as it ambled toward him. Rasp opened his mouth to scream, but a swell of sour bile crested over the top of his throat and swamped his tongue, turning his hollering into sputtered gagging.

"Get . . . back!" he managed, angling his open hand at his slowly advancing quarry. The last of his magic swelled within his palm in anticipation for the final blow. Gods, he hoped this worked. He had one last good push in him before his powers were spent. Timing it just right required both patience and precision—attributes that weren't exactly his forte.

Hold it, hold, hold it, he told himself as the lumbering shape neared. *Miss now and you're royally screwed.*

Power built within his hand until it was too hot to hold any longer. The magic pulled at his flesh like an unruly dog on a leash, begging to be let go.

"Rasp, wait!"

Faris's warning sounded a split second before something slammed into the back of Rasp's head. He lost his footing, spinning to catch himself as the magic shot from his hand, sending a torrent of howling wind hurtling in the wrong direction. The gale thundered across the battlefield, snapping several spindly trees from their roots as it tore a path through the forest.

The aftermath of his blunder probably would have been a lot louder had it not been for the raven attacking the back of Rasp's head. It was difficult to hear much of anything over its ear-piercing shrieks. The bird was a furious flurry of feathers and fast beating wings as it stabbed at the back of his neck.

"What the fuck?" Rasp stumbled forward, throwing his arms over his head to shield his face from the raven's razor-sharp talons.

The raven continued its noisy assault, yanking at his hair as its large wings beat him into submission.

"Who the fuck are you calling a spoiled mountain brat?" Rasp's desperate attempts to fight the raven off had the opposite effect. Instead of proving victorious over his smaller, albeit vicious assailant, he ended up falling over himself in an undignified pile of flailing arms and legs. "Get off me, stupid bird! I don't even know you! You've got the wrong Stoneclaw!"

Croak! Father's call rang out as he swooped down from the treetops to assist. The feathery snap of Father's powerful wings stirred the air as he battered the other raven into a forced retreat. Having successfully warded off the other bird, Father settled onto the upturned rubble with a hiss. He waddled over and delivered Rasp's elbow an admonishing peck for losing to a bird a fifth his size.

"I take back everything nice I said about you this morning," Rasp moaned. He lay still, refusing to uncover his head in the event the fighting was just getting started. "Why is Miss Angry Feathers over there attacking me and not the bear?"

Father gargled his reply.

"She's family?" Rasp lifted his head, confused. "Wait, the bear or the raven?"

Unfortunately, Rasp wasn't able to get anything further before Father and the mystery raven turned on one another. If nothing else, it explained the newcomer's tendency for unbridled violence. Their rancorous screaming match certainly felt like the family reunions Rasp had grown up with.

He eased into a sitting position with a moan, running his fingers through his tangled hair. Parts of his scalp were wet and sticky with blood, but aside from a little pain, the damage didn't seem detrimental. If anything, the pair's obnoxious croaking was doing more damage than the attack had. Rasp plugged his ears, trying to lessen the verbal assault hammering away at the inside of his aching skull. Each harsh croak felt like a red-hot poker being driven further into his brain.

"For fuck's sake," he said, "use your inside voices, please!"

To Rasp's surprise, the ravens listened. They were still too preoccupied with slinging insults at one another to address his mounting questions, but at least they were doing it at a more tolerable level now.

Faris crouched beside him. "That was rough to watch. You alright?"

"No!" Rasp's hands dropped uselessly to his sides. "I'm so confused right now. I don't know who the fuck that raven is, but they seem to know me. Father's not being any help and nobody seems concerned about the fucking bear!"

"The bear's on our side, actually."

"Since when? You hate bears!"

"Look, I'll explain everything, I promise. Just give me a minute here. Lots of fires to put out." The direction of Faris's voice changed, as did the volume. "Will you please go change already? Over there in the bushes out of sight, yeah? Just like we practiced? And for muck's sake, do something about your face before you come back over. Dinglehead here may not be able to see it, but I can. It's disgusting."

Rasp could just barely make out the bear's hazy shape across from him. It halted, stomping its front foot with a powerful thud.

"I don't care if it's natural," Faris replied. "So is shitting, and you don't see me pulling up a chair to watch that either."

The beast produced a high-pitched, wavering grumble as it turned and lumbered away.

"Dingle, I . . ." Rasp's voice trailed, uncertain of whether or not he'd truly lost his mind. "I think that bear just called you an asshole."

"Wouldn't be the first time," Faris sighed. "She's almost as bad as you."

"*She?*" Rasp angled his hands back in the direction of the retreating bear. Naturally, the one time he truly needed his powers to volley someone over the trees, it wasn't there for him. Stupid magic.

Faris slapped Rasp's hands away as he eased into the dirt beside him. "Cut it out. You're going to get Dagmar all worked up again." Fortunately, he answered Rasp's next question before he was even given the chance to ask it. "Dagmar's the other raven. Your great-aunt on your father's side, I think? Wrote that history book you had to translate?"

The picture was starting to grow a little clearer. Not enough to make out any of the important details, but there was some shape to it now. Unfortunately for Rasp it was a shape he'd never encountered and was, therefore, just as lost if not more than before. "How do you know all this? Last I checked, you can't talk to ravens."

"The bear told me."

"Huh." Rasp gave up trying to make the nonsensical pieces fit nicely together. There was only one real explanation for what was taking place. He slumped against Faris like a boneless bag of meat and ran his dirty fingers down the faun's scruffy face, knowing he had to enjoy the dream for as long as he could before he woke up again.

"Again with the face touching?" Faris said. "Why can't you just shake my hand and say thank you like a normal person?"

"Psh, you wouldn't have chased a normal person halfway across the United Territories." Rasp felt the warmth in his chest start to fade as the trickle of sadness returned. It felt so real this time, too. The highs, the lows, the throbbing pressure in his skull, all the way down to the numb tingle in his fingertips—it was disturbing just how accurate his imagination had gotten with this one.

"I wish you would stay this time," Rasp said.

"Am I going somewhere?"

"Afraid so, Dingle. Any minute now I'm going to wake up."

"You're not dreaming."

"That's just what Dream Dingle would say."

"If anything, this would be a hallucination. Considering one, you're not asleep, and two, you're interacting with your environment."

Now that really was something Faris would say. There was only one way to know for sure. "Hop?" Rasp's voice rang out, bouncing along the surrounding trees as the echo faded in the distance. "Are you still there? I'm not hallucinating again, am I?"

"Are you hallucinating that you're cradling a very uncomfortable-looking faun's face in your hands?" Hop called back from farther away. The fucker was probably still hiding among the cranberry bushes, sticking to his tried and true strategy of *don't get involved until the last second.*

Rasp's fingers stopped curling through Faris's beard in order to think about it. "Yeah?"

"Definitely not hallucinating then."

"And the bear?"

"Also real."

"Huh," Rasp said again, still not fully convinced. Oh well. If it meant extending the dream hallucination a little longer, who was he to question it?

Faris grabbed Rasp's hand and yanked it from his face. His grip was stronger than Rasp remembered, capable of crushing each individual finger to pulp. "Who is that?" The faun's voice was low and marked with caution. "Have you had someone else with you this whole time?"

Rasp wrangled his hand free, shaking the sting from his smarting fingers. "I am allowed to see other people, you know. You found yourself a bear and I got myself an artificer. I'm not saying it's a competition or anything, but I definitely won."

Faris responded with an irritated ear flap.

"You can come out now, Hop. The bear is Faris's girlfriend. She won't eat you." Rasp paused, allowing a shit-eating grin to pull across his bruised face. "You know, Dingle, I remember Rali mentioning something about you liking bears once. I didn't think she meant it literally."

"I don't believe this." Faris's voice was low and laced with the slightest hint of jealousy. "Another faun, really? Did you seriously try to replace me?"

"Faris." Rasp gestured from the smaller fuzzy shape to the larger fuzzy shape. "This is Hopalong Humphry."

"Hop, actually. A pleasure to meet you, Faris. I have heard so much about you." There was a notable pause before Hop found the courage to ask, "May I ask about your companion? It appears that she just shifted from a bear into a human woman."

"She did what?" Rasp whipped his head around, straining to catch some sort of glimpse of the shapeshifter, all while silently cursing his stupid aura vision for fading so early.

"Hello!" A cheerful voice hailed to them as soft footsteps crunched in the curled leaves.

"So, a lot's happened since we last saw each other." Faris stood and yanked Rasp to his feet. Placing one arm firmly behind Rasp's back, Faris forcibly walked him closer. "And, frankly it's hard to explain so we're just going to jump into the thick of it and wade our way through, okay?"

Rasp found himself fighting his next step, not entirely sure why. Standing made his head all woozy again. Light and dark shadows danced along his vision as his sense of balance started to slip from his control. "She's your girlfriend, Faris. I get it. Why do you have to make this so weird?"

"Rasp," Faris said, "meet Juneberry."

"Unfortunate name."

"Your sister."

Too much, his brain decided. Faris, shapeshifting bears, and a sister, which he most certainly did not have. What a shame. Once more, for what would hopefully be the last time, Rasp had managed to die without realizing it. As his world started to spin faster, growing dark along the edges like burnt paper, he heard Hop's voice murmur something before everything went impossibly black.

"That certainly explains the enthusiastic lack of clothing."

CHAPTER FORTY-FIVE

The Very Best Horsey

Daana descended the companionway from the orlop deck into the hold one tentative step at a time. She clutched the worn grab rail for dear life, cursing her vision for not making the transition from light to dark as fast as she needed it to. Steeper than a traditional stairway, the broad steps were built at a sharp fifty-degree angle, sacrificing ease of use for utility. The descent wouldn't have been nearly so bad had she brought a lantern, but such was the life of a fledgling spy.

Success meant learning to embrace the dark. Failure to do so was what separated the good spies from the dead ones. According to Ellisar, anyway— who, admittedly, may have just told her that simply to make Daana's assignments harder than necessary. Then again, this so-called assignment very well could have been an excuse to remove Daana from the cabin for the rest of the evening.

No, not maybe, Daana realized as her face scrunched in disgust. It was *definitely* an excuse to get her out of the cabin for a few hours.

Gross.

The pungent stench of filthy straw and animal dung clogged the stale air. Daana drew the collar of her thin tunic over her mouth and nose to keep from gagging. Alas, aside from pulling the cloth up and over the rest of her head, there was little she could do to prevent the harsh, salty air from stinging her eyes. Daana blinked the tears from her vision as she placed each foot as softly as possible, careful not to betray her steps. She could see the hazy yellow light from an oil lantern flickering in the animal pens below.

A disembodied voice drifted upward. The sound grated against Daana's ears like broken ceramic scraping across tiled floors. "Who's a good horsey-horsey-horsey? The best horsey? The smartest? That's right, you are. You are!"

Daana reached the end of the creaky companionway and stepped sound-lessly onto the straw-littered floor. Carefully, moving on just her tiptoes, she crept farther into the dim hold, hugging the shadows along the curved wall. The animal pens were across from her. A familiar shape stood inside the nearest one, bathed in the warm yellow glow of the lantern hanging from the hook above him.

"That's right," Snag said, voice brimming with affection. "'Cause you're the best, aren't you? Not like those stinky brats topside. You don't ask any-thing of me, do you? No 'go here, do this, fork over all your hard-earned coin.' That's 'cause you're a good horsey-horsey. Got manners, don't you?"

The goblin continued smooshing Wormy's whiskered face between his clawed hands, uttering soft praises under his breath. The small, scruffy horse grunted its appreciation as it bucked its head farther into his hands, demand-ing more affection.

Oh gods, she was going to lose it. Daana's ears burned hot against the musty air as she clamped both hands over her quivering mouth.

"Especially that elf brat," Snag continued. "She's the worst of 'em all. Can't even sneak down a ladder without hitting every squeaky step on the way down."

Daana's lower jaw tumbled open in disbelief. *Again?*

"Can you believe it, Wormy? A species supposedly gifted with grace and elegance, and that clodhopper can't help but stomp everywhere she goes."

Dammit! Daana had been so careful this time, too. She was certain she'd finally succeeded in catching the old goblin by surprise. Daana stuffed her hands into her pockets and she shuffled into the flickering light. "How? I barely made a sound this time."

"You did, I hardly noticed at all," Snag agreed, still lavishing unsettling amounts of love and praise onto his favorite horse. "Silence doesn't do you a lot of good when your smell sticks out like a sore tongue."

Daana's eyes widened. Instinctively, she lifted her arm for a quick pit check. "I don't stink."

"Exactly. But everything else does down here. You're like the aromatic candle next to the shit pit."

While it was a relief to learn she didn't stink, Daana wasn't so sure how she felt about Snag's vivid comparison. She trudged over to the short pen, kicking at a loose tuft of straw on her way. "I'm going to get you one of these days. Just wait and see."

"Of course you will." Snag's tone dripped like sticky-sweet sap. "I'll probably be deaf and blind from old age by then, but what does that matter? The important thing is that you'll have done it. And then I can finally die at peace, knowing I taught you one thing."

Daana knew better than to bait him with protest. She snagged one of the apples from the burlap bag hanging from the tack hook instead, content to eat her feelings away. Her teeth sank into the peel with a crunch—not the pleasant, fresh kind either, but the sort of sound made when stepping on a snail. The mealy flesh disintegrated over her tongue, filling her mouth with the foul taste of overripe melon.

Snag swiveled his head around at her. His wrinkled expression went from lovey-dovey to foul in the span of a single breath. "You thankless thief! Spit that out! Apples are for horsies, not terrible sneaky sneakers."

Daana didn't have any desire to finish the unpalatable fruit, but the old instinct to do the opposite of what she was told was suddenly alive and well. She forced herself to take another bite, speaking around the mouthful of sad apple. "Is it really stealing if you stole all this in the first place?"

"I'll have you know I purchased that," Snag said, with the sort of venom in his voice that suggested he was more upset about forking over good silver than he was at being accused of theft. "We all agreed, no bad behavior while on the blasted boat. It draws too much attention."

"I don't remember agreeing to that." Daana chewed thoughtfully for a moment. While tensions had simmered between her and Snag since the awkward heart-to-heart from a few days before, it probably would have been wise not to push her luck. Unfortunately, the temptation to poke the proverbial bear was one she simply could not ignore.

She heaved herself up onto the half wall that made up the front of the animal pen. "Does that mean I should put back that spyglass I found in the navigation room?"

"What were you doing in the navigation room?"

". . . Not snooping?"

The goblin shook his head at her, earrings jangling against one another softly. "I hardly even recognize you anymore. What happened to that sweet summer child who used to cry when told to clean the rabbits for dinner?"

Daana forced down another disappointing bite of apple. "Correction, I *still* cry when you make me do that. I'm just more subtle about it now."

"Hear that, Wormy? She's still a softie when no one's lookin'. That's sweet, innit? Not as sweet as you, though. Nope, nobody's as sweet as you. 'Cause you're the best horsey. Aren't you? Aren't you?" Snag said with the sort of fondness in his voice that made Daana want to shudder. It wasn't the open display of affection itself that was odd, but the fact that it was coming from Snag—someone who dedicated a good deal of energy convincing others that he had no soft side.

Snag selected a stiff bristled brush from a bucket on the floor and set about scrubbing Wormy's tusks with vigor. "Grab that other brush and start giving his coat a good once-over."

Daana remained sitting on the half wall, her legs dangling over the side of the stockyard pen. The musty smell of damp hay and animal dung was a lot stronger now that she was sitting directly above it. "Not happening," she said. "Your beast nipped me in the butt last time I got near him."

"Probably 'cause you keep munching his apples."

Daana opened her mouth to deliver an equally scathing reply when the ship lurched with a sudden, thunderous *boom*, knocking her from her perch. Pain surged up her wrists as she struck the deck in a half crouch, saving herself from what could have been a nasty tumble. The ship's timbers rattled like old bones as decades of dust and debris rained down from the low-hanging rafters. Above, muffled by several floors, Daana heard screaming and footsteps pounding against the upper deck. She looked to Snag, realizing he wore a terrified expression similar to her own.

Daana gathered herself into a crouch, not bothering to wipe the filth that clung to her clothes. "That was a powder charge."

The goblin watched the ceiling, his ears fanned wide and flicking from side to side, listening as the clamor swelled louder above them. "I warned Ellisar under pain of dismemberment not to use those unless it was an absolute emergency."

"There's always the chance she did it anyway."

"I wish that were the case, but it sounds like we might be in trouble. What kind of weapons do you got on you, girl?"

Daana's hands flung out to her sides defensively. "You said not to carry any weapons! Draws too much attention."

"I said to make it look like you *weren't* carrying any weapons. Not to forgo them completely!" As if to prove his point, Snag withdrew two hidden daggers. He noticed Daana staring and promptly hid them behind his back, out of reach. "Nah, you gotta learn your lesson the hard way. Go on. Find something to arm yourself with, quick like."

With a shake of her head, Daana darted across the straw-littered ground. The livestock pens were located just off of the cargo hold, a depressing distance away from the arms locker, unfortunately. While she wouldn't find a proper sword or shield anywhere nearby, there was a wide array of equipment stored in the tool area. She yanked a rusted pitchfork from the wall and tested its weight in her hands. It wasn't ideal, but it would do.

Fast footsteps came pounding down the stairs as three weathered individuals burst into the cramped hold. The lead goblin pointed her curved saber at Daana and shouted something too loud to understand. It sounded like Laftak, the language of the flatlands, but the dialect was a far cry from the formal conversations Daana had learned back at the academy.

Daana tilted her head at the grizzled intruder. "What?"

The goblin repeated herself with as much success as her previous attempt.

Shrugging, Daana replied in Laftak the best way she knew how. The goblin stopped shouting and stared back at her unblinkingly. The two ruffians behind her, a rather scrawny-looking elf and what might have been a human, exchanged confused glances.

"Did you just tell her where the fucking library is?" Snag said.

Daana shrugged. "I thought that's what she was asking."

"They're pirates, girl. They want us to surrender quietly so they can hold us for ransom and all that crap."

"Oh. Well in that case, forget I said anything." Daana's feet shifted into the fighter's stance that had been hammered into her after many, many painful training sessions. None of the pirates had a bow, fortunately. Just swords and various other sharp, stabby implements of death. Most of which Daana was certain she could outrun if necessary.

For several seconds, the trespassers continued to stare at her in varied stages of bewilderment. "Snag," Daana shouted over her shoulder, "why aren't they attacking?"

"No offense, but I think they were expecting us to surrender. You an' I don't exactly have the look of warriors, you know."

With an infuriated scream, the goblin pirate waved her sword at her companions. Spurred back into action, the trio split. The goblin and elf advanced in Daana's direction while the third went for Snag. Daana couldn't help but feel slightly flattered by that. Sure, Snag may not have been armed with a super menacing pitchfork, but they obviously took her for the more accomplished fighter.

Idiots.

A shrill scream from the other side of the stock pens indicated Snag's opponent had already met their gruesome end. There wasn't time to double-check, however. Daana charged, brandishing her pitchfork like a spear. The goblin stepped out of the way in time, but the elf was a hair too slow. The prongs scraped along his ribcage, ripping a hole into his tunic that ran red with blood when Daana tugged her rusty weapon free.

She spun in time to block a blow from the goblin's sword. The pitchfork's wood handle shuddered violently between her hands as the strikes rained down. Daana saw her opening, ducked to the side and kicked, sending her smaller opponent sprawling. The elf lunged at her, screaming unknown obscenities. To be honest, even if Daana was fluent in the language, it would've been difficult to make out what he was saying over the sound of thundering hoofbeats.

Hoofbeats?

Daana looked just in time to jump out of the way. Wormy reared, striking down the elf with his front legs and then landed on top of him with a bone-crunching slam.

"Get on!" Snag shouted.

Still clutching her trusty pitchfork, Daana swung onto Wormy's back before the little horse took off again, picking up speed. It was like riding a furry, temperamental barrel. "Snag!" Daana screamed, cinching her arms around the goblin's waist. "Slow down, we're going to run out of ship!"

"We're taking the stairs."

"Horses can't climb!"

"Hush, girl! I'm hoping Wormy doesn't know that!"

CHAPTER FORTY-SIX

Hands Make the Best Souvenirs

The companionway drew closer as Wormy barreled toward it at full speed. Daana pressed herself flat against Snag's back and screwed her eyes shut. She felt the little horse's body lurch upward at an unnatural angle. Wormy's movements were short and jerky as he traversed the steep stairs with the sort of agility one would expect to find in a mountain goat and not a horse.

Daana refused to open her eyes. She held her breath, waiting for the inevitable moment Wormy lost his footing and the three of them plummeted to their deaths.

To her surprise, the rotund horse hopped all the way to the top of the companionway without issue. Wormy's lurching gait evened out beneath them as he galloped forward onto the orlop deck. He continued his mad dash, spurred onwards by tender words of encouragement from Snag. Daana reluctantly opened her eyes to find the deck in utter chaos around them. A mix of pirates and sailors clashed together, filling the crowded space with the deafening roar of a fight.

Only a few of the fighters stopped to gawk back at them. The rest appeared to have more pressing matters on their hands than to worry about the strange, tusked horse barreling through their ranks.

"Go on, then. One more. You got this." Snag maneuvered the small horse with a sharp turn, directing Wormy up the next flight of stairs.

It was official, Daana decided. Wormy was not a horse, but a force of nature. She vowed to never eat another one of his treats ever again. In fact, she owed him a full bag of apples after this. No, two bags! As many as his little heart desired if only they made it to the top deck without breaking their necks.

Panicked voices drew Daana's attention ahead of them. A slew of grungy pirates were making their way down the companionway directly in the path of the oncoming horse. The pirates spun around, screaming as they scrambled over one another to get out of the way. The closest individual tripped and was subsequently trampled. As were the second and third, each producing a muffled *crunch* that would undoubtedly haunt Daana's dreams for years to come. Wormy reached the top of the companionway several jostling leaps and bounds later, right on the heels of the sole survivor. While the pirate may have escaped the stairwell, his getaway was cut regrettably short by Snag, who plunged a blade into his throat as Wormy surged past onto the quarterdeck.

Topside was even more chaotic than below. A thick blanket of mist swept over the sides of the ship, making it impossible to see anything more than a few yards ahead at a time. The smell of sulfur and smoke wafted on the breeze. The main source of smoke appeared to be coming from the navigation room behind them. Flames lit the interior, visible from the outside via the smoldering hole where the door had previously hung. From the damage, it looked as if the navigation room had erupted from the inside out.

The wet air stirred with smoke, sulfur, and ash. There was something else as well. Something the others likely didn't notice. It buzzed against Daana's skin, causing every hair on her arm to stand on end. Awoken by magic, the dark veins within her arms were suddenly alive and wriggling. Daana bit back her scream as pain flooded her body.

"It's about fucking time!" Ashwyn's booming voice snapped Daana from her pain-induced stupor. "You two get your scrawny asses over here so I don't have to carry your shit anymore."

Daana spied Ashwyn's bulky form through the churning mist and smoke. The orc had her back to the mizzenmast, with a circle of pirates gathered loosely around her. The enemy hung back, as if afraid to be the first to breach the orc's deadly range. Their hesitation was not unfounded. The scattering of fallen bodies at Ashwyn's feet made it quite clear that the first pirate to volunteer his or her neck stood to have it snapped in half.

Wormy broke through the ring of pirates, scattering the already hesitant fighters into a disorganized retreat.

Ashwyn swung Snag's tattered leather satchel from around her neck and tossed it to him. She jutted the hilt of Daana's sword in her direction with less fanfare. "I don't know what sort of depravities you keep in that bag of yours, Snaggy, but after seeing the destruction it caused, I'd rather not carry it."

Snag peered inside his satchel, voice laced with fury. "It's half-empty!"

"Yeah, sorry 'bout that. Whatever Ellie pulled out of there sure packed a wallop though. Ain't ever seen a door blow off its hinges before." Ashwyn stopped talking only long enough to take a breath. No longer burdened with an extra sword hanging from her hip, she adjusted her stance to accommodate the sudden shift in weight. "Do I want to know where you two have been all this time?"

Daana slid from Wormy and got into position alongside Ashwyn, feeling relieved to have traded the pitchfork for something more familiar. If only there had been time to find a shield, some chainmail, and maybe a nice, sturdy helmet. Oh well. Worst-case scenario, she supposed she could use Ashwyn as a shield if needed. "We were belowdecks when we heard the explosion. What's going on?"

"Ambush." The ring of pirates had regrouped and were starting to close in again. Ashwyn busied herself with making faces at the advancing enemy, silently daring one of them to be the first to make a move. "There was a galley hiding in a cove along the coast here, waiting for an unescorted target to sail past. They used the fog as cover and caught the watch unaware. Our dear, sweet captain offered them cargo and hostages to appease them."

Daana nodded as she followed along. "The pirates didn't go for it?"

"Oh no, the deal was fine with them. It was Ellie who took offense to the bargain. She's not one for being a hostage unless it's her idea. She blew a damn hole into the ship and tossed the *Ducky Luck*'s captain overboard. Now it's just chaos with everyone fighting everyone because no one knows what to do."

A crackling bolt of lightning erupted from the dark, churning clouds overhead and struck the mainmast in a shower of yellow and white sparks.

"Oh, and the other side has an air elemental. I probably should've mentioned that earlier. The witch didn't take kindly to her beloved pirate captain being split from ear to ear. She's currently in a game of cat and mouse with the missus, out to exact her revenge or whatnot."

Daana gawked up at the brown and black thunderclouds swirling overhead, as thick as cotton. "The witch can control lightning?" Most air elementals stuck to wind, sometimes rain, but few were capable of harnessing lightning—not safely, anyway. Lightning manipulation was a highly unstable ability that hardly anyone ever got right, often at the expense of their own life.

"Seems that way."

Snag's voice rang out over the surrounding commotion. "That's all very nice and all, but do we have a fucking plan? We are literally standing targets right now."

Unlike Snag, Ashwyn didn't seem all that concerned with the ring of pirates slowly tightening in around them. "Well, I was supposed to be securing the four of us a longboat, but I got held up. Then you two arrived and I daresay you're caught up on everything I know insofar."

"Then what are you waiting for?" Daana demanded. "Do that thing you do."

"What thing I do?"

"Where you convince the enemy to do what you want them to do. That way we don't have to fight our way out of this."

"That only works if I mean it. Considering these no-good swine dogs interrupted a moment of privacy, I'm really not feeling all that merciful right now," Ashwyn said. "Besides, these are pirates. It's not like they'd believe me even if I was telling the truth."

"Oh my gods." Snag rolled his head back with a groan. He was still seated on Wormy's saddleless back, content to remain as far above the action as possible. "You two go get the boat. I'll find Ellisar."

Daana saw the flicker of a match seconds before he lit the charge in his hands. She ducked for cover the same time Ashwyn did. Snag whipped the powder charge into the enemy ranks, reducing the closest pirates to bloody clumps of flesh. Judging from the array of scattered, screaming bodies, those unfortunate enough to survive the blast would only do so for another few hours before succumbing to blood loss.

"Don't let her do anything stupid!" Snag shouted as he started off toward the bow at a quick gallop, disappearing into the mist.

Ashwyn raised her eyebrow at Daana. "Was he talking to me or you?"

"Could have been either or, honestly."

"Right." Ashwyn sprang back onto her feet with inexplicably spryness. "You heard him, Peaches. Time for you and me to secure us a ride out of here."

Daana tugged the collar of her tunic over her mouth and nose as she scurried after the orc's hulking frame. Smoke stung her eyes as she stole silently into the gloom, trying not to lose sight of Ashwyn. The rest of the ship was in chaos. Around them, crewmembers raced through the fog and ash, looking as lost as Daana felt.

Ashwyn darted down the steps from the quarterdeck to the main. She met resistance halfway and was forced to reconsider her strategy. Gripping the handrail, the orc kicked with both legs, sending the front two pirates hurtling into the deluge of bodies pressing at their backs. "Stairs are out of order, Peaches! Up and over that rail and, for goddess's sake, land with those knees bent like I taught you!"

There wasn't time to question the command. Daana swung her legs over the side and jumped, only realizing she couldn't actually see the main deck below until she was already plummeting through the ash-laden air. She hit the rickety deck, shockwaves of pain jolting up each leg. Daana was still shaking off the sting when a dark shape leapt out of the swirling haze at her.

She threw up her blade in time to block the blow. Instinct kicked in and she shifted her footing, trading blow for blow with her assailant in rapid succession. Harassing her opponent into a semi-retreat, Daana saw her opening and ducked low, throwing her leg wide in a sweeping arch. The leg sweep caught her opponent by surprise and they tumbled backward onto the deck with a muffled thud.

The pirate's hood fell from his head and Daana found herself staring back into the wide-eyed face of an elf. Taking advantage of Daana's hesitation, he rolled, reaching for the sword he'd lost while being dropped on his ass.

"Oh no you don't!" Daana brought her sword down with all her might. Her blade met resistance when it struck bone, but the initial force of the swing carried it through, severing the elf's dominant hand in a single slice. Her opponent screamed, grabbing his bloody stump as he writhed helplessly on the deck.

Daana screamed too. And then, for whatever reason, felt compelled to add insult to injury by kicking the severed hand away from herself.

A heavy *thunk* landed on the deck behind Daana. "A hand, nice," Ashwyn congratulated. "Why you kicking it for? You gotta keep that, you know."

Daana made a face, her queasy stomach performing an acrobatic flip at the mental image. As if the elf's stump spurting blood every which way wasn't bad enough. "Why?"

"As a souvenir, obviously. Just think of the puns, girl!" Ashwyn approached the still-whimpering elf as she spoke. "Need a hand? Give a hand? Take a hand? You're passing up quite the opportunity here."

"You're demented." What was possibly even more demented was the way Ashwyn dealt with the maimed pirate. Seeing her coming, the elf started to crawl away, leaving a trail of blood in his wake. Ashwyn caught up to him in a mere matter of strides and hoisted the screaming elf over her shoulder before dumping him unceremoniously over the side of the ship.

"Oh, I know!" The orc spun around on her heel, eyes wide with excitement. "String the hand on a necklace and give it to Snag. Guilt him into wearing it as a show of appreciation for everything he's done for you."

Now *that* was a tempting idea. Except the part where Daana had to carry a severed stump with her in the meantime. "You know, I think maybe this is what he meant by 'don't do anything stupid.'"

"Huh. You might be onto something."

"Just like we should be finding our way onto a boat, maybe?" Daana reminded her.

"Look at you, being so responsible today. Makes my heart proud." Ashwyn broke into a pearly grin that was as genuine as it was terrifying. "You're right as rain, of course. And just for that, I'm going to let you take the lead."

Flattery wasn't going to work this time. "Gods, no. We both know I'm using you as a shield."

"Fine, but I get to keep the hand."

CHAPTER FORTY-SEVEN

Not Your Nanny

The churning gray and brown sky lit as a lance of lightning struck the foremast, illuminating the chaotic deck in eerie white light. Wooden splinters and cinders rained down as the mast ripped from its rigging and fell. Ashwyn yanked Daana to the side. They huddled against the railing, watching wide-eyed as the broken mast toppled over the side of the *Ducky Luck* and hung limp above the raging sea.

Ashwyn's face was drained of color. Daana knew it wasn't the state of the ship that concerned her. She gave the orc's hand a reassuring squeeze. "I've seen Ellisar survive worse than that."

"Yeah. Probably just makin' a mess to prove a point. I'm sure Snag will slap some sense into her shortly." Despite her bold words, Ashwyn's voice had lost its brazen confidence. Still watching the churning sky, the orc rose and pulled Daana back onto her feet with her. "Come on. We've got to get to that boat, pronto."

Daana followed Ashwyn through the swirl of fog and ash without protest. From her evenings spent absentmindedly wandering the upper deck, Daana knew the *Ducky Luck* had two workboats designed to pull double duty as emergency crafts in a pinch. Unfortunately, she was not alone in this knowledge. When she and Ashwyn arrived at the first davit, they found the boat missing, having already been deployed.

Ashwyn changed course, tusks grinding against the flat of her upper teeth as she dodged bits of fallen mast and burning debris in the direction of the second longboat station. Sailors and pirates alike darted through the misty gloom around them.

"Why aren't they retreating?" Daana demanded between ragged breaths. With their captain slain and their best fighter, the air elemental, set on exacting her revenge at any cost, including the lives of everyone around her, Daana was surprised the rest of the pirates hadn't simply called it quits. "Even I can see this is a lost cause."

"Desperation, Peaches." The pirates were not alone in their desperation, apparently. The distress in Ashwyn's tone was damn near palpable. "I noticed it when the mast fell. Didn't want to say anything to get you riled, but we might be in a pickle here if that other longboat's gone."

"How so?"

"To your left, Peaches. Look, but don't stop moving your feet." Ashwyn slowed down beside her, looping her arm through Daana's. She guided the elf's steps, allowing her to take in the scene without sacrificing their speed. A decrepit galley bucked on the churning waters beside them, tethered to the *Ducky Luck* via a twisted tangle of ropes and grappling hooks. The stern sat abnormally low in the water.

"It's sinking?"

"Yeah, well, you know Ellie. Couldn't leave well enough alone. Had to go put a hole in the enemy ship. Unfortunately for us, that means these buggers are desperate to seize this one for themselves." With Daana's attention back on her feet, Ashwyn released her arm and assumed the lead once more. "Which is why we need to get that last longboat. Even if it means I have to toss you overboard to swim for it."

Daana tensed at what she sincerely hoped was an offhanded jest. While she had come a long way with her deep mistrust of boats, her disdain for water and any activity short of bathing had yet to improve. "Now that definitely qualifies as something stupid."

The pair were nearing the second davit when Ashwyn's fast footsteps ground to a halt. She ducked down beside the taffrail and signaled for Daana to do the same. Wordlessly, Daana slipped into the shadows beside her.

To her relief, she saw the second longboat was not yet deployed. Not from a lack of trying, from the looks of it. Judging from the blood and bodies scattered haphazardly on the deck, several of the crew had been in the process of lowering the longboat when they were set upon by the enemy. The pirates may have won, but their victory had come at a loss. The left arm of the davit had snapped away during the scuffle, forcing the pirates to guide the longboat down by hand. A feat made significantly harder by the raging swell that threatened to smash the smaller boat to pieces against *Ducky Luck*'s barnacled side.

Daana whispered to Ashwyn, "Is there a reason we're hiding and not seizing the boat?"

"Never work harder than you have to." Ashwyn's gaze was cold and calculating, watching their progress with the expression of a hungry scavenger about to capitalize on someone else's hard earned kill. "We'll wait here, catch our breath, and as soon as they've got it in the water, we'll jump 'em. Remember, wait for the lead to be secured first. The last thing we need is for the current to whisk our ride away without anybody in it."

A second lightning bolt erupted against the quarterdeck above them, sending a shockwave of smoldering wood and splinters in its wake. Startled by the blast, one of the pirates glanced worriedly over his shoulder at the destruction. His frightened gaze dropped lower, settling over Ashwyn and Daana.

"Change of plans!" Ashwyn surged forward, her sword already drawn and ready to taste blood. "Go for the rope, Peaches! I'll take care of the sea dogs."

The pirates dropped the rope in favor of their swords. Throwing herself into a dive, Daana seized the end of the lead before it disappeared over the side. The rope bit into her hands, splitting open the calloused skin on each palm. Screaming, being dragged on her ass along the rough deck, Daana kicked out with her legs and braced them against the siding. The boat jerked to a stop below her. Every muscle in her back and legs strained in protest as she slowly guided the rope down, hand over hand, until the boat reached the water and the line went slack.

By the time Daana had the lead tied, there were already two pirates dead on the ground, soon to be followed by a third. The remaining pair decided it wasn't worth their lives and turned tail and ran. Ashwyn's broad shoulders dropped in exhaustion as she trudged back over to the davit. In lieu of *Excellent work, Daana. Way to save our boat and our bacon*, the orc's disgruntled stare settled onto the knot Daana had used to secure the lead to the ship's rail.

"Who the fuck taught you to tie rope? That's just shameful."

"Seriously?"

"Yeah, yeah, you did good. Soak it all in and get a fat head, why don't you?" Ashwyn slung her leg over the side of the railing, preparing to climb down. "Good news. Subpar knot work aside, thanks to you, we're not going to have to swim for it after all."

Daana didn't trust the orc's unnerving grin. "Why do I get the feeling you're about to deliver some bad news?"

Ashwyn's pearly smile widened past the point of comfort. "I sincerely hope you're better at climbing than you are at knots, because this next bit might get a little hairy."

Another blast rocked the ship from stern to bow. Daana whipped her head in the direction of the commotion. The fog parted, revealing the navigation room fire had spread across the quarterdeck, steadily working its way up the mizzenmast. A single figure stood backlit by the flames with arms thrown wide, whipping the wind into a frenzy to encourage the flames higher.

Ashwyn called to Daana from below, her voice muffled by both the distance and the roar of elements. "What's the holdup?"

"It's the air elemental." The weight of magic in the air took Daana's breath away. She closed her eyes and extended her open hand, opening her sixth sense to her surroundings. Undulating waves of static buzzed across Daana's skin, building, before the full force of the magic slammed into the center of her chest.

Daana's eyes shot open with a gasp.

Tearing her gaze from the quarterdeck, she leaned over the heaving side of the ship and looked down. Ashwyn was almost all the way to the longboat now. The rickety boat bucked and heaved among the choppy waves, pulling at the rope tethering it to the bigger ship like an unruly dog. Daana raised her voice in order to be heard over the raging din. "I think I have to go do something stupid."

Ashwyn stared up at her, face wet and dripping from the ocean spray. "Sweet goddess, Snag's gonna kill me."

"It's the air elemental. She's lost control." When this didn't have the desired impact, Daana was forced to add, "I don't think Snag or Ellisar are going to get away if I don't intervene."

"Ugh, fine!" Ashwyn dropped the remaining distance into the small boat, gripping the sides for dear life as it heaved beneath her. "I'm not your nanny. If you want to go get yourself killed, have at it!"

Daana had hoped for something more encouraging, but it would have to do. Ensuring her sword was still secured at her side, she sprinted across the main deck. The magic grew stronger as she neared. The black lines under her skin pulled harder, and harder, like a ravenous tiger on a chain.

Daana climbed halfway up the splintered stairs to the quarterdeck and peeked over the side. The elemental paced back and forth across the destroyed deck with her head tilted upward at the sails, scanning the yards for telltale signs of life. Even with the mist and smoke to cloak Daana's movement, the deck was too open to risk it. The witch would obliterate her before she even got halfway.

Daana searched the area around her for an alternative form of cover, silently cursing herself for not finding a shield along the way. Just as she was considering something *really* stupid, a small spherical object rolled off of the roof of the navigation room and clattered toward the pacing figure. The witch leapt out of the way, throwing up a protective gust of wind a split second before the powder charge erupted.

Daana flew up and over the stairs without thinking. She pounded across the smoky deck, avoiding the small pockets of scattered fire. Alerted by her footsteps, the witch spun around and threw up her hands the same moment Daana slammed into her. They struck the upturned deck and rolled. Daana kicked, clawed, and punched to gain the upper hand. A close-fisted strike to the windpipe left the witch temporarily stunned, gasping for air.

Daana straddled the witch's body beneath her, using her knees to pin her to the deck. Magic crackled between the witch's hands as she threw them forward, choking on a spell lodged in her swollen throat. Daana caught the witch by the wrists, skin burning as the magic poured into her, and screamed, *"Exhaurire!"*

Blistering heat surged up her arms in waves, burning its way through her body until each nerve ending screamed in agony. The witch struggled beneath her, attempting to wrestle free, but Daana held strong. Power pooled in her chest, crushing her lungs as it whipped, whirled, and swelled, threatening to burst free. Bright lights popped across Daana's vision as hot stomach acid scalded the inside of her mouth.

Too much, her mind screamed. Cold panic surged forth, snapping Daana back to her senses. She released the witch's limp hands to sever the connection, but the power disobeyed. Blue magic arced between them, independent of a conductor. The dark veins within Daana's wrists squirmed with hunger. They pulled, pulled, pulled, draining the witch, who had since gone still.

Fuck. Fuck, fuck, fuck!

Head swimming, Daana staggered to her feet, but her sense of balance was gone. The once solid deck undulated like ripples across water beneath her unsteady feet. *Release it*, the still-functioning part of her brain commanded. *Now! Before the darkness takes control.*

A spell danced across her tongue unbidden. Dazed, barely able to keep her eyes open, Daana threw her arms into the air and screamed. Lightning erupted from her hands and rocketed high into the air. The magic erupted with a blast so loud, it deafened Daana's hearing. The force of the explosion pulsed downward, bowling her backward like a dry leaf in the wind.

Daana staggered, catching herself against the railing, her world still spinning. Ash and embers rained down from above, catching the remaining sails alight in flame. She still couldn't hear, but her sense of touch felt magnified tenfold. Every creak and groan from the ship reverberated through her screaming bones. Behind her, a steady *clump, clump, clump* grew stronger. Confused, Daana turned and squinted at the horse-shaped blur that burst from the companionway toward her.

A familiar hand reached for her. Some nagging instinct ordered Daana to jump and her legs obeyed. She mounted, managing to not slide off the other side of the horse as the ship shot past. Wormy didn't stop when the deck ran out. Clinging to Snag, unable to hear the shrill scream that leapt from her mouth, they sailed over the side of the ship and plummeted for several heartbeats before plunging into the icy depths below.

CHAPTER FORTY-EIGHT

The Fire Witch

The stench of smoke and charred flesh clouded the damp forest air. It burned the inside of Oralia's nose and throat, causing her eyes to water. She ignored the swell of hot tears, knowing any movement, even to quickly wipe away the moisture clouding her vision, could give up her position. She remained perfectly still, crouched low among a tangle of overgrown bracken, catching only glimpses of the witch that paced restlessly between the trees looking for her.

"Always have to do it the hard way." Grettie shuffled along, twisting and turning her hands in a manner that did not appear nervous, but compulsive. "You accidentally burn one acquaintance to a crisp and suddenly you're labeled 'untrustworthy.'"

The witch's muttered grumblings grew faster and more frantic, working herself into a rage. The twitch in her fingers worsened until the building impulse was simply too strong to ignore. With an infuriated yell, Grettie whipped around and threw her hands into the air, channeling a surge of flame skyward. The spell incinerated the lower boughs of a black cottonwood in a volatile flash of red and black.

More smoke filled the air as Grettie turned back around, scanning the dim forest floor for her troublesome quarry. "How's that for untrustworthy, huh? Now you get on out here before I'm forced to do something we both regret!"

Oralia kept painfully still, forcing slow breaths through her irritated nose as her thoughts raced behind her eyes. Of all the types of witches, why did it have to be a fire elemental? Those were the worst of the worst! Fire elements were often hotheaded, temperamental bastards who, against all odds, managed to survive a childhood rife with accidental fires. Only the most successful survived into adulthood, for grim reasons.

The challenge often left its mark, resulting in highly unstable individuals with a perverse sense of conscience. Grettie was clearly no exception, considering she'd incinerated her orc companion without a second thought.

A disembodied voice slipped among Oralia's panicking thoughts. **If you don't move, you'll end up in the same way. An unrecognizable, charred corpse.**

"I'm thinking," Oralia hissed under her breath.

I see, drawing the witch right to us then. An excellent plan if you wish to die!

This was, admittedly, a most unusual situation. As Oralia was playing the part of the unwilling host, the dark magic could not afford to let her die. If she perished before it had a chance to infect another vessel, it, too, would go belly up—or something like that. Truth be told, Oralia wasn't too keen on the exact details. What she did know was that, no matter how much it detested her, it was in the entity's best interest to keep her alive. For the meantime, anyway.

Oralia grimaced as the skin on her right arm crawled, as if swarming with insects. A quick glance assured her there was nothing there.

You're sensing magic, you fool, the entity hissed. **Dodge to the left, now!**

Ignoring every instinct screaming at her to do the exact opposite of what the entity said, Oralia obeyed. She threw her body sideways in an awkward roll, crashing through a tangle of barbed vines as she did so. The thorns dug into her wool clothing and marred the exposed flesh on her arms with deep red scratches. The pain was preferable to the alternative, however. A quick glance over her shoulder confirmed that the bracken was now nothing more than a smoldering pile of burnt ash.

Fucking witches, Oralia cursed within her head. If she allowed that to happen to her, Sascha would resurrect her from the dead just so he could kill her all over again.

Are you going to allow your beloved to bury you, as you did for Curly?

Oralia tensed. Amid the fear and fury stirring within her mind, she couldn't help but wonder how the spirit had learned which vulnerabilities were best used against her.

I am one with your thoughts and dreams. I see what Curly's death did to you. Poor Sascha isn't as resilient as you, I'm afraid. Poor fool wouldn't survive the heartache.

What made Oralia even more furious was the fact that the spirit's motivation was working. She gathered her knees beneath her and took off between the trees. The forest became an undistinguishable blur of green and black as she slammed her feet against the slippery ground, doubling her speed.

"Looks like the rabbit's been flushed from hiding!" The craggy voice rang out behind her. "Run, run, little rabbit. You're not getting away from me."

Oralia ducked and weaved as she sprinted, attempting to lose her psychotic tail. A white oak burst into flames to her left. Over the ragged in and out of her own smoke-infused lungs, she could hear Grettie's fast footsteps gaining on her.

Foolish orc. You cannot outrun the human. Use your smarts. The only way out of this is to best her in battle.

Fuck. That.

Oralia might have been an accomplished fighter, but that meant nothing next to a fire elemental. The moment she stopped running was the same moment her body was rendered into an unrecognizable pile of ash. No, there was another way. Her years on the battlefield had taught that all species, humans included, had shortcomings. Humans were fast on their feet, yes, but they lacked the finely tuned senses of an orc. Their senses of smell and hearing, in particular, were poor in comparison. If Oralia could put enough space between her and Grettie, she'd be able to give her the slip and bunker down somewhere out of sight. And then, come nightfall, she could pick her way back to camp under the cloak of darkness.

It wasn't the best plan, granted, but it was still miles ahead of taking on a witch head-to-head by herself! Of all the ludicrous ideas Oralia had ever heard, the spirit's suggestion was by far the absolute wo—

A wall of flame erupted across the ground in front of her. Oralia changed directions, only to find herself running parallel with the raging barricade of fire. She whipped around, eyes taking in the flickering expanse, desperately searching for a way out. It was too late. She was fully encircled now. The dancing tongues of red and orange flames fused together, allowing a small figure to slip through seconds before the ring sealed shut.

Grettie shuffled closer, appearing entirely too at ease for being in the middle of a raging inferno of fire. She was average size for a human woman, which was substantially smaller than Oralia. Unfortunately, a thing like size didn't matter much when your adversary could incinerate you with a snap of their fingers. Grettie's hair was a wild tangle of dirty brown curls nearly the same color of the matted furs she wore on her back. Other than a small knife tucked into her belt, she wore no weapon—not a great sign when dealing with elementals.

The scruffy human curled her nose in disdain. "There's something off about you, orc."

The magic holding the fire together kept the worst of the smoke at bay as well, allowing Oralia both the ability to not only breathe, but talk as well. While she had never been one for talking her way out of these sorts of situations, Oralia supposed there was no time like the present to put her serious lack of skills to the test. She stood straighter, mimicking the way Grettie tilted her head. "You do not know who I am?"

Grettie raised one dirt-encrusted finger to scratch the inside of her left nostril. "Should I?"

"You chased me all this way, went through the trouble of trapping me within a ring of fire, and you do not even recognize me? Me? With my face plastered on every wanted poster from here to Castle Bay?" Oralia threw her arms wide and spun around. She dragged the toe of her right boot into the muck as she did so. The results weren't a perfect ring, but she didn't think a seer's trap required perfection in order to work.

Oralia pinched the bridge of her nose with a sigh. "What is the point of being infamous if no one recognizes you?"

The sneer slipped from Grettie's curled lips in confusion. "Am I supposed to know who you are?"

"Yes! I thought that was why you and your gang were chasing me."

"We was chasing you to kill you and steal your things."

Oralia neatly stepped free of the seer's trap before sealing it with a final smudge of her foot. She didn't know whether the dark magic in her veins meant that she too could get caught within the rune, and held no desire to use this as an opportunity to find out. "Are you telling me you do not recognize your own Protector of the Realm?"

Grettie removed her finger from her nose and studied the contents trapped beneath her filthy fingernail.

"Former protector, I suppose." Oralia folded her arms over her chest in the same manner she had seen Daana do countless times in the past. She had always found it a bit snobbish and hoped the bandit would think so as well. "Before the whole traitor to the realm thing came into the light, of course."

"I—"

"Are in the presence of an outlaw legend," Oralia finished, helpfully. She peered down her nose at the smaller human, lifting one eyebrow higher than the other skeptically. "Can you do something about the fire, by the way? It is getting unbearably hot in here."

"That's kinda the point, actually."

"This much smoke exposure cannot be good for the lungs."

"Now see here!" Grettie took a challenging step forward. "Stop trying to run this. I'm in charge. Me! Not you. Got it?"

"Fine, fine." It was difficult to maintain her air of superiority when Oralia wanted to rip her clothes from her back. The temperature within the ring bordered on sweltering. "Now, how do you want to do this? I would rather skip the threats and move on to the part where I pay you handsomely to look the other way, if you do not mind."

Grettie's scrutinizing eyes looked Oralia up and down before coming to a fast conclusion. "You're not carrying any money. Not enough, that is."

"Yes, because that would be incredibly impractical. The money is back at my camp, obviously." Oralia challenged the bandit's stare with one of her own. After a moment of intense silence, she took things a step further. "I am getting the impression that you are not the one in charge. Where is your leader? Perhaps I will have better luck with someone less"—she withdrew the word "incompetent" and selected the slightly less insulting—"fiery."

"Or I could just kill you as planned and then go find your camp. The rest of the crew are probably already pillaging it as we speak."

"Sounds as though you have it all figured out then," Oralia said. "Carry on."

Grettie squinted at her, seemingly aware a trap had been set but unsure of where or when it was going to snap shut on her foot.

"For your sake," Oralia muttered at a volume barely loud enough for the witch to overhear, "I hope your leader is the merciful type."

"Alright, enough whispering to yourself, orc. You either tell me whatever it is you've got to say or I'll turn you to cinders right here."

"You finding the money on your own would be quite a feat, considering I alone know where the chest is stashed. You do not just leave that sort of wealth sitting out in a saddlebag for all the world to see, after all. But if you are certain you can do it without me, all the best to you."

"Fine. Tell me where it is then." A slow smile spread across Grettie's soot-covered face as a plan slowly unfolded behind her glassy eyes. "And I'll let you walk away."

"As tempting as that sounds, you will need me to lead you to it."

"This just sounds like an overcomplicated plan to force me to keep you alive."

"Well of course it does. That is exactly what it is. This is not the first time I have run into trouble on the road. When traveling with large sums of money, the easiest way to safeguard your life is to make sure no one else knows where it is hidden. That way you always have a bargaining chip in the event you are forced to barter for your survival."

They stared at one another for an unbearable stretch of silence. The broiling heat from the fire crackled and snapped at Oralia's back, causing a sheen of sweat to drip down her forehead. The air was thick and smoky, stinging the insides of her nostrils as the irritation crawled down her throat, clogging her airways.

Finally, greed won over, lessening some of the fire raging behind Grettie's wild eyes. "Fine! But we're doing this my way. Understand? No funny business. You make one wrong move and I cremate you on the spot!"

And to think, just earlier that day, Oralia's biggest concern had been ensuring she returned to camp with Sascha's favorite pot. That seemed almost laughable now. Almost. Alas, the dark entity had been right about one thing. Sascha would not survive the heartache of losing both his favorite pot and his fuckmate on the same day. For both of their sakes, Oralia needed to do whatever it took to return to camp in one piece. Even if it meant playing prisoner to an unstable fire witch.

She lifted her hands in compliance. "Understood."

CHAPTER FORTY-NINE

Undeserving

Red and orange flames burned bright against the surrounding sea of dark trees. The sweltering air within the burning ring was thick with smoke and ash. Hands held aloft, unable to wipe the sheen of sweat that dripped down her brow and collected along the tips of her eyelashes, Oralia relied on blinking alone to clear her vision. It was working as well as was to be expected. She persisted, her gaze locked on the scruffy witch across from her.

"First things first." Grettie unslung the rusted dagger from her belt and gestured to the mossy forest floor. The sprawl of ferns and short grasses were bent and wilted, sagging closer to the ground to escape the oppressive heat. "Throw down that sword and any other stabbies you got on you."

Oralia unbuckled the sword belt from her hip and dropped it. She slid the weapon farther away with her foot, hoping to put the fidgety witch at ease.

"Good, good," Grettie said with a bob of her head, frizzy hair bouncing. The persistent twitch in her fingers seemed at odds with her confident smile. "Now put your hands behind your head and get on the ground. Nice and slow like."

Oralia glanced out of the corner of her eye at the symbol etched into the dirt behind her as she eased down. Even to the discerning eye, the seer's trap would be hard to spot.

"I said slow!" Grettie slashed the air with her rusted dagger for emphasis. "And watch those hands! You even think of trying something, and I'll burn you to the ground."

Moving at the speed of cold molasses, Oralia dutifully placed her hands on the back of her neck and slowly sank to the ground. She couldn't help but note that the dark entity writhing beneath her skin had gone suspiciously silent. It wasn't that she missed the additional voice, per se, but even the slightest distraction from the dread boring a hole through the bottom of her gut would have been appreciated.

Oralia eased onto her stomach. With her head tilted at an uncomfortable angle, she watched as Grettie edged closer, unraveling a coil of rope from her pocket as she did so.

Five, four, three . . .

Grettie's cautious footsteps sidled by, disappearing from Oralia's line of sight as the witch moved to secure her hands. Oralia remained still, heartbeat pounding as she controlled her breaths, slowly counting down the seconds as they ticked past.

Two, one . . .

Grettie stooped to loop the rope around Oralia's wrists the same moment the orc shot to her knees, throwing her head back with all of her might. The back of Oralia's skull struck Grettie's unprotected face with a soft *crunch*. Screaming, thrown off-balance by Oralia's force, the witch stumbled into the awaiting seer's trap. The rune flared to life as a ring of red light shot skyward. Severed from Grettie's magic, the dancing ring of red and orange flames sputtered out.

Oralia leapt awkwardly to her feet. She managed three steps before her balance gave out and she crumpled back onto the ground among the wilted ferns and grasses. Her lungs burned with each ragged breath as she clawed her way forward, dragging her disobedient legs behind her. The polluted air wreaked havoc on her mind, jamming the inner cogs of wheels with the same smoky grime currently clogging her airways.

She was nearly to the dark ring of scorched, smoldering earth when the seer's trap flickered. Oralia glanced over her shoulder, watching in terror as Grettie's magic overpowered the symbol. With one final flare, the seer's trap erupted in a plume of smoke and ash. Grettie's dark shape leapt free and charged in Oralia's direction, throwing her hands into the air above her head.

Oralia rolled, narrowly avoiding the burst of flame that incinerated the drooped groundcover in her wake. She crashed through a patch of wilted bracken as a blistering heat engulfed her right leg. Searing pain jolted up her thigh, traveling along the nerves straight to her brain. It struck like a kick to the teeth, clearing the mental fog from her mind.

If nothing else, her undignified flailing served to extinguish the flames eating away at her pantleg. Her haphazard roll eventually came to an end and Oralia found herself hidden among a wild tangle of overgrowth. She moved onto all fours, using the thick blanket of smoke as cover as a trickle of energy returned to her weary bones. Eyes fixed on Grettie, Oralia steadily worked her way backward.

You won't make it if you run.

Oralia ground her teeth together as she slunk farther back. Whether it was due to sheer stubbornness or the fact that she detested the idea of listening to a predatory spirit hitching a ride inside her body, she vowed to do the exact opposite of what the entity wanted.

Charge her.

Dead, Oralia decided. The dark entity clearly wanted her dead! It was the only logical conclusion to such an asinine demand.

You'll die if you don't.

The nearest trees were only paces away. A few more seconds, that's all she needed, and then she would have the cover necessary to turn and run, using her second wind to carry her as fast and as far as her legs would go. Alas, unable to see where she was placing each foot, Oralia made a misstep, inadvertently snapping a twig beneath her heel. The sound drew Grettie's attention. The witch's eyes narrowed as she whipped about, twitchy hands already poised for the killing blow.

The dark entity's voice thundered across Oralia's thoughts. **Charge her, now!**

Fuck it. She was dead anyway.

Oralia surged forward and body-slammed Grettie to the ground. Hot magic erupted against her skin. The snap of flames crackled and popped. Bursts of color flashed across her vision. The dark magic flooded down Oralia's arms, cooling the blistering heat as it pooled into her hands. It was too much. The searing heat and blistering cold intermixed with the crushing weight in her lungs as every ounce of energy drained from her limbs. Oralia's eyes rolled upward, her surroundings nothing more than a smoky blur as her body went limp.

She struck the ground, incapacitated by the waves of debilitating pain causing her chest to tighten.

"What the fuck?" Grettie was back on her feet, blood streaming from her broken nose, staring wide-eyed at her hands. The twitch in the witch's fingers was gone, replaced instead by a familiar inky darkness that wriggled like leeches beneath her paper-thin skin. Already, Oralia could see the infection had spread from Grettie's hands and was traveling up her scrawny arms.

"Was that supposed to weaken me, orc?" A maniacal grin spread across the witch's blood-smeared face. "It barely hurt. In fact, I feel stronger than ever!"

Grettie curled the fingers of her right hand and lifted it overhead. A blaze of fire shot skyward, nearly twenty feet in height, and engulfed the upper branches of the nearest tree.

"Oh shit! You see that, orc? You see what you did to me? Watch this!" She lifted both hands and a blaze of fire sprang up from the earth and encircled them once more. The dancing wall of flames was twice as tall as the last one. Clouds of smoke, thick with ash and soot, churned within the circle, blanketing the interior in darkness.

Grettie stepped closer. The flickering red and orange flames illuminated the witch's dirty skin in an unnerving yellow glow. Her bloodshot eyes were wide and rimmed in white. From beneath her shirt collar, Oralia saw dark, branching tendrils snaking their way up Grettie's slender neck.

Her voice was distorted, brittle and cracking along the edges like weather-worn paper. "Now just wait to see what I do with you."

Grettie raised her hand once more. Red magic crackled down her arm and gathered in her fingertips. The magic built until it was blinding and then, without warning, flared black. The entity burst to life, spiraling back up Grettie's forearm in a plume of shifting darkness, consuming all in its wake.

The sinister smile bled from Grettie's face as her laugh turned to a scream. The witch's skin pulled taut as the muscle and flesh underneath turned to dust. Her face shifted in color from tan to white, to a sickly blue. With her withered hand still outstretched before her, the final scream faded from Grettie's hollowed mouth and her empty husk crumpled to the ground, disintegrating into a pile of bone and charred ash.

The ring of fire went out in a puff of black smoke.

Acid shot up Oralia's throat and pooled inside her mouth as she stared at what was left of Grettie. She heaved herself into a sitting position, coughing the burning particles from her lungs as she drew back her shirt. What she saw caused a second volley of acid to fill her mouth. The dark veins snaking along her collarbones were still there.

The witch was an undeserving vessel. The entity's voice rippled across her panicking mind. **Fit only for a quick meal. You and I are still intertwined, orc. As we will continue to be until you find me a vessel fit for service.**

"But you transferred bodies. I felt it. I felt you leave—"

I gave but a piece. You may not possess the magic I require to form a new body, but you are unusually resilient for an inferior being. You will continue to serve as my vessel until you are no longer useful to me.

That had only been a piece. With only a sliver, the darkness had consumed the witch from the inside out in the blink of an eye. This time, when the nausea clawed its way up her tightening throat, Oralia gave in to it. She folded over, retching the contents of her stomach onto the smoldering ground as her body trembled, helpless against the onslaught.

Overcome with fear, Oralia didn't hear the voices calling out to her, or the hurried thunder of feet against the ground. She barely noticed the two blurry forms that broke through the shifting blanket of smoke. Their shouts were distant and muffled, like a stranger calling from the bottom of a well. Oralia remained hunched over, barely cognizant of the pair of strong hands that seized her below the arms and dragged her from the smoldering ring of ash and death.

CHAPTER FIFTY

When Brothers were Brothers and Blankets were Blankets

Rasp awoke from the strangest dream. Reuniting with Faris had been nice—a bit bittersweet now that he was slowly starting to rouse and grasp that it wasn't real, but enjoyable while it lasted. He still found the part involving the bear who was also somehow a sister rather confusing. All in all, it hadn't been the craziest dream he'd ever experienced, just odd. An odd dream for an odd man, he supposed. Given the events of the past year, he wasn't sure he knew what normal looked like anymore.

Rasp's eyelids fluttered open and took in the muddled gloom around him. Nightfall, likely, given the stark absence of light. A cold wind rattled the dry leaves overhead. Normally he hated the sound as it meant another miserable night without the warmth of a fire, but the fur blankets strewn across his numb body were warding off even the fiercest chill. Lulled into complacency, Rasp tucked his chin into his arms and closed his eyes. He was already drifting back asleep when a pesky thought wiggled its way to the forefront of his mind.

You don't own any fur blankets.

"Hop!" Rasp shot upright. Tried, anyway, as the pelt draped over him now felt less like a blanket and more akin to a boulder. A warm, furry boulder, with an inexplicable amount of fat and muscle bulging beneath its loose, shaggy skin. Rasp shoved with his hands, desperately trying to squirm out from under what he feverishly hoped wasn't a bear.

His rough movements elicited a low growl from his stubborn blanket. Waves of vibrations rippled through the pelt and buzzed against Rasp's skin, similar to that of a giant, purring cat. He froze, not entirely from fear this time, but with an equal parts mix of anger and confusion as well.

"Boney asshole?" Rasp repeated. While being able to understand the bear probably should have come as a shock, it was her response itself that bore the brunt of his bewilderment. "Who taught you to name-call? That sounds like a painful medical condition, not an insult!"

The bear lamented her woes with a low-pitched wine.

"I don't see how growing up without a father applies in this scenario." Rasp supposed he should have been grateful the bear wasn't trying to eat him. Would have been nice to be able to feel his legs though. He reached up and gave her a tentative pat, signifying his wish to tap out before the suffocation set in.

The bear preferred airing her grievances regarding her upbringing to a captive audience instead.

"Believe me, you didn't miss out on anything. Our brothers are terrible."

Our brothers? Rasp wasn't sure when he'd decided to go along with the sister story, but something about it felt unusually natural. Too natural, in fact. The lack of air was clearly getting to him. Gathering his heavy limbs, he pushed with both hands and knees in a futile attempt to prevent the damn beast from smothering him. It was not going as well as he'd hoped.

"Get. Off!"

Finally, the unmovable weight lifted and Rasp scrambled out from under it. He didn't make it very far before his wobbly legs gave out beneath him. Whipping his head from side to side, he gathered what limited information he could with his slow-moving senses. It was definitely nightfall, he was still in the forest, and—judging from the suspicious lack of commentary from either Hop or Faris—he and the bear were alone.

Also, he was suddenly cold. So cold, he almost considered worming back under the bear. Pride won out, however, and Rasp drew his arms over his chest and settled for a dignified shiver. "Where are the others? You didn't eat them, did you?"

The bear huffed an incensed reply.

"I'm sorry, that *was* insensitive of me, wasn't it?" Strange, stomach-churning noises came from the bear's direction. The series of wet pops and cracks were eerily similar to the time Mul dislocated a shoulder—minus the screaming, of course. Rasp decided he didn't want to know, and carried on talking. "How dare I accuse you of eating anyone. It's all a hurtful bear stereotype. Never mind the fact that you were eating a witch earlier."

"I wasn't eating the witch!" a woman's voice roared back at him, sounding deeper and more gargled than it had any right to.

Still mid-transition, Rasp supposed. From the gruesome sounds, his inability to watch the spectacle was probably for the best.

"Look, we've all dabbled in cannibalism from time to time," he carried on. "I accidentally swallowed a toe and you ate a witch's face off. I'm not saying they're the same, but I get it. Sometimes your mouth is just in the wrong place at the wrong time."

"Your mouth is about to be in the wrong place."

Rasp was about to tell her where she could put her mouth when the response withered on his tongue. The shapeshifter was under the false impression she was his sister. And while Juneberry was obviously mistaken, Rasp couldn't shake the feeling that incestuous jokes hugged a line even he didn't want to cross.

"Oh, come on. You were about to say something snarky, I can tell. Don't hold back on me now."

"You never answered my question." Gods, it was really saying something when Rasp had to steer the conversation back on track. "Where are the others?"

"Faris and that other fellow went to go collect your stuff. Said something about fetching a mule. I'm not sure if that's a euphemism, so I didn't question it." The woman's voice grew louder as her footsteps approached. Rasp assumed she'd finished shifting forms. For one, her voice sounded more human than it had before and, two, the oppressive smell of animal musk and fur was no longer trying to jam its way up his nose.

Juneberry settled onto the leaf-littered ground beside him, adding, "Faris thought we could take the time to get acquainted."

Rasp failed to see what for. Just because Faris was entertaining Juneberry's delusions didn't mean he had to follow suit. He tilted his head to the side instead, suddenly noticing the suspicious lack of squabbling. "Did they take Father with them?"

"Who?"

"The other raven." Describing Father would have been a waste of effort, as "volatile" and "stabby" were not generally linked with one's physical appearance. "Loud? Abrasive? Rather pecky?"

"Oh, you mean the 'no good, dirty rotten, sad excuse of a man'!" Juneberry delivered the line without malice, as if this were simply the way she'd been taught to refer to her father. She patiently waited for Rasp's wheezing fit of laughter to stop. She gave up when it didn't, sounding less confident than before. "Do you suppose that's why he flew off in a huff? I didn't mean anything by it. That's what Aunty always called him."

"No, that's great. Keep at it. He'll learn to love it."

"Father left shortly after you passed out." Juneberry spoke the name as if it were a foreign word with a difficult pronunciation. "I'm sure he said where he was going but, between you and me, I've never been around this many people before. Keeping track of who said what is really hard! Is it normal for everyone to talk on top of each other all the time?"

Rasp stared straight ahead into the murky gloom, feeling the last tickles of mirth fade away. He had no interest in getting to know Juneberry. He didn't see the point, considering they weren't actually related. "In my family, we just hit each other. Talking was for those who didn't know how to use their fists."

"That sounds lovely. I can't wait to meet the rest of them."

It was time to shatter some realities, it seemed. "Look, Juneberry—"

"Call me June. Sounds like you're talking to a pie otherwise."

That definitely wasn't helping the "you're not my sister" case Rasp was currently trying to make. "I'm grateful for you helping Faris find me and keeping him safe and all, but I think you've got the wrong person. Just because you happen to have an equally shitty name doesn't make us kin. I'm starting to think having unfit parents might be a universal thing."

June crept closer. Dried leaves crunched beneath her knees as she leaned forward and placed both hands on either side of Rasp's face.

It was strange being on the receiving end of unwanted physical contact for a change. "What are you doing?"

"I've heard twins sometimes have an otherworldly connection. Like they can talk to each other without using words. I'm testing ours," June explained as she adjusted her grip on his face. "Can you feel anything?"

Rasp didn't think embarrassment was the answer she was looking for. He slapped her hands away and sat straighter, deciding it was time to put his foot down. "First of all, that's stupid. Secondly, we're not twins. My twin was a boy and he died at birth."

"Oh no, that's just the story Mom told everyone," June replied matter-of-factly. "She made it up to keep both of us safe."

Lies and hearsay!

Unable to refute June's claim without relying exclusively on every expletive in his vast repertoire of indecent language, Rasp settled for saying nothing at all.

Alas, June continued the conversation regardless of Rasp's lack of involvement. "In case you hadn't caught on, I'm a shapeshifter. A bear, specifically.

Gave Mom quite the scare when she found a cub in the cradle where her newborn daughter should've been."

"I see."

"You don't believe me, do you?"

"I do not."

"We actually look a lot alike. Obviously you're the ugly twin, but the resemblance is there."

"Insulting me isn't going to win me over."

"Then maybe you could try asking thoughtful, adult questions instead of sulking like a baby, yeah?"

Fuck, she sounded just like their mother—his mother! Not theirs. Not yet, anyway. Rasp sank lower to the ground, feeling as if another life-shattering revelation was about to smack him across the face.

As it turned out, thoughtful, adult questions were difficult to ask. June was alarmingly patient for a hot-blooded Stoneclaw. She explained her existence in the most digestible way possible and, in the end, with the help of small words and repeating her answers until they were hammered into his thick skull, Rasp felt he had a decent handle on the events surrounding their birth.

His mother—*their* mother—was an underhanded, bold-faced, two-timing liar! And he loved her all the more for it.

The best way to tell a convincing lie was to take the truth and twist it ever so slightly. Tal Stoneclaw had indeed borne twins during her sixth pregnancy. One boy, one girl, and, for magical reasons, the girl became a bear several hours after birth. At that moment, Tal realized two things: baby Juneberry was magical, and her son Raspberry was irrefutably the sixth son born of a mighty Stoneclaw leader. She feared superstition would not allow either child to live.

So Tal lied. She claimed the twins were male and that only one survived the night. She had Juneberry whisked down the mountain and placed in the care of an estranged family member. While her husband, Paler Stoneclaw, may have been the head of the clan, Tal was the voice that whispered in his ear. "The sixth son is dead so that the seventh can grow into the mightiest warrior the Stoneclaw clan has ever seen." And it worked, at least for a little while. Due to her quick thinking, Rasp's differences went unnoticed long enough for him to grow into adolescence.

June, on the other hand, thrived. She was brought up in secret by their estranged aunt, living just outside of the Mossborn territory. The aunt kept

June squirreled away in the dark woods where the only people who could find her were the ones she wanted to. It was an ideal arrangement. Juneberry had all the room and support a fledgling shapeshifter needed to grow. In addition to teaching her to read, write, and all the survival skills necessary to survive on her own, Aunt Dagmar also passed on her love of magic and the true history of the Stoneclaw people.

"You're awfully quiet," June remarked once the epiphany had had a chance to settle. "You got all that?"

Rasp sat in stunned silence, realizing he'd been handed irrefutable proof that he was the sixth son born of a mighty Stoneclaw leader, destined to bring death and destruction upon the world. While he'd always had his suspicions, at least there had been a convenient layer of doubt to keep his fears at bay. The benefit of plausible deniability no longer applied now.

Dazed, Rasp failed to notice the sudden gust of wind overhead. He brushed the hair from his eyes with a defeated sigh. "I think so—"

The sentiment was drowned out by the predatory growl that rumbled in the back of June's throat. She shot to her feet, snarling, "*You.*"

Rasp's only comfort was in the knowledge that June was not growling at him. "Who?"

"The blue porcupine from the mountain." June called out, "I know you're there, you little shit. I'd know that smell anywhere. You're not spiking me with your toxin quills this time!"

CHAPTER FIFTY-ONE

The Schemiest Schemers

The hair-raising growl rumbling from the back of June's throat would have made an ordinary man turn and run. Rasp, alas, was not an ordinary man. And while unordinary was an apt description most days, he feared what he was about to attempt landed him squarely in "stupid man" territory. He reached out, searching along the ground until he found June's bare foot. He heaved forward, wrapping all four limbs around the trunk of her leg like an unruly child clinging to the equally unruly parent about to kick some ass at a children's stoolball game.

June tried to shake Rasp from her leg. Other than rattling his brain a little, her attempts were unsuccessful. She settled for dragging him with her, one stubborn step at a time. She gritted out between clenched teeth, "What are you doing?"

"Preventing unnecessary death." Despite Rasp's admirable efforts, they were moving at a speed far too fast for his liking. He dug his heels into the dirt, shouting, "Your death, specifically!"

"My death?" June ceased dragging Rasp's ass across the bumpy terrain. The air of incredulousness in her voice seemed to imply her hands had already gone to her hips. "That blue porcupine may have gotten the jump on me before, but I'm ready for it this time."

"That's not a porcupine, that's a fae." Rasp raised his voice, for June's benefit, but probably not in the way she thought. "A fae who wouldn't dream of smiting an unfamiliar human while their apprentice is clinging to her leg, I imagine!"

Whisper's voice carried on the breeze. "You're right, because dreaming would be irrelevant. I could drop her from this distance regardless of your proximity."

"But you won't, *right*?"

Whisper grumbled intelligibly.

Having ensured the pair weren't going to kill one another, Rasp could finally get around to the more important things. Like answers to his many, many questions. "Do you two know each other?"

"Intimately," June said.

"No, *not* intimately," Whisper snapped. "Don't say it like that."

"That's Whisper. They fancy themselves my mentor, when really it's me doing most of the teaching," Rasp said. While June may have stopped uttering animalistic growls, that didn't convince him to release his grip on her leg just yet. He knew from personal experience the lengths a hotheaded Stoneclaw would go to settle a slight. "Whisper, this is June. She's family. Don't be a dick."

Whisper's quills rattled back, promising nothing.

At least his mentor wasn't throwing things. A good sign, all things considered. "Now that we've got introductions out of the way, enlighten me as to how you two know each other."

"We don't," Whisper replied.

"We do!" June insisted with a stomp of her foot. It sent an unpleasant rattle up Rasp's spine. "I looked a little different last time, is all."

Whisper's silence was effective in communicating their absolute disinterest in the matter. With a huff, June's voice changed back in Rasp's direction, explaining, "I was hunting on the ridge last summer when a flash flood struck, nearly sweeping me off the mountain. I was making my way to higher ground when I heard shouting and came across a faun trapped under a tree limb. Having grown up around Lonebrook, I knew of Faris even if he didn't know of me. I was in the midst of trying to rescue him when this one—"

Rasp assumed from the jerk of her body, June was pointing accusingly in Whisper's direction. That, or giving the finger, both of which the fae definitely deserved.

"—showed up out of nowhere and started whipping toxic quills at me!"

"Did I?" Whereas Rasp would have expected confusion, defensiveness, perhaps even a tiny smidge of remorse, Whisper proved him wrong once more by sounding more amused than anything. "I seem to recall a magic bear, not a woman."

"I *was* the bear! And whatever you hit me with knocked me on my ass for three days! By the time I awoke, all the chaos had already ended! There was no one left on the mountain. It was very confusing."

Rasp's eyebrows lifted. Not in reaction to what June had said, but what his mentor *wasn't* saying. "Magic bear?" he repeated. "Whisper, you knew she had magic?"

"Of course. Just as I could tell you had magic the first time we met."

"And you still attacked her?"

"You say that like it surprises you, little bird. I was under the impairment of severe iron poisoning and I needed Faris to get to you. I simply didn't have time to deal with any other distractions, so I made the distraction go away."

The taut muscles in June's leg relaxed. Rasp suspected her will to fight had deflated along with her pride. Not without getting the last word, of course. "I could have helped."

"Considering your version of helping involved trying to rescue a prey species while in bear form, I maintain that I made the correct decision." Whisper's soft footsteps tentatively approached. "Her magical signature is similar to yours, little bird. You mentioned family, but there is a resemblance that would suggest this one is more than just a Stoneclaw."

"I'm his sister."

"Fascinating." Whisper's curiosity got the better of them and the small fae scurried closer. Still clinging to June's leg, Rasp felt Whisper press past him as they poked and prodded at the very human they'd intended to kill only moments ago. "Your magic is markedly more controlled than his. Were you dropped on your head less as a child?"

Heat stung the tip of Rasp's nose. "What happened to not being a dick?"

"Asking innocent questions does not make one a dick, little bird. Wishing aloud that you had been brought up under the same circumstances as your sibling, thus allowing you to have a competent grasp on your abilities and therefore decreasing my workload, would be dickish. I said nothing to that effect." To add insult to injury, Whisper delivered this with a patronizing pat to Rasp's head. "I only thought it."

Rasp was debating whether a fae hex would be worth snapping Whisper's fingers off with his teeth when the sounds of approaching footsteps spared him from yet another stupid decision. Still clinging to June's leg, he felt her upper body shift in the direction of the oncoming commotion. "Oh, hey, look. They're back. And there was a mule. Guess it wasn't a euphemism after all."

Faris sounded remarkably similar to a parent who'd just walked in on a roomful of children caught painting the walls with jam. "What in the gods' names are you doing?"

Rasp decided now was as good of a time to let go of June's leg as any. Well, actually, several minutes prior would have been better, but that ship had already sailed. He untangled himself from his sister and scooted away. "Saving lives, Faris! What's it look like?"

". . . Not that?"

"Definitely not that," Hop agreed.

Rasp threw his hands in the air. "Oh shut up!"

Rasp wasn't the only one upset by the pair's unannounced arrival. The wind whipped overhead, stirring the blanket of dried leaves from the forest floor in a flurry of crinkly movement. "Faun." Whisper greeted Faris with no warmth in their voice whatsoever. "I should have known you were behind this."

Faris mirrored Whisper's enthusiasm. "Oh look, Rasp still hasn't managed to kill you yet. Impressive."

"Why are you here?"

"Why do you think I'm here?" Faris countered. "For him, obviously."

Well, this certainly was a rare treat. In the past, the only people who'd ever fought over Rasp were those seeking to kick his ass. And while both Whisper and Faris wanted something from him—be it awakening their magical egg or simply for the sake of friendship—it was rather nice knowing the end result wouldn't be a beatdown for a change. Not for him, anyway. Based on the severity of their dislike for one another, there was a good chance the pair would be at each other's throats in no time.

"June, right?" Hop stammered, acutely aware of the tension hanging over their heads like an anvil on a string. "Do you think you could assist me with something? Away from here, preferably."

"And miss the action?"

"Yes, that was the point. I was trying to be discreet, but I can see how that may have been misguided of me."

"No way. This is just getting good," June grunted. "Take Rasp."

"I got the idea that he needs to be here for this. Unlike you and I, who could be anywhere else right now. Far, far away, ideally."

"You can go, June," Faris said. "I know how to handle myself."

"Handle yourself? Is that what we're calling running and screaming nowadays?"

Faris's hoof struck the dirt with a *thump*. "Will you go already?"

Hop, fortunately, was well-versed in the art of getting stubborn Stoneclaws to fall in line without the need for superfluous hoof stomping or ear fluttering. "Have you ever had a corn cake?"

"Corn cake? What's a corn cake? Is it food?" June perked up at the idea. Her footsteps were fast and light, already pitter-pattering off in Hop's direction, mirroring the sudden eagerness in her tone. "Please tell me it's food. Shapeshifting is such strenuous work and I'm always so hungry. Faris is a stickler for rations."

June's voice faded in the distance as the pair moved away, affording those remaining the privacy needed to hash things out. Rasp found himself conflicted. On the one hand, he knew he had to stay and help smooth over whatever altercation was about to take place between Whisper and Faris. But, at the same time, the other hand promised corn cakes. What rightfully should have been *his* corn cakes.

And yet, the other-other hand, the third, oftentimes forgotten hand, insisted he could do both. Surely Faris and Whisper wouldn't kill each other in the few, short minutes it took to secure a bite to eat while they got all of their pleasantries out of the way.

"Not you," both Faris and Whisper said together the moment Rasp started to gather his feet beneath him.

Rasp settled back down with a groan. "You know why you two hate each other? Because you're too much alike!"

"Don't compare me to this psychopath."

"At least this psychopath isn't stupid!" Whisper shot back. The agitation in the fae's voice was damn near palpable. "Every competing power in the United Territories is scouring the countryside for the little bird right now. You know that, yes? You could have led any number of enemies right to us!"

"They didn't need me for that. You two have been leaving a nice trail of destruction in your wake wherever you go." Twigs and leaves crunched under hoof as Faris drew closer, his voice growing markedly louder as the gap between them diminished. "And yes, I am very much aware every power in the territories is out to get Rasp. You want to know how I know that? Because Geralt Lazuli placed a mucking bounty on my head! I've spent the last two months on the run because suddenly everyone wants to use me to get to the realm's most powerful witch!"

Aw, Faris thought he was the most powerful. That was almost as flattering as it was sad.

"And that's not the half of it," Faris continued. "I managed to slip Geralt's snare, so he set his sights on my village instead. He's got the place locked down, no one in, no one out, trying to lure me home."

A sudden hurt struck Rasp square in the chest. "Mom and Dad?"

"Alive and well, last I heard. But I'm not sure for how much longer. Which is why I need you to come back with me before that changes."

Rasp did not claim to be a brilliant strategist by any stretch, but even he saw the obvious holes in such a plan. ". . . Wouldn't Geralt be expecting that?"

"As I said before, stupid," Whisper agreed with a disapproving tsk. "That is exactly what Geralt Lazuli is expecting you to do. I haven't spent the last four months keeping the little bird out of enemy hands just to let you run headlong into a trap with him. Forget it, faun. It's out of the question."

"Rasp doesn't need your permission," Faris argued.

Whisper said something cutting in return and two voices rose in volume as tempers flared, leaving Rasp to ponder an alternative that could save his adopted family while skirting Geralt's trap. "You know what they wouldn't be expecting?" he said, slowly, still piecing the ideas together. "Me *and* a wind shifter."

"Do you know why they wouldn't be expecting that, little bird? Because it's assumed the wind shifter is too intelligent to go along with something that idiotic!"

"Faris's family is my family too. And whether you approve of it or not, I'm going to help them. So if you want to keep me around to hatch your egg, then you'd better find a way to make it work."

There was an uncomfortable pause before Whisper muttered under their breath, "It's not an egg."

Un-fucking-believable. Him, the king of petty squabbles, was having to act as referee to his betters. Rasp should have been stuffing his face hole with a hot corn cake right now, not playing peacemaker! "I meant what I said earlier," he replied. "You two are the same. The schemiest schemers I know. For the gods' sakes, put your differences aside and figure something out! If I have to form a plan all on my own, we're as good as dead. And then you both would look like idiots."

CHAPTER FIFTY-TWO

A Final Deal

The forest giants swayed overhead in a symphony of quaking leaves and groaning boughs. Without light, Rasp had no way of telling what either Faris or Whisper were doing. The severe lack of angry pacing painted a picture within his mind. He envisioned the pair staring the other down, face-to-face, seconds from verbally ripping into one another all over again.

It was Faris who conceded his silence. With a full-body sigh, the faun bit back his anger and extended the proverbial olive branch in a manner that *almost* sounded sincere. "What's this about an egg?"

Whisper's first instinct, naturally, was to set the olive branch on fire. "Nothing. It doesn't concern you."

"Whisper," Rasp groaned, running a heavy hand over his face, "do you really want the explanation to come from me? I mean, really-really? Because if that's the case, I'm going to make it as uncomfortable for you as possible. Lots of *intimate* details, if you catch my drift."

The fae rattled their quills so fiercely, Rasp swore he felt the aftershock thrum within his achy bones. At least it got them talking. Sort of. "It is not an egg." A second glare from Rasp managed to extract further information from Whisper in the most insulting way possible. "The little bird calls it that because it's the closest comparison he can wrap his feeble mind around. It is an unawakened of my kind."

"A baby, you mean?" Faris said.

Whisper's tone seemed to suggest the use of "baby" was only slightly more tolerable than "egg." "Essentially."

"Great, glad we got *one* thing clarified. What does that have to do with not saving my village?"

Whisper took their sweet time saying nothing at all, prompting Rasp to fill in the necessary blanks. "Because it's the only egg left of their species and Whisper lost it. We've been running up and down the whole countryside for months looking for it. Whisper's under the impression it's among a collection of magical artifacts, which may or may not be located in the military settlement not far from here. Owned by Geralt Lazuli, of course."

"Of course it is," Faris said with a groan.

Rasp tilted his head in Whisper's direction, flashing a threatening smile. "See how easy that was? That's what you should be doing. *Not* me."

He wasn't sure at what point he'd managed to break Whisper but, at last, with one final quill rattle, the fae stopped being a stubborn stick in the mud and offered something actually useful. "Today's scouting mission confirmed that the artifact is indeed within the settlement. I couldn't breach the tower itself, but I could feel the unawakened calling to me." Whisper's irritated voice shifted to Faris, explaining, "I need the little bird's help to awaken it once it's been recovered. Which is why I cannot risk losing him to one of Geralt's traps."

The answer seemed fairly obvious to Rasp. "Then we break into the settlement, steal the egg, and *then* go save Faris's family. There, solved."

"It is not a task to be taken lightly, little bird. The artifact is being safeguarded against fae magic. Due to the nature of the charms, I'm unable to step foot within the tower walls. I need someone of the magical variety who is unaffected by both iron and silver in order to do so on my behalf."

"Okay, but I can still do it."

"For your sake, I hope that was a misguided jest. I should not have to state the many obvious reasons as to why that would not work."

"Fine." Rasp rolled his eyes. So many stipulations. It was as if Whisper didn't actually want the job done. "*Faris* and I can do it."

"Forgive me for not being clearer. While you and the faun could breach the tower without harm, neither of you would be able to locate the object itself. It is a magical artifact, under the guise of glamour, being stored in a vicinity filled with every other sort of magical artifact imaginable. The sheer abundance of power would overwhelm your magic sensitivity beyond repair, little bird."

"So what you're saying is that you need an expert. A whole team, from the sounds of it," Faris said. "Do you know how long it would take for you to assemble one? A proper one? Weeks, if not months. I don't have that kind of time."

"You don't," Whisper agreed. "But I do."

"Except you're not great at dealing with people. I am. Free Lonebrook and I'll help assemble the best gods damn specialists money can buy."

"But—"

Whisper barely got a word out before Faris cut them off. "You get one chance at recovering your egg. If you fail, Geralt will know someone's discovered his hoard. Which means he's going to bring half his army down here and move it again. You can't afford that possibility. You've found your artifact and it's safe. It's not going anywhere. We take care of my crisis first and then we'll fix yours."

Whisper said nothing, resigned to their hostile silence. The wind whipped overhead in unnatural circles, signifying that, even if they didn't like what Faris was saying, the faun was arguing sense.

"You know Rasp is going to come with me anyway," Faris persisted. "You might as well ensure he comes back in as few pieces as possible."

The wind whipped harder as Whisper's fury doubled. "As my apprentice, he is to accompany me until I have released him from service. That was our contract that he and I agreed upon. If I don't go, then neither does he."

Rasp had only one card left to play. Ideally, he'd planned to hold onto it, squirrel it away for as long as he could, but it seemed time to reveal his winning hand already. "If Faris doesn't get his family back, then neither do you."

The wind dropped without warning. "Come again?"

"You just said so yourself. Our deal stated I was to be your apprentice. Agreeing to help awaken your egg was never part of the original contract."

"'I vow to find a way to give you the happy ending you deserve,'" Whisper quoted back at him. "That's what you told me only last night."

A saner man would not have laughed at a fae to their face. As unhinged and stupid seemed to go together like butter and toast, Rasp did so with great relish. "That's the thing, though. What I said and what you *think* I said are two different things. I could have been flirting with you for all you know."

Unable to argue with Rasp's surprisingly sound logic, Whisper switched tactics, the edge of their voice fraying ever so noticeably. "You don't even want your magic!"

"But *you* do."

"But . . ." For the first time ever, the fae appeared to be at an actual loss for words.

Rasp considered offering a patronizing pat to the side of Whisper's scaled face. Alas, with darkness making it damn near impossible to pinpoint the fae among the gloom, it wasn't worth the risk of accidentally pricking himself on one of their quills again. Rasp settled for a shit-eating grin instead. "I may not be the brightest, but I pick up things along the way. A good fae contract is supposed to be watertight and you overlooked several holes in yours."

"Unbelievable," Whisper said, finally.

"I know, look at me, learning shit. Who would have thought?"

Rasp felt a scaled hand grip his shoulder and pull. "We need to speak in private. *Now*."

Whisper wasn't physically strong enough to drag him, but Rasp sensed it would be best to go willingly. He stood and Whisper's grip shifted from his shoulder to his elbow, still pulling with the desperation of a leashed dog set on being the first to piss in the yard.

"Rasp," Faris said, voice laced with unease, "are you sure about this?"

Fuck no. Everyone knew you weren't supposed to waltz hand in hand with a psychopathic fae into the dark woods at night. But Rasp also knew that whatever Whisper was about to tell him likely couldn't be said in front of Faris. "I'll be fine, Dingle. I'll scream for you if I need anything, alright?"

"You sure?"

Faris really wasn't letting this one go. Probably best to put his fears at ease. "I'm sure. In fact, go start packing your bags. I have a feeling we'll be on our way back to your village in no time."

"I don't have any bags to pack, but I appreciate your confidence."

"Well, you should go get some bags then. And a few cute outfits too. A splash of color, maybe? You know, something to bring out the adoration for me in your eyes."

"You can't see my eyes!"

"It's the thought that counts, Dingle," Rasp called over his shoulder as Whisper pulled him away. They walked for a short ways—some more effectively than others as Rasp did quite a bit of tripping. Eventually, the pair reached a suitable distance and Whisper halted. And then they just stood there in awkward silence glaring at one another. At least that's what Rasp assumed they were doing. Short of reaching out and touching Whisper's face, he had no real way of knowing what sort of expression was curled across their ugly mug.

"Is this really what you want, little bird?"

"You mean saving Faris's family?" *Want* wasn't the word he'd use. Need to do, morally obligated to do, would never forgive himself if he stood back and did nothing? Yes, a thousand times over. Want? No. Nobody wanted to run headlong into a trap designed specifically to use you against your will. "Yes."

"Why?" Whisper demanded.

"What do you mean why? You're doing the same thing, aren't you? You're risking your neck to ensure the fate of your people. It's not any different than what I'm doing."

"These people are not your own. They're not even the same species!"

"So?"

"So?" Whisper repeated, voice raising several octaves in indignation. The wind picked up again, ripping through the quaking treetops before it stilled. When the fae spoke again, they sounded as though a few deep breaths had done them some good. Their tone was calmer, more collected, less likely to smite Rasp on the spot. "I do not like this, little bird."

"I know."

"It's stupid and reckless."

"I know." Rasp waited patiently for Whisper to add the inevitable "you are stupid and reckless."

"But your loyalty to those you consider kin will always be the driving force in your life. It is, in some ways, commendable. Stupid nonetheless, but commendable." There was another reluctant pause before the fae added, "I will not stop you. If this is what you need to do, then so be it."

"Really?"

"However—"

Ah, the catch. Rasp had known to expect one.

"—if you want my help, which you will undoubtedly need if you expect this venture to not go up in flames, then I will ask something of you. A trade, if you will." Whisper waited for Rasp's resulting protest. His mentor continued when it became abundantly clear that Rasp didn't intend to offer one. "Your magic. You already agreed to gift some in order to awaken the youngling, but for this, I want all of it."

All of it? Rasp was caught between relief and suspicion. "You said you didn't want to do that before."

"It wasn't fair before. By taking all of your magic, I would have been ridding you of a life extended beyond regular human years, of power, and influence. I could not ask that of you for nothing. And now I have something to offer. My help for your magic."

Rasp didn't see a downside. A shorter lifespan, maybe. Not that it meant much. He'd already exceeded everyone's expectations for how long he would live anyway. Besides, what good was a long life if he didn't have a weird faun family to share it with? Oh, and there was a bear now too. June seemed like she would make a lively addition to his list of furry relatives.

Common sense dictated that he give life-altering decisions extensive thought. Thus, Rasp waited at least ten seconds before agreeing. He offered his open hand in Whisper's blurry direction. "Deal."

"Deal?" The calmness drained from Whisper's voice. "Just like that? No consideration at all to how this affects you?"

A fine layer of confusion settled over Rasp's preexisting suspicion. "Why are you so angry? You're the one who asked for it. Shouldn't you be happy?"

"No! I'm not happy!"

"Why not?"

"Because you're not thinking! I'm asking for the most important piece of yourself and you're giving it away without any forethought. This is how it starts. This is how people take advantage of you!" Whisper stomped off, their tiny footsteps slamming against the dried leaves as they paced back and forth, working themselves up into another frenzy. "Why is it I'm the only one who can see that? No matter what I say, how much I demand, you're not going to change, are you?"

Rasp shielded his face from the flurry of leaves stirred into the air by Whisper's tantrum. "Why are you getting mad at me? It was your deal. I was only agreeing to it."

"Exactly! You're blindly agreeing to something without considering what it means for your future. After everything I've taught, you're still thinking with your heart and not your brain!"

"I don't see why that's a problem."

"Because you're going to end up the same as them if you don't stop!"

"Them?"

"Yes, *them*! Like you, they were too blind to see the greed of mortal-kind." Whisper's restless pacing lost some of its vigor. "They gave and gave, not because they had to, but because they wanted to. And it cost them everything. As it will you."

The dots started to connect within Rasp's mind. Whisper wasn't mad at him. Not entirely, anyway. "I believe you when you say it will cost me everything. The difference is I don't care."

"You should!"

"Why?"

"Because!" Whisper hesitated, their voice marked with desperation as they searched for an answer Rasp could wrap his mind around. "It's . . . it's not natural. It goes against self-preservation. Why would anyone give up everything for another?"

Rasp shrugged. "Stupidity?"

The dried leaves fell back to the ground as Whisper issued a long, wearisome sigh. "Sometimes I think you might be more like my people than I ever was, little bird. I've been the last of my kind for centuries and yet, I'm beginning to realize that perhaps I've always been alone."

"Nah, I call bullshit." Rasp stifled any ensuing argument with a wave of his hand. "Are you a selfish, self-serving little prick? Absolutely. No ifs, ands, or buts about it. Despite all that, you may not be giving up everything, but you are dedicating a substantial effort to bring your people back, no? I think that counts for something."

Whisper gagged at the implication, sounding like a cat with a hairball lodged in its throat.

"In fact, I think saving Faris's village presents a very unique opportunity for you. For the first time ever, you could go against your conniving nature and help simply out of the kindness of your heart. You know, baby steps and whatnot."

"Over my dead body."

Worth a shot, Rasp supposed.

"There is a fine line between generosity and allowing yourself to be robbed blind, little bird. Helping your family is noble. Walking headfirst into a trap in order to do so is the opposite of that. I would hate for you to lose everything in order to learn such a valuable lesson, so I will not take everything. Just your magic. If you want my help, my offer still stands."

"I'm not changing my mind."

"I know. Which is why I need you to take this more seriously than you have anything else in your life. You are about to strike a fae contract. Once the deal is struck, the conditions are binding."

In that case, Rasp realized it was probably worth stating his conditions aloud. "You will journey with us and use your power to spare Lonebrook and its people from destruction. In exchange, Faris will help you assemble a team to rescue your unawakened egg. Afterward, my magic is yours. All of it."

Whisper's scaled hand grasped his and magic sparked between them, sealing the covenant.

CHAPTER FIFTY-THREE

Beneath a Sea of Stars

Consciousness slowly returned to Daana's body. The first thing she noticed was how the jolting gait beneath her lacked the smooth roll and sway of the ocean. Confused, Daana forced her heavy eyelids open and squinted at the pale light stretched above. Orange and pink clouds streaked across the sky like brushstrokes on a lavender canvas. The breeze tickling her nose was wrong as well. The familiar stench of salt and water rot had been replaced with the sweet undertones of fireweed and tundra grass.

The cool night air stung the skin on her face, but the rest of her body was warm, wrapped tight in a mound of blankets. The warmth was lulling her back into another dreamless sleep. Daana was already drifting off again when her hearing returned, transforming the low hum of background noise into distinguishable voices.

"Shh, Ellie, look. I think she's finally coming around. For real this time."

Ellisar's dry voice replied, "And that requires us to be quiet *because?*"

"In case she tries to say something." Ashwyn spoke notably lower, almost quiet enough to be considered a whisper—had the loud orc any concept of what constituted a whisper. "I want to be able to hear."

"Should we hide and shout 'surprise' too?"

"I wouldn't. She's a jumpy little thing. Might kill her. Probably best just to smile and wave."

"For the gods' sakes, how about you two just don't do anything?" Daana recognized the third, scratchy voice as Snag's. It was coming from the opposite direction of the other two. "Give her some space. Let her come around on her own, would ya?"

Like a moth drawn to flame, Daana followed the voices, fighting the weariness that bogged her down. After several unsuccessful tries, she was able to keep her eyes open long enough for her blurred vision to clear. She found herself swaddled like an infant, lying on her back in what appeared to be the back of a small wooden cart.

Cart.

A swell of relief washed over her. Cart meant land. They'd reached land! Overcome with joy, Daana tried to sit upright. To her credit, she got nearly halfway before her body remembered it was broken. Every muscle seized tight, squeezing the air from her lungs. Daana slumped back down, unable to scream.

"Maybe don't do that," Ellisar said helpfully.

Daana rolled onto her side, drawing her knees to her chest as she breathed through the waves of pain radiating from her lower back. Squinting through hot tears, she could just make out Ellisar's and Ashwyn's respective shapes trailing behind the cart. "Fuck," Daana gasped between tightly clenched teeth. "It hurts just to breathe. What did I break?"

Everything? Definitely everything. It was the only explanation for the sheer agony coursing through her veins.

"Nothing important," Snag assured her, his voice drifting down from above. He was bent over the back of the seat, staring back down at her. His expression, a combination of relief and concern, seemed to be at odds with itself. The creases around Snag's yellow eyes softened when he said, "You're just beat up is all."

In that case, Daana hated to imagine what it felt like to break something important. "Is everyone else okay?"

"Ashwyn lost her hand," Ellisar said.

Daana's stare shot back in their direction in time to see the orc's shoulders slump miserably. "Why must you keep reminding me? Damn seagull swooped down and swiped it right out of my clutches! It was going to be your anniversary present, Ellie dear."

"Eh. Probably for the best. You know how I feel about handouts."

Ashwyn raised her hand to her forehead dramatically. "My poor heart. It's been backhanded with your callous words."

The pair were acting stranger than usual. While lighthearted banter was commonplace for Ashwyn, it was rare for Ellisar to partake so willingly. Daana peered at the latter more carefully. The elf's normally pale face had a touch of color and there was a twinkle in her eyes Daana hadn't seen before. Was she . . . giddy? Dear gods, it looked downright unnatural.

Daana twisted around, gritting at Snag through clenched teeth as stabbing pains rippled across her bruised rib cage. "What's wrong with El?"

"She blew another hole in the *Ducky Luck* before jumping overboard. Been quite pleased with herself ever since."

Ellisar tilted her head up at the darkening sky with a dreamy expression on her face. "Best night of my life."

Ashwyn promptly forgot all about the severed hand. "The best night of your life, really? Nothing else comes to mind, like, oh I don't know, a particularly passionate night with your wife, perhaps?"

"I recall we kissed quite passionately after I sank the ship."

"I was resuscitating you!"

"And I came to beneath a sea of stars, with the flickering firelight of a sinking ship in the background and your beautiful face whispering sweet nothings in my ear."

"I was screaming 'don't die, don't die, don't you fucking die on me.'"

"Best night of my life."

Daana's eyebrows furrowed as the pieces of the night in question slowly emerged from the dark recesses of her mind. The effort resulted in a noxious stabbing sensation deep within her skull. She massaged her aching temples with her fingers, stammering, "I-I remember the fire. Was it the powder charges that caused it? The rest is all a blur."

The gathering grew suspiciously quiet. Daana glanced up in time to catch the nervous glance Ashwyn and Snag traded over the top of her head. The fact that neither was volunteering information even after getting caught was even more troubling. Gritting her teeth, Daana held a hand to her side and eased into a sitting position. The change in elevation made her head swim.

"Alright, out with it." Daana pressed her fingers to her temples, willing her vision to stop spinning. "What is it you aren't telling me?"

Snag and Ashwyn still had their eyes locked together, engaged in a silent conversation Daana hadn't been invited to. Their efforts to break the news gently were thwarted by Ellisar. "You killed an air elemental by siphoning all their magic in a single go and then made it rain lightning fire from the sky," the elf said nonchalantly. "Hands down, the most impressive thing you've ever done."

Ashwyn swiveled her head at her. "Ellie!"

"What? I gave her a compliment. No mention of the spread, as requested." Ellisar crossed her arms over her narrow chest triumphantly. "You're welcome."

Spread? Gripping her sleeve, Daana peeled the fabric away from her skin, unable to contain the startled gasp that leapt from the back of her throat. The black veins snaking up her arms had spread. It branched past the elbow, already halfway to her shoulder. A quick examination of her other arm proved the same.

Panicked, Daana searched their faces for a sense of reassurance and found none. "You're all looking at me like I'm a sick puppy. It's bad, isn't it?"

"You were convulsing when we got you out of the water and onto the longboat," Snag admitted. "You should have been chilled to the bone after a dip in the ocean, but your skin was hot to the touch. I wasn't sure you were going to make it through the night."

"How long have I been out?"

"Four days."

Ashwyn interjected with what was clearly forced cheerfulness. "The good news is, while we didn't make our intended port, we made it ashore and are in the flatlands. A little farther south than expected, but we made good progress while you were out. Traded the boat for a cart and are already halfway to our destination. If we keep going at this rate, we should reach your mother in three days' time."

That was good news, right? Her mother would have answers and maybe even a cure. Her mother who just happened to be a witch, surrounded by an army of witches, all with powerful magic. Magic Daana could siphon at any moment and use to destroy everyone without meaning to. The more she considered it, the more it sounded less like good news.

Ashwyn noticed Daana's dismayed expression. "I know those marks seem like an impossible setback, Peaches. But your mother will have answers. Her people will have you fixed right as rain before you know it."

Daana drew her knees to her chest and slumped over them, wincing at the twinge of protest in her back. "What if it doesn't work? What if she doesn't have answers? What if she takes one look at me and tells me to turn back around again?"

"Sounds about right," Ellisar agreed.

"Ellie!"

"Her mom's a bitch. There's no sense in telling her fantasies."

"We all know what sort of high opinion you have of Larkspur. You never fail to bring it up at every opportunity."

"So?"

"So I'm saying maybe this is the opportunity *not* to bring it up."

"Say, was that a rabbit I just saw?" Snag's nervous smile bordered on manic as the severity of his glare wilted the arguing pair into submission. "Maybe you two should go do some hunting, yeah?"

Ellisar wrinkled her nose. "Why? So you two can have another heart-to-heart?"

"El, so help me, another smart word out of you and I'm gonna drive a stake through *your* heart."

"Goddess, what I would do for a steak right now," Ashwyn muttered wistfully. "Almost as good as a hand. Except you can eat it."

Whereas Ashwyn was oblivious to the lethality of Snag's glare, Ellisar took note. In a rare show of compliance, she threaded her hand through Ashwyn's and pulled the orc off of the narrow, winding road and into the sea of swaying tundra grass. "Come on. Let's find you that steak. Let these two get all their touchy-feely shit out of the way."

"We're actually hunting, right? That's not some sort of euphemism? Because I might cry if you drag me all the way out there just to take your pants off."

"Food first," Ellisar said, disappearing into the grass. "Then pants off."

Daana waited until the pair had disappeared from sight before gathering her leaden legs beneath her. The left side of the cart struck a bump, causing her to lose what little balance she had. Daana caught herself against the short wood siding, saving her battered body from a painful spill. She waited, allowing her equilibrium to return, before swinging one leg up and over the back of the driver's seat. It was tedious work. She could feel Snag's concerned gaze watching her the entire time, but he kept his reservations to himself.

Finally, breathless, convinced her bones had turned to jelly from four days of unuse, Daana settled triumphantly onto the hard seat beside him.

"Do I want to know what you're doing?" he said.

"Sitting."

"Can't argue with that logic."

"I feel like you, of all people, could," Daana replied.

"You're right. But I won't." Snag clutched Wormy's reins as though he feared they'd rip free of his gnarled hands. The shaggy horse clomped along ahead of them, tail swishing back and forth without a care in the world.

Daana slumped over and rested her head against Snag's bony shoulder. She half expected him to shove her off, but he didn't. The goblin only clutched the reins all the tighter as some of the lovely green color drained from his pained face.

The pale lavender sky stretched on overhead, steadily giving way to the inky blackness spreading from the east. The sun was low. The last of its brilliant orange rays caught the edges of the clouds, making them appear more gold than gray. A sea of tall grasses sprawled across the undulating hills on either side, as far as the eye could see.

As she took in the cool evening air, listening to the distant calls of the crickets and frogs, she recalled how her freedom had not come so freely. The weight in her chest grew heavier at the realization that the greatest cost had yet to be paid. Daana had never known family, not in any traditional sense anyway. And now, days away from reuniting with her own flesh and blood, something screamed at her to turn back. She'd forged her own bonds and the thought of closing that chapter of her life in order to start anew suddenly felt like a fate worse than death.

Snag would be fine without her, she was certain of that. She just wasn't sure if the reverse was true. Blinking the tears from her eyes, Daana swallowed the grief building within her throat and resolved to make the most of the time she had. She rode the rest of the night with her head bouncing against his shoulder, savoring the sounds of the night, as remorse clawed at the back of her mind like a cat begging to be let back into its cage.

CHAPTER FIFTY-FOUR

The Great Larkspur Denari

For three days, Daana's company traveled along the winding dirt road. The flatlands stretched around them in an endless sprawl of yellow and tan tundra. The days were warm and the nights were cool, harried by a relentless wind that swept from the south, filling the air with the constant quiver of dry grass.

It was well after sunset. A dense blanket of charcoal-gray clouds stretched overhead as far as the eye could see. The moon, a waning sliver of pale light, glowed faintly in the distance, obscured by the overcast sky. Given the late hour, Snag normally would have called it quits and settled down somewhere off the road, but tonight he kept going. It wasn't until they crested a particularly steep hill that Daana realized why. A settlement sat nestled in the shallow valley below, made up of hundreds of clay houses surrounded by a curtain wall of solid stone. Firelight from within the huts poured through the square windows, illuminating the settlement in a warm, homey glow.

Daana sat wrapped in a blanket in front of the cart with Snag. The goblin's gaze was not focused on the town itself, but the sea of tents encircling the settlement walls. Orange and yellow campfires dotted the dark landscape like stars in a clear dark night. "Don't like the looks of that," he murmured, left ear twitching, filling the air with the soft, metallic jangle of hooped earrings. "You're all seeing this too, right?"

"Aye." Ashwyn gave a low whistle of approval as she moved to stand alongside Wormy. "If I didn't know better, I'd say Lark's amassed herself an army."

"And that's our cue." Ellisar looped her arm through Ashwyn's and started back down the winding dirt path, calling over her shoulder as she did so, "Daana, it's been terrible. You're home safe now. Our part in this is done."

Ashwyn slid her arm free with practiced ease. "My goddess, Ellie. We've come all this way. The least we can do is introduce the poor girl to her mother."

"Daana defeated the dark entity! Escaped Geralt's clutches! Burned Alkurth to the ground with a flick of her fingers! She needs no introduction."

"I don't believe it." Daana feigned surprise. "That's what, two compliments in almost as many days? Ellisar, I fear you must be losing your edge."

"You wore me down. Congratulations." Ellisar hooked her fingers through the back of Ashwyn's belt and continued her futile pulling. "Goodbye."

Despite Ellisar's increasingly desperate attempts to usher her along, Ashwyn remained where she stood. The harsh lines around her eyes softened as she twisted her upper body in order to gaze back at Ellisar. "This is because you don't want to see Larkspur, isn't it? I was really hoping that after all of this time, you would have set your bad blood aside."

"She got us captured. And instead of taking any of the blame, she let us stand trial in her stead! And don't get me started on the fucking ship." Ellisar ceased her struggle and spun around. Her eyes lacked the fire laced within her words. "*Before the Fall* was the closest thing I had to a child and she fucking sank it!"

"She wasn't even onboard when it sank," Ashwyn reminded her.

"Well, it would have been better for us all if she had been!"

"You did love that ship." The orc tapped her chin as she considered a solution that would appeal to them both. "Look, if you would rather stay out here with the cart, that's perfectly fine. I'll pop in, say hello, and then I'll be out again before you know it."

"You said the same thing on our honeymoon. Next thing I knew, we were smuggling a cargo load of escapees across the border."

"That was one time."

"It was twelve!"

A pearly smile split across Ashwyn's tusked face. "Made for an unforgettable honeymoon, no?"

Ellisar's sour expression agreed for entirely different reasons.

"I'd like it stated for the record that I've been free a total of twenty-nine days now and I have volunteered us in exactly zero causes, no matter how noble they might've been. If you don't trust me, then you're welcome to act as my escort." When Ellisar's fixed expression refused to budge on the matter, Ashwyn started off without her, gesturing for Daana to follow. "Come on, Peaches. Let's go spring a surprise family reunion on your mother."

Daana clambered down from the cart, glancing up at Snag as she did so. "Are you coming too?"

Snag remained seated on the driver's bench, wearing an expression nearly identical to the one stretched across Ellisar's face. He shook his head no. "As much as I would love to traipse through the middle of an unknown army to meet the elf whose daughter I sold to her worst enemy, I think it's best that I stay with the horse, thank you."

Daana's heart felt as if it'd been yanked from her chest and stomped on. "You won't leave without saying goodbye, right?"

His ears flattened against the back of his head as he peered down his nose at her. Despite Snag's best efforts, a smidge of sadness managed to leak through. Not in his words, of course, which remained as stubbornly apathetic as ever. "I won't *now*, I guess."

"Good. Because I'd never forgive you if you left before I could give Wormy a hug and kiss." Daana started off down the hill after Ashwyn, noting how Ellisar slunk along behind them with slow, reluctant footsteps.

Swaying rows of cotton grass flanked either side of the winding path. Daana drew her cloak tighter around her shoulders as they followed it past row after row of wedge-shaped tents toward the settlement. The trio's passage did not go unnoticed. Several figures clad in leather armor stood and watched their progress, content to let them pass in peace. It wasn't until they reached the gates that anyone bothered to speak to them.

A guard appeared at the top of the gatehouse wall, holding a lantern aloft as they peered down at the trio assembled below. Their greeting was as painfully generic as the giant wood and iron doors barring Daana's company from entry. "Who goes there?"

Even after stating their business, it took several back-and-forths for Ashwyn to convince the guard that no, it couldn't wait until morning and yes, they would like for the Sage Superior to be roused in the middle of the night just for them. She assured the guard that they *really were* that special. Ashwyn's persistence won out and the guard grudgingly disappeared, leaving the trio to stand in the middle of the path and wait.

The wait was unbearably long. Daana was considering spending another night in the back of the wagon when one side of the double doors drew open with a heavy groan. A small armed party was assembled on the other side, ready to receive them. A faun festooned in a red cloak stepped forward, his bespectacled eyes darting between the three of them before settling on Ashwyn as the obvious leader. "Commander Pride," he greeted with clinical coldness.

"Hear that, Ellie? Barely been sprung free of that dungeon a month now and I've already earned myself a title. Not sure what for, though." To the untrained eye, Ashwyn's smile was easy, almost friendly, but Daana saw the unease that pulled tight around the corners of her slate-gray eyes. "And who might you be, friend? Gotta say, I'm a little disappointed Larky didn't come greet us herself."

"I am Havershire, the Sage Superior's chief advisor. I have been instructed to escort you inside." The faun was all business, wasting few words and even fewer fucks. Daana couldn't blame him. From the unkempt state of his salt-and-pepper-gray hair, he'd been dragged out from a warm bed to deal with the riffraff assembled at the gate. "I ask that you bring only your key people. The rest of your forces can make camp outside of the wall, along with the others. There is not enough room and board for everyone."

"Forces?" Once more, Ashwyn glanced at Ellisar for clues.

The elf merely lifted her shoulders in a shrug.

"That won't be necessary," Ashwyn said to Havershire. "As you can see, it will be just us three. Ellie and I aren't even planning to stay the night. A quick in and out and we'll be on our way."

Something about this caused the faun's irritated expression to change. He took another gander at the three. Whatever answers he sought, however, did not appear to be found. "Very well," the faun said, pushing his glasses back onto the bridge of his nose. "As a final request, the Sage Superior asks that you leave your weapons at the gate. You may collect them upon your return."

His request snapped Ellisar from her hostile silence. She edged a daring step forward, snarling, "Is Lark out of her fucking mind?"

The glare the faun shot her way would have stopped an ordinary opponent dead in their tracks. Being that the recipient was Ellisar, it did the opposite, encouraging several more steps from the outraged elf. Havershire stood his ground, as if dealing with unhinged swordsmen was simply part of the job. "It is a standard request. And, given the upheaval surrounding the two of you as of late, a sensible one."

"Oh come on, Ellie. Everyone knows you're just as deadly with a sword as you are without one. It encourages creativity." Ashwyn stripped her weapons from her side and delivered them to the guards. "Do be careful with those, please. They're family heirlooms. Not mine, of course. But whoever I stole them off of probably cares."

Daana followed suit, as did Ellisar, albeit with a substantial amount of muttered cursing.

"This way then." Havershire led as the armored escorts fell into a strategic formation around them.

The trio were escorted through a maze of cramped side streets, crisscrossing their way into the very heart of the settlement at what felt like the most convoluted way possible. Eventually, countless confusing twists and turns later, a towering structure rose up over the clay houses. It was three stories high and, unlike the neighboring stone and clay huts, built from wood. The flatlands were tundra, making trees a sparse commodity. The fact that someone had built an entire building out of wood meant the lodge was significant to the town in some way.

Hopefully not a prison, Daana thought, given the way the armed guards kept stealing wary glances over their shoulders at her.

They arrived at the lodge from the back and were ushered in through the servant's entrance. Havershire led them through a dark room cluttered with stacked chairs and linens before crossing over into the main room. Long tables took up most of the interior. There was an unlit fireplace in the corner next to a raised platform with a variety of ornately carved chairs on display. Timber beams stretched high above them, crisscrossing along the underside of the steeply pitched roof.

"Wait here," Havershire instructed as he dismissed the armed escort with a wave of his hand. "The Sage Superior will be along shortly."

"You keep saying that like it's a real title." Ellisar's gaze wandered the great hall. "Probably made it up herself. Nice to see Larkspur's ego is as inflated as ever."

Havershire's brow wrinkled. His mouth opened, poised to volley venom-laced words, when he thought better of it. Snapping his jaw shut, the aged faun offered a tight-lipped smile before exiting the way he'd come, taking care to close the door in his wake with an ungentle slam.

"Sweet goddess, Ellie. You saw the army assembled outside the gates. You can't say things like that." Ashwyn ran a broad hand over her worried face, uttering, "I don't know what in chaos is going on but, given the circumstances, it wouldn't hurt to be on our best behavior for the time be . . ."

The statement died on Ashwyn's tongue as she watched Ellisar move away. Using the natural grooves in the log siding, the elf worked her way up the wall like a squirrel on a tree. She reached the nearest beam and jumped for it, pulling herself over until she disappeared from sight entirely.

"What in the goddess's name are you doing?"

Ellisar's dry voice was accompanied by a faint echo. "If Larkspur's going to waste our time playing games, then I'm not going to participate. Holler for me when you're done getting jerked around."

"She's going to be the death of me," Ashwyn whimpered.

Daana left them to argue as she moved to inspect the rest of the space. Judging from the tables, the room appeared to be a formal dining hall. The main entrance was across from her and made up of a pair of grand, ornately carved double doors. There was a third door off to her left which, given the lingering smell of cooked onions and stew, likely led to a kitchen area. Had Ashwyn not advised them to be on their best behavior, Daana might have considered picking the kitchen entrance open and seeing what sort of goods were on offer.

Making a good first impression. Not stealing from your mother, Daana reminded herself as she shuffled along. Eventually, weary from boredom and a lack of sleep, she joined the table Ashwyn was unceremoniously strewn over the top of. Daana plopped down onto the bench seat across from her with a groan. "I'm starting to think Ellisar had the right idea. How long is this going to take?"

Ashwyn spoke with the side of her face plastered against the table. "To your mother's credit, we did show up in the middle of the night, Peaches. It's to be expected. A few more minutes won't kill you."

"Savor them," Ellisar's dry voice called from above. "Soon you'll look back fondly on the time before you met the great Larkspur Denari."

"I know you can't see my hands, but I'm holding up ten fingers nonetheless," Ashwyn replied.

Daana slumped over the table, cradling her head in her hands. She was nodding off when the main entrance jerked open behind them, allowing a cold wind to stir the stale air. Daana twisted around, heartbeat drumming loudly in her ears, watching wide-eyed as a sharply dressed figure stormed into the unlit hall, looking fit to set it afire.

"Ashwyn Pride." The elf's velvety voice was like spider silk, soft but unbreaking. "What in the seven realms of chaos took you so long?"

CHAPTER FIFTY-FIVE

Cutthroat Snakes

Two red-robed soldiers followed in the Sage Superior's wake. The metal armor fitted beneath their robes clinked softly as they moved at an awkward pace, caught between keeping up with their esteemed leader and maintaining an air of regality. Sadly, they failed on both accounts, looking less like imposing escorts and more akin to crabs scuttling along the beach amid low tide. The soldiers heaved the ornately carved doors shut before taking their positions on either side of the grand entryway.

Daana's sixth sense told her the pair were magical. She felt their power from across the gathering hall. That, however, was nothing compared to the raw energy emitting from the elf who strode confidently toward them. The call of magic rippled over Daana's skin, teasing every hair into the air. She took a breath, trying desperately to ignore what felt like ants crawling up her spine, and focused on the Sage Superior instead.

The elf in question was several inches taller than Daana, with dark, spiraling curls, and features so sharp, they could cut with a single glance. She wore a cropped blue cape over a thick, padded doublet. The paired skirt was plain but sensible, unlike her boots, which had more buckles and ties than a carriage harness. Considering the amount of time that had gone into securing the Sage Superior's footwear, it was a small miracle she'd arrived in a timely manner at all.

Not important, Daana told herself. *Here we go. Play it cool. You're a competent, badass, long lost daughter not looking for anyone's approval, just answers.*

Daana's legs wobbled as she stepped away from the table, intent on meeting the approaching elf halfway.

The Sage Superior swept past. "Ashwyn Pride!" Her voice caused the rafters to shudder in protest. "Where is my army?"

Ashwyn drummed her fingertips against the stained wood, utterly unintimidated by the Sage Superior's curt greeting. "Outside the settlement walls, last I checked." She tilted her head to the side and flashed a winning smile. "Are you in the habit of losing your armies, Larky? Kind of hard to miss a thing like that."

Larkspur's brisk steps stopped short of the table. "How many did you bring with you?"

"Three."

"Three hundred or three thousand?"

"Three thousand?" Ashwyn said with a strained laugh. "Look, if you're really desperate to stretch the numbers, I suppose we could bump it to four if you counted the horse. He's an honorary member of the team at this point."

The Sage Superior held her tongue as a flush of color tinted her brown skin an unflattering shade of red. And then, just as she looked to be on the verge of losing her temper, the fury vanished, dismissed with a wearisome roll of her dark eyes. "Oh dear gods," Larkspur murmured, raising a hand to massage her forehead. "It's been so long since someone has dared utter a witticism in my presence, I fear I no longer recognize them."

Ashwyn only smiled as her gaze darted to Daana as if to say, *what the fuck's a witticism?*

"Forgive my sharpness, old friend," Larkspur continued. "As all of my correspondences have gone unanswered thus far, I feared that I was being willfully ignored."

Ashwyn, like Daana, had absolutely no idea what the elf was rambling on about. Unlike Daana, Ashwyn decided she didn't care. The orc saw her opportunity and seized it, neatly steering the conversation back in the direction she intended it to go. "No apology necessary." She gestured for Daana to approach. "Now, as to why I'm here. Larkspur, allow me to introduce you to—"

"You can introduce me to your officials soon enough. First, I want to hear the news on Oralia. Surely she is well on her way by now, yes? With an actual army in tow, I should hope."

". . . I think there may be some confusion here, Larky. I didn't show up on your doorstep on Oralia's behalf."

"Enough with the useless jests already. I do not enjoy them. Just as I am not enjoying the course of this conversation. Stop stalling and tell me where your sister is." Larkspur continued in spite of Ashwyn's obvious confusion, as if hoping a spew of critical information would jog the orc's poor memory. "I issued a call to arms months ago. Four months, Ashwyn. That should have warranted a response by now. I cannot keep sitting idle while Oralia traipses the countryside uprooting every insignificant realm outpost she stumbles across. Her place is here, by my side. I—"

Larkspur stopped mid-rant, noticing the way Ashwyn's open-mouthed gaze had wandered back to Daana. The Sage Superior's eyes narrowed. "Why do you keep looking at the elfling? Should I be demanding answers from your inferior instead? I swear, it's like you don't even realize . . ."

A flash of clarity extinguished the fire burning within Larkspur's umber eyes. "You," she started, forced to try again when the rest of her sentiment neglected to roll from her tongue in a single go, "you don't know what is going on, do you?"

"No idea," Ashwyn assured her.

"And you don't have an army with you?"

"Definitely not."

"And Oralia?" Larkspur's eyebrows lifted high on her head, almost pleadingly.

"Could have settled down and started an orphanage for wayward criminals for all I know. Oralia and I haven't spoken in years."

The fire within Larkspur's dark eyes rekindled with twice the fury as before. "That cutthroat snake! I knew she couldn't be trusted." Her foot slammed against the hardwood floor as she looked up and down the gathering hall with sudden, dead-set purpose. The Sage Superior's harsh glare passed over Daana only briefly in her search. "Where is she?"

"Larky, I told you. Oralia's not here."

"Not Oralia. Your damned wife!"

The snap of Ashwyn's tusks was so powerful, it elicited a flinch from everyone gathered, including the guards. The orc stood. "Speak about Ellisar in that tone again and I will walk out that door without another word. Is that understood?"

Larkspur's proud shoulders dropped. For the first time since her arrival, she looked something other than angry. "Ashwyn, my dear friend, forgive me. I think we both may have been misled. Will you allow me to explain my side? And then I will hear yours?"

Daana met Ashwyn's gaze once more, the orc circumventing the need for words with a single, raised eyebrow. While this was not the homecoming Daana had hoped for, they were here and her mother was present. It wouldn't hurt to push the introductions until everyone was on the same page, she supposed. Daana waved her hand, signifying that it was alright with her.

Larkspur noticed the curious back-and-forth and, from her curled expression, was biting back a myriad of questions. Why in the seven realms of chaos Commander Pride was taking orders from a lowly elfling topped the list, undoubtedly.

"By all means, then," Ashwyn said. "Explain to us what is going on."

Larkspur's explanation was well-rehearsed, as if she'd spent a lifetime rearranging the words within her head until they were perfect. "After I fled the realm, I did not simply disappear into obsoletion. I have been planning, plotting, designing a way to make everything right again. For the last seventy-four years, I have been training refugee witches with the sole intention of overthrowing the Division of Divination and, by extension, the United Territories of the Realm."

There was an uncomfortable drop in conversation as Larkspur waited, watching Ashwyn's blank expression for a tell. If she was expecting some sort of grand response, she didn't get one. Ashwyn offered the verbal equivalent of a thumbs-up. "Good for you, Lark."

"None of this is supposed to be a surprise to you. You were supposed to have been kept in the loop!" Larkspur pinched the bridge of her nose. "I am on the cusp of war. This is not the time to be discovering that the person tasked with delivering my messages willfully neglected to pass the information along! Is this why Oralia isn't here? Did your wife conveniently forget to tell her as well?"

"Can we circle back to that, actually? I'm still not sure what any of this has to do with Ellisar."

"She was my point of contact! I've been sending Ellisar correspondences ever since her enlistment into Oralia's faithful four. She's been acting on my behalf for the better part of a century: siphoning witches from the Division of Divination, sending and receiving intelligence, sowing dissension, paving the way for revolution. While she wasn't my first choice, her resilience to death made her an ideal courier. I had no reason to doubt Ellisar's competence." Larkspur paused, adding, "Until recently, that is. When all contact from her stopped completely."

"Huh," was all Ashwyn managed.

Larkspur's body language softened as she stepped tentatively closer. "She really didn't tell you?"

Slowly, as if in a daze, Ashwyn shook her head no.

"I'm sorry. As her partner I thought surely you, out of everyone, would have known." Larkspur gathered the orc's right hand into her own and clasped it. "At the very least, consider what I'm offering. What it could mean for the realm. We would be starting over, just like you always wanted. I need Oralia to handle the military operations, but I need you to rebuild. I always told you I would find a way to repay your generosity, and this is it. Together, we could make this land a haven for all. Isn't that what you always wanted?"

Poor Ashwyn looked like she'd been roused from a nightmare. She opened and closed her mouth uselessly, still having some trouble separating reality from fantasy.

"I am offering you a position as one of the key advisors. There is a long road ahead, yes, but after everything you have sacrificed, you deserve to see your ideas come to fruition. I need you by my side."

Gingerly, with marked care, Ashwyn removed her hand from Larkspur's grasp. "That's thoughtful of you, but I'm not here to join your cause, Larky. I came to reunite you with your daughter."

Larkspur's head swiveled back in Daana's direction. Her stare settled this time, actually taking Daana in versus simply glancing over the top of her. "This is your worst joke yet."

"Funny how the truth works that way." Despite her nervous smile, the gleam in Ashwyn's flint-colored eyes was heavy. The orc held out her arm and ushered Larkspur in Daana's direction. "It's a bit of a long story. The short of it is, there was a shipwreck, your daughter was found and smuggled back into the realm, raised by your mortal enemy, and is just now discovering her roots."

Daana lifted her hand and offered a nervous wave. Whatever words started to form on the tip of her tongue died the moment she was swept up in Ashwyn's path, forcefully herded toward the door.

"Obviously you two have a lot of catching up to do," Ashwyn said. "I'll leave you to it."

"Hold on!" Daana dug her heels into the slick hardwood. Alas, all she got for her efforts was a horrific squeaking sound as the worn tread of her boots skidded along the top of the floor unhindered. "You said you were going to introduce us first!"

"I just did."

The Sage Superior was equally helpless against Ashwyn's strength. "I don't have time for this. We have a rebellion to go over!"

"See to the door please, gents," Ashwyn told the soldiers, who, caught in a moment of bewilderment, followed her orders without question. "We can discuss your war afterward, Larky. You and Daana catch up. I have to take care of a few personal matters in the meantime."

In a mere matter of strides, Daana found herself ushered out the doorway, down the front steps, and standing in the cool night air. From Larkspur's perplexed expression, she appeared equally as confused as to how they got there. The Sage Superior glanced over her shoulder, blinking in surprise as the double doors drew shut behind them.

Larkspur's frown deepened around the edges. "I forgot how persuasive she can be."

CHAPTER FIFTY-SIX

Love of a Mother

A frigid breeze whipped overhead, laden with the soothing scents of dry cotton grass and smoke from wood-burning fires. The overcast sky was dark, but the cobblestone beneath Daana's feet was bathed in the warm yellow glow from the street lamps lining the outside of the gathering hall. A growing unease churned within Daana's stomach. It twisted her intestines into slippery knots, tugging tighter, tighter, tighter as each agonized second ticked past.

Larkspur Denari, the witch, the rebel, the idealistic revolutionist, possibly mother, stood only paces away wearing an expression of absolute indifference. Nay, it was worse than that. For a second, the Sage Superior's mask slipped, and Daana saw utter revulsion burning within her dark, umber eyes. The elf inhaled sharply through her nose and said, "And here I thought I'd finally put this behind me."

Fearful of sounding stupid, Daana said nothing. It came at the price of merely looking stupid.

"Go on then," Larkspur said with an impatient flick of her wrist. "Spin your lies. Paint me a picture. Convince me how you're my long-lost daughter, just like all the other fakes that've cropped up over the years."

All the hours spent rehearsing what she was going to say slipped through Daana's grasp like loose sand between tightly clenched fingers. Her left shoulder lifted, as if possessing a will of its own. "How?"

"How? You travel all this way and that's the most you can say? You dare waste my time with a measly *how*?" Larkspur peered down her nose at Daana, debating whether to use her heel or words to squash her into unrecognizable pulp. The latter won out, for the time being anyway. "You are not the first to turn up on my doorstep claiming to be my long lost child. If money is your intent, I have none. I am also regrettably short of patience. So if you wish to keep your head, remove it from my sight immediately."

The tips of Daana's ears burned against the crisp night air. "I don't want your money!"

"Of course you don't. No one ever admits that right out of the gate." Larkspur rolled her eyes. It looked entirely out of place on someone who was the visual epitome of elven grace and nobility. She shooed Daana away with a halfhearted wave of her hand. "Spare me the theatrics and go away."

"Ah! Right there! Did you see that? You just rolled your eyes."

"You are supposed to be roleplaying *my* child, child. Not the other way around. What of it?"

"It used to drive Uncle—" Daana nearly bit her tongue on the word. Hating his guts didn't make it any less of a hard habit to break. "It used to drive Geralt Lazuli mad. And now I think I know why. Every time I gave him disrespect, all he could see was you."

"That does not prove anything."

"Watch!" Daana mimicked the facial expression. "Do you see it? You probably got in just as much trouble for it at the division as I did."

The disgust burning within Larkspur's eyes shifted to confusion, laced with the tiniest trace of pity. It was the sort of look typically reserved for two-legged dogs and particularly ugly babies. ". . . You are a very strange elfling."

"Yeah, I grew up hearing that a lot too." Daana's shoulders slumped miserably. Meeting her mother wasn't anything like she pictured it to be. She could feel the weight of disappointment creeping up from within, threatening to drag her under. "Look, I just want answers, okay? I don't know if I'm your daughter or not. But Ellisar seemed to think so and Geralt Lazuli told me the same. I'm not here to con you. I just want to know who I am."

"And why would I be able to tell you that? How would I know who you are?"

"My gods, Ellisar was right. You *are* a bitch." Daana threw her hands into the air as she spun on her heel, suddenly intent on being anywhere else. A tavern, a hayloft, the bottom of a pig trough, all sounded better than being berated by some stuck-up snob. "Forget it. Obviously I'm just wasting both our time."

"Wait."

The sheer force of the command bore down on her like a sledgehammer. Daana hadn't intended to obey, but her feet betrayed her. She froze mid-step, unable to do more than set her raised boot onto the ground to keep from falling over. Clenching her jaw, Daana resolved to keep her back to the Sage Superior. It was a rather pitiful attempt as far as acts of defiance went, but it was something.

Larkspur's boots scuffed softly against the cobblestone as she approached from behind. At last, having drawn out her steps in the most aggravating way possible, she came to a standstill directly in front of Daana. The older elf's gaze was that of an unenthusiastic judge, tasked with evaluating prize heifers at the fair. "Did you just call me a bitch?"

Now was probably not the time to ask if the Sage Superior's ears were working. Daana offered another shrug, trying not to draw attention to the sudden sheen of sweat dripping down her brow. "If the shoe fits."

"Hm." The start of a smile cut across Larkspur's sharp mouth. "Now *that* does sound like me. What's your age, elfling?"

"Seventy-six?"

"Are you asking me or telling me?"

"Considering I don't even know my real name, let's consider it an optimistic guess." Daana's gaze dropped to her hands. The darkness stirring beneath her skin sensed Larkspur's magic. It pulled at Daana, urging her to reach out and take it, to feed the hunger gnawing at her from the inside.

Daana took a breath to steady her nerves instead. "You were just telling me to leave. Are we doing that or not?"

She didn't like the way Larkspur's intense stare bored right through her, rooting out her darkest secrets without having to lift a finger. Finally, with her mouth pinched to the side, the Sage Superior uttered a single word. "Ren."

"Blen. Look at that, I can say nonsensical words too. Is that what we're doing now?" Daana winced the moment the words left her mouth. That might have been a step too far. Regrettably, the more time you spent around the dredges of society, the more your own propriety tended to slip.

"Ren is what I named my daughter," Larkspur said. "I will admit, there is some resemblance. Although that nose and those hips did not come from me."

Un-be-lievable. They had known each other an entire five minutes and her mother was making unwanted comments about her appearance already.

Larkspur stepped closer, cupping Daana's chin in her hand as she lifted her face, allowing her to peer deep into her eyes. "What sort of witch are you?"

"The terrible kind?" Daana offered. The joke landed as remarkably as she expected it to, prompting her to provide a more substantial answer. "I'm magic-sensitive."

"Then why do I sense magic?"

Damn. Apparently it was time to move on to that nasty bit of business already. Pulling free of the elf's grasp, Daana drew back the corner of her sleeve and exposed the marred skin underneath. "Because of this, I think. It's the other reason I'm here, actually."

Larkspur withdrew her hand as if she'd touched a leper. Curiosity piqued, taking care to clasp her hands safely behind her back, the Sage Superior leaned closer and examined the dark veins writhing beneath Daana's skin. Her tight-lipped expression was a mix of unease and morbid fascination. "What is it?"

"The remnants of a dark entity. A small piece, anyway." Daana paused, recalling the name Whisper had used. "Referred to as an old one, I think?"

Larkspur's gaze lifted from Daana's wrist to her face. The older elf's eyes were wide and rimmed in white. "You encountered an old one? And survived? How did it mark you in this way without its power consuming you?"

The intensity of Larkspur's stare made Daana want to shy away. Unfortunately, her traitorous feet were still fixed in place. "It was a joint effort. Another witch trapped the entity while I channeled its power into a powerstone."

"Dear gods, child. I've heard rumors of an incident on the Iron Ridge. I even sent my best people into the territories to investigate the wild claims circulating around the Stoneclaw witch, but I have yet to learn anything useful. You were there when it happened? You helped?"

The slight hint of admiration in Larkspur's voice was enough to pick Daana's spirits back up off the floor. "You heard about the battle on the mountain?"

"Anyone who is anyone has heard. Every world power is in a mad scramble to find those responsible." Larkspur lowered her voice, glancing around them as if to check for unexpected eavesdroppers. It seemed like overkill considering it was the middle of the night and the only other people within earshot were the guards, who were keeping a respectable distance. "Do you have it with you, child? The powerstone? I would very much like to see it."

Daana gripped her wrist, feeling her queasiness return. "Uh, no. I don't have it."

Larkspur's dark eyebrows rose high on her head. "It is with the Stoneclaw witch then?"

Those left on the mountain after the battle had agreed it would be best for someone of the non-magical persuasion to keep the powerstone. It was fine by Daana, as she wanted to be nowhere near the damned thing. "I have no idea." She adopted her best look of innocence. "I went into shock shortly after the ordeal. When I awoke, the other witch was already gone."

Carried off by a dragon. Gone. Po-tay-toe. Po-tah-toe. Same difference, as Snag was fond of saying.

"You didn't inquire about the stone's whereabouts?"

"Of course I did. But nobody tells me anything." As she'd learned from Ellisar, the best lies were the ones that encompassed a partial truth.

Larkspur's expression grew unreadable as she drew back, her brown skin illuminated by the flickering lantern light. "Who else was on the mountain with you?"

Crap.

A knowing smile hovered over her mother's lips. "The stone is with Oralia, of course."

How? How had she gotten the answer without being told? Daana scrambled to recover some of the ground she'd unknowingly lost. "Actually, I'm not sure where the stone is. You would be better off asking—"

"Say no more, child. I understand the need to keep it secret. It would be devastating for something of that magnitude to fall into enemy hands. I have no doubt that my most trusted general is keeping it safe." Larkspur tilted her head skyward, muttering, "Provided Oralia remembers her place and returns to my side before I am forced to retrieve her myself."

There wasn't any way to backpedal now. Daana chose silence instead. After a moment of deep thought, Larkspur offered Daana a soft pat on the shoulder. It felt like the pity touch one gave to a spurned suitor. "I think it would be best to revisit this in the morning, after everyone's had a chance to sleep. Tomorrow, you and I can get to know each other better. You can tell me all about your adventures on the mountain then."

CHAPTER FIFTY-SEVEN

After Everything

Ashwyn heaved the heavy double doors shut. She felt a twinge of guilt for throwing Daana out into the cold, especially with someone as inhospitable as her mother, but there were more pressing matters at hand. An inescapable pressure swelled within her chest, clawing its way upward and outward, until the pressure reached her eyes. She had been betrayed many times in her life, but this was more than the usual hurt. She felt cut open and split in half with her insides spilling out, exposed and vulnerable.

Ashwyn leaned against the door, fighting the urge to drive her clenched fist through it. "Is this why you didn't want to come?" Her voice echoed along the steeply pitched ceiling. "Because you knew Larkspur had a position here waiting for me? And instead of being upfront about it, discussing it like a grown adult, you chose to hide it from me?"

There was a soft rustle behind her. Ashwyn turned, breath bated as Ellisar dropped down in front of her. At the very least, she was willing to do this face-to-face. That meant something, didn't it? Ashwyn clung to the hope that this was all merely an oversight. Ellisar could be cruel and fickle at times, yes, but surely there was an explanation that could alleviate the pressure building behind her eyes.

As the seconds slowly ticked past and the pair stared without speaking, the hope for a simple miscommunication flickered out. Ashwyn's hope transformed into a pit that threatened to swallow her whole. Her tongue was suddenly so unbearably dry she felt the words scrape along the roof of her mouth on their way out. "Is it true?"

When Ellisar's eventual answer came, the only thing telling about it was the way she artfully dodged the very question itself. "I just spent the last sixty years working my ass off to free you from that dungeon. Don't throw that away."

"I know you sacrificed, Ellisar. I will always owe you that. But right now you owe me the truth. Is what Larkspur is saying true?"

Ellisar locked her jaw. Ashwyn could hear the elf's molars being ground into powder in the back of her mouth.

"Answer me!"

"I wasn't going to let her talk you into throwing your life away for another lost cause, alright? So yeah, it's true," the elf said. "I told Larkspur what she wanted to hear to keep her from meddling in my affairs. I didn't earn your freedom just to have you taken away again. I earned it so that we could spend it together. Forgive me for not wanting some power-hungry maniac to get in the way of that!"

"You are my partner. A partner does not get to make unilateral decisions without consulting the other half. You know this. You agreed to this."

Ellisar narrowed her eyes. "Just like you volunteered us to pick up all those escaped witches the night of the massacre? Or how about after your sister caught us, when you single-handedly volunteered to sacrifice yourself to the realm so that Larkspur could run free? Funny how you didn't need my input back then."

Ashwyn held the swelling pressure at bay, trying her damndest to remain level-headed when every instinct screamed at her to fight fire with fire. The fear of what might slip out if she did was all that held her back. "That's not fair, Ellisar. I was transparent with you on both of those issues."

"Yeah, to tell me you were doing them! You never asked bloody permission, did you?"

Once more her wife successfully managed to reroute the conversation. "Stop changing the subject. You should have told me about Larkspur, and the war, and my supposed role in all of it."

"I didn't tell you because you would have considered it."

"Of course I would have considered it!" Ashwyn's own words caught her by surprise. Anger was awakening something in her. Something that had slowly festered during those long years in confinement. As much as she tried, she could never rid herself of the resentment. For years, she shoved the feelings down, trying to make do with the hope that one day it would not matter. But the resentment did not dwindle. It merely went dormant, slowly breeding resentment in the dark, unvisited corners of her mind.

For the first time since her escape, the resentment bubbled over. "I'm allowed to have dreams too, aren't I? Yes, you got to work your ass off, Ellisar. Don't remind me. But I didn't. While you were off fighting in wars and risking your life with your friends, I sat for seventy-three years in that dungeon waiting for the chance for my life to start again."

"Unbelievable," Ellisar said. "You're jealous? Because I got to run myself ragged serving your sister? I'm sorry you're the one who got left behind, but how is that my fault?"

"It's not."

"Then why are you bringing it up?"

"Because you act like I owe you for it!"

Ellisar blinked, taken aback, but said nothing.

That was the funny thing about buried issues. As soon as you uncovered one, the rest had an unfortunate way of clawing their way to the surface. Ashwyn couldn't stop the words coming from her mouth had she tried. The sad part was, she didn't want to. After years of trying, maybe it was finally time to stop. "I never asked you to save me. I told you to cut and run the moment Oralia's back was turned."

Hurt glimpsed Ellisar's stoic face. It was replaced almost as quickly by rage. "I stayed because I love you!"

"I know." Hot tears slipped from Ashwyn's eyes. She didn't try to stop those, either. There wasn't any point. They both knew what was coming next. "And I love you, too. But is that enough to keep justifying this? First the massacre, and then the escape, our trial, now this. Are we just using another crisis to stall the inevitable? Could it be that it's easier to be mad at our circumstances than it is to stop and evaluate whether or not we ever worked to begin with?"

"Don't you fucking say it."

"We were growing apart, Ellie. Even before all of this. There is no sense in denying it."

"Fuck! You're calling it *now?* After everything?"

"I'm not calling anything. I am telling you where I stand. Whether this relationship is still worth it is for you to decide." Ashwyn stood straighter, drawing an unsteady breath. "My place is here. It always has been. I would love nothing more than to have you by my side."

"Ashwyn, do you even hear yourself? Larkspur is insane!"

"Others have said the same about you."

"So that's it then? One lousy speech about how the two of you are going to make the world a better place and you roll over like an obedient dog? Just like that? Larkspur will do to you what she does best. She will chew you up and spit you out the moment you're no longer useful to her. Is that what you want?"

"Now you suddenly care what I want?"

"You are playing right into her hand! This is what she does." Ellisar made a gesture with her hands, as if gripping an invisible object and ripping it to shreds. "She takes good things, things that are whole, full of promise, and she dismantles them piece by piece, until there's nothing worth keeping. And then she throws them away, because that's all people are to her—disposable trash."

Ellisar's animated hands uncurled and fell uselessly to her sides. "She broke me, Ashwyn. Just as she is going to do to you."

For years, Ashwyn had tried to pry behind those stubborn golden eyes, to glimpse the inner workings, to learn what had happened to render Ellisar so mangled beyond repair. For the first time, Ashwyn was starting to see the hairline cracks. Had she persisted, she may have been able to break the very wall down itself. But that required the willpower to do so. And, after fighting an unwinnable battle for so long, she found herself not lacking the power, but the will itself.

Hardness settled in Ellisar's golden eyes at the realization that her bout of openness was too little too late. "I'm not going to stand by and watch her turn you into an empty shell of a person."

Ashwyn had unknowingly been preparing for this moment for years. It had been hard in the dungeon, sometimes going months between correspondence, all the while wondering if each letter from Ellisar would be her last. That might have been easier. At least she could have written the failings of their relationship off to circumstances outside of her control.

This hurt so much more. "Then it seems we've reached an impasse."

"I'm not coming back. Not this time. If this is really what you want, then you'd better be damned sure."

How could anyone be sure of anything? The only certainty Ashwyn felt was the suffocating tightness that coiled around the base of her throat. Filling her lungs to capacity felt impossible. Her breathing grew short, springing forth in small, short gasps as a second burst of tears welled within her eyes. "I'm sorry, Ellisar. I think this might be goodbye."

She looked like she wanted to kill something. Ellisar's eyes were wide and gleaming with murderous intent. Her upper lip curled back but whatever vile words danced across her tongue died there. A half second later, she turned swiftly on her heel and strode back across the gathering hall, wrenched the side door open, and slipped soundlessly away.

The urge to call out, to race after her, to gather the stupid elf in her arms and demand she come to her senses, all of it pulled at Ashwyn. But she remained still. Watching, with tears streaming down her face, as the love of her life disappeared into the night, stealing her heart one final time.

CHAPTER FIFTY-EIGHT

The Unsurvivable

Oralia awoke to a deafening absence of noise. She drew air in through her nose and out the gap between her tusks. The customary stench of wet soil and forest rot had been replaced with dusty, leatherbound books and the sweet undertones of burnt incense. Tentatively, her heavy eyelids eased open.

The blistering light convinced her to snap them shut again. Head swimming, Oralia felt around her with her dominant hand, intent on piecing the clues together without the use of vision. The nest of warm, fluffy blankets piled beneath her was far too soft to be her own. There was a pillow as well—a commodity unfit for life on the road.

Wherever she was, Oralia concluded, it was certainly not camp.

This time, when Oralia forced her reluctant eyes open, she realized that the surrounding brightness was not from the spirit realm calling her home, but from the large bay window to her right.

Not dead. Good start.

Her eyelids clamped shut once more, allowing the noxious boiling sensation within her gut to die down to a simmer. Logic slowly stirred back to life as she waited. The presence of the window meant she was inside. The next question then became, where? Unfortunately, answering that required opening her eyes again—a task which seemed far more difficult than usual. After a few steadying breaths, Oralia turned her head away from the window and took in as much of her surroundings as her weak vision could bear.

She was propped up on a makeshift cot of patchwork quilts and pillows strewn across the floor. Oralia's proximity to the ground gave the illusion that the room was large but, at her full height, the top of her head would have grazed the ceiling. The walls were painted a faded yellow and adorned with homely decorations of dried flower wreaths and aged parchment framed in wood. A myriad of potted plants hung from hooks on the low ceiling above, suspended by artistically woven hangers made of knotted hemp rope. There was an ancient green settee behind her. Beyond that, she suspected, was the open entryway leading to the rest of the house.

What Oralia found most peculiar, however, was the lack of people.

Her nose told her that there'd been multiple persons in the house recently. Fauns, primarily, based on the lingering presence of musk and fur. Oralia could not hear anyone moving about. An opportune time, perhaps, to be on her way before the residents returned.

Sitting upright proved downright torturous. Every muscle in her swollen abdomen seized the moment Oralia lifted her shoulders from the pillowy cot. Stifling a snarl, she eased back down, allowing the spasms to run their course. When the worst of it was past, she stubbornly unclenched her jaw and attempted once more.

Oralia's forehead was coated in a hot sheen of sweat by the time she'd managed to gather her knees beneath her. Sucking in a gulp of incense-infused air, she planted one bare foot against the cold wood flooring and heaved her unwilling body into a wobbly stand. She managed two steps before her legs gave out. Oralia caught herself against the green settee, saving herself from a more painful fall.

"I'd tell you to stop being an idiot and sit your ass back down, but listening to reason never was your strong suit."

Oralia's shoulders bristled. Lifting her head, her gaze followed the voice to its source. A brown and tan faun leaned against the archway, stirring a cup of tea with an unamused expression hovering over her fuzzy eyebrows.

Oralia's voice came out dry and gruff. "Briony?"

"Hello, Protector," Briony replied, still stirring her tea, looking every inch the epitome of boredom. "Although I suppose you probably don't go by that anymore. Do you fancy Oralia these days or is there a new title I should call you by?"

"What are you doing here?" The words had the misfortune of leaving Oralia's mouth before she realized her energy would've been better spent on something more along the lines of: where am I? How did I get here? And why in the seven realms of chaos am I as weak as a newborn?

"This is my home. I live here," Briony stated matter-of-factly. "The better question is, what are *you* doing here? Last I heard, you and your ilk were causing havoc along the Adderwood border. So strange of you to pop up in Lonebrook without warning."

Her team! For the gods' sakes, why hadn't she asked about her team? Tearing her eyes from Briony, Oralia searched the hallway beyond for signs of her people. She forced her mounting panic down with a difficult swallow. "My team is not here, are they?"

"Gods no. We found you all by your lonesome in a most unusual situation. I've got eyes and ears all over these woods, though. Your crew isn't far. I was reluctant to extend an invitation without knowing what sort of trouble would be walking through my doorway first."

Fatigue got the best of her. Grasping the settee's wooden frame for support, Oralia twisted around and eased her trembling body to the floor. The couch would have been undeniably more comfortable but, given its size and age, wasn't worth the risk of it breaking and further upsetting her already irritated host.

The resonating click-clack of Briony's hooves grew louder as the faun moved from the archway. Her tan and brown shape appeared on the opposite end of the settee. Briony sat on the edge of the green cushion and crossed her legs at the ankles, keeping her steely amber eyes locked on Oralia.

Suspecting the faun wasn't going to offer the location of her team without having her own questions answered first, Oralia obliged Briony the best she could. It was a shame she was too weary to remember what the original question had been. "What is it you wish to know?"

Briony gave her tea another thoughtful stir. "Why you're here."

That much was easy at least. Oralia didn't even have to lie. "To find Faris. We have reason to believe that the realm is using him to lure Rasp out of hiding."

"You sure you're not here hunting witches?"

That was probably meant as a verbal jab, but Oralia answered truthfully on the off chance it was a legitimate question. "We are not hunting witches."

"Then why was it I found you with a fire elemental?" Briony lifted the teacup to her chin and took a breath, inhaling the warm steam through her nostrils. "At least that's what I assume it was. Hard to tell given the state of the remains."

Warm bile pooled in the back of Oralia's throat as the memory of burnt flesh and crackling flames flashed to the forefront of her mind. She sank lower, feeling an inexplicable chill roll across her bare arms. She used her palms to rub the life back into the forearms, but the cold persisted.

Something soft descended over her shoulders, causing Oralia to flinch in surprise. She settled back down once realizing it was a blanket. Confused, her wary stare returned to the faun beside her.

"You were shivering." Briony tilted her horns in the direction of the unlit hearth. "I can get a fire going if you want."

"No." Oralia squeezed her eyelids shut, attempting to drown out the sounds of the hungry, lapping tongues of flame that danced along the edges of her frayed memory. Through clenched teeth, she gritted out, "No fire, thank you."

"That witch did a number on you, didn't they? How in the gods did you manage to defeat a fire elemental?"

"I . . . I do not know. My memory of the incident is foggy at best."

Although she couldn't see Briony's expression, the faun's words sounded utterly unconvinced. "It wouldn't have anything to do with that curious-looking rash you've got on your chest, would it? Or the powerstone you carry around your neck?"

Instinctively, Oralia reached for the pendant. She didn't know why she felt a rush of relief when her fingers made contact with the stone's cool, smooth surface. By all rights, she should have wanted it gone.

"You nearly broke my hand when I tried to remove it," Briony continued. "Which was alarming, considering the tonic I'd given you for the pain was supposed to have put you under."

Oralia eased her eyes back open, fearful she already knew what direction Briony's line of interrogation would be taking. "Did I? My apologies."

The withering look the faun imparted rivaled even Oralia's best *don't fuck with me* glare. Briony's tone was as cold as the ice rampaging through Oralia's veins. "In case you've forgotten, I was on the mountain with you when all the shit went down. I know what that stone is, Oralia. And know what's in it. Your wounds are identical to Daana's. Which means whatever is afflicting you was caused by the dark entity. I think all of this would go a lot easier for both of us if you were up-front about what's going on."

Right. Oralia actually *had* forgotten about Briony's involvement on the mountain. If she was not mistaken, trapping the dark entity into the powerstone might have been the faun's idea. With a pained sigh, Oralia pulled the collar of the billowy nightshirt—not her own, might have even been a bedsheet at one point in its life—and exposed her collarbones. "We did not defeat the spirit on the mountain. Not completely. While Daana was able to contain the dark entity within the powerstone, a small piece of it burrowed into each of us."

Briony interrupted her recount, raising one eyebrow in concern. "Even Rasp?"

"No one has had any contact with either him or Whisper since the incident. I do not know for sure, but would not be surprised. Rasp was in closer contact with the spirit than any of us."

"That's not good."

Exhausted, Oralia nodded her agreement. Briony was right, of course. If the dark entity was having this much of a toll on her, a non-magical person, she hated to imagine what sort of consequences it would exact on an overpowered, highly unstable witch. Hopefully Whisper and Rasp were faring better than she was. Oralia drew a breath and picked up where she had left off.

"On its own, the infection is mild. I feel more drained than usual, but it is not unbearable. When paired with the powerstone, however, it can . . ." She paused. "It speaks to me."

Briony's eyes went wide. "It what?"

"Here." She pressed her index finger to the side of her head. "Telepathically. In the same way Whisper used to."

"So why wear the stone then? Why not delegate it to someone else, or just, I don't know, not wear it at all? Keep it confined somewhere safe?"

"Ralizak would tell you it is because I am an unwavering martyr that enjoys making myself suffer." It wasn't wrong, Oralia supposed. "The truth is, I cannot afford to have the stone fall into the wrong hands. Between the constant travel and rearranging and repacking of bags, having the pendant misplaced or stolen was simply too great of a risk to gamble. Carrying the stone comes with its own downsides, which is why I took on the task personally."

Sascha and Rali insisted on taking turns as well, but that was not something Oralia felt the need to share. Briony had the information she needed. And, judging by the pinched look on her face, she was sifting through it for all the little details Oralia *didn't* say.

"Gods, woman," the faun muttered at last with a disapproving shake of her horns. "You are the living epitome of pigheadedness."

"So I am told. Quite often." Oralia eased into a position a little less murderous on her back, pausing to wait for the room to stop spinning, before speaking through her tusks. "Now that I have satisfied your curiosity and, hopefully, reservations as to why I am here, I would appreciate it if you would point me in the direction of my team."

Briony's attempt to withhold her laughter resulted in a choking snort instead. She dipped forward, holding her shaking sides as if Oralia had told a particularly humorous quip. "Oh you precious thing. You're just not accustomed to anyone else being in charge, are you? You may as well make yourself comfortable. Neither of us are leaving this room until I learn how you killed the fire elemental."

CHAPTER FIFTY-NINE

Logical Solutions for an Illogical Problem

Briony's tea had to have gone cold by now. The faun didn't appear to notice. She continued to swirl the lukewarm beverage with slow, deliberate twirls of her spoon as she sat on the edge of the green settee, looking every inch like a hungry lioness poised to pounce. Her amber eyes narrowed, allowing a haughty smile to pull at the corners of her mouth. "Thought I wouldn't notice, did you? You gave more information than I expected, I'll grant you that. But the way you skirted around your encounter with a fire elemental was quite telling."

Shit.

Oralia had been so careful, too. While the obvious answer was to lie, she feared Briony would see right through her deceit. The alternative, unfortunately, wasn't any better. The truth was so utterly outlandish that anyone with a lick of sense would dismiss it as pure fantasy. Oralia sighed, running a calloused hand down her broad face. "I had hoped it would slip your notice."

Briony's ears flicked in irritation. The leathery snap wasn't nearly as threatening as a hoof stomp, but the warning came through crystal clear regardless. "Stalling isn't going to reunite you with your team any faster. As I said before, I need to know what sort of trouble you're in before it becomes my own."

Sascha is out there searching for you right now. Probably thinks you're dead. The sooner you get through this, the sooner you can ease his suffering. Maybe he'll even feed you when he's done grieving the loss of his favorite pot.

Reluctantly Oralia opted for the truth. "The fire elemental and I crossed paths during an ambush. I and another member of my team were out fetching water when we were set upon by her and her bandits. My companion and I ran in opposite directions to divide their numbers."

Okay, *mostly* the truth. Oralia's recount was, admittedly, an over-generous description for what truly happened. It certainly beat "my idiot companion ran screaming at the first sign of danger." Oralia continued, gaze focused on the rhythmic stir of Briony's spoon as she spoke. "The fire elemental took chase and used her magic to corner me with the intent to kill. Nearly succeeded, in fact."

The stench of smoke and burnt hair flooded Oralia's senses once more. The flush of heat that scorched the skin on her forehead was at odds with the ice thrumming deep within her aching bones. Her heartbeat galloped along, steadily gaining speed, like a runaway horse. The only thing that kept Oralia centered was the mesmeric stir of Briony's spoon. She kept her gaze locked on it, fighting the growing swell of panic stirring to life from within.

"By all rights you should be dead."

"I should," Oralia agreed, marveling at how hollow the words came across.

"And yet you're not. *How?*"

"The dark entity saved me. As I am its host, it is reliant on me for survival. The one thing I cannot provide is food. The fire elemental's mistake was trapping us together. At such close proximity, the entity used the elemental's magic to jump hosts, or at least a piece of it did, in order to feed." The words flowing from her mouth did not sound like her own. Oralia felt detached, as if severed from her mind and body, allowed to sit back as an unconscious part of her filled in the necessary blanks. "The spirit consumed the witch from the inside out in a matter of seconds."

Briony's hand froze in place, halting the rhythmic stir of her spoon. The faun's amber eyes were wide and rimmed in white. She said nothing, resigned to an alarmed silence as she mentally sifted through Oralia's recount, arranging and rearranging the pieces to make sense of it all.

"I don't know what sort of answer I was expecting," Briony said. "Admittedly not . . . that."

"You actually believe me?"

"I wish I didn't, but yes. That's far too creative for you to have come up with on your own." Slowly, Briony started stirring again, too caught in thought to notice the drop of brown liquid that dribbled down the side of her cup and landed between the folds of her skirt. "You realize what sort of problem this powerstone presents, right?"

Problem was a gross understatement. In the wrong hands, the wielder could use the powerstone to wipe out the world's most powerful witches without having to lift a finger. It came at the cost of playing host to an evil entity, of course, but Oralia suspected that wouldn't deter those hungriest for power. "I do."

"This is the sort of problem I *didn't* want to welcome into my home, Oralia."

"You could solve that by allowing me to walk out."

"No, I know about its existence now. I may not have much of a conscience, but there's enough of one to realize that would be a bad idea." Briony drew a breath of incense-infused air in through her nostrils and out her mouth, before summoning the courage to ask, "I don't suppose you've tried destroying the stone?"

Ah yes, the desperate search for a logical solution to an illogical problem. Oralia knew that dance all too well. "The stone cannot be destroyed by ordinary means. Believe me, we tried. Daana and I nearly died when Ellisar cast it into the fire. The answer, I fear, is in its creation. The powerstone was created by magic and, therefore, can only be destroyed by magic."

"Magic?"

Oralia was fairly certain she'd said the word correctly. She was not given the opportunity to confirm her statement as Briony gave a sudden snap of her fingers. "That's why you're here!"

Confused, Oralia said nothing, allowing the faun to reveal whatever thoughts were racing behind her wide, gleaming eyes. It was not a long wait, fortunately.

"Oralia, you snake." The contemplative look slipped from Briony's face and was replaced with a sly smile. She shook her fuzzy head, chuckling, "You were lying through your teeth before, weren't you? And to think I fell for it so easily."

"I beg your pardon?"

Briony lifted the spoon from her teacup and set it daintily onto the side table beside her. "You're not here for Faris. You're here to seek Novera's help regarding the powerstone and its hold on you."

"Novera Belfast?" Oralia failed to see what connection existed between the infection coursing through her veins and Faris's mother. "I am afraid I do not follow."

"Oh please, you can stop pretending. Finding Faris was a believable cover while it lasted, but I've seen through it now. There's no sense in sticking with an obvious lie."

Oralia allowed her confused silence to speak on her behalf.

"That is why you're here, isn't it?" Several more uncomfortable seconds lapsed before Briony realized her error in judgment. A sheepish blush transformed her tanned cheeks a warm shade of pink. "Oh good gods, you really don't know?"

"Obviously not."

Briony lowered the untouched cup of tea and rested it against the top of her legs. "Huh."

The faun's sudden, tight-lipped silence was telling. Alas, for the life of her, Oralia couldn't pinpoint what information she was supposed to be gleaning from it. And, at the moment, it wasn't her primary concern. Her first priority was reuniting with those still looking for her. "I am unaware of what Novera Belfast brings to the equation. If she is able to assist in any way, I will gladly seek her out but, as I mentioned before, I am here to find Faris. The realm cannot be allowed to use him to get to Rasp. Finding Faris first seemed like the obvious way to prevent this."

"That's it?" Briony's ears lowered. "That's really the only reason you're here? You're not here for Novera? Or on the behalf of the resistance, maybe?"

"I am in no way affiliated with the Sons and Daughters of Resistance." Oralia was quick to stamp out that misconception.

Unfortunately, it did not seem to matter as Briony regurgitated the same misinformation Oralia had been combatting for months. "Everyone else seems to think otherwise. Your fellow figureheads, for one. According to the realm, you single-handedly spearheaded the rebellion yourself."

Oralia pinched the bridge of her nose, sighing. "I helped move witches from the realm into the flatlands to keep them out of the hands of the Division of Divination. That was as far as my involvement went. I did not intend to spark a full-blown rebellion."

"But it did. And now you're helping."

"I have no issue helping the people win their freedom, as I did with Adderwood. My involvement, however, was not on the behalf of the Sons and Daughters of Resistance. I refuse to help transfer the reins of power from one dictator to another."

". . . Oh."

Oralia raised her eyebrow at the crestfallen faun. "Why does this knowledge upset you?"

Briony stared at the worn floorboards as she spoke. "The realm's taken Lonebrook hostage. They came looking for Faris, as you suspected, but the little weasel managed to slip their nets. Geralt's got a stranglehold on the village. He's trying to lure Faris back by tightening the noose around the people's necks. When we found you, I had hoped that Larkspur had sent you. That you were here to free us, as you had Adderwood."

It was Oralia's turn to utter, "Oh."

"Yeah. For a second I thought maybe we had a chance. I'll save you from wasting any more of your time. Faris isn't here. I haven't heard from him in months." Briony's crestfallen stare swept to the window, adding, "Novera might have some secret means to contact him, though."

Oralia considered this information. It was bait, most likely. A last-ditch attempt to rope her into another rebellion without begging for her help. "If Geralt has the village on lockdown, as you say, I imagine securing an audience with Novera would be next to impossible then?"

Having given up on actually drinking her tea, Briony set it into the small side table next to the spoon. "Difficult, not impossible. That is with the right help, of course."

"And the price for securing this help?"

Briony dropped her act for what might have been the first time in, well, probably ever, really. Her amber eyes widened and her ears drooped, looking like a shivering dog begging to be let inside. "Stay? Help us? There are a lot of good people trapped in that village. The realm is growing impatient. It won't be long before they start applying the pressure. And unfortunately, it's going to be to our necks."

Oralia ignored the urge to blindly agree. "I cannot make a decision of this magnitude on my own. Your cause is worthy, make no mistake. But I am one person, and I cannot dictate the lives of my team without consulting them first."

The puppy dog expression faded and Briony's face went blank once more. "The only leverage I have over you right now is that you are separated from them. Bringing them in before a deal has been struck defeats the whole purpose."

Oralia pulled the blanket tighter over her shoulders. She couldn't remember the last time she'd felt this cold. She was indoors, protected from the elements and still, she was shaking like a damn leaf. "This may come as a surprise to you, Briony, but it is not always necessary to use blackmail in order to get me to do something. I helped Adderwood without them having to resort to extortion."

"Adderwood had an army," Briony replied.

That much was true. And, without knowing the numbers or the stakes, it was a factor that was going to weigh heavily on Oralia's decision. She wasn't going to say that, of course. First and foremost, Oralia had to assure Briony that she would not turn and run the moment she was reunited with her team. "You implied that Novera may have insight about"—she gestured to the dark veins branching beneath her collarbones—"this?"

The faun perked up a little. "No promises, but this sort of thing is up her alley."

"And she may have a way of contacting Faris?"

"I think so."

"Then that alone is enough to at least stay and consider our options."

"Alright, I'll go fetch your precious team. But if any of them try to stab me, I'm not above shattering kneecaps!" With a breathy snort, the little faun stood.

Oralia attempted to do the same with less success. A withering glare from her host prompted Oralia to sink back down onto the floor.

"I said me, not you. For the gods' sakes, woman. You're in no shape to go trampling through a forest."

Oralia had to give credit where credit was due. For being nearly two full heads shorter than her, Briony could certainly put on an intimidating front when she wanted to. The orc lifted her hands in defeat. "Yes, ma'am."

Briony went over the house rules, accentuating each command with a hoof stomp. "No leaving the house. Don't go through my shit. If you see any soldiers, run. If you get caught, you and I never saw each other."

Oralia considered pointing out that the *no leaving the house* rule was in direct conflict with the *run in the case of soldiers* rule. Not wanting to make an issue of it, she bit back her tongue and offered a nod of confirmation instead. "Understood. I will stay here and await your return."

Oralia waited for Briony to leave before dragging her aching carcass back over to the makeshift bed on the floor. It was a pathetic, undignified, and horrifically painful process that Oralia did not wish for anyone to witness, especially not the person who was depending on her to save their village. Briony knew she was weak, undoubtedly. It just made Oralia feel better not having her watch.

Oralia eased into the nest of soft pillows and blankets. She had no intention of sleeping, but the quiet combined with the velvety softness of the cot soon lulled her into a dreamless slumber.

CHAPTER SIXTY

One of Those Living Dead Situations

"Welp, it's official. The boss's dead."

"She's not dead. For fuck's sake, Lingon, she was snoring when we walked in."

"'Twas but a death rattle, dear brother."

The voices, one thin and nasally and the other deep and guttural, roused Oralia from her dreamless sleep. Her heavy eyelids eased open to find two human men crouched on either side of her. Regrettably, she recognized the pair instantly.

"Not dead," Mul grunted at his brother. "Told you."

Lingon peered closer, brushing a stray lock of long brown hair from his narrow face. "How do we know this isn't one of those living dead situations?"

"Because she's not dead! You want me to kill her to prove it to you?"

Oralia held up her hand. "That will not be necessary, thank you."

Lingon narrowed his eyes at her. "Just what an undead would say."

Clenching her jaw, Oralia heaved into a sitting position. Pain lanced up her spine and erupted within her aching skull like lightning, spawning a cloud of blinding spots that blinked along the edges of her vision. A crippling wave of nausea followed. Oralia closed her eyes and breathed through it. It was only after the tightness in chest and abdomen had eased that she regained the ability to form words.

"Where are the others?"

"Still tearing the forest apart looking for you, probably." Mul straightened his posture. He hooked his thumbs into his belt loops and swaggered a few steps away, eyeing the yellow walls in search of something worth stealing.

"Me an' Dingleberry were actually not far from here. We'd found a hidden trail and were following it when this mouthy little faun popped up out of nowhere, insisting she knew your whereabouts."

Oralia found that scenario highly unlikely for several reasons. One, as Briony possessed a fully functioning sense of self-preservation, she would have known not to approach either Mul or Lingon outright. Secondly, of the many, many qualities the Stoneclaw brothers lacked, a deep distrust of strangers was not one of them. The pair would have never blindly followed a strange faun into the woods.

She clicked her tusks softly and sighed. "None of that is true."

"That bit about us being close by was!"

"We did actually find a secret trail," Lingon insisted. His reluctant expression implied there was more to the story than either of them were letting on. Fortunately it took only a few seconds of uninterrupted eye contact to coax the rest of it out of him. Lingon hurried through it, hopeful, perhaps, that if he blurted it out all in one breath, Oralia would only catch half of what was said.

"And then we came across this giant tree and I bet Mul I could climb to the top faster than him. While I was proving my mettle, a faun came up out of nowhere and stole our packs. We raced after her and it wasn't until we got to this here cottage that the little thief announced that you were inside and that if we didn't believe her, we could go see for ourselves." He dipped forward, small chest heaving as he gulped in a giant breath of air. "There, happy?"

Mul nodded in agreement. "The faun also said not to steal her shit before disappearing back into the woods. Which seems a little hypocritical, if you ask me."

Oralia mentally sifted through the wealth of information for the important pieces. Her efforts produced only one. "Briony is not here?"

"Fetching the others, likely." Mul scratched the underside of his beard. "We broke up into groups for the search. Most of them went in the other direction."

"The whole camp was worried sick about you." Lingon moved to the red brick fireplace and rearranged the trinkets along the mantle. "Not me an' Mul, obviously. But everyone else's been tearing the woods apart trying to figure out what happened to you after the bandit attack."

The mention of the attack sparked Oralia's memory. She lifted her head from where it was buried between her hands. "The bandits—"

Mul cut her off with a flippant flick of his wrist. "Didn't stand a chance. Thanks to Kalihn's screaming, we heard them coming a mile away."

"And Sascha?" Oralia asked timidly. Her fuckmate worried excessively over even the most mundane of things. She hated to imagine what toll her disappearance was taking upon him.

"In a fucking mood," Mul replied.

Lingon spun around on his heel, throwing his slender arms out at his sides. "He kept going, morning, noon, and night, insisting he wouldn't stop until he found you. And of course all the rest of us felt bad, so we kept going, too. Sascha refused all breaks. Wouldn't even stop to catch his breath. You should 'ave seen the look he gave me when I politely asked him to stop and make me a sandwich!"

An unexpected tap at the window spared Oralia from answering. She twisted her head in the direction of the noise, squinting through the barrage of sunlight filtering in from outside. "What is that?"

Both brothers acted strangely indifferent to the ominous tapping. Together, they answered as one, "Nothing."

"It is not nothing." In addition to the increasingly loud tapping, Oralia swore she heard the harsh, rattling croak of a raven. "There is a bird outside clearly trying to garner your attention."

Now that she thought of it, this was not the first time either. While Rasp may have been the only one of his people capable of understanding the ravens, it did not stop the ravens from communicating with the rest of the family. Trying to communicate, anyway, as Mul and Lingon obviously had no intention of listening.

Lingon stormed across the room and threw the window open. "Go away! We already told you, we're not interested!"

The raven fluttered past him and circled the room twice before coming to rest on the green settee. Ruffling its feathery head, the raven slung open its cavernous maw and argued back just as loudly.

Oralia spied something fastened to its spindly leg. "It appears to have a message for you."

Mul dropped onto the opposite side of the couch with a huff, glaring daggers at the noisy bird. "Yeah, we know. And I guarantee you it says the same thing as the last three."

Lingon paced in front of the couch, pointing his finger at the raven as he passed. "And you can tell that ugly fuck that our answer is still no. We're not coming home. He can have the throne. We don't bloody care!"

Throne? Oralia's thoughts churning. She strung the bits and pieces of information together until it produced something, if not cohesive, then as close to it as she was going to get. "Lingon," Oralia said, taking care to keep her voice level. He already looked like a spooked horse prepared to bolt. There was no sense in sending him dashing out the front door prematurely. At least not until her curiosity was satiated. "Has Bil been trying to reach you this entire time?"

"What?" Lingon scoffed, still nervously pacing. "No. Of course not."

Bil Stoneclaw, the eldest and possibly most competent of the royal siblings, had vacated Mount Hook prior to the battle. With their home destroyed and their warring neighbors in an active scramble to seize territory, Bil and the Stoneclaw clan had vanished without a trace.

"How long has your brother been trying to reach you?" Oralia demanded.

Lingon had the expression of a child caught pinching sweets from the kitchen. He collapsed onto the ancient settee beside Mul, uncaring of the fact that he nearly squashed the raven messenger doing so. "I don't know. A few weeks maybe? A month, tops."

"I do not understand," Oralia said. "You told me you did not know the location of your clan. I thought it was the only reason keeping you here. When the truth is, not only do you know where Bil is, but he has been summoning you home, and you could have been well on your way a month ago?"

Lingon's face reddened as his gaze dropped sheepishly to his feet. "The thing is we don't want to go home."

"Come again?"

"We don't want to go home, alright? This is the most adventure Mul an' I have ever had and the thought of going back is just . . . well, horrible."

Mul nudged Lingon in the ribs with his elbow. "Tell her about the banana."

Lingon elbowed him back twice as hard. "I don't want to tell her about the stupid banana!"

"We tried a banana for the first time back in Adderwood." Mul took on the task himself. His eyes were wide and his expression was unusually sincere. "It was the best thing I'd ever tasted. I ain't ever going to see another one of those if I go back to the Iron Ridge."

Oralia's tone was woefully unimpressed. "A banana?"

"It's not just the banana." Lingon tried to explain their reasoning better, which, for whatever reason, involved an excessive amount of hand gestures. He grasped at the air with his fingers as if plucking the answer from nothing. "The banana is just, I don't know, symbolic of everything we haven't tried, I guess?"

Oralia wished there was someone else present with whom she could exchange confused glances. Her only option was the raven, however. And she was not quite prepared to stoop to that level of desperation yet. "If you stay, you forfeit your claim to the throne. Neither of you can lead your people if you are not *with* them."

"Yeah, we considered that." Lingon continued talking to his shoes, unwilling to meet Oralia's unflinching stare. "Bil can have it. It's better he doesn't know what he's missing, else you'd have one more of us tagging along after you. Seven realms, probably a whole clan."

"I do not want a clan behind me! Not even one as formidable as the Stoneclaws." Oralia's unexpected outburst was as much of a surprise to the brothers as it was to her. "This is only temporary. I have no intention of traveling the land and freeing each individual territory from realm control one after the other."

Mul nudged Lingon with his shoulder as a grin slowly pulled across his bearded face. "Temporary, right."

The younger brother nodded his agreement. "She's got the fever something fierce."

Although Oralia understood the majority of the words that came from the pair, their meaning was often lost in translation. This case being no exception. Oralia massaged the growing ache from her temples. "I am not ill."

"Martyr fever," Lingon clarified. "You can act detached all you want, but it's as plain as the tusks on your face. You could have been free of this mess months ago, but each time you were given the chance to step back, you plunged right back in. This 'temporary' schtick ain't fooling anyone but yourself."

"I . . ." Her voice trailed as she could not outright deny it. If it was this obvious to these two, it meant everyone else already knew as well. Everyone but herself, of course. That seemed to be the nature of how this sort of thing worked. Oralia was always the last to fully understand her own motivations. "I do not wish to talk about it."

Although the pair themselves said nothing, the smug delight on their faces assured Oralia that her days of secrecy were long gone. Somewhere along the line she'd become completely transparent. Not that she was about to open that up for discussion either. "You are the subject here, not me," she said sternly. "Am I to understand that the two of you would rather follow me, to your own detriment, possibly death, than return to your people?"

"Why is this so hard for you to wrap your head around?" Mul's eyebrows shot high on his head, as though offended by the very question itself. "Our lives were utterly boring before all this. All we did was drink and fight each other."

"That is all you do now," Oralia reminded him.

"Not true. We fight other people now, too."

"And make love afterward." Lingon added, quickly, "With other folks, not each other. Or the dead bodies."

"So glad you clarified that last part," Mul told him.

"Shut up!"

Oralia had always kept strange company. She supposed this wasn't any stranger than her previous team. More annoying, perhaps. On some level, she almost felt honored. To have not one, but two capable Stoneclaw warriors in her personal company spoke volumes. Their impact probably would have been more meaningful could she convince them to let their reputation speak for itself, versus opening their mouths to let every thought pass through unchecked. Mouthiness aside, the pair would be imperative to the trials that loomed ahead. Possibly enough to swing the fate of Lonebrook in her favor.

Lingon lifted his head curiously. "Anybody else feel the ground shaking?"

Mul hurried across the room and poked his head out the open window. "Looks like the mouthy faun found the rest of the party after all." He glanced over his shoulder at Oralia and waggled his eyebrows in a manner that begged to be slapped. "Your beau looks to be in an awful hurry. Do you think he'll slow down or just snap the door off its hinges on his way in?"

Oralia rose onto stiff legs and reached for Mul, using him as a means to keep her balance. He didn't offer much in the way of support, but at least he didn't shrug her off. Every step was excruciating. Oralia stubbornly persisted, shuffling one foot in front of the other, knowing speed was of the essence.

"If you want to sleep with a roof over your head tonight," she said, gasping as a surge of pins and needles moved down her legs, "get me outside before he knocks the house down."

CHAPTER SIXTY-ONE

Too Stubborn to Die

Three days had passed since. Three. Blasted. Days. And *still*, the unsteady tremble in Oralia's hands persisted. The tremors made even the most mundane of activities a challenge. Eating, in particular, topped the list. The few times she got a spoon to her mouth without spilling its contents down the front of her tunic were for naught, as the food came back up almost as quickly as it went down.

And, as if body trembles and the constant, pendulous swing between ravenous and nauseous wasn't enough, her sleep was plagued by unrelenting nightmares as well. Each time Oralia closed her eyes, the fire elemental's death replayed over and over. Her dreams always ended the same—trapped within a ring of red and orange crackling flames, choking on stomach acid as the putrid stench of singed hair and flesh slowly filled her blistered lungs.

Her temper suffered the worst. Oralia found herself short, snippy, and acting so utterly out of character, she feared her mind was ripping apart at the seams. Her team graciously took it in stride. Too graciously, which revulsed her even more. The lack of back-talk, the pitiful glances, the way everyone suddenly volunteered for extra work outside of the cottage—it was belittling in the worst of ways.

Briony's homestead was situated several miles outside of the village of Lonebrook, hidden so deep within the trees, the realm soldiers had yet to find her. Briony insisted they were safe so long as no one did anything to draw unwanted attention. In spite of the warning, Rali, the unofficial face of unwanted attention, convinced Briony to take her closer to town. They were there now, with Dewpetal in tow, scouting the outskirts of Lonebrook for whatever it was Rali was looking for.

Mul and Lingon slipped away soon after, promising on each other's lives that they'd stay out of trouble. For reasons unknown, they took Kalihn with them. What was even more surprising was how Kalihn, who normally avoided the brothers like the plague, accepted their invitation without any of her usual bellyaching. She practically ran out the door to be free of the cottage.

It was all highly suspicious.

"Moonflower," Sascha's voice disrupted Oralia's internal stewing, "is something upsetting you?"

Oralia ceased drumming her fingers absentmindedly against the linen tablecloth. She was seated at the table tucked into the corner of the balmy kitchen. Sascha was across from her, laboring away on another broth. This one smelled faintly of ginger, garlic, and green onion. "Not at all. Why do you ask?"

"You're grumbling like a badger in heat."

What a horrifically descriptive comparison. At least Sascha had the decency to call her a badger and not a sow, she supposed.

Sascha had his back to her, scraping a handful of finely minced herbs from the cutting board into the cauldron hanging over the fire. He normally hummed while he worked, but today his carefree noises were strangely absent. "Are you sure there isn't something eating at you?"

"A dark entity."

Oralia heard the exasperated click of his tusks from all the way across the room. Had her answer been overly-literal? Of course. But ridiculous questions deserved equally ridiculous answers.

Sascha used a broad, wooden spoon to stir the pot's simmering contents. "Anything else?"

"Nothing at all." As if on cue, her left hand spasmed, causing her fingers to curl painfully in on themselves. Oralia slammed the flat of her palm against the table and held it there. She gave her right hand the side-eye, warning it to stay in line else it would suffer the same fate as the left. "Do not even think about it," she cautioned. "I am not above drawing blood."

Sascha stared over his shoulder at her with both eyebrows raised high on his forehead and mouth held slightly agape.

"What?" Oralia demanded.

"You're the one threatening your own appendages, Moonflower. You tell me."

Oralia released her hand from the table and curled it into a fist. "I have, admittedly, not been feeling like myself lately."

"I noticed," Sascha assured her. "Which is why I bribed the others to make themselves scarce for the evening. It's time to stop tiptoeing around the issue and address it head on."

Dear gods help her. She'd been a little crankier than usual, yes. But surely not anything intervention-worthy! Also, why hadn't any of the others warned her? At least given her a head start. Useless legs be damned, Oralia would have made it work. She sank lower onto the wooden bench and studied the exit from the corner of her eye, wondering if it was too late to slip out the back door and catch up to Rali and Briony. She could drag herself the whole way if need be.

Sascha turned to face her, wiping his gargantuan hands on his flower print apron. His expression fell the moment he saw her face. "Why do you look like a child about to be reprimanded?"

"Because I *feel* like I am about to be reprimanded."

"I mean, if that's what you want." Sascha narrowed one eye as he wagged his spoon at her playfully. "Eat all of your dinner or it's straight to bed."

While he had meant it as teasing, she was seriously considering the straight to bed option.

Sascha withdrew a set of wooden bowls from the cupboard and held the pair in one hand while ladling hot soup with the other. He delivered both bowls of steaming broth to the table without spilling a drop. He offered Oralia a gentle smile, under the false assumption that a little reassurance would be enough to keep her from bolting the moment he sat down.

"It's just me, Moonflower. I won't say a word if you drop the soup. There's always plenty more." A look, caught somewhere between genuine concern and playfulness, pulled at the corners of Sascha's eyes as he eased onto the bench beside her. "I could try spoon-feeding you again if you wanted. You might get more in your mouth if you refrained from biting me this time."

She refused to let his charm soothe her fraying nerves. "Stop trying to flirt with me. You said there was an issue to be addressed. Seven realms, get it over with before I die of suspense."

Oh gods. Too harsh, Oralia realized as the smile slipped from Sascha's mouth and transformed into a pained grimace. Moisture started to collect around the edges of his sorrowful eyes. Oralia reached for his hand, the words already curling over her tongue, when he beat her to it.

"I'm sorry," Sascha said.

"No, do not be." She winced. "That was uncalled for."

He flipped his hand over and clasped hers with a gentle squeeze. "I sent the others away because I have some groveling to do. The soup is my very pathetic attempt at an apology. The start of one, anyway."

And here Oralia thought she could not possibly have been any more confused. She should have been the one begging for forgiveness, not him. "I do not follow."

"I was reckless and put you in danger," he started. "I was the one who sent Kalihn with you to fetch water the day of the attack. She was annoying me. I thought it would be more fun if she annoyed you instead. My carelessness nearly got you killed."

Oralia waited for more. When Sascha's agonizing admission stopped there, she was forced to ask, "Is that all?"

"I understand if you want space. I can sleep in another room, or outside if you would prefer—"

"No need. You are forgiven."

He blinked in confusion. "Just like that?"

There wasn't anything to forgive as far as Oralia was concerned. She'd merely said it to stop him from making a fool of himself. Oralia reached for her bowl and raised it to her mouth, fighting to control the unsteady tremble in her hands. The broth was light and savory, with a pleasant kick of heat at the end. "Ellisar used to try to kill me all the time. Kept me on my toes. She came to the eventual conclusion that I am simply too stubborn to die."

Come to think of it, Ellisar might have actually said stupid, not stubborn.

"Oralia, please," Sascha said. "You've been in a silent rage for the last three days. Will you stop pretending that everything is okay between us? You're allowed to be mad at me."

Half of that statement was true. Not the critical part, though. Oralia set the bowl back onto the table, fighting the sudden urge to roll her eyes. "Sascha, I am not mad at you."

"You threatened to disembowel Lingon earlier."

"He was chewing with his mouth open like a damn horse!" Oralia said. Unfortunately, Sascha's resulting stretch of silence left her with no other choice but to explain herself. "I am mad at my circumstances. Not you."

"Well, you should be mad at me."

"Should I be?" Oralia repeated, feeling the floodgates of rampaging emotions begin to open. *No, no, no, not now. Not here. Hold it together!*

Unfortunately, like the rest of her confounded body, her tongue rebelled, spilling every volatile emotion churning within her tightening chest. "My own body is betraying me. And you think I should hold you accountable for that? Should I blame you for the nightmares as well? Why stop there? I could blame you for the way I wake up each morning weaker than the last. Or how my strength does not recover the way it used to? Is that what you want to hear, love? That this is all your fault somehow?"

"You almost died."

"I almost die all of the time!"

He wrapped one burly arm behind her back and tugged her closer. The tightness felt good, even if she didn't want to admit it. Regrettably, instead of simply accepting forgiveness and fetching her another bowl of soup, the big lug kept trying to assuage his guilt. "How can you say that? How can you dismiss it so casually like it's nothing?"

"Because the alternative is not any better. I will let you handle the dwelling for both of us."

Unfortunately, he did just that. "This is twice now I thought I had lost you."

Twice that Sascha knew of. Oralia decided against bringing up all the other near-death experiences she hadn't bothered to tell him about.

Sascha buried his face into her neck. His hot breath tickled her skin as he spoke. "I'm not sure anyone else would have survived what you did."

Oralia hadn't spoken in depth about her encounter with the witch. Other than a short, not-entirely-accurate description, she avoided even thinking about it. She tried to play it off as a joke but her words rang hollow instead. "As I said, too stubborn to die."

"Will you please take this seriously? Briony says they pulled you out of a fire, Oralia. Most people don't survive being engulfed in fire."

Against every instinct urging her to turn this into a heated debate, Oralia bit back the poison on her tongue and leaned into him. She reached up and threaded her fingers into the curl of Sascha's beard, feeling every shake and tremble of his unsteady breath. "I wish I could tell you that this was the last time. That, from here on out, I would avoid every risk to cross my path. But you and I both know that would be a lie."

Wordlessly, he squeezed her tighter.

"Assisting Lonebrook is going to put me right back in the path of death and danger," Oralia reminded him.

"You haven't had your meeting with Novera yet. It's not too late to back out and give retirement a try."

A harsh laugh caught within Oralia's throat. It was woefully inappropriate given the utter lack of humor in her next words. "For you, maybe.

As Rali would say, 'that ship has sailed.' I would not fault you for leaving, however."

"Why would I leave?"

"Because I have already made up my mind."

"You act like it's your job to save everyone. It's not. You are one person."

"Believe it or not, but I am capable of being selfish as well. I am not trying to save everyone. I am trying to save myself." Oralia peeled back her tunic to reveal her collarbones. As overdramatic as the gesture may have been, she had every right to be as dramatic as she wanted. Her opportunities to embrace the melodramatic were running regretfully short. "The infection has spread, Sascha. Time is not on my side. Any hope for a cure lies in the hands of Novera Belfast. That said, she cannot help me if she is dead."

At the very least, the reason for her underlying rage was becoming clearer now. Whatever Oralia did, no matter the choice she made, death awaited her at the end of each turn. The question was now whether she chose the short path, and fought, or opted for the slightly longer one, and spent her remaining time sipping soup with Sascha while her body slowly wasted away.

There was no choice, as far as Oralia was concerned. Death by the sword was preferable to the agony of being consumed alive. "I can either fight or I can run," she said. "There is a small chance I survive both the battle and the illness. Running, on the other hand, only postpones the inevitable. A few months, maybe. A year, tops. That is not a life I wish to live."

Sascha fell painfully silent. Fresh tears welled within his eyes as he slowly came to terms with the gravity of the situation. Oralia's attention swept back over the rest of the kitchen, unable to hold his gaze any longer. Unlike his hand, which she was currently squeezing to a pulp.

"How long have you known?" he asked.

"I've had my suspicions since the mountain," Oralia admitted. It had been easy to dismiss at first. But as time went by, and her symptoms worsened, ignoring the problem only allowed it to grow. "I fear the incident with the fire elemental may have accelerated the severity of my condition. I feel weaker now than I ever did before."

Her next words were the most painful to say. "I am sorry, Sascha. I understand if this is too much to ask of you."

And there it was: the ultimatum she'd been unknowingly fighting for the past three days. Perhaps the lashing out had merely been a last-ditch, subconscious effort to drive the others away, Sascha included. After all, just because Oralia had accepted her fate, didn't mean the others had to follow suit. They could go on to live perfectly happy lives without her.

"Seven realms, woman." Sascha threw both arms around her and pulled her close, burying his face back into her neck. "Stop being ridiculous. You know what my answer is."

Tears streamed freely down Oralia's face. Somewhere along the way she'd forgotten how to breathe. She took in a sudden gasp of air, only now realizing how dry her throat felt.

"Did you think I was going to say something different?" Sascha demanded.

"Yes? I am being rather pigheaded right now."

"That we can agree on." Like his voice, Sascha's arms shuddered with each shaky breath. "Just promise me you'll be more careful. Let someone else sacrifice themselves in the face of danger every once in a while, yeah?"

A weak smile pulled at Oralia's mouth. "But I am so good at it."

"The best," he agreed. "I believe the run-in with the fire elemental has met your yearly quota, however. And, seeing as I cannot possibly stomach another heart attack, I think it's best you retire from that aspect of martyrdom."

Oralia held two fingers into the air. "On my honor, I swear to never go near another fire elemental so long as I live."

CHAPTER SIXTY-TWO

The Very Best Idea

Croak, croak, croak! Dagmar's lecture carried far and wide on the crisp breeze.

It was morning, too early for the sun to be out judging from the gray shifting light. Plumes of mist wafted along the forest floor, soaking everything, including Rasp, to the bone. He sat in the center of the encampment with a blanket pulled over his shivering shoulders, listening as Hop and Whisper hurried about, preparing for their departure. June was off to the side, receiving a loving earful from their Aunt Dagmar. June herself said little, giving small grunts and sighs of acknowledgement every now and then, as if to confirm that she was indeed listening and not shriveling up inside from humiliation.

Rasp wriggled the tip of his pinky finger into his ear with a grimace. He found himself in somewhat of an awkward situation. For what may have been the first time in existence, he was not the recipient of a raven's frenzied lecture. That in itself wasn't so bad, actually. It was the fact that he, unlike the others, understood every embarrassing word spilling from the raven's croaking maw. He felt like a creep, listening in from the other side of a closed door on a deep, sentimental conversation.

He also might have been a teeny, tiny bit jealous that no raven had ever showered him with such unbridled adoration.

"Are you sure Dagmar and June are both Stoneclaws?" Rasp whispered under his breath to Faris.

Faris was hunched on the damp ground beside him, trying to savor a steaming cup of hot nettle tea. Trying being the keyword as there was no way in the seven realms of chaos anybody, not even stubborn Faris, could enjoy the taste of boiled spinach and dirt. "Why?" the faun said, failing to stifle the reflexive gag after braving another sip. "What's Dagmar saying?"

"Terrible things."

"And what part of that strikes you as unusual? Sounds like typical Stoneclaw behavior to me."

"No, not that kind of terrible. Terrible lovey-dovey things, Faris. Like 'I love you. Please don't do anything stupid. Watch out for cliffs, and deep running water, and consider everything out of your brother's mouth a lie.'"

Faris patted Rasp's back, feigning sympathy. "Must be tough to learn that not everyone in your family is an asshole."

"Drive that blade straight into my heart, why don't you?" Once upon a time, Rasp wouldn't have thought twice about smacking the faun upside the head for his blatant disrespect. Being a reformed person, however, came with changes. The most prominent was allowing his words to do all the heavy hitting. "You know, your in-depth knowledge of my family really speaks volumes about you, Dingle."

"I'm afraid to know what it says."

"Really highlights your obsession for me. Not only do you have the ins and outs of my family dynamics committed to memory, but you apparently missed me so much, you had to go and find my twin as a replacement."

"That was as insightful as I expected it to be." Faris managed another sip of the foul-smelling tea before gritting out, "Although, at the risk of deflating your ego, I would like it stated for the record that it was June who found me. Not the other way around."

"A likely story."

"It's actually a rather funny story. Or at least she thinks so, given the amount of times she keeps bringing it up."

Rasp supposed it was only fair to return the favor and take an equal interest in Faris's life. He twirled his fingers in the air, motioning for the faun to get story time over with.

"June was my neighbor. Not that I knew that, of course, considering she and Dagmar kept to themselves. They lived their whole lives just outside of Lonebrook without anyone ever realizing it. June knew about me, about you, about the realm, all of it. It wasn't until Geralt Lazuli seized control of my village that she finally decided it was time to stop hiding. She tracked me down after I fled so we could join forces and find you together."

"I thought you said this was a funny story," Rasp said. Unless Faris had meant funny in the ironic sense. In which case, Rasp was still severely disappointed. He had a deep dislike of irony, particularly the way it kept sticking its hand uninvited into his life and giving the shit a vigorous stir.

"Can I keep going or do you want to keep interrupting some more?"

Another unenthusiastic hand wave got the faun going again.

"Turns out a shapeshifter's forms have both positives and negatives. June's human form can talk, but it can't run, not as fast as a faun anyway. She had to use her bear form to keep pace with me. Chased me for three days straight until I collapsed from absolute exhaustion."

"That's not funny, Dingle. What you're feeling is sad."

"You're an expert on feelings now, are you?"

"Oh, yes. I have to be now that I'm all mature and in tune with my emotional side," Rasp said, listing the most common culprits. "Happy. Sad. Angry. The whole spectrum."

"You know there are more than three emotions, right?"

"I prefer to stick to the basics, thank you. Any more than that and it starts to get confusing. Anyway, was that the end of your sad story, or is there an actual funny part?"

Faris paused thoughtfully before admitting, "Well, I did eventually wake up with a bear sitting on top of me. To keep me from running away, she insists."

That would have been *almost* funny if Rasp had not experienced something eerily similar only the day before. The terror of waking up pinned beneath a living fur blanket, however, was still too fresh in his mind to crack jokes about.

"It was not my best moment," Faris carried on. "There was a lot of screaming after that. From me, mostly. Until June shifted into her human form and explained who in the seven realms she was and why she was following me."

"Was she naked?"

"Is that honestly all you're getting from this?"

"It's a legitimate question!" Rasp knew for a fact that Whisper possessed a magic cloak to avoid winding up naked as a jaybird each time they went from dragon to angry porcupine. Whisper jokingly threatened to gift Rasp the magic cloak upon their death to spare the world from having to witness his bare ass ever again. The final joke was on Whisper, of course, as Rasp intended to wear it as a hat.

Faris's blurry shape slumped forward as he shook his horns from side to side in exasperation. "Yes, Rasp. It's not like a bear can wear human clothes."

"Ha!" Rasp was starting to see the humor in the story now. "The nude form makes you all squeamish. She's lucky you didn't keel over with fright."

In what could have only been an attempt to make his tea more palpable, Faris snapped the tip of a pine twig between his teeth and chewed. His words were muffled slightly by the sounds of his back molars grinding the sprig to pulp. "The whole thing's given me something of a complex, truth be told. I have nightmares about being hunted by bears now."

It was Rasp's turn to offer his friend a patronizing pat to the back. He aimed too high and got the back of Faris's neck. But, as with most things, it was the thought that counted. "I appreciate the hardships you endured to come find me. Bears. Naked women. Two of your biggest fears."

"If only you meant that."

"Of course I do."

Faris's tea sloshed against the tin cup as he swirled it from side to side, lacking the motivation, much less stomach, to drink it. "In that case, I might feel a smidge better if you finished my tea for me."

"Gods no. I wouldn't have traded with you if I'd intended to drink that shit in the first place."

"You did what?"

"I switched the mugs when you weren't looking." Rasp allowed a devilish grin to split across his face. "Hop's always brewing up the most horrible concoctions for me, insisting it's for my health. Normally I just toss 'em when he's not looking, but my mouth felt like a desert after that third corn cake this morning so I drank yours instead."

"You gave me poisoned tea?"

"Medicinal tea," Rasp corrected. "Your cup was lovely, by the way. Floral with just a hint of sweetness."

"This tastes like ass!"

Rasp raised a single eyebrow at Faris. "Which begs the question why you're still drinking it."

"I'll tell you why," Faris said in that huffy sort of voice that implied he was building toward something profound. Whether or not it would be profoundly stupid was yet to be determined. "Because, for the first time in two months, I woke up to someone waiting on me hand and hoof for a change. I opened my eyes and there was a plate of warm food and tea waiting for me. Do you know how rare that is?"

Considering Faris had effectively described how Rasp awoke most mornings, he couldn't say he did. "So you're forcing yourself to endure the taste of ass out of gratitude?"

"My reasoning made a lot more sense before you started poking holes in it," Faris grumbled. "Honestly, sometimes I don't think you even realize how good you've got it. All of these strappingly handsome fauns coming out of the woodwork to keep you alive and well fed and you barely notice. It's downright criminal."

Rasp gnawed the corner of his lip as he considered Faris's words. Not the part about the lack of gratitude, of course. It was far too early in the morning for that sort of self-reflection. "Are you implying there are two strappingly handsome fauns in this scenario?"

Faris chose the wrong moment to finish the final dregs of his tea. Choking, the faun's blurry shape heaved forward with a wet sputter, coughing droplets of foul tea from his lungs as he beat his chest with his fist. "What?"

"You refer to yourself as strappingly handsome all the time, that's nothing new. Couldn't help but notice you used the plural, though."

Speaking clearly was still proving to be a bit of a challenge for Faris, who could do little more than cough and gag, trying not to upend all of the breakfast he'd worked so hard to swallow down in the first place.

Rasp tilted his head back, wondering aloud, "Then again, maybe I just misheard."

"Yeah, that's it," Faris said weakly. "Obviously."

"Obviously," Rasp agreed.

From the sudden swell in obnoxious croaking, Dagmar's fond farewells were coming to a close. Rasp supposed it was only proper to see the old bird off. He heaved to his feet, calling loud enough for the entire camp to hear. "Hey, Hop! Faris says that's the best nettle tea he's ever had and he's too bashful to ask for another. Would you be a dear and remedy that for him?"

With Faris's hissed "I hate you" still ringing in his ears, Rasp shuffled out across the leaf-littered encampment. He kept his feet close to the ground, sliding each boot through the damp forest debris to avoid getting snagged on any unseen obstacles as he followed the sounds of Dagmar's lively chatter.

"Aunty Dagmar," Rasp called in his best singsong voice as he drew dangerously within pecking range. "I thought the point of leaving was to, you know, actually leave at some point?"

June spoke on the raven's behalf. "Sorry. She's almost on her way. Just saying her goodbyes, is all."

"Yeah, I heard."

". . . Oh, right."

Rasp managed to make the entire journey without tripping. Almost. A tree root caught him by surprise at the very end and he fell forward with a startled yelp. June reached out and caught him before he made impact with the spongy ground. Grumbling his thanks, Rasp placed his hand on her shoulder as he steadied himself. Amid the rush of relief, he could not help but feel a slight ping of annoyance at the realization that his sister was taller than him.

We're just going to pretend that didn't happen.

Unfortunately, June hadn't yet perfected the ability to read the annoyance on his face and asked with disgustingly genuine concern. "You alright?"

"Fine, fine." Rasp wiped the stringy hair from his eyes as he steered the conversation to a topic unrelated to his fall. "We're going to be traveling again soon. Aunty Dagmar might have to wrap up the goodbyes if she wants to reach Lonebrook before we do."

Faris's plan involved sending Dagmar ahead of them to deliver a message to a contact hidden outside of the village. Blessed with wings and a familiarity with the area, she was the logical choice for a messenger. That, and because Father flat-out refused. The successful delivery of the message, however, hinged upon the raven actually reaching her destination. An impossibility if Dagmar never actually got around to the departing part.

"Aunty," Rasp said, putting on his best grownup voice, "I promise I won't let anything happen to your precious bear cub. You can be on your way now. June will be safe with me."

Croak!

Out of habit, June started to explain, "Aunty said—"

"I know what Aunty said!" Rasp took a breath, allowing it to wash away the sting of Dagmar's insult, before offering an alternative. "June will be safe with Faris."

Croak.

"Fine! Hop, then. He's always telling me not to do things because they're too dangerous. On his life, I swear Hop will keep your precious bouncing baby girl safe."

"Excuse me?" Hop's voice called from across the encampment. "Why did I just hear my name?"

"No reason." Rasp turned back to the raven, squinting up at what he hoped was her blurred shape perched in the bare boughs above him. "We are in a race against time. Please go. I promise you there will be no shenanigans whatsoever."

Dagmar fluttered away, muttering something about the dramatic decline in recent Stoneclaw leadership.

June waited until the old bird had flown out of hearing. "That was all a lie, right? I was looking forward to the shenanigans, personally."

"Every word. Now, completely unrelated, I have a pressing question for you." Rasp tilted his head up at June as his most brilliant idea of the day, possibly his life, nearly burst from his chest with excitement. The words practically leapt from his mouth on their own accord. Fearful, perhaps, that if he didn't get them out as quickly as possible, the idea would disappear into the aether itself, destined to go uncommitted for all of time. "Do bears wear saddles?"

CHAPTER SIXTY-THREE

Bear Don't Wear Saddles

Rasp adjusted his hips as he gathered great fistfuls of musty fur into his hands and leaned forward. The smell was a lot stronger than a mule. Not in a bad way, either. Unlike Bonecrusher, the scent of June's fur was oddly familiar, like tundra and sweet grass in the fall. Tightening one's legs was an important aspect to bareback horse riding. Unfortunately, try as he might, the same principle did not appear to apply to bareback bear riding.

Note to self, Rasp told himself as he felt his left leg begin to slip, *don't say bareback bear riding out loud. Ever.*

Finding a stable riding position atop a bear was like trying to wrap one's legs around a fuzzy barrel made of jelly. Each time Rasp thought he'd finally found the sweet spot, the layer of fat beneath June's shaggy hide would shift and he'd lose his grip, causing him to list dangerously to one side. It might have been easier had his sister been a little bear, but alas, it was not so. June was hands down the largest bear he'd ever encountered. Unnaturally big, in fact—close to the size of the fabled warbear spirits that haunted the cliffs of the Iron Ridge territory.

Oh for fuck's sake.

For what was not the first time, nor last time, Rasp found himself marveling at just how badly the Stoneclaw clan had butchered their own history. "June?" he said, making the final adjustments to his form. "Warbears aren't the reanimated soul of a witch, are they?"

June's rumbling reply reverberated up through her ribs and into Rasp's legs, settling deep within his narrow chest.

"Magical shapeshifters." Rasp repeated her answer from a lack of having anything else to say.

"Are you sure this is wise?" Hop called from off to the side, where he was undoubtedly wringing the life from his hands with worry. "It took a lot of effort to fix your teeth and I am going to be vexed if I have to do it all over again."

"Honestly, Hop, do you even hear yourself?" Rasp said. "If this was wise, I wouldn't be doing it."

June stamped her front feet.

"Of course we're still doing it." Rasp wrangled his legs into position the best he could before wiping away the hot sheen of perspiration that clouded his eyes. Wicking the sweat off didn't improve his visibility any, as his surroundings appeared as bleak and blurry as ever, but it lessened the sting at least. "Alright." Rasp took a breath and let it out slowly as he leaned forward. "Ready?"

June gave a raspy grunt of acknowledgement.

"Good, now hurry up. Let's go! Before Faris has time to chime in and tell us why this is going to fail."

"Oh no, no, no. Don't mind me." Faris's voice hailed from a reasonable distance away. He sounded far enough away not to get caught up in the inevitable consequences, but still within range to enjoy witnessing said consequences in all their stupendous glory. "I'm just here for the show. Carry on."

Hop offered a final, meek protest. "But he could get hurt."

"How else do you get him to learn anything?"

Rasp applied slight pressure to June's sides with his heels. "Yah!"

June took off at a lumbering gallop. The dark green and brown outlines of the trees flew past at a blurred rate. Rasp heard the heavy crunch of dried leaves and broken branches as June plowed over the forest floor at a steady gait. The bear's shoulders were taller than her hips and with each long, mismatched stride, Rasp felt himself slide farther down her back. He held on with all the strength in his hands, unwilling to ruin such a perfect experience with something as lame as falling off the back of a charging bear.

For the briefest of moments, his heart soared. This was the first spot of fun he'd had in what felt like ages. He was going home, his best friend had found him, and on top of all that, Rasp had discovered a sister who was just as easily swayed down the path of impulsive recklessness as himself. The fact that said same sister was unopposed to allowing him to ride piggyback on her bear form was simply the cherry on top of whatever dessert people put cherries on top of—he honestly didn't know, because he always ate the cherries before they could be made into something.

But, much like the debilitating stomach cramps that came from eating a whole bucket of cherries, all good things had to come to an end. The end to

Rasp's fun came at the bottom of a rather steep hill several moments after he slipped from June's bounding form and hit the leafy ground and rolled. He tumbled head over heels, cursing each time he struck a rock or half-buried tree root on his way down. With one last stomach-wrenching summersault, he slammed face first onto the ground and slid to an undignified stop.

It was Faris who reached him first. "Muck, are you alright?"

"Yeah, yeah, I'm fine." A jolt of pain coursed down his lower back as Faris helped ease him into an upright position. Rasp ignored it, squinting at Faris's blurry shape. "Have there always been two of you?"

Faris's head twisted around, calling back over his shoulder with a distinct waver in his voice. "Hop?"

"Kidding!" Rasp surged forward, pushing Faris to the ground as he leapt upright and started back up the hill, ignoring the twinge of pain in his left shoulder. The loose leaves slipped underfoot, making his progress uphill far less impressive than he'd intended. Rasp grabbed at whatever handholds he could find as he dug the tips of his boots into the slick hillside. Unfortunately, the harder he attempted to climb, the faster he slipped. After about the third attempt, Rasp gave up and slid to a standstill at the base of the hill.

Faris's blurry shape stood waiting for him. "This is sad, Dinglehead. I'm getting secondhand embarrassment just watching."

"You try doing this with your eyes closed and tell me how it works out for you!"

"Ooh, I touched a nerve, didn't I? Don't tell me you're embarrassed."

Heat stung the tip of Rasp's smarting nose—and not just where the rough ground had abraded the skin, either. As much as Rasp wanted to deny the accusation, he could feel the heat already working its way to his ears. There was no use in denying it when his complexion was already giving him away. That didn't mean he had to admit to it, of course. He crossed his arms over his chest and turned away.

"Touchy, touchy, touchy," Faris tsked as he hooked his arm through Rasp's. "Come on then. We'll go together."

"No." Whisper's voice rang out from the hilltop above. "Don't help him. He was the one who insisted on behaving like a fool. He cannot expect someone to pull him out every time he gets stuck attempting something stupid. Stand back and allow him to find his own way."

The intensity of the heat stinging Rasp's face doubled. "Seriously?"

"You have more magic in a single pinky finger than most witches could hope to achieve in their lifetime. Use it."

"What's the point? You're just going to take it away anyway!"

"I cannot do that if you don't know how to first use it."

Rasp unthreaded his arm from Faris's and stood back, considering his options. He knew asking for a hint would only result in a sternly worded lecture about how he needed to actually try before giving up. It would be best to hem and haw for several minutes before throwing in the proverbial towel.

Giving up already?

Dammit. He hated that Whisper could read him even from a distance. *I'm thinking.*

About giving up. Yes, I know.

This would be easier if you weren't breathing down my neck. At least give me a chance to fail first. Rasp felt Whisper's buzzing thoughts detangle from his own. He probably could have thought that nicer, but unscheduled training sessions made him grumpy. Not that regular training sessions didn't do the same, but at least he had ample time to complain about those beforehand.

Besides, Faris was watching. The same Faris who had gone out of his way to find him so that they could save Lonebrook together. The last thing Rasp wanted was to give his best friend second thoughts, not after everything he'd gone through to get here.

Perhaps it would help if you stopped fawning over the blasted faun and focused.

"Shut up!"

"Rasp," Faris said after a moment of unease, "nobody said anything."

"Well they were thinking it. Now hush, Dingle. I need to *focus.*"

In an unexpected show of encouragement, Faris reached out and touched Rasp's shoulder. "You can do it. I believe in you."

Rasp fought the full-body cringe that shimmied up his spine. He gagged, "Gods, Dingle. Don't do that. It's so much worse."

"Fine. But if you don't hurry it up, I'm going to do it again. Except this time I'm going to tell you how good you are, and how proud I am, and how you've come so far just to make your skin crawl."

Forget disappointing Faris, that was motivation in itself. Rasp corralled his wandering thoughts to the back of his mind and focused on his senses. Both fire and water—the easiest elements for him to manipulate—were in short supply. He could feel the wind on his face, however, and hear the creak of the trees overhead, and feel the solid dirt beneath his feet. While he could bend flora to his will to a degree, it wasn't easy and without sight, nearly impossible to get it to do what he wanted. Thus, he chose the wind.

This would require a second, working pair of eyes however. Someone to tell him how high to go and whether or not it was safe to let them drop. "Dingle." He outstretched his hand in Faris's direction. "I'm going to need you for this."

Faris was rightfully suspicious. "What for?"

Rasp seized him by the arm all the same. "It helps to have someone who can see how far the ground is below me."

CHAPTER SIXTY-FOUR

Out of Place

Rasp drew inward, pulling the wind in his direction. A raging gust swept beneath them, lifting their feet from the leaf-littered ground. Faris abandoned his futile attempts to squirm free and threw his arms around Rasp with all his strength, wailing something about this being a terrible idea. Rasp paid the panicking faun no mind. For the gods' sakes, they were barely even off the ground yet! He wouldn't have to take Faris's screaming seriously until they were a little higher.

With a flick of his hand, the gust swept them upward. And while this worked as well as intended, Rasp may have misjudged one tiny detail—the thick canopy stretched overhead. Gnarled, twisted branches, thick with leathery leaves, tore at his face and clothes as the pair broke through the treetops.

Faris, fortunately, was a bit of a natural at his role as the lookout. "Big branch! Go left, left, left!"

Rasp twitched his finger and they banked left, barely missing the thick limb that Rasp swore had come out of nowhere. Faris insisted otherwise, but that's why he was the lookout, after all. A few narrow misses later, and the pair broke through the top of the canopy and into the clear airspace above. The bright blue light made Rasp's head swim.

Carried by the wind, they rose higher, higher, higher. The air was fresh, almost crisp tasting as it filled Rasp's lungs. For the first time in weeks, he felt the full power of the sun against his bare skin. The experience would've been divine if it were not for the icy winds hellbent on tearing the threadbare clothes from his body. The current howled as it pushed and pulled the pair in whatever direction it pleased.

Faris trembled against him. "Why are the trees *below* us, Rasp? You were supposed to get to the top of the hill, not the top of the mucking forest!"

"Poor planning? I dunno. It's not like I've done this before."

"You've never done this before?" Faris's high-pitched reply came out sounding more akin to a scream than a question.

"I can tell you're impressed."

"But you know how to get down, right?"

Of course he did. What a silly thing to ask. "I assume the same way we got up. Except, you know, the opposite direction."

"You're going to drop us?" Faris squeezed tighter.

"Gently, Dingle." Rasp took a shallow breath. "I'm going to *gently* drop us."

"Okay, it's fine. It's fine, it's fine, it's fine." Faris didn't seem to be listening to Rasp anymore. He self-soothed by talking himself through the situation instead. "Whisper's a dragon. They can come save us if we get stuck. Or if we drop too fast or—"

"Well, not anymore actually." Rasp hated to burst his bubble, but it was only fair that Faris knew the truth. "I mean, Whisper still has a dragon form, yes. But it draws too much power to use. It's sort of an emergency use only kind of thing."

"This is an emergency!"

"Now who's being dramatic?"

"Are you telling me we're on our own?"

"Oh please, I got us up here. I can get us down just as easily."

"It's surviving the going down part that's important, Rasp!"

"Now that you mention it, I am feeling suddenly weak."

"Don't you mucking dare!"

Old Rasp would have let them drop a few stories simply for the funsies. Old Rasp was a bit of a dick, though. The more Current Rasp distanced himself from his former self, the more he realized he was lucky he'd managed to retain a single friend at all. Also, if he wanted to *keep* his only friend, it was of utmost importance to get him to the ground safe and sound. "Alright, I'm done being an ass, I swear. We'll take it nice and slow, okay? In all honesty, I didn't actually mean to go this high."

Faris clung to him tighter, whimpering, "Not helping."

"I'm going to need your eyes though. You don't happen to see a clear spot around here, do you?"

After a few steady breaths, the faun worked up the courage to open his eyes again. It came with a bit of a shock, apparently, as every muscle in Faris's body seized in terror. "For muck's sake, Rasp! Do you realize how high we are?"

"If I knew that, I wouldn't need your eyes, would I?"

A dark shadow passed over Rasp's face. Instinctively, he craned his head upward, squinting at the blurred shape that circled soundlessly above. "Dad?"

"That's a hawk, idiot."

Certainly explained the lack of obnoxious squawking. "Kinda weird for it to be here, right?"

"What, in the air? Where they hunt? Spend their free time? No, Dinglehead. I don't think the hawk is the one out of place here!" Faris screamed. "Want to know why it's above us? Because it recognizes an easy meal when it sees one! Any moment now, it'll be stripping the flesh from our dead bodies. If there's anything left after we splatter across the ground, that is."

"Splattering would make the picking easier," Rasp conceded.

Eventually, once he got all of the death and doom out of his system, Faris composed himself enough to provide actual assistance. He spied a small, swampy patch devoid of trees and, between the cursing and muttered insults, directed Rasp over the top of it. On Faris's command, Rasp began the descent, slowly.

They were halfway down when the ache in Rasp's lower back transitioned from a dull thrum to pulsing spasms of lightning. The bolts lanced up and down his spine as it spread waves of white hot agony to his extremities. The familiar buzz of magic waned, giving way to pain and exhaustion. Rasp was barely holding on by a thread by the time the blurry ground rose up beneath them.

Long blades of grass, wet with morning dew, brushed against his trousers as Rasp's heels struck soft ground. With a wave of his hand, he severed his magical connection, leaving only the tingling loss of sensation in his numb fingertips. The numbness did not apply to his shoulder and, thus, he felt the full force of Faris's punch. Rasp stumbled several steps backward before falling flat on his ass.

"Don't ever do that again!" Faris emphasized his scream with a hoof stomp.

". . . Urg."

Rasp went limp among the damp grass, feeling the wet squish of the muddy ground splatter beneath him. Exhausted and magically spent, he laid perfectly still, listening as the sounds of the forest intermixed with Faris's relentless pacing.

It took half an hour for the rest of the party to find them. June was the first to arrive on the scene. Having shifted back from bear to human, her willowy shadow came bursting out of the trees at a full sprint. "That was amazing!" June's wet footsteps carried her all the way to Rasp's side. She bent over and tugged ruthlessly on his arm, not bothering to check if Rasp was even alive before attempting to heave his limp carcass from the grass. "Can I go next? Please, please, please!"

Hop was not far behind with the mule and Whisper in tow. Unlike June, he stayed tucked along the trees, allowing his baritone voice to carry across the clearing from afar. "Nobody should be doing that again."

Rasp raised his finger triumphantly into the air above his head. "I conquered the hill, as requested."

Faris was still angrily pacing back and forth. "You could have done it in a less dramatic fashion, you know. You got lucky today, Rasp. But you can't do that kind of shit when we're in real danger. My village is at stake."

'My family is in your incompetent hands' was the part he wasn't saying.

The breeze shifted directions, unsticking the sweat-soaked hairs that clung to Rasp's forehead. A swell of magic rippled across his skin as Whisper touched down beside him. **The faun may not be impressed by your feat of magic, but I am.**

That certainly came as a surprise. Rasp said nothing, waiting instead for the inevitable follow-up, which would undoubtedly include such words as "however," "but," or "idiot."

Unfortunately, Whisper had other plans, which, for some gods-awful reason, involved introspection. **Do you understand the importance of what just took place, little bird?**

I got over the hill like you asked me to? Without dying either, Rasp would have liked to have added. Seemed a little redundant though, considering Whisper would be attempting to converse with a corpse otherwise.

Indeed, you did. More importantly, you used the full extent of your magic without stirring the darkness.

Oh shit. He had, hadn't he? Rasp hadn't been able to do that since becoming an unwilling host to the dark magic. Small spells he could squeak past with, sure, but this hadn't been a small spell. No, in fact, he'd all but drained his power with the flying nonsense. He should have been elated, but he felt mostly confused instead.

This is not the first time, either. You achieved the same yesterday, when you first reunited with your friend. Whisper allowed the thought to sink in before asking, **Do you know why these two instances were different from the others? Why you were able to use the full extent of your powers without losing control?**

If you tell me it's the power of love or some shit like that, I might just hit you. Whisper's quills rattled together, daring him to try. **You were not angry.**

While it may not have been the power of love, Rasp still found the answer nauseatingly stupid.

Anger is what awoke the spirit in the first place. It is how it first reached you. By controlling your anger, feeling it without becoming consumed by it, you are denying the dark entity access to the rest of you.

That's it? That's all it took? This whole time Rasp could have been using his magic without the threat of losing control and all it would have taken was not being angry? For reasons perhaps too ironic to fully grasp, this knowledge served only to make him angrier. The scuffed skin on his face stung in the cool morning air as a ripple of heat flushed all the way from the tip of his nose to his forehead.

"Are you fucking kidding me?" Rasp didn't care if the others didn't know what he was yelling about, he had to get the rage out before it had time to dig its claws in and fester. "Is that why you kept pushing all this emotional wellbeing bullcrap? It actually had a purpose? I thought you were just trying to make me more tolerable to be around."

And you're back to being angry. Right on schedule.

CHAPTER SIXTY-FIVE

Hospitality

Breakfast was a simple bowl of cooked oats topped with simmered apples and a drizzle of honey. After months on the road, it was the best meal Daana had eaten in recent memory. Seven realms, even the water tasted better. Which failed to explain why her breakfast companion had barely lifted his spoon so far.

"You know it's not poisoned, right?"

"You hope," Snag replied.

Daana shoveled down another spoonful of sweet oats as she considered something smart to say. "Nah, you wouldn't let me eat it if it was."

Ordinarily, he would have said something quippy in return, but Snag appeared too preoccupied with checking his peripherals to bother. The pair were seated in the bustling meal hall at a table shoved all the way in the corner. Snag was across from Daana with his back to the wall, watching the morning's breakfast patrons come and go with his jagged mouth held in an uneasy grimace. Although the goblin clutched his spoon as if it were a weapon, his bowl of oats remained untouched.

After the bizarre introduction to her mother the night before, Daana had gone back outside of the walls to fetch her belongings. What had started as a pathetic attempt to say goodbye to Snag turned into her begging him to stay the night. After many tears—hers, not his—he acquiesced, ultimately insisting it was because he wished to replenish his supplies and not because Daana was making an idiot of herself.

She almost felt bad for inviting him inside now. Almost. The steady supply of food was doing wonders to keep the unpleasant feelings at bay. Daana lifted her bowl of oats and tilted her head toward the double doors behind her. "I can take this outside if you want. Bring yours, too."

No sense in letting good food go to waste, after all.

A flood of stark light swept across the inside of the great hall as the doors opened with a creaking wail. While the hall didn't fall deathly quiet, the volume certainly dropped in a noticeable way. Curious, Daana twisted around on the bench to get a glimpse of what was taking place. The disturbance was Ashwyn, whose height made her stick out among the hungry crowd like a shark fin across water. Despite the bustling crowd, Ashwyn was across the room in no time at all. Probably helped the way the other patrons practically leapt to the side to avoid crossing her path.

The shared bench wobbled under the orc's weight when she dropped down next to Daana. From there she just sort of melted, like candle wax on a hot day, and spread out across the top of the table.

"You look awful," Daana said around another mouthful of honey-drizzled oats.

Normally this would have provoked some sort of response out of the orc—a laugh, a quip, a hearty punch. Ashwyn said nothing, choosing to remain a sad, melted puddle of an orc instead.

Daana and Snag traded worried glances. His pinched brow warned her not to say another word. "This is a job for El," he said, hurriedly glancing about, as if expecting the elf in question to materialize out of the shadows at any moment. "Where is she?"

Ashwyn's hollow voice was but a ghost of its normal might. "Gone."

"What do you mean gone?" Snag's long ear shot into the air. "Gone where? To bed? The tavern? She's not already in jail again, is she?"

"We . . . uh . . ." Ashwyn's hand clenched into a fist, her knuckles draining of all color. "She left."

"Without you?" Daana prompted.

"Yeah."

"What the fuck!" Snag stood and threw his spoon across the table with a clatter. Those seated nearest them scooted farther away. "That's it? She just up and left? Without even bothering to say goodbye or tell me where she was headed?"

"We fought, Snag. It was ugly."

"Well, she's coming back, right? I mean, this is what she does, innit? You two fight, she burns something to the ground, gets blistering drunk, and then comes crawling back the second she's sobered up again?"

The sound that squeaked out of Ashwyn's mouth had more in common with a whimper than a sigh. "Not this time, mate."

Daana placed her open hand over Ashwyn's. "I'm sorry."

"Me too."

Daana didn't know what else to say. As fate would have it, it wasn't necessary to say anything. The double doors opened behind them once more. This time, the doors stayed open, flooding the room with natural light. Blinking the sunspots from her eyes, Daana glanced over her shoulder and watched as the faun from the previous night left his entourage at the entrance and approached, hooves clacking against the hardwood flooring with a resounding *click clack*. Havershire halted just short of their table, standing with his hands clasped behind his back and looking rather annoyed at having to see their faces again so soon.

"The Sage Superior will see you now." His hardened gaze swept from Daana to Ashwyn. "Both of you."

Daana glanced over at Snag, who had not only sat back down, but appeared to be attempting to camouflage with the wall. He'd be under the table soon, given the way he steadily inched down without a sound.

Alas, Daana was not the only one to notice. The aged faun peered at Snag over the top of his rounded spectacles with sudden, careful interest. "You're the goblin."

A cold look flitted across Snag's gnarled face. "What gave it away?"

"You are one of General Dawnsight's trusted four, yes?"

"Who?" Snag adopted his best look of innocence, this maneuver included blinking his eyes and tilting his head to the side like a confused puppy. "Oh, no. Not me, sir. I'm but a humble gobby guide. I'm just here to collect my payment from the nice lady for delivering her safe and sound."

Snag extended his open palm in Daana's direction expectantly. Armed with nothing else, Daana gave him her spoon.

"Thank you for your generosity," Snag said, tucking it into his clothes.

Unfortunately for Snag, Havershire was not an idiot.

"We have been expecting a message from your commanding officer for some time now. Come." The faun whirled around, his red robe billowing dramatically in his wake as he strode back the way he had come, calling over his shoulder, "You may explain to the Sage Superior in person why you are so late."

"But I—" Snag's protest petered out when he noticed the entourage of soldiers waiting for them. With a muffled whimper, he stood and followed after, casting nervous glances from left to right, searching for the nearest escape route.

Daana meant to place a reassuring hand on his shoulder, but all that did was make him jump a foot into the air. She quickly withdrew her hand. "Sorry."

"Don't do that! You're liable to lose fingers that way."

Ashwyn leaned closer, murmuring at a volume the others would be hard pressed to overhear. "You alright, mate?"

"I don't have a bloody message," he hissed. "Your sister never involved me in any of the resistance stuff. I mean, I knew about it, she knew I knew about it, but we both just pretended I didn't."

"You want me to cause a distraction so you can hightail it out here?" Ashwyn tried to smile but it was clear that her heart wasn't in it.

"And go where? Ellisar and I were supposed to travel back to the coast together." Snag walked between them, wringing his gnarled hands as he considered his options. "Should have run when I had the chance."

Daana didn't necessarily have any sway with her mother, but she supposed it wouldn't hurt to try to explain the situation on Snag's behalf. "I can vouch for you, if you want."

"Daana, I mean this in the very best way, but dear gods, girl, no. Just let me handle how I see fit, 'kay?"

"I'm not *that* bad at negotiating."

"I think it's safe to assume the person with a giant army outside her walls is going to be infinitely better at it."

With Havershire in the lead, and the soldiers flanking in what reminded Daana of the v-formation used by migratory birds, the trio were paraded down several bustling dirt streets. She tried to keep track of the twists and turns, but with so many new sights, smells, and sounds, she was soon too overwhelmed with taking it all in to remember if their last turn had been a right or a left. From Snag's worsening posture, he likely already had a mental map of the main streetways down.

At last, their travels brought them to a clay building that looked suspiciously like all of the others around it. They were herded down a short flight of stone steps and into the low-set doorway of the basement apartment below. It was an open room with various tables overflowing with books, scrolls, and loose parchment. The few half windows scattered across the walls were closed with their thick curtains drawn shut, cutting out all natural light from the outside. Candles littered the room, their melted wax spilling over the sides of their copper holders and leaving hardened deposits on the tabletops and floors.

Larkspur was bent over a table at the center of the stuffy room, trading low, heated words with an elf in a red- and gold-embroidered robe. She finished her conversation before straightening her posture and approaching her guests, meticulously placing one slender boot in front of the other as her dark eyes swept from one to the next. Her attire was the same as the night before. Ridiculous boots included. Daana only noticed this because the buckles rattled with each purposeful step.

Larkspur's gaze settled on Snag with the weight of an anvil. "Ashwyn, was it necessary to bring your stable hand?"

"Ha!" A nervous laugh erupted from Snag's mouth. He spun around and marched for the doorway. "Daana, Ashwyn, it's been a pleasure. If you'll excuse me, I'm off to go saddle a horse."

Havershire stepped swiftly into Snag's path, barring him from the exit. The wizened faun gazed over the top of him at Larkspur. "Sage Superior, this is one of General Dawnsight's trusted four."

"The goblin?" Larkspur's dark brows knitted together. After a moment of thought, she dismissed her confusion with a wave of her hand. "Of course she sent the goblin. He was the only one familiar with the territory."

"Who, by the way, loves being referred to as 'the goblin' and not his actual name," Snag muttered.

"My apologies, Mister . . ." Larkspur's words trailed as she realized her error. She searched the faun's face, probing the answer to a question she dared not ask out loud.

Daana nearly bit her own tongue to keep from speaking on Snag's behalf.

"Snuglebum Flint," Havershire answered with a remarkably straight-face. The same could not be said for the guards standing alongside the entryway who buried their faces into their sleeves to muffle their snickers.

"What? No! That's not . . ." Snag stopped trying to sidle around the red-robed faun and ran a clawed hand down his forehead, muttering, "I'm going to strangle that boy the next time I see him. Damn maggot calls me that *one* time and it's all anybody remembers."

Larkspur cut back in. "My apologies, Mister Flint. You must under—"

"Not to worry, Miss Daana's mum. No need for introductions. I was just on my way out." Alas, each time Snag nearly reached the door, the stubborn faun stepped in front of him once more. It was a very bizarre game that neither looked to be winning. Nor enjoying, for that matter.

The same could be said for Larkspur, whose stare hardened at the embarrassing display. "Mister Flint, you are late. And I do not like to be kept waiting. What news do you have from Oralia? Tell me she is on her way."

"How the fuck would I know?" Snag gestured to Ashwyn with an over-dramatic sweep of his arm. "I just spent the last month springing this one from a dungeon. And if that wasn't hard enough, I then got roped in making sure they got delivered safely to your doorstep. Which you're welcome for, by the way. Considering one of 'em's your long-lost daughter."

Larkspur studied his outstretched hand as her sharp features shifted from anger to confusion. "What is he doing?"

Daana looked to the ceiling above, stifling her reflexive groan. "He wants you to pay him."

"How bold."

"Worth a try," Snag said with a shrug, returning his hand to his side. "Anyway, I don't have a message from Oralia. She was in Adderwood last I saw her. I'd tell you to start there, but she doesn't stay in one place for long these days. So . . . good luck with your search then?"

The room went still as all eyes swept to Larkspur. Daana swore it suddenly felt ten degrees cooler. The seconds slowly ticked past until, at last, the unthink-able happened. A smile pulled across the Sage Superior's mouth. "Mister Flint, you appear to be in a hurry to leave. I hope that isn't my doing."

Snag, wisely, said nothing at all. Still didn't stop him from eyeballing the door with the subtlety of a sledgehammer, though.

"You went through all of this trouble to reunite me with my daugh-ter," Larkspur continued. "Please, allow me to show you the hospitality you deserve. I believe a seat at my table is in order."

"I, uh, don't want that."

"You seem to be under the misconception that I'm giving you a choice."

CHAPTER SIXTY-SIX

Damage Assessment

For as long as Daana could remember, there had always been a little fire demon that danced in the back of her head whenever an unfair situation arose. It had earned her a good deal of trouble in her youth. Suppressing it had been a matter of survival during her academy days. Try as she might, however, the fire never completely went away. Watching the standoff between Snag and her mother not only sparked the coals of Daana's inner rage, but incited live flame. This had the additional, unfortunate effect of wiping Snag's warning not to get involved from her memory.

Daana stepped boldly forward. "Where do you get off threatening him like that?"

Larkspur's annoyance shifted from Snag to Daana. A subtle wave of her hand kept her guards positioned near the doorway. The Sage Superior remained otherwise cool, content to watch Daana's fiery spiral peter itself out.

"He," Daana said as she gestured to Snag, who looked to be on the verge of melting into a puddle of green goblin goo, "is not a part of this. I asked him to bring me here as a favor. I will not stand idle while you threaten him." Daana couldn't be sure, considering her eyes were locked on her mother, but she swore she saw the low-burning candles flicker along the corner of her vision.

Several seconds crept past before Larkspur was forced to ask, "Well?"

"Well what?"

"You said you would not stand idle. What do you intend to do about it?"

Crap. Daana hadn't thought that far ahead. That was the problem with her inner demon. It was all flash and fizzle with no real heat. "I . . ." Daana's voice trailed as her mind desperately searched for an answer. For some terrible reason, the solution it settled on was one of Willem's old lessons about killing one's enemies with kindness. "I will have to ask you politely to stop doing that. If Snag wishes to leave, then let him."

Larkspur's expression was woefully unimpressed. She pivoted accusingly in Ashwyn's direction, hands on her hips, as if this was the orc's fault somehow. "All this time together, and that's the best she could come up with? What have you been teaching her?"

"How to throw a decent right hook, mostly." Ashwyn's teasing tone didn't match her posture. The orc may not have had any weapons on hand, but she looked prepared to make do with her fists if needed. "I suspect it will take someone far more experienced than me to teach her how to throw her weight around. Speaking of which, are you done having your fun? You stand to lose her again if you keep this up."

"She won't leave. She can't afford to." Larkspur gestured unenthusiastically to the red-robed elf still seated at the table. "I brought in my finest healer to assess Daana's condition. Walking out that door means walking away from any possibility of a cure."

Daana was damn near mad enough to walk out anyway. The tips of her ears burned as she ground her back molars to keep from saying something that would only make her situation worse. She flinched when a clawed hand touched her own.

Snag sidled up alongside Daana. For her own sake, she pretended the hand clutching was out of support and not to prevent her from doing something they'd both regret. "A healer?" he said, tone dripping with doubt.

Snag's skepticism was understandable. Even back at the Division of Divination, a place crawling with every type of magic imaginable, healers had been practically unheard of. Not due to rarity, but demand. Healers were a commodity, often snatched up by the rich and powerful the moment a fledgling witch showed a talent for it. Like all things deemed worthy of value, healers were a magical resource hoarded by those at the very top of the social hierarchy. To a commoner, a healer was the witch equivalent of a unicorn—rumored to be real and, yet, destined to never see one.

"I have several healers in my service," Larkspur told Snag. "Nevil is my personal attendant. The best in the land."

Snag mulled over this information with careful consideration. "And if we stay for your sit-down, answer your questions, Daana gets healed?"

Larkspur had them in the palm of her hand and knew it. With a tight smile, she turned and strode for the table, calling over her shoulder. "If there is any cure to be had, yes. That's the idea."

"Healer first," Snag said, giving Daana the silent side-eye to shut it and let him handle things. "Then we answer your questions."

Larkspur traded pointed looks with Havershire before conceding the matter with an unceremonious shrug of her shoulders. "Fine."

"This way, dear." On cue, Nevil, the red-robed healer, stood and shepherded Daana into one of the open chairs clustered around the table. His nervous stare was not fixed on her, but Ashwyn and Snag, who both hovered too close for his comfort. "I don't normally allow spectators, but I get the distinct feeling these two won't be leaving without a fuss."

Snag allowed his unblinking stare to confirm the healer's intuition.

"You're welcome to stay so long as you sit and promise not to interfere."

Ashwyn slid into the open chair beside them and clapped Daana's shoulder in what was probably meant as a reassuring gesture. "You've got this, Peaches. We'll be right here if you need us."

"Not interfering," Nevil reiterated.

"Not interfering," Ashwyn said with the sort of toothy smile that warned she would decide what constituted "interfering."

Finally, the healer gave Daana his full attention. "If you would show me the markings, dear."

Daana unbuttoned her sleeve and pulled back the fabric, bunching it at the elbow. Although the dark veins snaked higher now, almost to her shoulder, she was not about to yank off her top in front of a room of her mother's closest advisors. She still had some small semblance of dignity, after all.

With a reassuring smile, Nevil stepped forward and took Daana's hand into his own. His slender fingers started at the wrist and moved upward, humming to himself as he worked. Daana felt the heat of magic pass between them. She opened her mouth to protest, but it was too late. Pain struck her behind the eyes as the dark magic surged forward like a ravenous dog on a chain. She tried to pull away but the elf had gone into a full trance. His eyes were closed and he swayed back and forth, holding Daana's arm in a viselike grip.

Dark magic rippled beneath her skin, pulling at her flesh as it tried to bridge the connection. Pain radiated in her arm like a thousand hot needles stabbing her at once. It was too much. Daana folded over, fighting the waves of nausea as sour bile trickled up her throat and flooded across her tongue. The room faded in and out of focus around her. Pinpricks of flashing light danced across her vision even after she screwed her eyes shut tight.

Chair legs jerked against the wood floor as several voices thundered in the background all at once. The noise swelled, filling the room with a heated exchange of words. The only voice Daana could distinguish among the fray belonged to Snag.

"Snag, help me!" Daana screamed.

The din crescendoed in sequence with the pain radiating within her arm. The darkness was growing. It spread out, its undulating tendrils weaving a vast tapestry across the inner workings of her mind. The barbed hooks pulled tighter, tighter, tighter, until the last of the dancing pinpricks of light faded into nothing.

At first, there was only darkness. Pitch black, like the inside of a cave that stretched on endlessly in every direction. And then, above her, a calming light flickered. It didn't crackle or pop, but flowed as effortlessly as water as it doubled in size. Its shimmering waves branched outward, transforming from rippling rivers into babbling brooks and streams as it overtook the darkness.

The pain subsided. A cooling calmness swept over her. Daana relaxed, lulled into a tranquil trance as the strange magic shrouded her in its comforting embrace. It didn't pull tight like the darkness. It was as light and airy as muslin cloth on a crisp spring morning. Even if she possessed the strength to fight, she no longer had the will. It was peaceful here.

Daana sank further into the magic, allowing it to course through her veins and heal the blistering ache.

"Daana!"

No, she thought. She didn't want to return to the outside. Not yet. Not now that she had finally found a small sliver of peace. The pain was gone; nobody was trying to run her down; she was reunited with her long-lost mother. For the first time in ages, all was right with the world again. And she so desperately didn't want to let go.

The voice hovering on the outside of her consciousness was annoyingly persistent. "Daana! Come out of it."

The glowing light faded. It dissipated into nothing as Daana slowly emerged onto the outside. It was only then that she realized her eyes were open. The warm candlelight caused her to blink the swell of hot tears from her murky vision. The fuzzy shapes around her gradually shifted back in focus. Snag and Ashwyn were crouched on either side of her, wide-eyed, with the color drained from their bleak faces.

"Thank gods," Snag muttered as his ears drooped in relief. "Ashwyn looked like she was about ready to slap you. Probably would have just sent you back under."

"I know my strength," the orc retorted. "It would have only been a little baby slap."

The red-robed healer stood between them. His narrow arms were hugged to his chest and he trembled. Nevil was incapable of tearing his gaze from Daana. Behind him, Daana caught a glimpse of her mother. Larkspur was bent over the table, fervently whispering with Havershire.

When Daana found her voice again, it was weaker than she expected. "What just happened?"

Ashwyn and Snag both looked to the healer for clarification, as if they weren't quite sure themselves.

"I was assessing the damage," Nevil stammered, unable to break eye contact with Daana. The poor thing looked like a wounded animal staring down the predator as it steadily closed in. "The infection is unlike anything I've felt before. I-I was doing the best I could to fight it, but then I lost control—"

"Oh!" Daana's eyes widened. "I wasn't thinking, I'm sorry. I should have warned you. The darkness responds to magic. It can take control and—"

"It wasn't the darkness, child. It was you."

CHAPTER SIXTY-SEVEN

A School of Hungry Sharks

It was you. The healer's ominous words echoed within Daana's mind as she gazed up at his stricken face.

Nevil's hazel eyes were rimmed in white and his lower lip quivered. The worry lines marring the tanned skin around his face were noticeably deeper than before, more akin to trenches than wrinkles now. The elf held his hands protectively to his chest and edged a step backward. "It was your power that tapped into mine."

"Nevil?" Larkspur was already halfway out of her chair by the time Nevil finished his statement.

"The dark entity is not consuming you. *You* are consuming *it*."

"Say no more, Nevil." Larkspur strode swiftly around the table and placed a firm hand on the quaking elf's shoulder. "There's no need to frighten the poor thing. Daana's been through enough as it is. I apologize if she caught you by surprise, my friend. It was an accident, I'm sure."

Broken from his trance, Nevil turned and glared venomously at Larkspur. "You said she was magic-sensitive. I'm telling you right now, that girl is—"

"Is talented beyond her years, I know," Larkspur agreed. For the first time since they'd met, Daana watched the cold mask slip from her mother's stern face. A genuine warmth lit Larkspur's eyes, coaxing the start of a smile. Even her words seemed less severe than before. "She is my daughter, Nevil. It is to be expected."

The dread fluttering in Daana's gut settled. A fuzzy sensation blossomed within her chest instead, matching the warmth of her mother's smile. The feeling was infectious. It spread all the way to her head until Daana was so dizzy with joy, she was afraid she might float to the ceiling. Tears slipped from her eyes again uninvited. Hurriedly, she brushed them away with the back of her sleeve, hoping no one noticed.

Nevil stood with a puzzled look on his long face. "She's your . . ."

"Daughter," Larkspur said, still smiling.

"That certainly explains some things," he muttered as relief vanquished some of the fear pooling behind his eyes. "A warning would have been nice. I'm more successful at warding off power drain when I know to expect it."

"Again, I apologize. I was not certain of her lineage, myself. Until now, that is." Larkspur's gaze moved over Daana. "Your powers work much like mine. To a lesser extent, mind you, but the similarities are undeniable."

Larkspur allowed the information a moment to sink in before returning her attention to the elf healer. "Were you able to purge the infection?"

Nevil rubbed his hands together, attempting to warm them. "I was able to diminish the infection, lessen the spread some, but it is only a temporary means. What is ailing your daughter is only a small piece of a bigger entity. The only way to completely remove it would be to eradicate the original source."

"And if we fail to do so?"

Nevil's grim stare wandered the room, unable to look either Daana or Larkspur in the eyes. "Best case scenario, over the course of the next year, your daughter dies a slow, painful death."

"And worst case?" Daana interjected when Nevil left the rest of his assessment unsaid.

"I don't think anyone knows what happens when a mortal absorbs the ancient power of an old one. If it were the whole entity, you would die. Since this is only a piece, I cannot say for certain. Not anything good is the only conclusion I can offer."

"Daana, I will do everything in my power to ensure it does not come to that." Larkspur's face grew somber as she drew inward, consumed with thought. Finally, with her mind made up, she turned to Snag and Ashwyn. "I have offered my best healer's services, as promised. At this time, I can do no more for my daughter. Her cure lies within the powerstone currently in Oralia's possession. Before we decide how best to retrieve it, however, we must address the recent breakdown in communication. It has become abundantly clear that none of us are on the same page."

"Here we go," Snag muttered under his breath as he took up the empty chair on the other side of Daana. He scooted it closer, ensuring there was enough room to kick her under the table if and when the need arose. From his firmly wrinkled brow, it was some small wonder he hadn't already started.

Reseated at the head of the table, Larkspur studied Snag in the same way an apex predator watched a scavenger approach its hard earned kill. She leaned forward with her lithe hands steepled under her chin. "You really have no message from Oralia?"

"No." He was still nervously eyeing the exit and trying not to look suspicious about it. "Like I already said, I wasn't even supposed to be here. Got guilted into it."

The Sage Superior eased back in her chair, unconsciously gnawing the edge of her bottom lip as she fit Snag's information into the wealth of thoughts stampeding behind her dark eyes. "May as well get this over with." Larkspur gestured to Ashwyn with a halfhearted roll of her wrist. "Where is Ellisar? I was told she was at the gate last night. As much as I'd love for us to continue avoiding one another indefinitely, my patience is running thin. There are a number of questions I'd like for her to answer."

Daana had never seen Ashwyn so miserable before. The orc's long face looked like it was about to slide off onto the floor and wallow in a pool of its own tears. "She left."

Larkspur raised a single eyebrow higher than the other. "I hate to pry, dear friend, but in what capacity? Did she leave in the sense that she is currently wandering the wilderness inebriated? Is she waiting for you to join her at the next closest settlement or—"

"Left for good," Ashwyn clarified, her voice barely a whisper.

"Oh." After an uncomfortable moment of silence, Larkspur added, "You have my sympathies then."

Larkspur at least had the sense, if not decency, to abandon her line of questioning. Such courtesy did not apply to her faun advisor, Havershire, who braced the flat of his hands onto the table and leaned out over them to get a better view of the grieving orc. "Is it true that all this time you were unaware of our activities?"

"You mean the resistance? Not a fucking clue."

"Ellisar never told you?"

Ashwyn bristled defensively. "Are you expecting a different answer from me each time you ask the same fucking question? I already told you, no. Ellie did her best to keep me from getting involved."

Larkspur's knuckles rapped softly against the tabletop, garnering the attention of her advisor. Once more, the pair communicated through a series of meaningful expressions, each in turn growing more exaggerated in effort to sway to the other. Finally, settling back into his chair, Havershire conceded the argument. "This would at least explain why your call to arms has gone unanswered," he said to Larkspur. "It is very likely that Protector Dawnsight is simply unaware that we have need of her here."

Larkspur's mouth twisting to the side and she glared at the center of the table with conviction. "I already don't like where this is going."

The elderly faun offered only an amused smile. It looked more smug than pleased.

"You're going to propose sending a company to fetch her," Larkspur continued. "I should not have to remind you that we just sent reinforcements into the United Territories to handle the rogue witch situation. I cannot afford to stretch my remaining forces any thinner than they already are."

Havershire tilted his horned head at Ashwyn. "Then it is fortunate that our solution is sitting in front of us. After having sat in a dungeon all this time, I'm sure Commander Pride would be more than happy to take on the task and prove herself to you."

Happy was not an accurate description of whatever expression Ashwyn's face was attempting to pull together. "Whoa, slow down, mate. I barely just accepted Larkspur's offer to be a part of this. Give me time to breathe."

"We don't have time," the faun replied sharply. "There will be no part for you to play if things remain as they are. We need your sister. Bringing her here is a task for which you are uniquely suited, given her notorious lack of trust in others. You are our best option."

"About that," Ashwyn said with a pained grimace. "After what I dragged Oralia through last time, trust is probably the last thing she feels for me. Love, fondness, sure. I'm afraid it's going to be a while before I can unburn the trust bridge, so to speak. Oralia is not likely to listen to a word I say."

Havershire went quiet as he considered an alternative solution. With a forlorn sigh, the aged faun slipped the round spectacles from his face and set about cleaning the lens with the edge of his robe. "We have no choice then," he said to Larkspur. "We'll have to send Daana with her."

"Me?" Daana squeaked.

"Her?" Snag shot to attention, choking on his surprise. "She's infected, barely fit to travel! Would sooner sink in quicksand than find her away across the flatlands."

"First of all, rude." Daana narrowed her eyes at Snag. Her next words were aimed at her mother. "Secondly, who said I wanted any part of this? I came here for answers, not to run your errands."

"You came here to save yourself," Larkspur corrected. "I will not mince my words. The fact of the matter is, you are dying. Regardless of whether it's the dark entity absorbing your power, or vice versa, the effects will kill you within the year all the same. Your cure lies within the powerstone, which happens to be with the very person whom I need delivered to my side. Our end goals may be different, but the answer to both is the same. Accompany Ashwyn to bring back both Oralia and the powerstone, and you will get your life back."

Daana sat back in a stupor, processing her mother's blunt words. It was one thing to know you were dying. To have it stated aloud, in such certain terms, hit entirely different.

"That's all fine and dandy, Larky," Ashwyn said, "but it still doesn't negate the fact that Daana and I don't know the way."

Larkspur's fingers drummed against the table as her stare settled back over Snag for what felt like the umpteenth time that hour. If her furrowed eyebrows were any indication, her opinion of him had not improved. "If only there was a guide willing to show you the way. One, preferably, who already demonstrates an unusual investment in keeping my daughter alive."

Snag loudly sucked his teeth. "You'll be disheartened to hear I've stopped taking on charity work. My services are in high demand. A lot of the deep-pockets types are scrambling to find passage between the territories. I stand to make a fortune on this upcoming war."

Havershire leaned over and whispered into Larkspur's ear. Her expression darkened. "We will give you ten days' worth of supplies, fresh horses, and ten gold now, with another ten upon your return."

Snag's lower jaw slung open, momentarily taken aback by the offer. "You're offering actual money?"

"I could arrange to pay you in rocks if you'd prefer," Larkspur replied smartly.

"No, no, uh, money's good. It's just whether or not it's enough, you see. Awful long way . . . and, uh . . ." Caught in an unexpected daze, Snag was unable to form the necessary words to bargain. Probably wasn't used to people attempting to meet him halfway right out of the gate.

Ashwyn kindly stepped in on his behalf. "Twenty gold now and another twenty upon completion."

This seemed to do the trick. The goblin shook his head with a rattle of earrings, blinking up at the orc in confusion. "If I agree, you realize you're on the hook to tag along, right? I only mention it 'cause you didn't seem all that keen on the idea a moment ago."

"I'm not going to be much help moping around here. Besides, it might be good to see Ra Ra again. She always was the best at pulling me out of my relational slumps."

Snag wrinkled his nose at her. "You sure you got the right sister? I seem to recall Oralia threatening to drop the others over the nearest cliff any time one of them brought up their romantic woes."

"I said the best, didn't I? A strong kick in the pants might be just what I need."

"You have a . . . point." Snag refused to admit whatever Ashwyn's point was, it was obviously a terrible one. "Well, sounds like it's all settled then. The three of us go fetch Oralia for, what was it again, fifty gold?"

Larkspur's annoyed expression remained steadfast. Her voice cut back in with an edge as sharp as a well-honed blade. "Fifteen gold now, and another fifteen afterward. Final offer."

Nobody said anything. A swift kick from Snag soon told Daana why. Both he and Ashwyn were staring rather expectantly in her direction, awaiting her say. It caught her by surprise, actually. All her life, Daana's opinion had not been one held in high regard. Her wishes were often swept to the side with little to no concern. The moment might have been a tender one had everyone else in the room not been watching her like a school of hungry sharks.

"Fine. So long as long as you don't make me step foot on another boat," she said. Two sinking ships was already two too many for a single lifetime.

Ashwyn flashed her a pearly smile. "Hope you're a strong swimmer then."

"I'm with Tadpole on this one. No more water," Snag said with a shudder. And then, in what was quite possibly the most daring move Daana had seen of him yet, Snag spat into the palm of his hand and offered it to Larkspur with a needled smile. "Sounds like we've got ourselves a deal."

She ignored the outstretched hand, offering only a solemn nod of her head. It was difficult to see but, behind her mask of cold disinterest, Larkspur's dark eyes danced in the flickering candlelight, reflecting the smile her mouth refused to form. It was the smile of a predator. All teeth and venom.

CHAPTER SIXTY-EIGHT

Questionable Stability

There were many things fauns were known for. They were unmatched in endurance, speed, and cunning. The one characteristic Oralia had never expected to find on such a list, however, was digging. Dwarfs were excellent diggers, goblins too, but Oralia had never thought to lump a cloven-footed species in the same category. As it turned out, the fauns of Lonebrook had not only mastered the art of underground tunneling, they'd managed to do it without anyone from the outside catching on.

Briony's cottage was the epitome of quaint homespun living, with its stacked stone walls, straw thatch roof, and picturesque gardens. All part of the guise, Oralia concluded. On first glance, no one would've suspected they were standing over the secret underbelly of Lonebrook's smuggling operation. The entrance to the tunnel system was located in the root cellar, hidden behind several shelves of preserved goods and crate upon crate of vegetables. Hers was but one of many tunnel exits scattered throughout the village, Briony had explained. The passage she intended to lead Oralia and Rali through would deposit them in the wooded lot along the backside of Belfast Manor.

"Under our feet this whole time," Oralia said as she stood at the mouth of the tunnel, reluctant to follow Briony all the way inside. The size of the shaft had been built with a faun's height in mind, not a seven foot tall orc. The stooping didn't bother her so much. Unlike the crawling, which Briony warned was definitely going to happen as several sections of the tunnel were narrower than others.

"How many witches came through here?" Oralia asked.

"Anywhere from a few dozen to a few hundred every year," Briony replied. She stood several paces within the tunnel, lantern in hand, waiting for Oralia and Rali to follow. "Couldn't give you an exact number. That wasn't something we ever dared write down. Now, are you going to insist on a breakdown of its construction too, or can we mosey along?"

Rali lingered outside of the entrance near Oralia, shifting her weight from one foot to the other. "I would, actually. For comfort reasons."

Briony started off into the dim tunnel system without them. "We're burning candlelight, let's go."

Oralia noted the way the dwarf wrung her hands, causing the tips of her fingers to turn pink. "I could task you with guarding the entrance if it would make you feel better."

"Excuse me?" Rali dropped the hand wringing and adopted a withering glare instead. "Remind me again, what's our rule?"

"No more lone martyr shit," Oralia sighed.

"That's right, missy! And just because I have to follow you into a dark, dingy tunnel of questionable stability doesn't mean you get to go at it alone!" To prove her point, Rali swung her arms dramatically at her sides and marched in after Briony. "Your fuckmate and I have a new arrangement. One of us must accompany you at all times. Seeing as he's more liable to get stuck down here, the honor fell to me."

Oralia ducked inside, forced to bend at the knees to avoid scraping her bent head against the low ceiling. Thanks to bedrest and Sascha's insatiable need to shove soup in her face, she wasn't as miserably weak as she'd been only a few days before. Still, there was no doubt in Oralia's mind that her lower back would be screaming in agony by the night's end. "I am forever in your debt, Ralizak."

"Oh believe me, I am aware!"

"Not so loud," Briony hissed from her position at the front of the procession.

"It's because the tunnel is going to come crumbling down on us, isn't it?" Rali whispered to Briony. "I knew I should have demanded some blueprints before stepping foot in this place."

The light of the lantern bobbed on ahead, obscured slightly by Briony's and Rali's respective shapes as they walked single file. Unlike Oralia, the pair could stand at their full height without banging their heads on the blasted ceiling. "The tunnel is perfectly stable," Briony insisted. "It's your volume I'm worried about. The last thing we want is to alert the local forces that we've got an escape route right under their noses."

"Yeah, about that. How come the Belfasts aren't utilizing it? Kind of defeats the purpose of having an emergency escape tunnel, doesn't it?" While the questions were genuine, Rali was most definitely using it as a way to alleviate her mounting anxiety. The rigidity of the dwarf's shoulders suggested she was a few panicked thoughts from slipping into an episode.

Maybe they should have swapped for Sascha, after all.

The cavernous shaft amplified Briony's whisper, allowing Oralia to catch the majority of her response without having to strain to listen. "Too suspicious. Our occupiers would know something was up the moment either Trant or Novera went missing. The Belfasts insisted we move the most vulnerable out first: the old, the young, folks nobody would notice. But progress was slow and the soldiers were starting to get suspicious. They've tightened their stranglehold on the place since. We haven't been able to spring anybody in weeks."

The air grew staler as the trio traveled farther into the maze of tunnels. Eventually even Rali stopped talking, allowing the rest of the walk to pass in silence. Relative silence, at least. The few times Oralia had to crawl to squeeze through a narrow passage involved a plethora of muttered snarls and cursing. The instances were few and far between, thankfully, and after half an hour, their underground journey came to an end at the bottom of a ladder.

"You didn't mention there'd be any climbing involved." Rali crossed her arms over her chest and glared suspiciously at the ladder.

"I thought it'd be best to wait to tell you. You know, limit the complaining to the least amount possible. Now, do me a favor and hold the lantern. I've got to go check for Novera's signal." Briony pressed the lantern into Rali's hands before scuttling up the wooden ladder with practiced ease. Although the worn wood appeared rather old and somewhat rickety, it held strong against the faun's weight. Oralia only hoped it would extend her the same courtesy.

Metal hinges opened and closed above them with a soft creak, sending down a small cascade of loose dirt. Dingy light from the outside filtered down for a few seconds before Briony snapped the secret door shut behind her. Oralia was content to wait in silence. The same could not be said for her dwarf companion.

"Alright, now that she's gone, I'm gonna say it." Rali twisted around to look at Oralia with disbelief dancing in her dark eyes. "How the fuck did we miss this? An entire tunnel system for moving witches in and out of the realm and we never noticed?"

"How would we have known?"

"Just look at the place, Oralia! It's not your small-time operation. This thing's elaborate."

Oralia could not help but smirk at Rali. "Are you upset they did not invite you into their secret tunnel system sooner?"

"I'm just saying we spent a whole lot of time around Faris. I thought we'd achieved the status of friends by the end there, actually. And not once did the little bugger mention any of this!"

"I suspect there is a lot about the Belfast family we do not yet know." Including whether they would offer information on Faris's whereabouts. Traitor to the realm or not, there was still the sticky issue that Trant and Novera held Oralia personally responsible for the death of their daughters. It would be nice if Faris had cleared up that misconception prior to fleeing the territory, but she wouldn't hold her breath on the matter.

The squeak of rusted hinges sounded once more. "It's clear," Briony whispered from above. "Leave the lantern behind."

Rali's uneasy gaze shifted from the ladder to Oralia and back again. She stepped dutifully aside. "Bosses first."

"To be clear, you want me to climb ahead of you? So that if the ladder gives out you cushion my fall? Am I understanding that correctly, Ralizak?"

"Oh no, no, no," Rali clucked with a simple shake of her head. "You see, I'm going to be standing back a ways. That way if the unthinkable were to happen, help will be administered immediately and, most importantly, not flattened in the process."

"I feel so much better about this already." Oralia tested her weight against the first rung. So far so good. The rest of the climb was pleasantly uneventful except for the step that snapped in two midway up. Oralia caught herself on the rung below it and, after a few steadying breaths, continued all the way to the open hatchway. The little wooden door was open, allowing a glimpse of the dark, star-speckled sky between the treetops above.

Oralia heaved herself free of the hatch door, grateful that her wide shoulders and hips passed through without much undignified wriggling. Briony sat in the tall grass beside the entrance, waiting for her.

"The loud one?" the faun asked, quirking an eyebrow at Oralia.

A tentative glance back down the shaft confirmed Oralia's suspicions. "It might be a few minutes." Had it not been for the *no lone martyr shit* rule, she would've considered telling Rali to stay behind and await their return. As doing so would only result in more shouting, Oralia settled into the cool grass alongside Briony and waited for the dwarf's eventual arrival.

Rali emerged minutes later, muttering unintelligible curses under her breath as she fought to pull herself free of the hatch. "Should . . . have . . . been . . . Sascha," was the only part Oralia was able to make out. The dwarf pulled herself all the way over the lip and slumped face-first onto the ground with a whimpered groan.

"Are we finished with the dramatics yet?" Briony asked. "Novera can only stay out so long before someone notices she's missing."

"We could go and you can catch up," Oralia offered.

"Over my dead body!"

"To be clear, I'm not hauling anyone's dead body anywhere," Briony said. "The best you can hope for is a shallow grave and a nice bed of moss to decompose you quicker."

A toothy smile split across Rali's dirtied face as her gaze shifted from Briony back to Oralia. "Now hear me out, boss. I know you keep saying we're out of the game and no more faithful followers, and yada, yada, yada, but this one's got real potential. She just talked about dumping my body without even batting an eye."

"Most people would be concerned by that notion, Ralizak."

"Come on. At least let me swap her for the two dingleberries. Briony's worth twice what they are put together."

"I don't know who or what the 'dingleberries' are, but I'm good, thank you. Now let's get a move on."

Briony led them through the dark forest at a fast walk. She would stop from time to time, her large ears twitching as she listened for sounds too soft for Oralia to hear. After several starts and stops, she delivered them into a thicket. From a distance, the large patch of gnarled, twisted branches appeared impenetrable. Briony proved this was nothing more than a cleverly arranged illusion the moment she turned and disappeared through a hidden entrance.

The faun weaved her way through the tangled maze with the sort of confidence that came from having done so many times before. Each time Oralia thought they'd hit a dead end, Briony would duck to the side, revealing yet another hidden passage. At last, they reached the center, where a cloaked figure stood awaiting them.

Novera signaled for Briony to go keep watch. At least that's what Oralia hoped it meant. She tilted her head for Rali to do the same.

"What? Got a crick in your neck, boss? Trekking underground bent in half will do that to you, I suppose."

"Go keep Briony company, please." Oralia looked to the dark canopy above with an exasperated groan. To her surprise, she saw something unexpected hidden away among the gnarled branches.

"Oh, you mean recruit her," Rali said with a wink so blatant it was practically audible. "Say no more. I'm on it."

CHAPTER SIXTY-NINE

Resilient

Oralia felt naked without her sword. Leaving it behind was not a decision she'd made lightly. Ultimately, given the uncontrollable tremors in her hands, it was the realization that she'd be more likely to drop it than swing it that'd convinced her to go without. She had other weapons, of course. All of which were strapped on her person, tucked conveniently out of sight. She was relieved Novera didn't ask her to remove. While Oralia had no reason to suspect the Belfasts of selling her out to the enemy, it was better to be cautious than dead.

"Madam Belfast." Oralia halted paces from Novera's cloaked figure and dipped her head in respect.

Novera did not return the bow. From her hollow stare, Oralia sensed it was not out of disrespect. Novera's far-off expression was one Oralia had seen many times before on battle-stricken soldiers returning from the field. The faun's sad brown eyes searched Oralia's face as she spoke. "I'm afraid I don't know what to call you anymore."

"I prefer Oralia, but 'traitor' seems to be the more popular option in these parts."

Several stunned seconds passed before the edges of Novera's downturned mouth attempted a smile. "Was that a joke?" The faun shook her head slowly, causing the ringlets of coiled hair gathered around her shoulders to bounce and sway. "I never thought I'd live to see the day."

The joke had taken damn near three months to craft and Oralia was quite proud of it. In addition to landing, it did as Oralia intended, breaking the silent tension that hung thick in the air around them.

"It's good to see a familiar face." Novera's smile faded. "But I suspect you're here for the same reason the realm is. I'll spare you the runaround.

No one knows where Rasp is. Faris left several months ago to find him and I haven't heard from either since."

It was mostly the truth, but there was more Novera wasn't saying. Such information would only come with trust. Something Oralia currently lacked. "I understand why you would be reluctant to trust me, Novera. My reputation, the horrible things I have done in the name of the realm, it is a lot for anyone to overlook. But I swear to you, whether you realized it or not, you and I have been on the same side since the massacre in Sunstorn."

Also only partly true. As Oralia understood it, Lonebrook had been working hand in hand with the resistance since the Night of Stolen Lives. Oralia had only let the resistance *think* she was in their pocket. Playing both sides was infinitely easier when both parties thought they owned you. Naturally, this was not something one uttered aloud when trying to win favor with someone who'd already picked the losing side.

"Faris told us as much." Novera's left ear flicked as the sadness slowly trickled from her somber expression. "Which, if it were true, makes me wonder why you're here. If your loyalty is to Larkspur, then wouldn't you be with her now? Trant and I are no fools. We know Lonebrook is not worth saving. Pragmatically speaking."

Fuck. So much for keeping her questionable allegiances unsaid.

The faun narrowed her eyes. "Whose side are you really on?"

"The people's. I have no desire to be a revolutionist. I am simply trying to right a wrong before it hurts more people." Oralia neatly steered the conversation back on track while conveniently skipping over the part that mentioned saving her own skin as well. "As you know, Rasp cannot fall into the realm's hands. Finding your son first will prevent that from happening."

"I told you, I don't know where Faris is."

"While that may be true, I suspect you have a way of communicating with him." Oralia lifted her head and squinted at the gnarled branches above. She spied three ravens disguised among the dark foliage. "If I am not mistaken, these individuals belong to Rasp's flock. Would be quite useful for running messages between you and others on the outside, I imagine."

Novera stomped her hoof against the ground. "I don't know where Faris is and that's the truth! My last message forbade him from coming home."

"At the expense of you and your village?"

"It is a price we are willing to pay." Novera lifted her chin and locked eyes with Oralia. The downcast faun from earlier was gone, replaced with the steely-eyed determination of someone who'd already accepted their fate.

"Faris cannot be allowed to return. I know my son. He'd travel through the seven realms of chaos to get back here. Whatever happens to his father and me, I ask only that you keep him away."

"I could," Oralia agreed. "Or I could eliminate the problem at its source. Faris will have no reason to come home, risking capture, if his village is already saved." As noble as Novera's intentions were, she was right about one thing: Faris would fight. And he would keep fighting, tirelessly, until his parents were dead and he turned around and blamed Oralia for standing by and doing nothing. And he would be right for doing so. Perhaps if he learned someone else was already stepping in, he'd do the smart thing and stay hidden.

"How?" Novera challenged. "Do you have an army Briony isn't unaware of? According to her, your crew is looking awfully skeletal these days."

"I do not have an army yet," Oralia admitted. "But I do have a number of favors to call in. How long do we have?"

"A handful of weeks at most." Novera allowed a moment of silence to pass between them, still searching Oralia's face for unspoken truths. She must have found her answer because the creases around her eyes softened. "I believe you when you say you want to help the people. But I'm not convinced your motivations are entirely selfless."

There was no sense in denying it. And yet, the willingness to admit it felt equally wrong. Oralia opted to say nothing at all, allowing Novera to come to her own conclusion.

"You must be in dire need of my help to risk everything for a village that amounts to little more than a speck on a map."

"I am," Oralia said. "Although, I still do not know what it is you do." Briony had not been very forthcoming with those details.

Wordlessly, Novera raised her right hand into the air and a spark of silver magic rippled across her fingers.

That. Explained. A. Lot.

Of course Faris's mother was a witch! His sisters had to have inherited it from someone. Forget tunnels, how they'd managed to miss this was well beyond her. For the life of her, Oralia could do little more than gawk like a fish gasping for air. She found her words several stunned seconds later. "You are a healer?"

"The term healer is a bit of a misnomer. As with most things, it is a spectrum of power. There are those that can make a person's condition better, and those that can only make it worse. I'm afraid my abilities fall somewhere in-between. I cannot heal, I cannot hex, but I can detect afflictions and abnormalities. My real gift is in the research that comes afterward. Unlike most healers, I rely on knowledge and medicine to help people, not magic."

Novera started to move forward. "May I see the affected area?"

Oralia stepped swiftly away. "I cannot allow you to do that. The last time I came in contact with a witch, it ended . . ."

The crisp autumn air faded away as the stench of smoke and charred flesh filled Oralia's nostrils. She knew it was a hallucination, a cursed byproduct of her own tortured mind, but she felt the singe of ash against her skin all the same. The heat clawed its way inside her mouth, lighting her throat on fire as it seeped into her blistered lungs. Blinking the invisible sting from her eyes, Oralia took a steadying breath. "It ended horrifically."

Novera's voice worked as an elixir, soothing the blistering ache tearing at the fabric of Oralia's mind. "I have examined many curses before," the faun assured her, coaxing Oralia's eyes back open. "I know how to take precautions."

Oralia hesitated. This is what she wanted, wasn't it? Someone who could provide definitive answers? Suddenly she wasn't so sure. Either her condition was treatable, and there was a chance she'd survive the dark magic coursing through her veins, or it wasn't. At least not knowing left her options open. A definitive answer meant she couldn't cling to the safety net of denial any longer.

Fighting the constant tremble in her fingers, Oralia unfastened the top row of buttons and drew back her tunic, exposing the dark branching veins that snaked along her collarbone.

Novera placed her hand against Oralia's sternum. A warm pulse of magic rippled from the faun's palm and spread across Oralia's clammy flesh. She felt the darkness respond. Unlike Novera's magic, it didn't push, it pulled instead, attempting to draw the power into itself. Novera's eyes flared an eerie, silver blue. Her hand lingered only a moment longer, before she pulled away.

"I am afraid to ask," Oralia admitted.

The light in Novera's eyes faded to normal again. "It will prove fatal if left untreated. Although you do not possess the magic necessary to increase the dark entity's strength, it is slowly sapping yours."

"Untreated." Oralia rolled the word around in her mouth as she considered the gravity of Novera's diagnosis. "That would imply it can be reversed?"

"The easiest way would be to allow the spirit to switch hosts. Given what I've heard about your encounter with a fire elemental, I should not have to explain why that would be a very poor idea."

The smell of smoke teased at the corner of Oralia's mind as her thoughts returned to the nightmare that awaited her each time she drifted to sleep. She saw the terror in Grettie's wild eyes as the dark entity consumed her from the inside out. 'Unfitting' had been the spirit's words. It wished for a host more powerful. For the fate of the world, it was imperative to prevent that from happening.

Novera wrung the last of the magic from her fingers as she spoke. "How to extract it without the use of another vessel will be more difficult. Especially given your unique situation. I will need time to research the answer. Time I may not have unless the realm's stranglehold on the village is removed."

There it was—the unspoken deal Oralia had known to expect. There was no sense in dancing around the topic any more than necessary. They both knew the severity of the stakes now. "I require a healer with your talents. You need a warrior to liberate your village. Assisting one another is the only way either of us makes it out of this damned conflict alive. Will you accept my help?"

"I will, gratefully." Novera's tone was unconvinced, as though she was holding back many unspoken doubts. "In order to uphold my end, I will need to know more about the affliction. Any particular changes or symptoms I should be aware of?"

Oralia rattled off the list of usual suspects: weakness, nausea, muscle spasms, and body aches. It wasn't until she reached the end of her very extensive list that she realized Novera was fighting to constrain an amused smile.

Oralia furrowed her brow. "Did I say something humorous?"

"I thought perhaps you were feigning ignorance before, but you really don't know, do you?" Novera shook her head. "My dear, yes, you are infected. Beyond a shadow of a doubt. But did you ever stop to consider that perhaps there was an additional explanation at play? The dark entity is not the only life-form sapping your strength."

Oralia's gaze followed Novera's pointed stare all the way down to her midsection. "No."

"Afraid so."

"That is not possible. I have always been careful." Admittedly, after surviving the magical showdown with an ancient, awakened spirit back on the Iron Ridge, she *may* have been less than careful a few times. But only a few. And it shouldn't have mattered anyway! Oralia thought her age had put the matter to rest a century ago.

Novera's timid smile was now a full blown smirk, accentuating the worry lines around her tired eyes and mouth. "It's early. A few months at most. Orcs normally carry for ten, so you have at least eight more to come to terms with reality."

This was not reality. Not the one Oralia lived in, anyway. Sure, in the middle of the night, when her sleepless thoughts were left to wander unchecked, the occasional what-if scenario had crossed her mind. But that's all it had ever been. Magical thinking. Oralia hated how, slowly but surely, the fantastical was bleeding over into actuality.

Competing emotions tore at Oralia's racing thoughts. Alas, her body wasn't faring any better. It felt like she was drowning outside of water. There was air all around her and yet her damn lungs couldn't fill. "Is it . . . salvageable?"

"It?"

"If I call it by any other name, then my situation ceases to be a hypothetical."

"Faris was right. You are more melodramatic than you let on." Novera reached out and gave Oralia's hand a reassuring squeeze. "Rest assured, I sense it takes after you already."

Oralia didn't know what that was supposed to mean.

Fortunately, Novera spared her the awkwardness of having to guess. "The child is strong and, I daresay, stubbornly resilient."

Oralia sucked in a mouthful of cool night air as the weight of the situation came crashing down upon her. Amid the chaos, a single thought wormed its way through. *Oh dear gods. Sascha's going to have two of me to deal with.*

CHAPTER SEVENTY

A Proper Groveling

It was another cold, fireless night. Rasp's party had traveled until the sun was beyond the horizon before bunking down for the evening. Exhausted, Whisper had gone swiftly to sleep, leaving the others to settle. Dinner was a cold meal of hard cheese, dried meat, and corn cakes. Not that Rasp was complaining. Food was one of the few things in his life that remained consistently good. The right handful of ingredients could temper moods, foster harmony, brighten the soul, and all without a single complaint.

Unlike Faris. Who took every opportunity to complain, which was a real feat considering his commitment to the silent treatment. If there was anyone who could manage such an undertaking, it was Faris, of course. He made his complaints known by sitting as far away as possible, refusing to share his dinner, and, worst of all, giving an irritated flap of his ear anytime Rasp contributed to the conversation.

It was around the fourth unnecessary ear flap that Rasp finally said something. "Faris, are you still mad at me?"

Rasp received a breathy snort in response. While it may not have been words, it was enough to inform him that Faris was not only mad, but positively fuming.

Oh boy, here goes. Rasp pulled a face, realizing the only thing left to do was utter all of the mushy stuff his former self would have kept mum even under the pain of torture. "I'm sorry for being an ass, Dingle. I won't be so careless next time."

Claiming he wouldn't put Faris's life in danger again was a promise they both knew he couldn't keep. This was a sort of halfway measure Rasp could try to stick by.

Faris uttered a single, gruff word. "And?"

"And I'll be more considerate of your feelings next time." That sounded like something an emotionally mature human would say. Gods, he was getting good at this. The saying part—not the turning words into actions bit. But there was plenty of time to work on that along the way. The important thing was that Faris knew he was sorry and would put his grudge aside and maybe even share the rest of his cheese.

"And?" Faris repeated.

". . . I'm sorry I didn't realize you were scared of heights?"

"*And?*"

"Gods, what more do you want? Do you want me to get on my knees for you, Faris?" Rasp assumed the position with his hands flung out at his sides. He edged forward among the dried leaves and pine needles. "Grovel a little bit? Roll around in the dirt, maybe? I'm not a mind reader. Tell me what it is you want!"

Silence passed. Tense silence. The kind of tense silence that you just knew everyone and their dog was staring, judging you. Especially the dog.

"No, this is good. I just wanted to see how far I could push you." To add insult to injury, the bastard reached out and patted Rasp's head. "Your groveling could use some work but, frankly, I'm impressed you got this far. Well done."

"That's it. You're dead!" Rasp launched himself at Faris's fuzzy shape. The faun went tumbling backward into the dirt with Rasp scrambling over the top of him. Faris was quick to toss him aside, but Rasp was on his feet in no time. They rolled across the leafy ground with neither seeming capable of getting the upper hand on the other. This was surprising, actually. Faris normally put Rasp in his place a lot faster.

"I don't believe this! You're out of shape." Rasp wriggled free of Faris's grasp with ease. He switched positions, hooking the crook of his arm over the faun's throat from behind. "Four months without me was all it took to turn you soft."

"I'm not soft!" Faris choked out between sputtered gasps for air.

"Gross. There's such a thing as too much information, Dingle."

Over the strained huffs and grunts of their very sad attempt at reconciliation, Rasp heard June's voice announce to no one in particular. "You know, I've seen a thing or two about the birds and bees, but never anything quite like this. It's like they're trying to strangle each other with their love."

Hop, per usual, was focused on the unimportant part of what June said. "I have a feeling I'm going to regret asking, but you've *seen* a thing or two?"

"Well yeah, sure. My home was in this secluded bit of forest just outside of Faris's village. Aunty Dagmar hid our place real well using magic and whatnot. Very idyllic. Sort of became a secret nookie spot for all the local lovers."

"Dear gods, there's that regret. I feel it now."

"Hey, if they wanted to keep it private, they wouldn't have been doing it in my front yard," June said. "Oddly, I only ever saw Faris there once."

"No, no, no!" Faris sputtered in spite of Rasp's headlock. "June, whatever you're about to say next, *don't*."

"Relax, Faris. I'm not going to say anything scandalous. All I saw was you getting your heart broken by that Billings lad. Real tragic, actually. Was like watching someone's soul wither and leave their body," June said. "I suppose I should be congratulating you. It's good to see you finally found your special someone. Would prefer it if you two consecrated your love somewhere out of sight, though. Just saying. He is my brother. Feels weird."

Rasp's shoulders bristled at the implication. "We're just friends!"

"Right," June agreed, unconvinced.

"Tell her, Faris!"

"To be honest, I'm not even sure we're friends anymore." Faris panted as he tried to break free of the stranglehold Rasp had around his neck. "This is not how friends treat one another!"

"Agree to disagree." Over the drumming of the heartbeat in his ears, Rasp could pick out Father's faint call in the distance. He ignored it, adjusting his stranglehold on Faris's throat so that his friend could still breathe but not get away. This, after all, was far better than listening to his father gripe about Rasp scarfing down all of his dinner without sharing. "A true friend gives you the walloping you deserve. That's how you know I'm a true friend, Faris. I don't put on the kiddie gloves when it comes time to teach you a lesson!"

"I am not the one who needs to be taught a lesson!"

Croak!

"And yet, our circumstances would be switched if you were in better shape now, wouldn't it? Consider this my way of encouraging you to do better."

Faris broke Rasp's hold and rolled forward, flipping him over his shoulders and into the dirt with a slam. "I'm going to end you!"

The abrupt landing knocked the air from Rasp's lungs. "See?" he said weakly. "It's working already."

Rasp heard Faris's hooves scrape against the ground as he lunged. Given the lack of light, Rasp couldn't see the fucker coming but knew he was moments away from having his insides turned into outsides. Wind whipped between them a split second before Faris's dark form descended, throwing the pair sprawling several feet in opposite directions.

Crap. They'd gone too far, apparently, and awoken the only slumbering member of the party. Rasp rolled onto his side and covered his head, waiting for the whirlwind of debris to run its course. Whisper didn't have the energy to maintain the torrent for long. As predicted, the gale died down shortly after.

Rasp kept his arms over his head in the event he provoked a second whirlwind. "Look, I'm sorry. We didn't mean to wake you, but you could have used your words, you know."

Don't speak.

Somebody was grumpier than usual.

Stop running your thoughts and listen. Your father's mind is moving too rapidly for me to translate. Tell me what he is saying.

Father was no longer airborne. His clawed feet pitter-pattered in the dirt alongside Rasp amid a barrage of guttural clicks and caws.

"He says—"

Using your thoughts, little bird. I fear there are others listening.

The dots within Rasp's mind not only connected, but started to flash like giant beacons of fire. *We're being stalked,* he translated. *Father didn't get an exact count, but they've got numbers on their side and they're closing in. We need to move east before they surround us completely.*

I will communicate this with the others. Please remain silent.

Rasp heard a muffled squeak across from him. It came from June, the only one of the four yet to experience the displeasure of a second voice in their head. She was coping better than most, at least, given the stark lack of screaming.

Rasp unwrapped his arms from around his head and used them to push his body into an upright position. Tilting his head side to side, he strained to catch any signs of danger. He heard the rattle of the breeze blustering the treetops above and the harmonic songs of the frogs and crickets hidden among the undergrowth below, but nothing he deemed out of place.

Warmth rippled across his skin, warning him of a lurking presence that hadn't been there before.

Drawing within himself, Rasp cut off the outside world and summoned his sixth sense. Due to that afternoon's unexpected flying lesson, his powers had not yet fully returned. While this meant he didn't have the reserves necessary to cause mass destruction, he had enough to investigate. Rasp unclenched his hand and his magic swept across the group. With his aura vision activated, he could pick out the individual signatures of the magically-gifted members of the group. Hop's aura glowed pale purple, June's was beside the faun, a lovely pulsing green, with Whisper's sapphire energy glowing brighter than both of theirs combined.

The additional presence was a little farther away and . . . up? In the trees, likely, given its unusual proximity from the ground. It was small, too, and glowed with a green energy similar to June's. Rasp wasn't sure if any of the others were watching him, but he tried anyway. He lifted his finger, pointing in the direction of the unfamiliar aura.

Father provided the answer with a low hiss.

A . . . hawk? Rasp furrowed his brow, unsure of whether he'd heard right.

Whisper's voice rippled across his mind. **A shapeshifter.**

That explained why the hawk had similar energy to June then. Also, fuck. Rasp suspected he knew the answer, but didn't see the harm in allowing someone else to shatter his hopes for a successful escape. He channeled his thoughts to Whisper, asking, *So if we run?*

It will follow, Whisper confirmed. **Alerting the others of our movement.**

You got a plan then?

We kill it. And then we run like all of chaos is behind us.

Rasp's mind was already scattering in several different directions when his sixth sense pinged stronger than before, alerting him of another magical presence. This one was larger, human-sized, judging from the shape of its glistening silver aura. The magical stranger strode boldly out from between the trees and called out in a nauseatingly familiar tone, "Good evening again, gents! And lady. And . . ." There was a noticeable pause as Rasp assumed the speaker's stare settled on Whisper. "Whatever our fae friend goes by. I must say, it's a relief to finally have all of you together at once. It's going to make this so much easier."

CHAPTER SEVENTY-ONE

The Cruel Smile of Fate

Rasp's racing mind sifted through memories of the last several days to place the speaker. The pieces fitted together rather quickly—the voice, the distinct silver aura, the smug confidence that made Rasp want to drive his fist into the speaker's face repeatedly. "Dingle?" he called over his shoulder to Faris. "Is this the witch you hobbled the other day? You know, when I was saving your ass from the earth elemental?"

Faris's voice was laden with trepidation. So much so, he didn't bother to correct Rasp's totally accurate recount of the fight. "I could have sworn I broke his leg."

"Irvan." The approaching witch kindly reminded them of his name. "And you did indeed, Mister Belfast. Fortunately for me, broken bones are but a minor inconvenience."

Rasp cursed their luck. This was why it was essential to ensure every member of the decimated party was taken care of before moving on. Sole survivors bent on revenge had a nasty habit of causing unexpected hiccups down the road. Admittedly, sole survivors weren't usually this calm and collected. Irvan was behaving like a perfect gentleman so far, which, in Rasp's limited experience with perfect gentlemen, meant there was a wolf lurking beneath the polished veneer.

Faris must have sensed it, too. "How do you know my name?"

"We know your importance now, and how the Speaker of the People is using you to draw the devil witch into his net. I'm afraid we had to take steps to keep that from happening." Irvan's silver aura came to a standstill at the edge of camp. Rasp heard the creak of old leather being drawn open. A momentary rustle followed before Irvan withdrew something from his bag and tossed it before them. Regrettably, without the aid of light, Rasp couldn't tell what it was. All he heard was the soft thud of something feathery strike the ground.

"Aunty!" June's shriek turned to an agonized wail. Her howl morphed into something deeper, an animalistic, guttural roar. With a series of wet pops and snaps, her bones rearranged into a form better suited for ripping out throats with her teeth.

"Sorry about your messenger bird." Irvan remained hauntingly apathetic to June's transformation. His next words were the same as the first, calm, collected, and dripping with feigned sympathy. "And your mule."

From the corner of his eye, Rasp saw the hawk's green aura swoop from its perch and hurtle past. A pained bray filled the still night air a split moment before Bonecrusher's heavy body struck the ground. Rasp whipped around, following her panicked screams to their source. The mule's cries of pain faded as her thrashing legs went still. The shapeshifter's aura stood beside the dying mule, glimmering notably larger than it had been only moments before.

The newcomer could shift faster than June, indicating either a surplus of power, experience, or an unfortunate combination of the two. Alas, such critical information was lost on June. Caught in the throes of bloodlust, her bear-shaped aura barreled toward the newcomer with a roar. The attacker shifted again, as effortlessly as before. Their feathery wings beat the air as they took to the sky, only to be slammed back down from a swipe of June's front paw. Their auras tangled together in a symphony of shrieks and snarls as the entire encampment turned to chaos.

Scalding hot magic filled the air. Rasp winced, feeling it singe the hair from his eyebrows as the blistering wind whipped in Irvan's direction. Irvan responded, his silver glow thrumming brighter as he willed an incantation to life. The spell surged forth like a wave across still water. Rasp was knocked off his feet when the two magics clashed. The competing auras flared, lighting the surrounding darkness ablaze with blue and silver. The tang of sweet fruit and moss permeated the gusty air, battling for supremacy against the over-powering stench of spoiled garlic and metal.

Rasp staggered to his feet, only to dive back down again to avoid being crushed by June as she and the other shapeshifter tumbled past, interlocked in battle.

Seven realms! He'd never felt so out of place during a battle before. Rasp was used to being caught in the action, center stage, with hot rage pumping through his veins. Not like this, utterly useless and stuck on the sidelines. Rasp clambered back onto his unsteady legs in time to see a wave of silver magic engulf the blue. A blazing pulse of light rippled from Irvan's phantom form as he chanted unfamiliar words. The spell burned as bright as a solar flare before blinking out entirely.

Darkness returned and blanketed the stony forest floor in night's shadow once more.

Whisper's small aura crumpled to the ground with an agonized whimper. Their magic flickered, steadily fading until its telltale blue glow was barely perceptible. Rasp stumbled toward Whisper's dimming form, feeling the ice cold grip of fear seize his heart. "No, no, no." He hollered over his shoulder, not a hundred percent sure where the fifth member of their party had ended up amid the shuffle, "Hop! A little help?"

Hop didn't answer Rasp's call for aid. Not in the verbal sense anyway. Rasp did hear the rustle of brush as the timid faun extracted himself from whatever vegetation he'd dove headfirst into at the first sign of trouble.

"Tell me what you see, Hop," Rasp prompted.

"Whisper's alive," Hop said with marked hesitation. "But it's not good."

Rasp altered course, moving in Irvan's direction like a suicidal moth drawn to a particularly annoying flame. "You're going to tell me what the fuck you just did," he said, putting on his best 'that's right, I'm in charge here' voice. "Or I'm going to pull your fingernails off one by one and feed them to you until you choke."

"You pompous little shit." Irvan's gratingly annoying voice was still as bold and brash as ever, but interlaced with an unmistakable thread of pain. "You burned two of my colleagues alive and crushed another. And you have the audacity to be angry at *me*?"

"That should have been your sign to stop trying to take us prisoner, yeah?"

"I offered you the chance to come peacefully. All you had to do was say yes!" Contrary to Irvan's rise in volume, his silver aura was steadily dimming. "'Make an example. Change his mind.' That's what the Sage Superior told me. Well, there it is, boy." Irvan spat at the ground, whether it was from a mouthful of blood or simple disdain, Rasp couldn't decipher. "Let's see how far you get without your fae master."

Fury rose up from the depths and flooded Rasp's tightening chest with molten rage. He dug deep, summoning any magic he could find. But there was nothing to spare. His reserves hadn't yet recovered from that day's flying adventure. Rasp's hands clenched as he considered doing something horrifically stupid. Fists didn't require magic. And, from Irvan's labored breath, it sounded as if Whisper had done more than half of the work already. Rasp would just be completing the job.

"Message received." A predatory smile split across Rasp's face. "I think it's time for me to send your boss a message back."

"Stay where you are or the fae dies!" Irvan's voice flooded with panic. His aura dimmed fainter and fainter as magic slowly bled from his body. "I already willed the iron poisoning deeper. Come any closer, I'll send it straight to their heart. Your master will be dead before you reach me."

"Rasp!" Hop's voice halted Rasp in his tracks. "For once in your life, think before acting, please. I don't know what we're dealing with yet. Don't go out of your way to make it worse."

All eyes were on him. Rasp could feel it. Somewhere among the chaos, June, Faris, and the mystery shapeshifter had ceased fighting. They'd all gone deathly quiet, save for the sounds of June's huffing breathing. "Is what he saying true?" Rasp asked Hop. "Can he make the iron poisoning go to Whisper's heart?"

"I don't know, but I don't think we can't risk finding out, either."

Shit. And here he was, blood pumping and ready for a fight. Rasp glared in Irvan's direction and scowled. "So how exactly do you see this ending? Is this one of those, agree to come with us and I'll lift the hex situations?"

Irvan's laugh was more unnerving than his speaking voice. The strength in the witch's legs gave out as his phantom aura sank to the ground. Talking sounded as though it'd become more a chore which, regrettably, still didn't prevent Irvan from doing it in the most annoying way possible. "No, no, dear boy. Such a plan would be far too easy for you to thwart. I just cursed your fae friend to death, you see. If you wish for them to live, then you will need the Sage Superior's mercy to lift the hex."

The witch carried on, "I can tell you're still thinking of running. And yes, you might slip through our fingers again tonight, but you won't get far. There are over thirty members of the Sons and Daughters of Resistance assembled all around these woods. They're not going to waste their energy on a direct attack, either. They have orders to hound you, run you ragged day and night, wait for exhaustion to set in as their net steadily draws tighter. When they finally make their move, none of you will have the strength to fight."

Dread hung thick in the air like smoke from a poorly ventilated fire. It clogged the airways, jamming Rasp's windpipe as doom slowly sank in.

Irvan issued his final ultimatum with the sort of smugness that implied he knew they were had. "Surrender, now, and it won't have to come to that. I'll take you back to the Sage Superior myself and get this all sorted out for you."

Caught in an internal whirlwind of racing thoughts, Rasp didn't hear Faris's approaching hoof steps until he pressed close, whispering, "If he possesses the power to hex, then he possesses the power to lift it as well. We don't need their leader. We just need to get it out of him."

"And how do we do that?" Rasp asked, hopeful that the answer involved fists.

"Adriel." Irvan disrupted their whispered huddle as he called across to the shapeshifter who, by some sheer miracle, was still apparently alive. "It's time. Return to the others and send word to the Sage Superior. Tell her they refused."

"Your rest was earned well, Brother Irvan," Adriel replied.

"Now hold on, we haven't decided—" The rest of Faris's sentence was swallowed by a gasping squeak, followed by a whispered, "Muck."

Rasp watched, mystified, as Irvan's weak silver glow was swallowed by the dark. He didn't want to ask. Feared to, in fact, but short of going up and prodding the body with a stick, there wasn't any other way to know. "Did he just . . . ?"

Faris sounded as stunned as Rasp felt. "Yeah."

While Rasp had fully intended to carry out the job himself, he couldn't help but wonder what powers could drive a man to such extremes. "Why?"

"To force our hand," Faris replied grimly.

Little bird. Whisper's voice rippled across Rasp's thoughts, sickly and weak. **Stop the shapeshifter. Buy us time.**

While he would never admit it, Rasp was secretly grateful someone was finally telling him what to do. He turned and charged in Adriel's direction. The shapeshifter saw him coming and shifted to something smaller. Too small to be a hawk, Rasp realized, as he watched the tiny green glow dart between June's paws. June's bear form was too cumbersome to catch it. She stamped about, snapping her jaws, and emitting frustrated growls each time the tiny creature eluded her.

Rasp cleared the stretch of encampment and threw himself into a dive, clasping his hands around the little green aura as his body struck the ground and rolled. The shapeshifter gave a squeak of terror, their tiny, fuzzy body clawing at Rasp's hands as it forced its mouse-shaped body through his fingers. The shapeshifter leapt free with Rasp hot on its tail.

Sharp branches whipped at Rasp's face as he scrambled on all fours after the mouse. In what was possibly the most undignified fight of his life, against an opponent a hundredth his size, Rasp flipped, flailed, and rolled his way to victory. Sore, bleeding, and desperately trying to fill his blistering lungs, he rose from the prickly undergrowth victorious. He proudly held his interlocked hands aloft.

"I got—ah!" Pain ripped through Rasp's body as the mouse sank its teeth into him. His hands spasmed, loosening his interlaced fingers enough for his quarry to spring free. Father's harsh cry reverberated within Rasp's ears as the raven swooped down from above. There was a furious flap of feathery wings and a sudden, piercing shriek before the ruckus went suspiciously quiet.

Rasp sucked the blood weeping from his hand, silently hoping magic shapeshifting mice didn't carry disease. He glanced back and forth, realizing he no longer saw the shapeshifter's tiny green glow. "Dad?"

Croak?

There were far more pressing matters at hand, undoubtedly. Still, Rasp couldn't move past the nauseating feeling churning in the pit of his stomach until he knew for certain. "Did you . . . eat him?"

Father confirmed Rasp's suspicions with a snap of his bill.

Rasp attempted to process this shocking information. Unfortunately, this involved stating all of it out loud. "You're a bird, who used to be human. Who just ate a mouse, that was actually a person."

"Rasp," Faris called, trying to snap him out of it.

Unfortunately, there would be no snapping of anything. Rasp feared his mind had beaten Faris to it. "On the scale of cannibalism, I think this might be a six." He listened to his father's resulting protest before nodding his head in stunned agreement. "You know what, I'll give it to you. It's a seven."

"I can't believe I'm saying this," Faris said, touching Rasp's elbow in that concerned way friends do when they realize they're the only sane one left, "but I think your father's cannibalism is the least of our concerns right now."

Right. Back to the hopeless reality of death and gloom. Rasp turned in Whisper's direction as the last of his phantom vision petered out, giving way to utter darkness. Rather fitting, given the circumstances. "How do we fix this?"

To his relief, it was Whisper who answered. Well, relieved until the weight of their words settled, at least. After that, there would be no relief. "We don't. There isn't time." Whisper's voice was weak and riddled with agony. "We have to move before our pursuers realize they no longer have eyes on our location."

"And then what?"

"I am going into a state of stasis within your pack."

Terrible start so far. Rasp hoped that whatever Whisper said next, it would be better and, most importantly, not delivered in riddle form. He really hated that. Clear-cut instructions were the only way to go.

"At which point," Whisper said between sharp gasps for breath, "you may have to try your hand at taking charge in my absence."

The impossible weight of responsibility settled onto Rasp's impetuous shoulders. Other than being born with a natural capacity for ordering others about, he didn't know the first thing about being a leader. Somewhere, beyond the veil of space and time, he felt the cruel face of fate smile down upon him, elated that he'd finally exhausted his ability to run. There was no other option now. The sixth son of a mighty Stoneclaw warrior, bearer of the silver-hair, was being called to step up and accept the role assigned to him.

Dear gods, Rasp thought as the overwhelming urge to crawl into a hole and hide swept over him. *Why couldn't it have been a damn riddle instead?*